Novels by Richard Helms

RICHARD HELMS

22 Rue Montparnasse

Wye Creek Books

For All the Wallys

CHAPTER ONE

OVER THE REMAINDER of his life, Beau Shipley would never forget the terrifying scream of incoming artillery.

His parents had taken him to France on vacation when he was a child. They had visited all the usual tourist sites in Paris and spent a week or so wending their way across the Riviera to Italy. Along the way, they had passed through dense forests of beech and oak and maple. Beau could never recall exactly which forest they had traversed. He hoped it wasn't this one.

The Meuse-Argonne Forest in the latter days of 1918 bore little resemblance to the lush, verdant woodlands he recalled from the childhood trip. The dense overgrowth had been decimated by tanks and howitzers and the long German guns and aeroplane-dropped bombs and the inevitable fires which trailed behind warriors like camp followers. Twisted scorched tree trunks remained in patches where it was inconvenient for the heavy machinery to travel. The denuded soil of the forest bed had long since been churned into mud by a million boots and ripped by long scars and webs of opposing trenches that stretched for miles in each direction.

Along with a million or so other American Johnny-come-latelies in the war, Beau Shipley had managed his life to this point with such inelegance that he now found himself at the age of twenty-two in the middle of the bloodiest battle of The Great War.

Designation: Cannon Fodder.

Well, he mused, as he watched the ash on his cigarette grow, *more likely machine gun fodder.*

He recalled his literature course at college, and how he had been saddled with reading Tolstoy. He remembered the reference to cannon fodder in *War and Peace,* and how he had wrestled with the inconceivable notion that anyone would voluntarily place themselves in a war's path, with death almost a certainty.

Then came the expulsion. It wasn't his fault the girl fell asleep in his room, but he was out regardless. The last thing he wanted was to go to work in his father's cigar-import business. His father seemed none too keen on the idea himself. When Wilson finally decided the United States should enter the war, Beau saw an opportunity. His plan was faultless. His execution may have left something to be desired. He enlisted before talking to his father.

Beau was only twenty-one when he enlisted. In his mind, his father would admire his industry and pluck, and maybe pull a few strings to get Beau a commission. He had heard such postings were for sale, and his father had the contacts to make it happen. He imagined assisting some general far behind the lines—in Paris perhaps—oiling the machinery of war from the rear during the day and cavorting with models and actresses at night.

His father had only recently reconciled to bring Beau into the business, perhaps at a satellite office with infrequent traffic, and he raged when Beau announced his enlistment. Among the many things Gordon Shipley hated, he hated changes in plans most, and he had already changed his once. After a period of furious silence, he clapped the boy on the shoulder, shook his hand, and wished him well. "It would suit me," he had said, "if you should survive this war. Please do be careful."

Beau was shuffled into the infantry. No commission. No cushy assignment in Paris. Mostly through attrition, he rose from buck private to corporal. Field promotions were rife after each sortie. For all Beau knew, some luckier kid would wear his stripes tomorrow.

Faggot Donnie had died during the night. Influenza. Beau could never remember the kid's real name. The British boys had dubbed him Faggot Donnie because he was a consummate forager and always had cigarettes for sale. Now he was dead of the flu, his jacket and ruck full of cigarettes, and nobody would get near them for fear of infection.

"What the hell," Beau mumbled, as he pulled another cigarette from the pack he had liberated from Faggot Donnie's ruck. "Something's gonna get you."

His engagement with the enemy so far had consisted of potshots over the lip of the trench. He tried to imagine what it would be like, charging over the top into the mud and muck and barbed wire. He had a sadistic imagination, and he could see himself stumbling through the mire, tripping over the dead, brilliant flashes lighting the night ahead of him, and knowing each flash was a bullet headed directly for his head.

If he was fortunate.

A head shot would be like turning out the lights, cutting all your wires at once. One second here. The next instant not. Beau found the concept boggling. He couldn't fathom the concept of instant death, the idea that everything—like, the *big* everything—would simply...*stop*. Instantaneously. Eternally. Beau torched three cigarettes trying to get his head around it and was no closer to comprehending.

Pain, he understood. What scared him most was charging over the top and taking a round in the liver, or the intestines, or becoming a fifty-caliber castrato. He had seen a kid named Jake at the aid station a few days earlier who had stopped a bullet with his crotch. Most of his manhood was still in No Man's Land. Miraculously, it looked like the kid might live.

But for what? Beau resolved on his fifth cigarette that if he took a bullet in the eggs, he'd put the next one in his own head.

Around midday, a grim squad of graves registry pukes bore Faggot Donnie away on a stretcher. Before they did, Beau cadged another several packs of smokes from Donnie's ruck.

He lit a cigarette and extracted the worn and muddied letter from his jacket pocket.

The words hadn't changed, despite his most fervent hopes.

Dear Beau—

This is the hardest letter I've ever had to write...

"Try reading it," Beau whispered.

I never expected...I know this is painful for you...He's a good man, Beau...I wanted to wait, but the news each day is so grim...For all I know, you'll never live to see this letter...I do so wish you won't hate me...At some level, I will always love you...

The lancing gut shot pain he'd experienced the first several hundred times he read the letter had worn off. Now he felt only numb resolution.

Beau rubbed his hand across the sandpaper beard of his face. An unpleasant aroma rose from his uniform, and he winced. He smelled. Everybody smelled. The Germans across No Man's Land smelled.

Corporal Caleb Styles plopped next to Beau. Everyone called him Keeby. Despite having lived in the States for most of his life, he considered himself Quebecois due to his birth in Montreal. Beau and Keeby had met in basic training and, against all probability, had billeted together ever since.

"Keeby," Beau said. "Want a cigarette?"

"Where's Faggot Donnie?"

"Died. Flu."

"Those his cigarettes?"

"No. They're mine." He paused and added, "They *were* his."

"Jesus," Keeby said. "Pass. I heard some guys talking at the latrine. We're going over the top. Tonight."

"Might as well take a cigarette, then," Beau said.

CHAPTER TWO

BEAU AND KEEBY spent the day writing letters to their families. Outgoing mail was unlikely until the battle ended. They'd each keep the letters securely inside their uniforms. With luck, if they fell during the sortie, the letters would be retrieved with their bodies and delivered.

The sun had settled a hand above the horizon in the west when burly Sergeant Wally Smith lurched in their direction. He must have been six and a half feet tall, and he was forced to scramble along the trenches hunched over lest he lose the top of his head to snipers.

"Corporal Shipley?" he barked.

Beau stood. "Sergeant?"

"You're needed at the Division HQ."

"Am I in trouble?"

"If you're lucky. Maybe they'll clap you in irons and you won't have to go over the top. You aren't that lucky though, boyo. Hustle on, now."

———

The Americans had been quick studies when it came to the construction of trenches. The network of rapidly dug ruts, barely the height of an average man, were as intricate as any anthill. Directional signs hung everywhere lest entire squadrons become hopelessly and permanently detached from their fellows.

The Division Headquarters was a hollowed out hovel at the intersection of two main trench channels. The inside smelled of earth and decay. Each time an artillery shell fell within a thousand yards, dust and loose soil flaked from the ceiling. Beau entered the HQ and stood at attention, waiting to be recognized. The Division Commander was a jowly, middle-aged man with pewter hair, whose eagle colonel insignia were so hastily sewn in place, Beau recognized immediately he was new to the job.

There was a lot of that going around.

The colonel was named Ritchie. He hunched over a portable campaign desk, reviewing communiques, apparently unaware Beau had entered. Finally, he said, "Got a cigarette, kid?" His voice was growly and carried a midwestern twang.

Beau took a pack from his jacket pocket. "Came off a guy who died of the flu."

"Did he smoke it first?" He took the cigarette Beau held out for him. "Okay, let's get the particulars out of the way. Name and rank, soldier."

"Beauregard Johnson Shipley, Corporal. Sir."

"So far, so good. Where from, Corporal?"

"Charleston, South Carolina, sir."

"Never been there. Nice place?"

"Except in August."

"What happens in August?" Ritchie growled.

"Everything melts. Sir. And the skeeters come out."

"Big ones?"

"Like crows, sir. My father tells a joke. Two Charleston city skeeters stole a calf. One of them said, *Let's fly him to the beach for a picnic.'* The other said, *'Are you crazy? The big ones will take it away from us.'"*

Colonel Ritchie didn't laugh as he lit the cigarette and stared at Beau through the cloud of smoke. "Your outfit is going over the top this evening."

"I've heard. Sir."

"You won't be joining them."

A balloon deflated in Beau's stomach. The relief that flooded through him made him dizzy and a little weak in the knees.

"My courier was recalled to Paris earlier today. Unexpectedly, I might add. The Brigadier suggested you would be a perfect candidate for the position. Do you know the Brigadier?"

"Never had the pleasure, sir," Beau said.

"Small world, Corporal. Neither do I. How do you suppose he knew your name?"

"I can't say, sir."

Ritchie took a deep drag from the cigarette and immediately collapsed in a paroxysm of coughing. He dropped the smoldering butt into an empty tin can on his campaign desk. "The position comes with a promotion in grade from corporal to sergeant, with—of course—a commensurate increase in pay. You want it?"

"Yes sir. Anything to avoid No Man's Land tonight." Suddenly aware he was already one step back over the trench wall, he quickly added. "Sir."

Ritchie dabbed at this tongue and spat a loose shred of tobacco onto the dirt floor. "Well, at least you're honest." He pointed to several empty bamboo cages in the corner of the HQ. "Sent out my last pigeon this morning. None have come back. Daresay the Kaiser's boys are using them for target practice across the mud. I have an important battle assessment to be delivered as soon as possible to the Brigadier, and no pigeons to carry it." He opened a desk drawer and tossed two sets of sergeant stripes to Beau. "I do have *you*. This is your opportunity to thank him. Put those on at your first opportunity. You know the way to the Brigadier's HQ?"

"I can find it, sir. The trenches are well-marked."

Ritchie settled back in his chair and surveyed his new courier. "Who in hell are you, anyway?"

"Beg pardon, sir?"

"Someone wants you to have this assignment, Sergeant. What kind of juice do you have?"

"I can't say, sir."

"Bullshit. This stinks of pulled strings."

"Sir," Beau said. "My father is a wealthy and connected man. He knows every congressman and senator in South Carolina. I believe he has considerable influence especially with one particular senator."

"As I imagined," Ritchie said.

"No, sir," Beau argued. "I enlisted without my father's knowledge. He was furious. I had hoped he might help me find a soft billet in Paris or London. Instead, he offered me a handshake and his best wishes. I've been eating and sleeping in mud ever since. With all respect, Colonel, if I had any pull, I'd be a hundred miles from the Argonne right now."

"I see," Ritchie said. "He isn't going to make this war easy for you, but he is willing to exercise his influence to save your life."

"I have no idea, sir. This new posting is as much as surprise for me as it is for you. I have no other explanation why the Brigadier requested me specifically, but I never asked for this. May I inquire, sir? The communique? It's important?"

"Important enough to risk your life instead of finding a new pigeon. Why do you ask?"

"Sir, we're going over the top this evening, possibly before I can complete the delivery. There is sure to be a German artillery barrage from beyond the river, and possibly even gas."

"Yes?"

"Sir, may I request an escort for this mission? Someone who could complete the delivery should anything happen to me?"

Ritchie rubbed his eyes and considered the request. "I suppose you have someone in mind?"

"Corporal Caleb Styles, sir."

"Another cigarette," Ritchie said.

Beau dropped the entire pack on his campaign desk. "Keep 'em, sir. There's a ruck full where they came from."

Ritchie lit a cigarette and scribbled a note on a sheet of paper. "I'm reassigning Corporal Caleb Styles to your direct command. This means I'm removing two valuable soldiers from your commanding officer, which will leave him shy during tonight's sortie. I hope you appreciate the hardship I'm placing on him, Sergeant."

"Bullshit," Wally Smith said when Beau showed him and Keeby the stripes. "They'll make anyone a sergeant these days. Hold on. Got a needle and thread around here somewhere." He rummaged through his pockets.

"There's more," Beau said. "I report to Colonel Ritchie now, and he's assigned Keeby to my command."

"What?" Keeby asked.

Beau pulled the orders from his pocket and showed the papers to both men.

"I'll be damned," Keeby said. "Now I gotta salute you."

"You don't salute sergeants, dummy," Smith said, as he handed Beau a sewing kit in an aspirin tin. "Shoulda taught you that first day of training."

"There was training?" Keeby asked. "Jesus. That explains a lot."

Beau set to tacking his new stripes on his jacket sleeve, straining to see in the dusky twilight. Smith watched and scratched at a fresh shaving scab on his chin.

"So, you two aren't going over the top tonight?" Smith asked.

"No," Beau said, threading the needle. "Soon as I sew these stripes on, Keeb and I head out to the Brigadier HQ."

"I see," Smith said.

It took a second for Beau to catch on. He and Keeby had been given a reprieve from hell. Smith was still going into No Man's Land. "Gee, Wally. I'm sorry. I didn't —"

"It's okay," Smith said. "I mean, it isn't, not at all. But it's not your fault. Can you do me a favor?"

"Sure," Beau said. "Name it."

Smith dug into his jacket and pulled out a folded piece of paper. "You guys got a much better shot at going home right now than I do. This thing's gonna be over in a few weeks, from what I hear. Keep your heads down and you'll be guzzling champagne in Paris in three months. If this damn Saint Christopher medal my Ma sent me works, maybe I'll be right there beside you. If not..." He held the folded paper. "I'd appreciate if you'd see this gets delivered."

"I'll hold onto it for you," Keeby said.

"Me, too," Beau added. "Return it to you when you come back over the wire."

"Good of you to say so, but I got a bad sense about tonight. I think my hourglass is out of sand."

"So turn it over," Keeby said. "That's how hourglasses work."

"Not tonight, I fear. First time I went over the top, I saw some poor bastard who'd fallen. Must have been weeks ago. He was already a pile of bones inside a rotting uniform. Nobody ever carted him off the field. A few more days, some more artillery rounds, a couple dozen tank treads, and he'll get buried in the mud. Maybe some archeologist will find him in a thousand years. I bet he's got a letter in his jacket nobody will ever read."

"Give me the letter," Beau said. "But you're coming back. First round in Paris is on me."

———

Beau and Keeby paused at a fork in the trenches to check the signs against their map. Keeby carried a lantern to help reading, as the sun had been down for half an hour.

"Did you mean what you said?" Keeby asked as Beau examined the map.

"What?" Beau asked absently.

"You told Wally he was coming back. You mean it?"

"Oh, hell no. He'll be dead in couple of hours." He pointed to the right. "But I'll see the letter gets delivered. We go this way."

"Wait. How can you say that?" They dodged a gaggle of soldiers huddled around a makeshift poker table. "He could make it."

"He's already decided to die. He's resigned himself to it. I could see it in his eyes and hear it in his voice."

"Kind of callous."

"If I'm wrong, I'll be as grateful as anyone else. I don't expect to see Wally Smith again."

"I suppose I owe you," Keeby said.

"Let's get out of this first. Wally was right. The hot poop says this war will be over in a few weeks. Some poor bastard is going to take the last round, and I sure as hell don't want it to be either of us. If we're sitting in a Paris café swilling bubbly this time next year, we can talk about who owes who. Deal?"

In the distance, shrill whistles shattered the evening quiet, followed immediately by desperate shouts and cries the men used to muster their courage as they rolled over the trench tops into a sausage grinder. Immediately, machine guns across the mud flashed in the darkness. Some of the shouts changed immediately to screams, or eerily stopped in mid-breath.

From far behind the American trenches, the large artillery cannons roared, and shells whistled overhead toward the German positions.

Keeby said, "How far?"

"Another hundred yards or so. Keep your head down, dammit! Those machine gun slugs can ricochet anywhere."

As if responding to a distant call, the German artillery opened fire seconds later. The haunting screech of the howitzer shells traveling well above the speed of sound reached their ears before the pounding boom of the cannons themselves.

"Duck!" Keeby launched himself onto Beau's back. They hunched together in the eastern corner of the trench as German shells pounded the scarred earth in No Man's Land, spraying geysers of mud and blood and metal and flesh skyward with each impact. Each time a high explosive projectile augured in, the ground in the trench lurched and the shockwave crumbled the dried mud wall.

"Let's go!" Beau shouted over the incessant din of the war. "It's all luck from here!"

Keeping their heads low, hunched over like hundred-year-old men, they dashed along the deserted trenches as clods of dirt and shards of twisted metal and indescribable gore rained down on them. The booming of the artillery had blended into a single long thunderous rumble that vibrated the earth beneath their feet.

"The Brigadier Headquarters," Beau shouted, pointing a few dozen yards ahead.

"Wait!" Keeby cried out. He pointed skyward, and they both instantly heard the crescendo scream of an incoming artillery shell, far too loud and improbably close.

20

"Oh, fuck—" Keeby said. The shell impacted directly on the Brigadier Headquarters. It penetrated the roof and exploded in a blinding flash. Channeled by the open doors, the blast wave followed the path of least resistance along the trench shafts, leaving no avenue for escape, until it blew Beau and Keeby into the air like bits of tissue paper.

CHAPTER THREE

AFTER A FEW SECONDS of stunned disorientation, the first thing Beau did was check his balls.

He appeared to be intact.

The ringing in his ears subsided, mostly, and he noticed a buzzing sound over his head, like monstrous mosquitoes. He lay on his back in a puddle of mud. Every second or so, something would zing overhead. The flashes of light reminded him of the fireflies who lived in the azaleas in his courtyard in Charleston. Then one of them splatted into the earth next to him, throwing a spray of muck across his face. He had been thrown entirely out of the trench and was now prostrate in the middle of No Man's Land. The fireflies were phosphorous tracer rounds zipping inches above his face.

Some sniper ensconced in the enemy trench had drawn a bead on him.

Beau rolled onto his belly as another round smacked into the mud, crawled the fifteen feet back to the lip of the trench and rolled over it to relative safety. Two bullets slapped the space where he had lain until only seconds earlier. Beau propped himself against the wooden wall of the trench and gasped repeatedly, trying to calm himself. His heart pounded in his chest like kettle drums beaten by a madman. His vision blurred and wavered at the edges. His gut lurched and he thought he might vomit.

The HQ was obliterated, a smoking hole which would have included his scattered remains had he been quicker and lot less lucky. After the world stopped spinning, he looked around for Keeby. His view was obstructed by smoke and dust thrown up by the artillery shell. It choked him and made his sinuses burn.

"Help," someone cried weakly. Beau felt his way along the trench wall toward the voice and found Keeby lying atop a pile of rubble. Every inch of exposed skin and hair were coated with light gray dust. His left leg hung at an unnatural angle, and a flitch of wood the size of a bowling pin had penetrated his side. His jacket and shirt were soaked with dark blood around the wound.

"How's it look?" Keeby asked when Beau knelt at his side.

"I've seen worse."

Keeby pointed with his trembling hand toward a human leg, still wearing a muddy boot, that had landed close to him. "Small comfort. If it's all right with you, I'm going to pass out now. Be a good man and get me to the aid station."

Losing consciousness was a kindness. Lifting Keeby off the rubble with his obviously fractured leg would have been excruciating. Keeby was two inches taller than Beau, and was twenty pounds heavier, but Beau had the adrenalin of terror and panic working for him. With great effort, Beau hoisted Keeby over his shoulder, taking care not to dislodge the splinter in his side lest it might hold something critical in place.

Now where? The explosion had ripped away all the posted signs. Beau couldn't recall seeing an aid station on the way, so he followed the trench network until he found some unmolested directions.

Luck held for him again. A hundred feet further along, another trench branched off to the west, and a sign indicated he should turn there for the aid station. It made sense, he reasoned. You'd want the medical facilities as far from the front lines as necessary to protect the medical personnel, but close enough to the action for quick access by the wounded.

In the distance, the staccato beat of machine guns melded with the rumbling explosions of artillery and grenades. With each shot, he imagined some poor son of a bitch boarding the off-world express. Ahead of him, the trench continued a hundred yards or more without interruption.

He was running out of reserves. Keeby was dead weight, and Beau stumbled along as quickly as his battered body allowed. His lungs burned with exertion, and his heart pounded against his ribcage. Halfway, he considered stopping for a rest. Each second wasted reduced Keeby's chances, though, so he trudged on until he came to an aid station sign and an arrow pointing to the left. As soon as he turned the corner, he saw it.

Later in the day, the station would overflow as other wounded found their way back to the trenches, but when he carried Keeby through the opening of the station, the place was deserted except for a couple of soldiers on cots, a body covered with a sheet, two nurses, and a single doctor. The nurses jumped as he walked in.

"Where can I drop this man?" he asked.

"Let us help you," the younger woman said. The doctor helped Keeby off Beau's shoulder and onto an empty cot to assess his injuries. Beau stepped out of the way and leaned against the back wall of the station. Sapped, he dropped to the filthy floor and considered sleeping for a hundred years.

"You're hurt," the older nurse said.

"I am?" he asked.

"Your head..."

Beau raised his hand and felt the side of his head. His hair was matted and sticky. During the artillery explosion at the headquarters, he must have been hit with a flying scrap of shrapnel. It had lanced a two-inch long gash in the side of his skull, above his ear. His head pounded and a trickle of blood dripped from his ear.

"Maybe I should lie down," he told the older nurse.

"That would be a fine idea," she told him.

———

The war ended four weeks later, with Beau and Keeby safely billeted in a hospital in Paris.

It was November 11th. Beau had been dozing quietly after being told he was ready to return to his unit. Keeby snored in the bed next to him, his leg still in a plaster cast. He had been lucky. The impalement had missed any vital organs. There had been a minor infection, and the doctors had fretted about Keeby's chances, but he pulled through in the end. Keeby and Beau would head back to the states with some fine stories to tell at parties.

Wally Smith, as Beau had predicted, had not been as fortunate. A man his size made a far too attractive target of opportunity. He had fallen mere yards after clambering over the trench lip. Among the first things Beau did on receiving the news was ask his nurse for an envelope, so he could deliver Wally's last letter to his family.

CHAPTER FOUR

BY THE TIME Beau and Keeby left the hospital, their active military services were no longer required. They both declined transport home temporarily, deciding to remain in France to further recuperate from their injuries.

In April of 1919, as the cherry blossoms appeared again along the Rue de Rivoli in Paris, they sat in civilian clothes in an open-air café at the nexus of the Rue Montmartre and the Rue de Turbigo, in the shadow of the ancient stone walls of the Eglise de St. Eustache. Keeby's cast had been removed a month before, but he walked with a limp, and the damage to his abdominal muscles from the impalement would yield an intractable ache when the winds changed that would follow him for the rest of his days.

But they were alive, when so many other youths were not, and it was spring in Paris, where the war was slowly becoming a tragic memory. People bustled along the thoroughfares repairing their lives and returning to normality.

A waiter brought Beau and Keeby two glasses of Bordeaux and a bowl of brined olives. They clinked the glasses in solemn camaraderie and sipped.

"To Wally," Keeby said.

"To all the Wallys," Beau added.

Young women in light, airy dresses strolled by window shopping. Some of them glanced at the handsome Americans relaxing at their café table. They made a striking pair, with Beau's sandy blonde hair and Keeby's jet black waves.

Beau's father had provided him with a generous allowance, delivered through Alphonse Rimbaud, the Shipley Company agent in Paris. He and Keeby had let a small pension in the First Arrondissement near Les Halles, five or six blocks from the Louvre and Jardin de Tuileries. His high school French fell about Beau's tongue, as Shakespeare's Henry V had stated, like a lovesick wife about her husband's shoulders. Keeby, being half Quebecois, fared better, but had discovered Canadian French had about as much in common with the mother tongue as American English did with British.

Still, they managed.

One might even suggest they had flourished, at least socially. Blessed by Beau's endowment, they spent their time exploring Paris' more sensuous delights. It had been fun, but Beau had grown restless.

"What is it?" Keeby asked. "Something's eating at you."

"It shows?" Beau chewed on an olive and sipped his wine. "I'm going home."

"Home! What's the hurry? Paris lies at your feet, young man. And the folks with broomsticks up their butts have guaranteed you won't find any more of *this* in the states." He hefted his wine glass. "Soon as the Volstead Act goes into effect in January, you won't be able to find a drink anywhere."

"Couldn't drink legally in Charleston even before we left," Beau said. "South Carolina's been dry since 1916."

"Ah. The Puritan ethic runs rampant in America. Why would you want to go back there?"

"What would you do if you stayed?" Beau asked.

"I could write."

"Write? What about?"

"Life. The war. Drinking. All sorts of things."

"People are sick of the war, Keeb," Beau said. "Who wants to read about it anymore?"

"I could write about Paris itself. I could work as a correspondent for a Canadian newspaper, or even one in the states. I have options."

"Aw, c'mon. Come back to Charleston. I'll introduce you around. Guy with your looks will get laid like a brick wall."

"I have that here already."

"Do I have to say it? I'd miss you. Okay?"

"And I'd miss you. But I have no appetite for America right now. Paris has grown on me."

"You'll tire of it."

"Then I'll go to Rome. Or maybe London."

Beau drained the wine, and the waiter appeared almost instantaneously with a fresh carafe. "You better be a hell of a writer. Without the stipend from my father—"

"I owe you a lot," Keeby said. "Let's say you'll always have a home in Paris."

"The real question is whether *you* will."

"Paris loves me. Paris will provide. And it isn't going anywhere. It'll be here when you decide to return. What's your rush, anyway?"

Beau refilled his glass and picked an olive from the bowl. "I have a wedding to derail."

CHAPTER FIVE

ON THE SECOND DAY of May 1919, bone-tired and constantly seasick from the transatlantic crossing on a crowded, rickety troop transport, Beau Shipley woke to a glimpse of the church spires of Charleston, the Holy City, for the first time in over two years.

As he was still tangentially attached to the Army, at least until he could officially muster out, he was able to secure passage on a crowded steamer out of Le Havre. The ship plowed the North Atlantic, grazing Greenland and hugging the North American coast, until it arrived in Charleston Harbor.

Beau watched as the city gradually hove into view. The ship passed the Civil War monument on Fort Sumter, and he caught his first glimpse of the dilapidated shipping docks on the Cooper River. Hordes of people had collected on the concrete loading platforms, many holding bouquets of flowers and waving frantically, hoping their returning family heroes would find them in the expanse of humanity. Beau searched the crowd for several minutes before he located his parents and his sister Adelaide. He waved, certain they didn't see him yet. He was home again.

Hours later, he placed his knife and fork on his plate and settled back in his dining room chair, fully sated. The Shipley family owned an eighteenth-century brick mansion on Wentworth Street, several blocks from the river. You could traverse the entire width of the Charleston peninsula in only a handful of minutes, and long-time residents of the Holy City had learned through sad experience that only the poorest or most foolhardy individuals lived in houses directly facing the water. The interior of the old city was the safest place when the periodic hurricanes struck, often with little warning, devastating everything in their path. The homes on the water were always the worst damaged. The interior homes, buffered by layers of lesser structures surrounding them, frequently emerged unscathed.

The housekeeper cleared the table. Beau's mother and sister retired to another room to relax, and Gordon Shipley invited his son to his study for brandy and a cigar.

People frequently observed that Gordon was an older version of Beau. He had the same cheekbones and chin, and their eyes favored one another. Like Beau, Gordon Shipley had brown hair so fair most people presumed it blond. Prosperity had made Gordon thick around the middle, but nobody would accuse him of obesity. Unlike Beau, he had cultivated a mustache which he kept meticulously trimmed. "We need to take you shopping for clothes," Gordon observed as he handed Beau a snifter. "You lost weight over there. Your suit hangs on you like old laundry."

"This is temporary," Beau said. "A few weeks of meals like tonight and I'll be back to fighting weight. But you're right. I do need something now. I'm shocked at you, by the way."

"Oh?" Gordon nipped the end of a Cuban Calixta Lopez cigar with a pair of scissors and struck a match. "Any particular reason?"

Beau held the snifter in the light and swished it. "Violating prohibition like this, and you a stalwart of the community."

Gordon chuckled. "I'll have you know the mayor of Charleston himself, Tristian Hyde, gave me this bottle. I enjoy special dispensation." He sipped from his own snifter and blew a smoke ring in the air, and was solemnly silent for a few seconds before saying, "Was it terrible?"

"The war?" Beau said. "Hell yes. Worse than anything you can imagine. Let's talk about something else."

"I admire you for going. You didn't have to, after all. I skipped out on the whole business in Cuba last century. Too busy making money. I swept in afterward to glean the profits."

"I'm not complaining."

"I knew where you were every minute. When I learned you had been sent to the Argonne Forest, I couldn't stand aside any longer."

"You pulled the strings to keep me from going over the top."

"I made some calls."

"Again, no complaints," Beau said. "Saved my life. Thank you."

"I needed you to survive, son. I hope you'll come into the business now if you've gotten all this romantic adventure out of your system. We've opened trade with several new Cuban and Jamaican cigar manufacturers. Business is booming. I can tell you've matured over the last couple of years. You could be a real asset now."

"To tell you the truth, I don't know what I want to do. Except for one thing. While I was away, Victoria Tradd took up with Alton Pinckney. She sent me a letter. The distance and the uncertainty of my return were too much for her. Well, I'm here now. I mean to break them apart and get her back."

"I see," Gordon said. "Clearly, you aren't current on the news."

"How so?"

"Alton Pinckney is dead, son. Along with his entire family, save for his brother who was overseas with you."

"Dead? How?"

"The epidemic. Spanish Influenza. It swept through Charleston like a tidal wave. Spared our house, I'm happy to say. But it took a lot of people. You want to be careful. It's still around."

"And Victoria's family?"

"Lost her mother. She and her father survived. Victoria had a particularly bad case, but it didn't kill her. So, you intend to court her?"

"If she'll have me."

"Can't imagine why she wouldn't. Let's get you properly dressed tomorrow, and you can call on her. If you dropped by tonight, they'd think their home was being invaded by a scarecrow."

"You're being uncommonly helpful," Beau observed.

"It seems Europe made you churlish as well."

"Realistic. What's your angle?"

33

Gordon placed the snifter back on the table. "You are my only son. The Shipley Company bears our family name, and you're the only Shipley left to run it. It's my legacy, but—before the war—I had concerns as to whether you had the steel in you. Now, here you are, a decorated war hero, world-wise, mature, practically a different man. You're ready. If Victoria Tradd can anchor you to this city and convince you to become my partner, I'm all for your pairing."

"About the business," Beau said. "I don't know—"

"Sleep on it. You've been through a traumatic experience. There's plenty of time for you to decide. In the meantime, let us enjoy these delightful cigars and sublime brandy. It's good to have you home, son."

CHAPTER SIX

THE NEXT MORNING found Gordon and Beau Shipley at the finest custom haberdashery in Charleston. Beau wore his best uniform, since he was still technically a noncommissioned officer, and it fit him better than his out-of-date suits.

His father's tailor, Talmadge Shaw, fussed over Beau from the moment father and son walked through the door. He insisted on creating five suits for the returning war hero—two in the finest lightweight wool, and a soft Scottish tweed for more casual evenings, along with the socially mandatory formal eveningwear. The tweed suit would sport two-inch cuffs and a belted jacket, the current fashion must-have for any sporty young man about town. Shaw took all of Beau's measurements, tutting and tsking at how his customer had slimmed in the army.

"You're practically skin and bones," he said, as he measured Beau's waist. "I will leave enough material to let these suits out once you fatten up a little."

"When can they be ready?" Gordon asked.

"Next Tuesday," Shaw told him. "Perhaps Monday. But certainly Tuesday."

Gordon dropped a hundred-dollar bill on the table next to the fitting mirrors. "Make it Friday. The boy must have something to wear. He's calling on a young lady."

"I can have the wool by Friday. The tweed? Monday at the earliest. The formal tails will take another week—the fabric is on order. But the rest? Tuesday. In the interim, may I suggest a *pret a porter* suit?"

"Off the rack?" Beau asked, recalling the term in French shop windows.

"I have your measurements. I can make alterations quickly. I could have it delivered later this afternoon. At the least, you'd be covered until the custom clothes are ready, and only another tailor would know it wasn't made specifically for you. In fact," Shaw said, glancing at the untouched hundred on the table, "I would be happy to include it *gratis*, in appreciation of your consistent custom over the years."

"Well, as I live and breathe," someone said from the entrance to Shaw's shop. "Could this possibly be Beauregard Shipley?"

Jamie Norton crossed the room and grasped Beau's hand. He was slightly shorter than Beau's six feet, but compactly and athletically built, with an aquiline nose and lantern jaw below smoldering eyes like a matinee sheik—a fact of which he was so aware, he had taken to slicking his hair back with pomade, though today he hid it under a fashionable herringbone tweed flat cap.

"It's good to see you," Jamie told Beau, smiling broadly. "How long have you been back?"

"Returned only yesterday," Beau said. "Need some clothes that don't have rank insignia all over them."

36

"Your suit is ready, Mr. Norton," Shaw said, obsequiously deferring to the much younger man. He stepped behind his counter to a rack holding completed orders. "And, I might say, it's a smart one." He held it out on a hanger for Norton to examine.

"Excellent work," Jamie said, fingering the fabric. "Mr. Shaw, you are an artist, well worth every penny."

"My blushes, Mr. Norton," Shaw said, with unmistakably fake humility. "Shall I box it for you?"

"Please do, but don't rush on my account. I want to catch up with Beau."

As Shaw retrieved a box from the storeroom, Jamie and Beau took a seat on the sofa in the fitting area. Gordon Shipley stepped out to the sidewalk to enjoy the warm spring sun and admire the passing women.

"What have you been doing with yourself?" Jamie asked. "The war's been over for six months, and you've only returned now?"

"Passed the winter in Paris. I took some shrapnel in the Argonne. My friend Keeby was much more badly injured, but he survived. I stayed until he was solidly back on his feet. To tell the truth, we're both adjusting to peacetime."

Jamie shuddered. "Nasty business, the Great War."

"I'm sure it distressed you terribly back here in the states. Shame you couldn't join us over there."

"Not everyone is a hero, old sport. And, besides, with half the eligible young Charleston bachelors occupied in the trenches, I became even more attractive to the ladies they left behind. No offense, but the Kaiser never did anything to me. I saw no reason to pick a fight with him."

"Sure," Beau said. "No offense."

"I'm studying law. Someone had to stay behind to witness the contracts."

"I suppose."

"Are you still recovering from your journey, or are you interested in a little fun?" Jamie asked.

"What did you have in mind?"

"As you may have heard, alcohol will be *verboten* all over the country in a few months, not only in South Carolina."

"We got the news in France," Beau said. "There was some discussion about it. The French have expressed regrets they wasted Lafayette on a revolution that led to abstinence."

"Old news around here, of course. We have a few years' head start on circumventing the restrictions. Been in the segregated district yet?"

"Nope."

"Oh, you're going to love it. Your father may have told you the city scions have tried to clean up the district."

"No," Beau said. "He didn't."

"Well, they have. Unsuccessfully, I might add. There are plenty of opportunities to skirt the blue laws there. Why don't we go tonight? I can show you around. Things have changed while you were away."

Despite its name, the segregated district had little to do with race. The area bounded by Queen, King, Beaufain, and Charles Streets in the middle of the peninsular city was largely populated by Negroes, which wasn't unusual, given almost half the city population was black, and they certainly weren't segregated from the white population. The city, prideful of its reputation as a community of churches, instead attempted to segregate its seedier activities to a single blue light district, within which one could find bars, bordellos, cockfights, bare-knuckle boxing matches, illicit hideaways where men danced with men and women with women, and all manner of behavior to make society matrons fan themselves into a dither. The city fathers had determined their best strategy was to separate Charleston's sins—and sinners—from the rest of the otherwise putatively moral town.

Alarmed by the increase in unlawful activity in the segregated district shortly after America's engagement in The Great War—frequently fueled by unruly sailors from the nearby Navy Yard—Charleston had attempted to close the district once and for all. Mostly, they had succeeded in driving the most offensive behaviors underground, which was a perfectly acceptable alternative, appearances being everything in the Holy City.

Any number of carnal delights were practiced out in the open before the war. Now, one suffered the inconvenience of having to know on which door to knock and which password would afford them entrance.

Beau knew neither. Jamie apparently knew them all.

"You said you could have the off-the-rack suit altered by this afternoon?" Beau asked Shaw.

"*Certainement!*" Shaw declared. "I can have it delivered to your door by four o'clock. Perhaps you are in the market for a new hat as well. I have a lovely fedora available in the finest beaver felt."

"Thank you," Beau said. He turned to Jamie. "Okay, Jamie. Sounds like we're painting the town red tonight. Drop by around eight, and we'll walk. First, I have an important errand."

CHAPTER SEVEN

TALMADGE SHAW was as good as his word. At precisely four in the afternoon, a courier arrived bearing a box with Beau's new off-the-rack suit, three fresh shirts and a dozen collars, two new ties, a hatbox containing the beaver fedora, and an assortment of socks.

After inspecting the package to ensure everything was there, Beau retreated to his room and dressed for the evening. He was delighted to discover Shaw's skills were undiminished during the war years. The suit fit perfectly and—as the tailor had promised—Beau couldn't tell it had started life on the rack.

He shaved carefully, polished his shoes to a blinding gleam, dropped several calling cards into the inside breast pocket of his new jacket, brushed two years of dust off his favorite straw skimmer from his wardrobe, and kissed his mother goodbye before walking the four blocks to Victoria Tradd's house.

The Tradd family, a branch of one of Charleston's most venerable family trees, resided south of Broad Street in a two-story brick home that had survived the great earthquake of the previous century. It had been reinforced, as had most of the city's structures, with threaded earthquake bolts that ran the length of the house and were anchored by six-pointed star flanges. It was believed, however untested, that the bolts would spare the buildings from collapse should the ground beneath their feet become irritable again.

A black servant named Silas answered the door. Beau handed the man his calling card. Silas invited Beau to relax on the wide veranda overlooking the garden courtyard while he inquired as to Miss Victoria's availability. Even in early May, spring had arrived in the South Carolina Low Country, and it was warm enough to relax outside.

Moments later, Victoria appeared in the doorway. She was smaller than he remembered, and her eyes had aged. Her wavy raven hair was piled and pinned high on her head, framing the beautiful and flawless skin of her face. Her umber eyes surveyed him from above her perfect straight nose, cupid's bow lips, and proud chin. Her skin had the pallor of mourning, as if she had sheltered far from the world for far too long. She dressed entirely in black. Silas remained behind her in the doorway.

"Beau," she said, surprised. "I had no idea you were back."

"I docked only yesterday. I called as soon as I was able. I wished to pay my respects. I wanted to tell you how sorry I am about your mother. She was a lovely woman."

"She was," Victoria said, before turning to Silas. "Could you fetch some iced tea and a few cookies, Silas? Mr. Shipley and I will chat on the veranda."

Silas walked back into the house.

"Please, sit," Victoria told Beau. He waited for her to sit before taking his own seat in one of the holstered white wicker chairs, facing her.

"Is your father home?" Beau asked. "I'd like to pay my respects to him as well."

"He had a meeting. He should return shortly."

"You look well," he lied.

"Thank you. And your family?"

"Faring nicely now the war is over. I…I heard just last night that the epidemic also claimed Alton Pinckney. Please accept my condolences."

"That is kind of you."

"Despite…what happened between you, I always considered him a decent and likeable fellow."

Silas reappeared with a tray bearing two glasses of tea and a small plate of cookies. He set it on the table between the two chairs and waited.

"Thank you, Silas," Victoria said. Silas returned to the house.

Beau pulled a stained and tattered sheet of paper from his jacket pocket. "About this letter—"

"Oh my goodness," Victoria said, her cheeks flushing, the first color he had seen on her ashen face. "You kept it?"

"Regardless of its contents, it came from you. In the trenches, any reminder of home is a priceless treasure."

"Beau, when I wrote —"

"You thought I would never return. We lost so many boys over there. It was touch and go several times. I nearly didn't come back, you know. I was almost killed during the battle of the Argonne Forest. An artillery shell destroyed a Brigadier Headquarters. I would have been inside it a minute later. As it was, I spent a month in the hospital, and this ringing in my ears still won't go away. But I did survive. I came home."

"Yes." She stood and walked to the edge of the veranda, peering over at the garden, as if gazing at Beau's face was too painful to bear. "And what are your plans?"

"My father wants me to join the cigar import business. He seems intent on the notion."

"And what do you want, Beau?"

"I'm still working through it. Except for one thing. Whatever I do, I dearly wish you would be part of it."

"I see," she said without looking back at him.

Beau crossed the veranda and placed his hands on her shoulders. "I don't care about the letter. You were justified in choosing Alton over me, but he's gone. I'm here. Victoria, can you forget about your loss and accept my attentions once again?"

"I can't say. Not yet." She turned to face him. "It's been two years. I steeled myself. I was prepared to hear you had been killed, or worse. I'm not a strong woman, Beau, regardless of what impressions you might harbor. I don't know if I could bear any more tragedy. If I accepted you back into my life, in the intimate way I did before the war, and anything happened to separate us, I couldn't bear it. It would break me."

"You're grieving," Beau said. "The world looks dark to you now. I know darkness, better than you can imagine. I lost dozens of buddies in the war, and I grieved for each one. If you'll allow me, I can help you through it. You remember Jamie Norton?"

"Of course."

"He wants to take me out tonight, to the segregated district. He says it's lively and sinful and even a little dangerous. Come with us. It will get your heart pumping and put color back in your cheeks. How long has it been since you got out and abandoned the rest of the world for an evening?"

"Too long," she said. "But not tonight. I want to go, but this is an...unexpected invitation. I need to prepare myself, and I can't see taking my first sojourn in weeks in... that place. I would be overwhelmed. I know. Alton took me there a few times before he died. Would you consider accompanying me to church this Sunday instead? We could have lunch at one of the nearby restaurants afterward. I do so want to rejoin the living, Beau, but my constitution tells me I should do it slowly."

"I would be honored," he said. "Please. I hesitate to put any more pressure on you, but I must know. Is there any chance for you and me? Is it too late to recover our lives before the war?"

"Perhaps," she said. "Time will tell."

CHAPTER EIGHT

JAMIE NORTON ARRIVED at the Shipley home only minutes after the family finished dinner. Gordon and Beau sat in the study when he knocked on the door.

"Mr. Shipley," Jamie said as he shook Gordon's hand. "Don't suppose we could talk you into joining us tonight."

"In the segregated district?" Gordon said, laughing. "I'm about twenty years beyond that sort of excitement, I'm afraid. Thank you for the invitation, though. You boys run along and have a fine time."

Despite the quiet, gentrified nature of Wentworth Street, one didn't have to walk far to reach the outer boundaries of Charleston's blue light district. Five blocks east and two south— how one measures distance on the Charleston peninsula—brought them to the intersection of Beaufain, Market, and Charles Streets. For the next four blocks south, the rules of gentility in Charleston were summarily suspended.

"So, when do you go to work for your father?" Jamie asked as they strolled.

"Haven't decided I will," Beau answered. "Why?"

"I overheard him talking with Talmadge Shaw this afternoon. He seems keen on the notion."

"We've discussed it. I'm on the fence."

"You know, with the war over, a lot of boys will be looking for work," Jamie said.

"What's your point?"

"The competition is going to be fierce. You're sitting pretty. A guaranteed job, and not any job, mind you. You won't be toiling in some mailroom or as an underpaid clerk. There's a lot of money in fine tobacco. And you could cruise to the tropics twice a year on business. Swing and sway under a coconut tree with Latin beauties. Guzzle rum like water."

"Did my father put you up to this?"

"Not a chance. Between you and me, he scares me a little. You pass on a deal like this, though, and I might hit him up for a job myself. So, if you don't go into the cigar biz, what would you do?"

"Still casting about. And I might work for my dad after all. I need some stability if I'm going to support a wife."

"A wife!" Jamie said. "Don't lose your mind, young man. Anyone in particular catch your eye?"

"I visited Victoria Tradd this afternoon."

"Anyone among the living?"

Beau stopped abruptly. Jamie took several more steps before he paused and looked back.

"Say that again," Beau said.

"You were serious? You're considering Victoria Tradd?"

"Some reason I shouldn't?"

Jamie pointed toward a bench off the street and palmed a flask from his jacket pocket. "Old son, you and I need to talk, and we both need a sip first."

Beau drank from the flask before handing it back to Jamie, who drained half of it in a single gulp. He screwed the lid back on.

"You saw her? Today?" Jamie asked.

"I was as close to her as I am to you."

"I recall you two were an item before you headed off to the shooting. How'd she look, compared to before?"

"Thinner, paler, quieter. She's been through a lot. Lost her mother. Lost Alton. She gets a pass on her looks. Life's been hard on her since I left."

"Life was hard on a lot of people. They didn't turn into Miss Havisham."

"What?"

"Dickens. The woman who shut herself away and sat in her wedding dress staring at the walls."

"I know who Miss Havisham was. What does that have to do with Victoria?"

"Nobody in this town has seen Victoria Tradd outside of church or her house since last year. She refuses all party invitations. She's never seen in the market. Sally Porter has visited her from time to time. The inside of the house is dark. All the drapes are drawn, day and night. It's as if she dropped off the planet. I don't know what you call a female hermit, but she's become one."

"That's terrible. And people allow her to do it?"

"They've tried to help her," Jamie said. "Sally, Dorcas Ravenal, Savannah Calhoun. She won't leave the house unless she's going to church, and she goes to church a *lot*."

"Why did it hit her so hard?" Beau said.

"I don't know, kid. I heard stuff, but it's just gossip."

"What?"

"Gossip, man. It's not worth repeating," Jamie said.

"Why mention it, then?"

"I thought about it a second time. Forget it You have enough troubles in your life."

Beau leaned forward, bracing his elbows on his knees, and stared at the ground.

"There is no place more hopeless than a battleground trench," he said, quietly. "It's one long open grave. You sit in mud, your back against mud, staring at a mud wall, under a muddy sky, and you see where it all ends. An eternity of mud. A man in a trench prays to whatever god or goddess will take his call and clings to any source of light there is. Mine was her letters, even the last one she wrote telling me she was marrying Alton Pinckney, and we were finished. They were my lifeline to home and a place where people weren't shooting at each other in anger they didn't understand and couldn't explain. If what you say is true, Victoria is in just as bad a place. She was the goddess who answered my call in the trenches. Maybe I can do the same for her here. But I have to know what kind of monster I'm fighting."

Jaime had lit a cigarette as Beau spoke, but he gazed at it, smoldering between his fingers, and ground it into the dirt with his heel.

"I didn't know," he said. "I mean, I saw newsreel film at the pictures, but they can't show everything. Don't want the women fainting in the aisles."

"It's in the past, mostly," Beau said. "Tell me the gossip."

"Alton didn't just die. He died a week before the wedding. Five days. Sally Porter was Victoria's maid of honor. They talked about everything. I mean, *everything*. I don't want to be crass, old sport, but you demanded the truth, and after what you've been through, I suppose you deserve it. I know you and Victoria…before you left. You know. She wasn't exactly going to the altar unblemished. Between you and Alton, there were a couple other guys."

"Who?"

"It doesn't matter."

"You?" Beau asked, the brittle steel in his voice unmistakable.

"Would you blame me? Everyone knows who does and who doesn't, and which side Victoria played for. But no. I wasn't part of it. You were gone, and Victoria went a little wild. Then Alton came along, and she fell hard. They were engaged four months after they met. We saw them in the segregated district two, three nights a week. She partied and danced and drank with the best of them. She was on top of the world."

"And then Alton died," Beau said.

"Not before he knocked her up."

Beau stared at Jamie in shock. Jamie flipped open his gold plated cigarette case and held it out. Beau waved it off. Jamie took one and blew a cloud of smoke into the air.

"She lost the baby shortly after he died," he said. "When she had the flu. This comes from Sally Porter, who'd know. There's no other way to say this, old bean. Victoria and Alton were racing the stork."

"Why did Sally tell you this?" Beau asked.

"I said I didn't have anything to do with Victoria, but I haven't been a monk. Pillow talk. People tell secrets in the dark, and Sally was vaccinated with a Victrola needle. Anyway, Victoria is grieving for a lot more than her mother and fiancé. It's made her a little…pal, I hate to say it, but it's made her a little crazy. True love's kiss might not be the cure for this brand of root magic."

"I'm obligated to try," Beau said. "I didn't have to go overseas. If I hadn't, she might be okay. I should try to make things right."

"I hope the cards fall your way," Jamie said. "But some battles are destined to be lost. Anything I can do, though, you let me know." He jiggled the flask back and forth. "Not much in here, and I'm thirsty. Let me buy the first round, okay? You look a little sick."

CHAPTER NINE

JAMIE NORTON led Beau to a praline and fudge candy shop on King Street, on the outer edge of the segregated district. The caramel aromas of sugar and butter and vanilla rolled over them as they stepped inside. Workers in white uniforms, wearing tight paper hats, pulled and tugged at still-warm saltwater taffy hanging from massive steel hooks set into foot-thick posts. Other confectioners poured sludgy pralines from a cauldron onto a marble slab near the front entrance to cool and harden.

Jamie asked the counterman for some Russian chocolate bourbon balls.

"I'm sorry, sir," the clerk said. "Fresh out. Hard to get bourbon these days, even for cooking."

"By any chance, might Vladimir have some in the back?"

"I believe he may," the man said. "Please, follow me. You can ask him yourself."

He led Jamie and Beau to a short hallway at the back of the store and pointed to a stairwell to the right. "Please, gentlemen, enjoy yourselves." He gratefully pocketed the four bits Jamie tipped him.

Jamie stepped aside to allow Beau to descend first. When they reached the bottom, they found a tunnel leading off to the left. The walls were old, mortared stone, only three feet wide. The arched ceiling was brick, barely tall and wide enough to allow Jamie and Beau through. The tunnel had recesses built into the walls, intended to hold candles. Someone had installed a string of electric lights along the length of the tunnel recently, and the candle recesses stood empty and cold.

Beau shuddered, flashing back to the constricting trench walls in the forests of France. Since the war's end, he had been anxious in closed spaces. He imagined the same applied to several hundred thousand other survivors of The Great War as well. Maybe millions. They had a term for it. He'd overheard the doctors whispering it in the hallways while he recuperated in Paris. *Shell shock.*

To calm himself, Beau said, "Vladimir?"

"The password. Ever since the Bolshies overthrew the tsar in Russia, folks on this side of the pond are bonkers about leftists. All the stuffed shirts behind the Volstead Act love to blame anything they don't like on Lenin and Trotsky, including secret drinking. *Vladimir* seemed a fun way to stick it to them."

"What is this tunnel? An old slave passage?"

"Before my time, old man."

The end of the tunnel was blocked by a massive polished wooden door on gleaming hinges. From behind the door, Beau could hear the thump of rhythmic drumming. The concrete floor vibrated. Jamie pressed a button set into the wall to the right of the jamb. A six-inch slide about head height in the door opened, revealing an intricate wrought-iron filigree. Beau could make out a face behind the shield, but only barely.

"Vladimir sent us," Jamie said.

Without a response, the peephole slid shut. The door opened silently on well-oiled hinges forged long after the need for a slaves' passage. The opening revealed an anteroom almost a dozen feet square, with another heavy oak door at the other end. The man behind the door was tall and lean, dressed elegantly in evening tails and white tie. His eyes, permanently bloodshot, glared demonically from his coal-dark face, but his mouth beamed in a grin.

"Mr. Norton!" he said, grasping Jamie's palm with his white-gloved hand. "What a pleasure to see you again." A scantily clad woman appeared at his side to take their hats. Both Jamie and Beau elected to retain their light wool jackets, mostly because—compared to their impeccably attired host—they felt underdressed.

Jamie turned to Beau, still grasping the black man's hand. "This is my friend Beau Shipley. He was in the war."

"Are you related to Gordon Shipley?" the man asked.

"He's my father," Beau said.

"He's a fine man. We've done business many times. So, you were over there?"

"I returned yesterday."

"Saw action?"

"My share. I was wounded in the last weeks of the war. The Argonne Forest. I recuperated in Paris," Beau said.

"Paris? Aw, I love Paris," the man said. "Perhaps, later, you can share the latest news from the City of Lights. Do you plan to join your father's business?"

"We're discussing it."

"Well, by all means, give him my regards." The man pulled a calling card from the inside of his waistcoat and handed it to Beau. It read *Chauncey Rutledge Howe*. Beau, out of the habit of carefully crafted manners, reciprocated with his card. Howe accepted it with a courteous but decidedly unsubservient bow.

"For now, please allow Miss Lovely to escort you to your table. And, in honor of your service, Mr. Shipley, and my long relationship with your father, I'll send a bottle of something refreshing to your table."

He shook their hands again and Miss Lovely, an aptly named young black woman wearing not much more than a bustier, pink tights, and a flourish of ribbons, took them lightly by the elbows and steered them toward a table near the middle of the main floor.

As soon as she opened the door at the far end of the anteroom, ragtime jazz blared through the opening and the room was suddenly flooded with light. Underneath the music was the muddled din of dozens of people talking at once. Cigarette smoke hung in an undulating milky cloud a foot below the ceiling.

The main room, apparently, was a basement storage area attached to the rear of a hotel one street over. Hidden within the walls of the larger structure, and accessed from the former slaves' tunnel, it was the perfect spot for an illicit watering hole. In case of a fire or—much less likely—a police raid, the partiers could escape surreptitiously into the hotel and from there back out onto the streets to pursue their hedonistic evening elsewhere.

"What's all that business about my father?" Beau asked, leaning across the table to be heard over the hubbub. "Who is this guy Howe?"

"You don't know?" Jamie asked. "I'm sorry. I figured you two must have met somewhere, the way he greeted you. And, even if you hadn't, you must know who he is. You never heard of Chance Howe?"

Beau cocked his head and glanced back at the bar, where Howe greeted a new couple who had arrived. "Chance Howe? That old man?"

"Everyone gets old, if they're lucky," Jamie said. "You are looking at a Charleston institution. His granddaddy sailed with Joseph Donovan's blockade runners during the Recent Unpleasantness. His daddy ran the original Charleston blind tiger, and Chance himself damn near won the welterweight championship of the world in a different century."

"And now he's a bootlegger."

"I suppose he'd have enjoyed a wider array of career opportunities if he'd actually *won* the championship. I wouldn't cry for him. This place is a little goldmine, and Chance Howe has two more like it scattered around. He takes it in hand over fist. And he likes you. I need to keep you close, kid. You might be lucky."

A waiter delivered a bottle of champagne in an ice bucket, and a tray with four glasses. "With the compliments of Mr. Howe," he told Beau. Beau slipped the waiter a tip and thanked him.

Jamie pulled the bottle from the ice and examined the label. "French," he said.

"It's champagne," Beau said. "Only place they make it is France."

Jamie filled two of the glasses and turned the bottle label to Beau. "Drink a lot of this stuff over in Paris?"

"Used to brush my teeth in it." Beau sampled the wine and raised his eyebrows in approval. "Mr. Howe has good taste. How in hell are he and my father connected?"

"Must be a cigar girl around here somewhere." Jamie craned his neck and scanned the room. "They don't roll 'em in the back, you know."

"And why four glasses?" Beau asked.

"Optimism," Jamie said. "Nature abhors a vacuum. Or at least an empty glass. Some destitute lasses who have no glasses at all will stroll along, and we shall generously share ours."

"Crafty," Beau said.

Suddenly solemn, Jamie lifted his glass. "To the guy who came home."

"The boys who didn't," Beau added, and they saluted the living and the dead with a clink as the band kicked into a syncopated rendition of *Tiger Rag*. Couples left their tables to congregate on the tiny dance floor in the middle of the room. The men were stylishly dressed and immaculately groomed, their immobile hair gleaming with oil. The women wore popular silk tunics over long skirts, and yards of pearls and turbans with peacock feathers.

Everyone smoked. The men dangled pre-rolled cigarettes from their fingers and lips as they talked. Some of the women carried elegant cigarette holders, in apparent competition to determine whose could be the longest without entirely losing its functional utility. Beau turned away from Jamie to listen to the band and scan the crowd for familiar faces. When he turned back, a woman with fiery red hair occupied the seat next to Jamie and smiled at Beau, her eyes twinkling with mirth.

"Damn, but that's a decent magic trick," Beau said to Jamie. "Can you conjure one for me?" He walked around the table to take Sophie Wildmon's hand.

"I'm glad you came back, Beau," she said.

"Strange greeting," Beau said. "You look beautiful, Sophie."

Sophie Wildmon batted eyes the color of ancient jade at him. Beau gave her hand a gentle tug, and she was instantly on her feet. She came to his chin, which Beau had always found the perfect height for a woman. Beau glanced toward the dance floor. She smiled, and seconds later she was in his arms swaying to *I'm Always Chasing Rainbows*.

Beau liked Sophie's face. He always had. Whether it was the light reflected from her hair, or some confluence of northern European genes, her skin always took on the tone of pink roses. Faint umber freckles spread across her cheeks and the bridge of her nose and didn't stop there. Long before he left for the war, and long before he had set his cap on Victoria Tradd, Beau had discovered Sophie Wildmon was a remarkably freckled creature.

"Have you been back long?" Sophie asked.

"My boat arrived yesterday. I ran into Jamie this morning while being fitted for a suit. He offered to show me how the town's changed while I was in the mud."

"Some things have changed. Most things are still the same. Tradition, right?"

"It can be a little stodgy. I spent the last five months in Paris, though. My perspective might be skewed. You can drink wine right out on the sidewalk there, you know."

"I'm glad I ran into you and Jamie. Some friends are planning a day trip to Sullivan's Island next Saturday. We're taking a sloop across in the morning, and we'll stay all day and have a cold lunch and get brown as nuts."

"You'll burn," Beau said. "As I recall."

"It's too cold to go into the water anyway. We'll likely stay bundled in blankets like mummies, and that can be fun too. There's space on the boat. You and Jamie should come along. It's going to be a riot. Please tell me you don't already have plans."

"I haven't been back long enough to make plans for next weekend," Beau said. "I'm taking Victoria Tradd to church and to lunch this Sunday. About as far ahead as I've planned."

"Well, aren't you the dear?" Sophie gave him a gentle hug as the song ended and they separated. Beau led her back to the table.

"Do you get seasick?" he asked Jamie. "We've been invited on an ocean voyage."

"You mean the day trip to Sullivan's Island next week? So sorry, old man, but I've already extended my regrets. Previous engagement. It isn't easy being Charleston society's most eligible bachelor."

"Maybe not for long, with Beau back in town," Sophie said.

"I'm not worried," Jamie said. "His eyes see nobody but Victoria Tradd."

Sophie's face clouded as Beau took his seat across from her. "Oh. I didn't know, Beau. I —"

"You thought I was taking her to church, and to lunch after, as a kindness," Beau said. "The way one might with a dowager aunt."

Sophie glowed bright red with embarrassment. "I recall you two were romantically involved before the war. I haven't seen Victoria in a long time. I don't recognize the woman who lives in her house now. I was simply…taken by surprise when Jamie said you intend to court her again." She placed her hand over his on the tabletop. "Please don't be cross. Come on the outing on Saturday. I insist. After all the horrors you've seen, you could use a day of gaiety on the beach. Invite Victoria. I suspect she'll decline, as she does with all social affairs, but she would be welcome, and everyone would love to see her. Perhaps you can sway her."

"Why not?" Jamie said. "Everyone else has tried."

Sophie shot him a warning look.

"It's okay," Beau said. "You're right. She's changed. The odds are against me. We're different people now. I'm not an idiot. I have my own doubts, and plenty of them. This isn't a crusade. It's more of an exploratory expedition."

"Or an archeological dig," Jamie said, and drained his glass. He held the empty bottle aloft. "Shall we order another?"

CHAPTER ELEVEN

THE NEXT MORNING, Beau suffered what his German brothers across the mud in the Meuse-Argonne would call a *katzenjammer*, following his revels with Jamie and Sophie in the segregated district.

Chance Howe had proven to be an expert on French wines, but less brilliant at moderation. Howe had delivered the second bottle of bubbly himself, and had shared their table for a bit, pouring and digging at Beau for all the hottest poop from Paris. The former boxer was a Francophile, and the war had prevented him from visiting his adopted country for several years.

"No, no, young Shipley," Howe cautioned when Beau described his lodgings with Keeby in Les Halles. "Sure, it's a safe area, and the Louvre is a short walk away. Convenient? Of course. But mark my words, when you go back you want to live on the Rive Gauche."

"I'm going back?" Beau said.

"You'll go back. And when you do, find a lovely little *pension* in the Latin Quarter, perhaps the Montparnasse, where all the smart young people are headed." He emptied the bottle and stood. "The Rive Gauche, young man. Where you want to be. By God, I do envy you. To be in my twenties and in Paris again. Please excuse me. It's time to circulate. I'll have another bottle sent over in a moment. Please extend my regards to your father, Beau. Mr. Norton. Miss Wildmon." He shook each of their hands earnestly, affected a slight bow toward Sophie, and disappeared into the crowd.

"What an unusual man," Beau said.

"You don't know the half of it," Jamie said, holding his glass to the light to watch the bubbles.

"How so?"

"He was a great athlete, but most people don't know he's a bit of a poof. I don't mind. Doesn't make a difference to me. But I'd say Chance Howe is a damned sight more than *unusual*."

The third bottle did them in. By the time they staggered through the hotel's marginally more respectable egress, fooling nobody, they were giggling and trying to compensate for a world which had suddenly canted perceptibly to the diagonal.

"Now where did I leave my automobile?" Jamie said, searching the street.

"We walked," Beau said.

"Walked! Damn. Silly me. Poor planning on my part. And the streetcars have stopped running. Didn't think it all through, and now I'm in no shape to walk."

"Driving would have been such a better option," Beau said, and giggled again. He pointed to a line of horse-drawn carriages parked in front of the hotel. "We are saved! Want to split a hack ride home?"

"I'm headed south," Jamie said, pointing in the general direction of Savannah.

"I'm only a few blocks north. Sophie?"

"I have a place on Bay Street, near Calhoun."

"Two go north, one goes south. I'm clearly odd man out," Jamie said, taking a congratulatory bow. "Have a lovely remainder of the morning, young lovers."

Beau escorted Sophie safely to her door. No southern gentleman would do otherwise, especially in her vulnerable and potentially compromising condition. He hailed one of the northbound carriages and held Sophie's hand to steady her as she stepped inside. Beau gave the driver the address.

"You moved out of your parents' house?" Beau took the seat facing her.

"I'm a rebel," she said. "Daddy always said going to college and reading all those books would ruin me. I suppose he had to be right about something. Got a cigarette?"

Beau lit a Gauloise from his cigarette holder and handed it to her. "Careful. They're strong."

She took a drag and immediately coughed. She gasped and coughed again, and wheezed, "Hot damn, Beau. You trying to get me hopped up? What is this? Pokeweed?"

"It's tobacco, mostly Turkish and Syrian. I warned you."

"They smoke this stuff over there?"

"It's considered patriotic."

She puffed on the cigarette again and exhaled a large blue cloud into the night. "Grows on you. You will have the decency to tell no one I was smoking in public. One must maintain standards in polite society. It's suddenly gotten chilly."

"Would my jacket help?"

Sophie crossed the carriage and sat on the same seat as Beau, facing backward at the receding lights and racket of the segregated district. She wrapped both arms around one of his and drew close to him, ostensibly for warmth. She leaned a head on his shoulder.

"*This* helps. I didn't exactly move out."

"Of your parents' house?"

"Right. I was…well, invited to leave."

"Your folks kicked you out?"

"My father couldn't cope with my political beliefs."

"Strange reason to cut you loose."

"I'm a suffragist, Beau. I've been working to get women the vote in this country. And it's going to happen. They're debating it in Congress right now. An amendment will pass later this summer. Too late for the Wildmons, I'm afraid. The issue has already fractured our family. I wouldn't be surprised if Daddy cut me out of the inheritance. If he does, I have a trust fund from my grandfather. I don't have to worry about money. I'd give every cent to be able to move home again, though."

"But you wouldn't give away the vote," Beau said.

"Never the vote. And that's what matters, isn't it? You see my priorities. I couldn't vote in the last election, but by God I will in the next."

"It's important to you?"

"It isn't to you?"

"I haven't given it much consideration. I've never voted. I was in Europe."

"Well, you'd better think about it. Times are changing. The war is over. It's time to shake the can a little, upset the status quo. You saw what happened over in Russia."

"I hope you aren't suggesting insurrection here in the States."

"No! I'm no trust fund anarchist. But the bad times are behind us. It's time to move forward. I can see a time when women won't only have the vote, but they also will be doctors and attorneys and college professors and captains of industry. Maybe even senators or governors. A president, perhaps. And it will be so common, nobody will think twice about it. It all starts with the vote."

"You're quite the modern woman, aren't you?" Beau said.

"Thinking about bobbing my hair."

"Please don't. A mane like yours deserves to flourish. I'd love to paint you one day."

"Paint me? Since when are you an artist?"

"It was part of my rehabilitation in the hospital. I took a piece of shrapnel to my head. They wanted to make sure I hadn't lost any of my faculties. Didn't have the heart to tell them I never had any before. I was fiddling with the brushes in the arts room, and people noticed. Turns out I had a talent for it."

"What do you paint?"

"Landscapes, mostly, but not what you're thinking. We aren't talking the Hudson River school here. I'm more of a post-impressionist. Not as abstract as Picasso or Braque, but a little looser than Renoir and Sargent, and positively never to be mentioned in their company again."

"And you want to paint l'il ol' me?"

"Backlit with the sun glowing through your hair, a rainbow of reds."

"Nude?"

"It's your picture. You can pose any way you want." They laughed, and he looked into her eyes, and he knew the true meaning of temptation. "Sorry. Champagne loosens my tongue."

"Yes. *In vino veritas.* It blows out all your filters. Removes the inhibitions that prevent you from saying what you mean."

"Inhibitions."

"Those books my Daddy said would ruin me? Included a couple by Dr. Freud in Vienna. I've become fascinated by psychoanalysis. Yeah. I'm kind of a modern girl. Read any of the works of Margaret Sanger?"

"Didn't she go to jail for advocating birth control?"

"She wasn't wrong. I'm that sort of modern too, Beau. I'm the future of womanhood in America. You'd better watch out. I'm afraid we're about to be a nuisance."

The carriage pulled to a stop outside a small two-story single house. The single house was a Charleston curiosity. Unlike most communities, where planners desired the front doors of houses to face the street, the limited space on the Charleston peninsula demanded a more economic architectural approach. By building long, tall houses with their narrow sides facing the street, they could erect more structures per square mile. Instead of the front door, visitors entered a gate on the sidewalk leading to a veranda overlooking a small, gardened courtyard. The arrangement provided greater privacy for the homeowners than the traditional front-facing houses, and if the gentry cherished anything on the increasingly crowded Charleston peninsula, it was privacy.

"See you to your door?" Beau asked.

"Thank you." He hopped to the ground first and held Sophie's hand as she stepped unsteadily from the coach. As she passed by him, she laid a hand on his chest and whispered, "Tell the coachman to wait."

Beau walked Sophie to her veranda gate and opened the latch for her. The house was dark, save for a gaslight at the corner that cast long shadows across the ancient sidewalk. She turned to him and leaned in close.

"This is the part where, normally, I'd invite you inside, see where things go. Of course, we already know the answer, don't we? A lot about tonight feels familiar."

"Sophie, I don't—"

"Stop there," she said. "I'm not asking you in. Not tonight. Not because I don't want to, and I'm drunk enough to cast caution to the winds, but I won't. I'm pleased we met again tonight, Beau. Between you and me, I have kind of an ache for you. Knew it the minute I laid eyes on you tonight. Took me back to the good times before the war. That boy is gone. I don't know this one yet. The war changed people here too. You're still working off an old program. Everyone's playing new roles now. So, maybe next time I'll invite you in. You have some things to do first. I'd suggest starting with your guilt over Victoria Tradd."

"My...my *guilt?*"

"That stuff by Freud sneaks into the conversation a lot lately. You chose to go to war. You left Victoria behind to lose everything except her dad and their spooky house. Maybe her life would have been different if you'd kept your nose out of Europe. Now you want to fix all her tragedies by marrying her. Sorry, my beautiful boy, but there are far too many conflicts in your head for you to give me the attention I deserve. I look forward to checking you for weird moles again real soon, but tonight's not the night. Go figure out your life. See if you can't do it before next Saturday, because when Victoria refuses to come to Sullivan's Island, you're my date."

She held his face in both hands and pressed her lips to his. It was more than a friendly kiss, and it promised far more to come. She hugged him once and disappeared behind the veranda gate. He heard her throw the latch on the other side, and her shoes clicked on the weathered cypress stairs as she climbed to the veranda and the front door. As soon as he heard the front door close, he walked out of the streetlight spill toward the carriage.

Confused, Beau took the carriage back to his parents' house on Wentworth Street. He undressed and fell naked into bed and thought for a while about death before finally falling asleep.

The alarm clock and the sunlight streaming through his bedroom window might have awakened him if the pounding in his head hadn't done the job first. In his exhaustion, he had forgotten to drink water before bed, and now he paid the price.

He soaked a washcloth in steamy hot water in the bathroom and lay back across his bed with the compress over his throbbing eyes. It was only a few hours after Sophie had summarily dismissed him at her veranda gate, and besides thinking about death, he had thought about whether she might be onto something.

The sudden rush of self-doubt only made his head hurt worse. He returned to the bathroom, rummaged in the drawers, and found a tin of Bayer's. He gobbled three of the tablets and forced back four glasses of water. He ignored the instant wave of nausea and focused on relaxing his facial muscles as he reheated his compress and returned to bed to resume his contemplations.

By breakfast, the rapid-fire artillery explosions in his head had dulled sufficiently for him to bathe, shave, dress, and make it to the table only minutes before the housekeeper cleared the dishes. His father, Gordon, sat at his place reading the morning newspaper. Gordon's plate and silverware had been cleared, but he seemed oblivious to a cup of coffee next to his elbow. Beau was transfixed with suspense as he watched his father turn the newspaper pages, each time coming within a hairsbreadth of knocking the coffee over with his elbow.

Perhaps he should have said something, but why spoil his amusement? He didn't have to wash the coffee stains out of the tablecloth anyway. He decided to allow physics and fate to take their various courses.

Gordon Shipley folded the paper, took a final sip of his coffee, and noticed Beau for the first time.

"Well, son, how was the segregated district?" he said, barely concealing his amusement at Beau's pallor. "I take it you found a way to pass the time."

"Jamie and I ran into Sophie Wildmon at a club. Chance Howe sends his regards."

Beau had hoped tossing Howe's name into the conversation would elicit a reaction from his father. He was disappointed.

"You visited Chance's club? Good choice. The man has exquisite taste. Give him my regards should you happen by there again."

"He said you and he did business together."

"Everyone does business with everyone else in Charleston, Beau. It's a small city. The options are limited. Is there something specific you want to ask?"

The cook delivered a plate to Beau. Two eggs over easy, country ham, grits with extra butter, and two biscuits. Beau's stomach lurched, but he suppressed the sensation. He was paradoxically hungry and nauseated at the same time. Perhaps if he picked at it slowly...

"Why did you marry Mother?" Beau asked, as he sawed at the slab of ham.

"Curious change of subject."

"I mean, why her and not someone else? What clinched the deal?"

"I'm not certain I follow the question. We found each other agreeable, I suppose."

"That's it?"

"That's everything, my boy. Your question suggests I had a wide choice of possible spouses. I suppose I did. I was your age not so long ago, and I had some wild oats of my own to sow. Each new generation believes it invented sex. Guess what. All those begats in the Bible? There's nothing new under the sun. I was strongly attracted to several young women, as I recall, in the way young men always are. I liked your mother, though. Oh, yes, there was attraction there. Had to be. But there was more. We found one another eminently agreeable. Instead of lustful tension, we found only pleasure in one another's company. We could talk to each other easily. It's the most important thing in a marriage. Everything else falls away with time and gravity. Eventually, all you're left with is whether you truly like being together. Why do you ask?"

"I'm questioning why I wish to pursue Victoria Tradd."

"Had a notion you might."

"She's changed. A lot."

"You both have. It's impossible to go to war and return unchanged. When you left, you were both children. What you need to ask is whether you're growing in the same direction."

Beau buttered one of the biscuits. "I don't know whether I'm pursuing this out of love, or obligation, or duty, or what. We only spoke for a few moments, but it's different. I know she was surprised to see me. I should have called first. I'm taking her to church tomorrow, and to lunch afterward. Maybe, with a day or so to prepare, she won't feel as awkward."

Gordon said, "Remember her before the war. Think about why you were attracted to one another."

"Okay," Beau said. "And what?"

"If it was for any reason other than you genuinely enjoyed being together, you're missing the most important thing. Perhaps it's different and awkward now because it was never right from the start." Gordon straightened his vest and retrieved his jacket from the coat rack. "Work calls. I can't tell you what to do, Beau. But here's something I do know. You're twenty-three years old. Short of murdering someone, there're few mistakes you can make at this age from which you cannot recover. So, you don't want to be in a hurry. If you marry the wrong person, well, you still had a lovely afternoon with all your guests, but otherwise you can work your way back from it. If you let the right woman slip through your fingers, it's a shame, but experience tells me there are a lot of right women in the world. Hundreds. Maybe thousands. If you're lucky, you find one of them. I was lucky.

All the Shipleys have been lucky. You give it enough time, and don't let impatience cloud your vision, and you might get lucky too."

CHAPTER TWELVE

WITH BEAU SHIPLEY'S DEPARTURE—and the loss of his father's stipend—Keeby Styles found himself in a Parisian pickle. Beau had graciously paid for their apartment in the Montorgueil through the end of July, but the lease didn't expire until the first of the year. Since separating from the Army, Keeby had sold several pieces of reporting to a magazine in his native Montreal. The checks had covered his half of the rent but left little else for the niceties of life.

It hadn't been a problem until recently. A month or two before deciding to return to Charleston, Beau had confided in Keeby exactly how much money he received each month from Alfonse Rimbaud, his father's agent in Paris. It was an appreciable allowance fully deserving of the low whistle Keeby emitted when he heard it. Wherever Beau and Keeby went, Beau caught the tab, because he could without raising a sweat or worrying whether his largesse would interfere with surviving the next day.

Now, with his benefactor an ocean away, Keeby faced harsh reality.

Worse, France was in an economic upheaval of its own. With the war over, hundreds of thousands of young men had streamed back into Paris hoping to resume their lives as they were before Gavrilo Princip spoiled the party. The infrastructure and economy they had enjoyed, before the war killed millions and the massive Spanish influenza pandemic wiped out millions more, simply no longer existed. Everything was in shambles as countries stumbled their way from a wartime to peacetime footing.

The French government, in a ham-handed attempt at normalization, made the tone-deaf decision to legislate limitations on workers' hours. No worker, the proposed law stated, would work more than eight hours a day or forty-eight hours a week. In a depressed economy in which overtime and multiple jobs barely kept pace, it was a devastating blow to the common man. Labor unions detested the new law. Skyrocketing postwar inflation had devalued the pay they received, and cutting hours only made the drawstring around their purses tighter. Talk of general strikes grew louder with each passing day.

It didn't matter much to Keeby. He didn't work at all, except when he pocketed a few francs as an interpreter for linguistically challenged American tourists. He could write into the wee hours if he pleased with no fear of the government telling him to stop. Seizing the opportunity, Keeby spent each day documenting the increasing strife between the government and desperate workers.

In addition, the former warring powers continued to wage the Paris Peace Talks through the winter and spring. Word had it they were on the verge of the first great treaty to emerge from the war's end, and it would be signed within the month. Paris vibrated with life and hope in the spring of 1919. Keeby tried to capture each moment of it in prose. He took copious notes, and typed manuscript pages through the entire night, pausing only to smoke a cigarette or pound back a glass of the cheapest drinkable wine he could locate. He fell into bed each morning not long before sunrise and rose again before noon to venture out and soak in as much of the Parisian experience as possible.

His plan was to collate all his Paris stories into a novel, a single account of the city's rebirth in the shadow of a war that nearly burned Europe to the ground.

In a perfect world, he would first sell the individual pieces to English language newspapers and magazines and enable himself to remain in his comfy apartment in Les Halles, preferably without the distraction or inconvenience of recruiting a roommate to share the costs. The plan had suffered in the execution, as the Paris Peace Talks had drawn correspondents from syndicates and independent periodicals all over the United States and Canada. Most of them had no problem knocking off human interest stories to pick some side money, cutting into Keeby's opportunities.

Keeby sat in an outdoor café in the Montorgueil, nursing the one glass of cheap Bordeaux he could afford that day, and scribbled on a notepad with the stub of a pencil he had sharpened in the ashtray with his penknife. It was late afternoon in early May. The trees had long since returned to verdant splendor. Women had doffed their heavy sweaters, and hemlines were rising again—a sure sign of oncoming recession. Keeby believed he could chart the rise and fall of great economies by the amount of skin women exposed to the world. In times of plenty, hemlines dropped. As money became tight and fabric more expensive, hemlines rose again. Keeby chuckled at the notion, and he jotted it on his pad. No idea—good or bad—was ever wasted.

A young man slipped into the chair beside him but didn't engage him at first. Instead, he gazed out at the passersby on the street. Keeby glanced at the man the way one does at a stranger. A rapid assessment—friend or foe? Something humans have done since the dawn of time. The young man was dressed cheaply, but not shabbily. He didn't smell, which Keeby appreciated. His hair was longish and stringy, as if he had used pomade the night before and hadn't washed it out. He had a thin dark mustache and wore thick eyeglasses. His woolen tweed flat cap showed some age but was otherwise in good shape.

The man ordered a *pastis*. The waiter left a bowl of olives and returned inside to fetch the drink.

"Bon jour," the man said, almost too softly for Keeby to hear. Keeby glanced over, smiling a greeting toward the man, and returned to his scribbling. He didn't mean to be rude, but he wanted to get the words down before the ideas in his mind took flight.

"Parlez-vous Francais?" the man asked.

"Tres peu," Keeby said without looking at him. His command of French was strong, but he had better things to do than engage the little man.

"Ah! *Americain!*"

"Canadian," Keeby said, which was mostly true. He wondered if the edge in his voice was as sharp as it sounded in his head.

"You are a writer? A reporter? Here for the peace talks?" The man's English was strongly accented, but otherwise precise.

Keeby traded the pencil stub for his glass. "You ask a lot of questions."

"I do. You are correct. My friends have often commented on this. What are you writing?"

Keeby's glass was empty. He debated finding a more private spot to work.

"I'll buy your next round," the man said. "I am only curious."

The waiter appeared. Keeby tapped the top of his glass and pointed to the strange little man with the thick glasses. "It's on him." The waiter glanced at the man, who agreed enthusiastically.

Obligated by the prospect of an unexpected second drink, Keeby turned to the man. "At the moment, I'm writing about the owner of a *patisserie* who had to remove the *et fils* from his shop sign because both his boys were blasted to atoms in the war. Now his business is failing because nobody can afford to buy pastries."

"This is for a newspaper? A magazine?"

"What's your interest, anyway?" Keeby asked.

"Perhaps I am in need of a writer."

"Unless your name is Hearst, you can't afford me."

"Forgive me," the man said as the waiter delivered Keeby's glass of wine. "My name is not Hearst. It is Remy Fousheé. Except, of course, it is not. But it is the name I go by."

"You are a strange little man," Keeby said. "But I appreciate the wine. To answer your question, I am collecting a series of vignettes about Paris and the recovery from the war. I sell a few here and there, but I don't have a regular publisher, and if you hadn't stopped by for a chat today, I couldn't have afforded a second glass."

"Ah. *Cassé?*"

"Not entirely broke, but close enough to it. I watch what I spend. I'm collecting these essays into a book."

"So you are a good writer?"

"Sure. I'm a regular Victor Hugo."

"Would you write for me?"

Keeby took a sip of the wine. "Maybe. Who are you? And what do you want written?"

"Your story about the *patisserie* owner. What do you make of his condition?"

"It's a damn shame. He hasn't done anything wrong, but everything is being taken from him. I make comparisons to Job."

"But what is your point of view?" Fousheé asked.

"I'm an observer. I report facts. I don't have a point of view."

"Oh, *merde,* my new friend. Everyone has a point of view. You compared a man who is being tested beyond his limits to Job. I could spend half an hour analyzing that one statement. You could have portrayed him as a fool, or as a man whose bad decisions were his undoing, a tragic hero undone by his own frailties. Instead, you paint him in sympathetic colors as a man undeserving of his fate. You yearn for a better world."

"Were you in the trenches, Remy?" Keeby asked.

Fousheé pointed to his eyeglasses. "Unfit to serve, I'm afraid."

"There is no worse world. Anything you crawl to from the trenches is an improvement."

"You found the war a grand mistake."

"Of epic proportions. You kind of had to be there."

"I suspect we share a great many opinions. I am a student at Salpêtrière, studying psychoanalysis. I am a member of a small cadre of students who also yearn for a world without war, forever. We believe in justice for everyone, not only the rich. We believe no man of conscience could ever horde a mountain of gold if he saw a single starving child, and therefore the rich have no conscience."

"Got it," Keeby said. "You're Bolshies. Spreading the Gospel According to Vladimir Lenin."

"Perhaps I was mistaken. Enjoy your wine." Fousheé drained his glass and rose to leave.

"Hold on," Keeby said. "Don't get touchy, Remy, or whatever your real name is. Relax. As it happens, I'm just poor and hungry enough to entertain questionable decisions. Tell me what you want."

"My friends and I operate a clandestine press on the Left Bank. We put out a new broadsheet each week. Only problem is, we are not writers. We hear things. People read the paper, and they agree with the ideas, but they say it is badly written."

"Most political diatribes are," Keeby said. "So, you need someone to transpose your bull goose crazy manifestos into readable prose."

Fousheé sat back in his seat and sipped from his glass. "I want to be a psychoanalyst because I believe I can read people. You are far more sympathetic to our cause than you admit. I need you to write what you are already writing. The shop owners squeezed like grapes until there is nothing left but the husks. The boy with a box full of war medals who can't find work. The young war widow forced into prostitution to survive. The poor man who is sent to prison and the rich man who walks free for the exact same crime. I want you to write about labor unions and workers' rights and the need to put the wealth back into the hands of the people who drive the engines of industry."

Keeby stared at Fousheé's bug eyes behind the thick glasses. "You knew who I was before you sat here."

Fousheé bowed his head.

"How?"

"I've read your articles. I sensed a fellow spirit."

"What's the pay?"

Fousheé told him. Keeby arched an eyebrow.

"Let's say I'm interested, mostly because I am. Where do a bunch of Bolshie students get the money to keep this broadsheet going, let alone pay the writer fees you're offering?" Keeby asked.

"We pool our resources. Some of us have money. Not all who yearn for equality are in poverty."

"You *do* need a writer."

"Regardless, there are those in the privileged classes also who wish things could be different."

"As long as the check clears, I don't care. I'm just curious. I don't want to sound ungrateful, but Bolsheviks aren't exactly welcome in Paris, and I'm a Canadian citizen and by extension a British subject. The last thing I need is to be deported—or worse, imprisoned—on insurrection charges, especially since I'm not entirely sympathetic to your goals or methods. I won't be writing any political screeds. I see what you're doing. The substance of your argument is dry as dirt, so you want to put a human face on the issues you're fighting to achieve. You need real stories of suffering and oppression to weave together with your polemic."

"You make it sound almost nefarious."

"It doesn't matter. The beast must be fed."

"The...*beast*, Monsieur?"

"I need the money. I have conditions, though. Nothing gets published under my own name. Ever. I don't know your friends, and I don't want to know your friends. You are my contact. I deliver the articles to you, and you deliver the money to me. I can write you five articles a week. You tell me what day and time to meet, and we meet."

"Where?"

"Right here's good. You bring the money; I'll bring the stories. You'll buy me a glass of wine and we'll make the exchange. The money stops, the stories stop. You don't show, the stories stop. My name ever gets connected with your little revolutionary cell, the stories stop. Are we agreed?"

Fousheé extended his hand. "I believe we are. I will return a week from today, and we will meet at this table. I will happily anticipate your five stories."

"Hold on," Keeby said. "First week in advance."

Fousheé squinted at him through his thick glasses. "Monsieur? Suppose I arrive next week, and you are not here?"

"Someone has to trust someone here, or none of this is going to work. I have no doubt you know my address, and I'm not about to skip town on what I'm making off a week's worth of stories. Besides, as I said, the beast must be fed. In this case, *I'm* the beast."

"I see," Fousheé said.

"Call it a retainer, if you like."

"I believe I will, Monsieur Styles." Fousheé dropped an envelope onto the table. He had expected to pay something that day after all. Keeby allowed himself to smile.

"And no names. I don't get to know yours, you don't get to spread mine around. I'm just words for hire. Got it? I'm not a revolutionary."

"You were clear the first time, Monsieur. Good day. I look forward to seeing you next week."

Relieved his money troubles had eased, Keeby boldly ordered another glass of wine. As he sipped, he reflected on the deal he'd made, and whether it was with some devil. His perception of the risks he undertook the moment he shook hands with Remy Fousheé—or whatever his actual name was—was not at all erroneous. It was dangerous to be a Bolshevik in Paris.

In 1914, the leader of the French Socialist Party, Jean Jaurès, was shot twice in the back of the head while dining in a bistro on the Rue Montmartre, around the corner from where Keeby now waited for his third glass of wine. There was no question about the identity of the shooter, a young French nationalist named Raoul Villain. The killing was witnessed by several other patrons, and Villain was identified almost immediately.

On the same day Beau announced he was returning to America, a French court acquitted Raoul Villain in the murder. Recognizing a complete breakdown of justice—and the apparent sanction of open season on leftists—French socialists, labor unionists, workers, and other downtrodden masses rose and marched in the streets, choking the Champs-Elysees with over three hundred thousand protesters.

The French government's response was rapid and summary. The traditional May Day festivities in the city, an international celebration of worker solidarity, were declared illegal. Instead of marching and reveling on the holiday, workers broke out in riots across the city. By the end of the day, three people were dead and thousands injured.

In the eyes of the city fathers and the French central government, the leftists were out of control. Crackdowns were inevitable. Similar movements were quashed across Europe in the wake of the Bolsheviks' decisive coup in Russia less than two years earlier.

Keeby was uncertain whether they should have been so worried. Affairs in the former Tsarist country were not moving smoothly. The revolutionaries had exposed themselves to the same lessons learned by rebels all over the world throughout history. It was one thing to take command of a country. Keeping the country running without collapsing into chaos was another.

So far, the Russians had fared little better than their French counterparts a hundred thirty years earlier. Having seized control, the revolutionaries' cobbled-together solidarity, smelted in the crucible of revolution, became a distant memory. In less than a year they had dissolved into bickering factions. Everyone agreed the end goal was to create a workers' paradise. Each cadre believed only they knew the correct path to achieving it. Russia's already rickety infrastructure crumbled. Anything useful was typically in short supply, if you could find it at all. Party *apparatchiks* enjoyed plenty, while the workers they pretended to represent went hungry and cold. Everywhere a person went, there were lines. To regain control over the day-to-day operations in the vast country, the Bolsheviks had reinvented bureaucracy, and had made a bit of a hash of that as well. As in every other political system in the history of man, the new Bolshevik government in Russia quickly devolved into a caste system of haves and have-nots. In their defense, if asked, they would have claimed they did it with the very best of intentions.

Other governments in the newly peaceful Europe, still nervously vibrating like a bell from the war, all observed the ongoing birthing pains in the new government in Russia with a keen eye, analyzing the events meticulously to prevent them from spreading it to their own countries. Surprisingly, resolving the conditions that produced unrest among the working backbone of the country in the first place always languished near the bottom on the list of intervention options. Repression of undesirable elements was always at the top.

That was the key. His stories would focus on those people whose lives were most affected by the greed inherent in any hierarchical social system. The poorest and most destitute among Paris's denizens would become his muses. Like Dickens a century earlier, he would mine the tragedies of the lowest classes—the sewage workers, the slaughter-house butchers, the rubbish collectors, the tavern keepers, the starving artists, the displaced factory workers forced into prostitution. He would give a voice to people who had no power. A virtuous but unfortunate worker is tormented by a greedy, cruel manager. Seeking help from the government sworn to serve, the worker is rebuffed due to a bureaucrat's interpretation of some obscure regulation, the true purpose of which was lost in antiquity. With nowhere to turn, the worker descends into destitution. What society would tolerate such conditions? Why, *all* of them, children.

He would make general observations of the human condition, which he could support with documented literary examples all the way back to Gilgamesh. Nothing seditious there. If it worked for Dickens, after all...

The students could do what they wanted with the stories, as long as they kept his name out of it. The money was worth the tiny sliver of risk he faced. What the Bolshie students wanted, Keeby could knock out in a day, leaving the rest of the week to write the serious stuff, the stuff he hoped would make him a famous and wealthy author.

He was, at worst, a part-time revolutionary.

Just enough to pay the bills.

CHAPTER THIRTEEN

THE TALK WITH HIS FATHER only confused Beau further. Their conversations had always tended that way. Beau suspected his father was a wise man, or at least a crafty one, who always withheld the greater part of his opinion on any given subject. As a result, he frequently appeared aloof or uninterested, but if you watched Gordon Shipley's eyes, you quickly observed nothing escaped his attention.

Even so, Beau dearly wished his father had given him a scintilla of direction. His feelings regarding Victoria Tradd were no less conflicted than they had been when he awoke.

It was a breezy May Saturday morning in Charleston. Soft clouds scudded about in a brilliant crystalline blue sky. Beau had no plans and no social obligations. It was almost his first moment to stop and reflect since he had shambled down the gangplank of the troop carrier two days earlier.

Two days? He shook his head in disbelief.

He didn't like sitting around the house contemplating existence like some Buddhist monk. The lack of plans only meant he was free to do what he wanted. He finished his breakfast, surprised he was no longer hung over at all anymore.

On the way back to his room, he was struck by a memory from Christmas several years earlier. Their parents had given Beau's sister Adelaide a pad of textured drawing paper and some pastel crayons. He stopped by her room and knocked. Adelaide sat by the window, reading a book.

"What are you reading?" he asked.

"Frank Norris. *The Octopus.*"

"Is it good?"

She cocked her head, as if weighing how to answer. Her eyes, blue like Beau's, were among their few similarities. She was darker and leaner, with sable brown hair compared to Beau's sandy blonde, and she seemed more fragile than he recalled from before the war.

"It's...thought-provoking. I suppose you're happy to be back in Charleston, especially after what you went through."

"It's proving interesting. The world kept turning while I was away and didn't let me in on the joke."

"I don't understand."

"Me either. Not yet. Working on it, though. I wanted to ask you about a set of pastels Mother and Father gave you a few years back. Do you still have it?"

"Of course," Adelaide said. "I never used it. It was Mother's idea. She wanted to encourage my artistic inclinations. I can't even draw flies. I never opened the box more than once or twice, so the crayons should still be fresh. Why?"

"I learned drawing when I was in rehabilitation. It calms me. I might do some sketches. Nothing else to do today."

"Hold on." She placed the book on a table and disappeared into her closet. Presently, she returned with a hinged and clasped wooden box and a pad of drawing paper. "Take it," she said, placing the items on the bed. "Better than rotting away in the closet. Show me your drawings later?"

"It's only fair, but I warn you, I'm a hacker. I don't know what I'm doing."

"Most geniuses don't," she said, smiling.

———

The amazing mid-spring weather lured Beau toward the southern tip of the peninsula to White Point Garden, an open park where, only sixty-eight years earlier, mortar fire heralded the opening of America's bloodiest years.

The bellicose scars in the earth had long since healed and glossed over with grass and palmetto scrub. One of the more popular sayings in Charleston was that, where Beau stood that morning, the Ashley and Cooper Rivers met to form the Atlantic Ocean. Being the lowest point in the city, the entire tip of the peninsula had been protected from the tidal surges at the confluence of the Ashley and Cooper Rivers by the erection of a great stone barrier wall, almost twenty feet from top to the bottom, sunk into the harbor silt. At low tide, ten feet of the harbor bed was visible from the seawall, littered with crabs and shellfish and various river flotsam. When the tide was high, water might climb halfway up the wall. He had never seen it, but Beau had heard, when hurricanes occasionally struck the city, the storm surges could breach the seawall, flooding East Bay Street with millions of gallons of water.

Beau was of a mind to sketch such an event. He closed his eyes and tried to picture it. He imagined a frying pan sky, undulating like sodden sheets, with bolts of lightning piercing the clouds and striking the spire of St. Peter's Church. He envisioned waterspouts in the harbor, and huge waves crashing over the seawall, with spray arcing higher than the chimneys of the houses along Bay and Water and Atlantic streets.

When he opened his eyes, the image vanished in the radiance of the day as it was. He stored the pieces of the storm picture as best he could in his memory and opened the wooden box to choose the colors for his sunny day sketch. He could always do a second quick sketch of the seawall and Bay Street and points north and fill in the hurricane stuff later if he wished, when the beauty of the sparkling spring day didn't distract him.

While the sky was perfect, a steady breeze from the south created chop in the harbor. Pleasure boats had ventured out, and they bobbed in the water like corks. Beau was reminded he'd likely be on one of them a week later, headed over to Sullivan's Island. He hoped the weather would be calmer. Jamie was right. He'd endured enough pitching waves over the last several weeks.

Beau sat on the seawall, faced north, cradled the pad in one arm, and roughed out his sketch. In the months he had spent in Paris with Keeby, he had visited many of the finest museums, and had found himself drawn to the impressionist works of artists such as Monet, Renoir, and Sargent. Then he encountered the next generation of painters—Cezanne,

Modigliani, Gauguin, Van Gogh—and examined their works meticulously from the perspective of inches, and he taught himself to how to paint. Most museum visitors admired the gestalt wholeness of the painting. Beau had looked at the brushstrokes, trying to determine how hard or lightly the artist had gripped the brush and pressed the bristles into the canvas. He analyzed each painting to determine how the artist had almost imperceptibly modulated the tint in a shadowed snowbank, or suggested chop in the harbor, or simply shrouded an entire painting in fog. When he found a knowledgeable docent, he asked every question that popped into his head, and he absorbed what he was told.

Precision, he had determined, was the domain of photographs. Instead of drawing out a detailed charcoal rendering of the waterfront, he instead squinted his eyes, blurring the scene enough to get the *idea* of the area, the suggestion of it. He drew patches of color and light. He drew with the side of the crayon instead of the point. Nothing was precisely to scale. An architect would survey the pastel and run shrieking into the night. Lines were left intentionally crooked. Nothing was corrected, only sketched over if it didn't work. Even so, once he was finished with his hazed impression, he believed people familiar with the area would recognize it.

As he raised and lowered his head, memorizing some component of the landscape and transferring it to the paper, he became lost in the process, and he was able to isolate the art from his other deliberations, and operate on two levels at once. Barely conscious of what his fingers were doing on the paper, he ruminated about the upended world to which he had returned, and how little of it made sense. He mused briefly on the possibility that the shrapnel which grazed his skull might have splintered, sending a shard deep into his brain, and the shard now controlled and skewed his perception of the world he had left behind. Not for the first time, he imagined he had died in the trench in the Argonne Forest, and this bizarre, disjointed Charleston was only his soul's interpretation of Hell.

CHAPTER FOURTEEN

BEAU APPEARED AT Victoria Tradd's front door on Sunday morning, half past ten. As he had on Friday, he presented Silas with his calling card and waited on the veranda for Victoria to appear so he could escort her to church.

His experience in the trenches had obliterated any faith he might have had in a higher being. No deity worthy of praise would allow men to rend one another limb from limb, gas one another, bombard each other with explosives, and leave millions of widows and millions of children orphaned. Faith was fine for a cloistered monk who never saw blood beyond the errant scratch. Step into the real world of global war for five minutes, he reasoned, and you'd question the existence of any deity, or at least their motives. Religion no longer held any fascination or interest for Beau, but church in Charleston was something beyond mere worship. If the segregated district offered one sort of social outlet, on the other end of the spectrum fell weekly church services, where saint and sinner were both expected to at least make an appearance.

Virginia Tradd's family attended the Circular Congregational Church on Meeting Street. One of

Charleston's oldest houses of worship, the stones and bricks of this sacred curiosity had stood since the early seventeenth century. Affiliated with the Congregational Association, the Circular Church services occasionally harkened back to the days of Cromwell and the Puritans. Beau had always been surprised at Victoria's carefree spirit, in contrast with the severity of her church's tenets. The war and her multiple tragedies seemed to have drawn her back toward her church, and away from the world.

The front door opened. Beau turned to speak to Victoria, but found her father, Norbert Tradd, standing in the doorway. For a moment, Beau didn't recognize him. When Beau left for Europe, Norbert Tradd had been dapper and meticulously groomed. His dark straight hair was always plastered to his skull, surgically parted in the middle. His handlebar mustache was waxed to within an inch of its life. His shoes were always kept spotless. His pince-nez eyeglasses permanently defied gravity. Norbert had always been a serious man, but he also had managed to make the best possible impression wherever he traveled.

The man standing in the doorway had Norbert Tradd's eyes, but little else was recognizable. The hair had gone silver, and he had allowed it to grow long and dry, hanging in clumps over his ears. The mustache was pewter, no longer waxed, and hung like willow branches over his mouth. He dressed entirely in the black of mourning. His face was a map of crags. If possible, he seemed to have shrunk half a foot in only two years.

"Young Shipley," he said, his voice raspy. "Please, have a seat."

Tradd pointed toward the chairs on the veranda and sat facing him.

"Victoria invited me to escort her to church today," Beau said, smiling.

In the time before the war, he and Tradd had orbited one another with a mixture of suspicion and grudging respect. Neither would claim the other as a friend, but at least one of Beau's potential futures included Norbert Tradd as his father-in-law, so it was in his best interests to speak to the man on the friendliest deferential terms possible.

"Yes," Tradd said. "That will not be possible."

"I'm sorry. Is Victoria not well?"

"She is in satisfactory health, I am happy to say."

"I'm relieved. Some friends asked me to invite her to an outing at Sullivan's Island next Saturday. Perhaps some fresh air and sunshine will—"

"What?" Tradd asked. "Fix her?"

"Beg pardon, sir?"

Tradd slumped in his chair. "Victoria's social reticence has not escaped my attention. I believe, given the great tragedies she has endured, a period of isolation and recreation can do nought but good for her. When she is ready, she will venture back into the world. However, at whatever point she decides to reestablish her social ties to the community, she will not be escorted by *you*."

A thousand shocked thoughts ran through Beau's mind at once. Had Tradd discovered Beau's and Victoria's affair before the war? Perhaps he knew about Victoria's miscarriage, and blamed Beau for guiding his daughter down the carnal path to her pregnancy? He searched his memory, trying to find any slight or insult he might have unwittingly made toward Tradd or his daughter. Nothing came.

"Excuse me, sir, but have I offended you in some way?" Beau asked.

"We are a devout family, Shipley. Perhaps we lost sight of it. Allowed ourselves to dwell too much in the domain of earthly delights. Victoria and I are all who remain of our family. God saw fit to look on us with displeasure for our wicked ways and rained misery on us with a fury. We were held to account for our sins, and the price was dear. I learned my lesson. I shall never turn my face from the Lord again. And you, young Shipley? Are you a devout man?"

"I don't see—"

"Because a devout man would know the importance of Second Corinthians, Chapter Six, Verse Fourteen. *Do not be unequally yoked to unbelievers.'* So I ask you again, Shipley. Are you a devout man?"

"No," Beau said, without flinching. "I'm not."

"It is to your credit, I suppose, that you did not attempt to lie about it. So, you see my dilemma. And Victoria's. We have found too much disfavor in the eyes of the Lord. I cannot allow her to engage in a relationship which would further endanger her soul."

"Allow? Excuse me, Mr. Tradd, but Victoria is an adult. She's *allowed* to make her own decisions."

"You visited my daughter two days ago, did you not?"

"I did."

"After you left, she remained in a great state of agitation for almost twenty-four hours. It was impossible for me not to recognize it. She did not confide the entirety of your conversation to me, but she told me enough to convince me she is not ready for your attentions, or the attentions of any young man. At whatever point in the future she emerges from her malaise, I am sure we can find an appropriate suitor from among Charleston's more godly bachelors. I should have communicated with you before you wasted a trip over here today, but I was curious to see whether you showed. Part of me regrets you did. It makes this situation so much more complicated."

"Yes. I can see how it might," Beau said.

"Don't be snippy. Even if you were adequately religious, I would have rejected you as a suitor."

"Why?"

"I don't believe our families would form a good union. I have great objections to your father."

"Father? What about him? What's he ever done to you?"

"To me? Nothing. I've said too much. In case there has been any confusion, you will not escort Victoria to church today, or next week, or at any foreseeable time in the future. She is not in fit condition to engage in other social activities, so you and your friends will be disappointed regarding her presence on this trip to Sullivan's Island. You will not offer to take my daughter into the segregated district again, ever, under any circumstances. This will not be a problem, I assure you, because you won't be taking her anywhere as long as she resides under my roof. Is there anything I've said that you still don't understand?"

"No," Beau said. "You've stated your position clearly."

"And, while we're speaking, I suggest you reexamine your life, young Shipley. You are not right with God. It would be a terrible fate you'd face should judgment befall us this morning."

"I'd manage. I'll see myself out." He crossed the veranda to the streetside door and opened the latch. Before leaving, he turned back to Norbert Tradd. "I'm not giving in."

Tradd lowered his head sadly, and said, "Young man, that is your folly."

Beau embarrassed himself by accidentally slamming the streetside door, and immediately regretted looking petulant. He pointed his feet toward Wentworth Street but chanced to look upward. He spied a figure dressed in black in the ancient wavy glass of a third-floor bedroom in the single house, a pale face framed by anthracite hair. The features were distorted in the refraction of the ancient window, until he saw a gaunt feminine hand press against the glass. It hovered there for several seconds, before it curled into a claw, dragged to the bottom of the sash, and disappeared just before the drapes closed.

CHAPTER FIFTEEN

KEEBY SAT at the same café table at the corner of Rue Montmartre and Rue de Turbigo in the Montorgueil, savoring a glass of burgundy and a plate of olives as he waited for his assignation with the man who called himself Remy Fousheé. It was a breezy middle spring afternoon. Overcast, but rain didn't appear to be in the offing.

As he had expected, Keeby had completed the five pieces the little man asked for in only a day or so. He had spent the rest of the week working on other projects and making silent wagers with himself as to whether Fousheé would even show. Part of him hoped he'd written the articles in vain.

The more he considered his strange business arrangement with Fousheé, the less he liked it. Within the last several days, he had read about mass arrests of political insurgents and sympathizers of the Russian communists. The French government, predictably, had once again decided their goals would be better served by suppression than by negotiation.

Keeby was no radical. Neither was he a particularly patriotic man, even if he had volunteered in the war. Whenever he marveled at the inconsistency, he reminded himself—as was often the case in stories like his—that there was a woman involved. In his case, it was a woman from a family who prided themselves on their military tradition. Blinded by his ardor, Keeby believed if he volunteered to serve, he might find favor with the woman's father.

She dropped him five weeks after he enlisted and married an accountant from Dearborn. Keeby was fully committed to his brief but dangerous and traumatic military career by then. At the time he enlisted, the United States had not yet entered the fighting, and President Wilson had been re-elected in 1916 on the boast he had kept the country out of the war. As he took the oath, Keeby had reasoned, *"There is no way I'll ever be sent over there."*

Keeby chuckled at the irony and popped another olive in his mouth. He wasn't a French citizen, and therefore owed the tricolor flag of the Third Republic no particular loyalty. His status as an American was equally conflicted, since he had been born in Quebec to an American father and Quebecois mother. Holding dual citizenships had left Keeby equivocal as to exactly where his native soil might lie. Not being tied to any specific geographic location, his allegiances were also fluid. He usually sided with whomever paid him best.

Now, he was being paid by the Bolsheviks. At least they had promised to pay. Considering their goal of overthrowing the bourgeoisie French government, Keeby hoped they held their bargain to keep his name and identity entirely out of the picture. Realistically, if it were discovered he, a French-speaking Canadian-American British subject, was materially involved in the activities of Foushée's revolutionary cell, the worst they would do was deport him and never allow him back in France. The idea didn't suit Keeby well. He had grown to love Paris. He had weighed making it his permanent home. He knew he was playing a dangerous game, but it paid the bills.

He was so lost in his reverie, he didn't hear Fousheé pull out the chair next to him and sit. He snapped out of it when Fousheé coughed.

"Do you suppose it will rain?" Fousheé asked.

"You're being melodramatic," Keeby asked. "We're a couple of guys sitting in a café. Nobody cares why we're here. Nobody's spying on us, and if they are, it doesn't matter whether we act casual and nonchalant. I have your pieces. You have the cash?"

Fousheé halfway removed an envelope from his inside jacket pocket. He showed Keeby the top half and slipped it back inside his jacket.

"Jesus," Keeby said, shaking his head. He opened his briefcase and handed Fousheé several paper-clipped sheaves of paper. A waiter appeared. Fousheé ordered a *pastis* and some bread.

Keeby sipped his wine and watched people stroll past the Eglise de St. Eustache toward the Les Halles market as Fousheé drank and ate and read over the articles. When he was finished, Fousheé folded the articles and placed them inside his jacket. He took out the envelope and handed it to Keeby.

"Pleasure doing business with you," Keeby said. "Same time next week?"

"I'm not sure you entirely appreciate the importance of the work we have undertaken," Fousheé said.

"*You* have undertaken," Keeby corrected. "I'm providing a non-political service. Are the folks who empty your trash cans and clean your windows Bolsheviks too? Does it rub off on us by touching you?"

"So you are only doing this for the money?"

"You find that curious?" Keeby asked.

"I find it...entertaining. A capitalist has thrown in with a pack of radicals but has no sympathy at all for the cause that pays him."

"The inconsistency has provided me a chuckle or two over the last several days as well. You're wrong about the capitalist thing. I'm kind of myopic when it comes to politics and economic systems, Remy. I don't write policy papers. I write about people, not movements. I write about their lives and their troubles and conflicts and victories and defeats. Maybe the politics of the day lie at the root of their problems, or maybe they don't. In the end, it doesn't matter. Every political system in human history has produced its share of misery. Your workers' paradise won't be any different. There's not one word about politics or economic systems or nationalism in my stories, because that's not what the stories are about. The stories I write are important to *me*. You want to buy them? Wonderful. They're for sale. As long as your money's good, what you do with them afterward is none of my business. Everybody wins."

"Everybody wins," Fousheé repeated. "I see. Well, as the Buddhists say, there are many paths to God."

"They say that, do they? Hold on a minute while I write that down."

"You don't have to be true believer," Fousheé said. "People serve the revolution in different ways. You may not be our ally, but neither are you our enemy, so we will remember your contribution. You may not understand yearning for universal solidarity, but your writings may stir an ember in the bosom of some young man or woman out there who is looking for like-minded souls."

"I'm not responsible for what people read into my words."

"I would like to meet elsewhere next week."

"So I'm still on the payroll?" Keeby asked.

"The pieces you delivered today are excellent. I can be open-minded regarding my associations as well, Mr. Styles, if it suits my purposes. Are you familiar with the Père-Lachaise Cemetery in the Twentieth?"

"I've heard of it. Haven't been there."

"Meet me at the front entrance, one week from today, at three in the afternoon. It is a peaceful place to conduct private business. Quiet, filled with secluded spots, and I have something to show you there. Good day. I look forward our meeting next week."

Fousheé drained his *pastis*, dropped the remainder of the bread into his coat pocket, tossed a few coins on the table, and walked away.

CHAPTER SIXTEEN

FOUSHEÉ WAS WAITING when Keeby exited the Paris Metro station at the entrance to the Père-Lachaise Cemetery on the Boulevard de Ménilmontant the following Friday. Compared to the dreary weather on the day of their last meeting in the Montorgueil, the afternoon was bright and clear and warm. Keeby had traded his wool tweed jacket for a lighter linen one, and he wore a skimmer instead of his heavier fedora. He carried the manuscripts in a light leather mail pouch slung over his shoulder.

He didn't extend his hand as he approached the little man, who was dressed exactly as he had been on their two previous meetings. He was cautious about giving Fousheé any false impressions. They had no more than a business arrangement in common. Instead, he patted the case.

"Hell of a trek from the First to the Twentieth Arrondissement, Remy. After my time in the trenches, I'm uncomfortable in the Metro. Holes in the ground make me antsy. I have the stories. You have the money?"

"Not here on the sidewalk," Fousheé said. "Please, walk with me."

He led Keeby to a set of stairs built into the walled enclosure of the cemetery. Paved and gravel paths led off in several directions, lined by rows of trees whose foliage shadowed and cooled the walkways and the visitors who strolled on them. As far as Keeby could see, crypts and gravestones and tombs and memorials sprang from the ground like mushrooms after a rain. There may have been a half dozen people in sight, most of them too far away to hear his conversation with Fousheé.

"There was a time," Fousheé said as they walked, "when, if you were the wrong religion, or of the wrong class of people, or the wrong race, you could not be buried in Paris. The church controlled all the cemeteries, and the church was uniformly Catholic. Muslims, Jews, Protestants—none need apply because there was never any space designated for them. Napoleon Bonaparte dedicated this magnificent boneyard, Mssr. Styles. In doing so, he said, *'Every citizen has the right to be buried regardless of race or religion'*. Think about it. A man might be denied food, shelter, work, love, education, all of it, for his entire life. In death, he has a right to a patch of dirt. What if that was all you had to look forward to? Wallow in penury for your entire life, and accept it as your due, because of the promise there might be a place to lay your bones when you've passed."

"Are you going somewhere with this?" Keeby asked.

"Napoleon started at the wrong end of life. We desire to guarantee each man the rights he is due from the moment of birth onward."

He paused in a small valley bounded by a great stone and brick wall.

"You are perhaps familiar with the story of the Paris Commune?"

"No."

103

"It was long before you were born, in the earliest days of the Third Republic. France was in chaos. When the war with Prussia ended, the national guard seized cannons placed around the city during the siege. They used the cannons to take over the Paris government. March 1871. Only forty-eight years ago. Doesn't sound like much. Not so long, eh? Less than a half century ago, Paris was at war with France. The national guard were populated largely by those the Third Republic called radicals. They had the audacity to believe in a decent working wage and freedom for the people and the end of the ruling proletariat. They were the direct ancestors of the Bolsheviks in Russia. They called themselves the Paris Commune."

"I take it their reign was short-lived," Keeby said.

"They had two months to establish a new order in France. It was a failure. They were wiped out. The Republic threw every soldier they could find at the Commune. It was…a bloodbath."

"The Parisians are fond of throwing one every hundred years or so."

"You joke," Remy said, his voice bitter. "On May twenty-first, forty-eight years ago, the army entered Paris. By the next morning, the Commune had erected barricades across the city. Over the next seven days, eight thousand Communards were slaughtered in the streets. The gutters ran with the blood of the rebellion. Here, the spot on which you stand, was the site of the final battle. The army had overrun Buttes-Chaumont earlier in the day. In late afternoon, they breached the cemetery walls with cannon. Inside, two hundred brave Communards made the last stand of the revolution. You can still see the marks of bullets on some of the tombs. Nothing was sacred to the Third Republic, not even a cemetery for all dedicated by the magnificent Napoleon Bonaparte himself. The Communards fought bravely, but they were outnumbered, and cut off from supplies. The end was inevitable. One hundred fifty people laid down their arms and surrendered as the sun set."

Fousheé walked to the wall and leaned against it with both hands. "They were stood against this stone wall in bands of ten, and a Republic firing squad slaughtered them. A pit had been dug along the wall, and after they were shot, they were tossed in to make room for the next party of condemned. The wall is pocked with bullet holes. See? This is the exact spot where one hundred fifty men and women who only wanted freedom were savagely murdered by the Third Republic."

He turned, and Keeby saw tears coursing down his cheeks.

"Including my grandfather and grandmother!" he shouted. "The last thing they saw was a band of Republic thugs with rifles amongst a garden of tombs. You are standing on hallowed ground, Monsieur Styles. It is soaked with the blood of revolutionaries. You stand on the graves of my ancestors. You are amused by the fervor with which my comrades and I pursue the same liberties my grandparents died to protect. Perhaps you now see it is no trifling matter."

"I see it's no trifling matter for *you*," Keeby said. "As a storyteller, I ask how the story would have gone had the Communards won the day here. Perhaps the Republic soldiers would have found themselves lined up against the wall instead? I see what you did here today. I know why you asked me to meet you. Your motives are kind of transparent.

If you believe you can win me over to your way of thinking, you're fighting a cause as lost as the Communards'. I'm a hired hand. I'll keep writing as long as you keep handing over cash. My commitment to your noble revolution ends there. You have a problem with me, I can walk away clean."

He pulled the stories from his mail pouch and handed them to Fousheé.

"You want to read them first?" Keeby said, pointing toward a nearby stone bench. Fousheé shook his head and handed Keeby the envelope from inside his jacket.

"I know they are good," he said, sadly. "I only wish they were sincere."

"You get what you pay for. And no more cross-country trips. We meet from now on at the same café off the Rue Montmartre. I should charge you extra for the Metro fare and my aggravation. Next week, you buy the drinks." Without another word, Keeby turned back toward the Metro station.

CHAPTER SEVENTEEN

ON THURSDAY MORNING, before the sun rose and the fog lifted, Beau Shipley rose and carried his new easel and art supplies to White Point Gardens at the tip of the Charleston peninsula. He erected the easel and laid out his crayons and waited. Presently, the hazy horizon over the eastern edge of the harbor glowed with a faint pink iridescence. Within minutes, the glow turned to a flare, and finally the sun itself peeked over the vista. The fog around Beau glimmered as it burned off. When the mist dissipated into isolated patches on the water, Beau began to sketch. He squinted, blurring his perspective, and wondered whether the original impressionist painters had engaged in this conceit. He knew Monet was slowly going blind. His vision problems were a recent affliction, and he had launched the entire movement with his works forty years earlier. Perhaps a long, progressive deterioration in vision had led Monet to paint what he saw.

Beau had no idea. He had only run into Monet once, at an exposition in Paris. The painter had become something of a recluse at Giverny. He seldom ventured into the city. Beau hadn't introduced himself, fearing he might be found presumptive and ingratiating.

In any case, squinting allowed Beau to see the world as an impressionist painting, and as a nascent artist he justified using whatever tools enabled him to achieve his artistic vision. The morning warmed, and the vestigial fog burned away. No matter. Beau had the image he wanted etched into his brain. He finished the sketch in time for breakfast.

He packed his kit and strolled the twelve blocks toward Wentworth. As he walked, he again tried to make sense of Norbert Tradd's rejection of his attentions toward Victoria. Even before he left to fight the war in Europe, relations between Tradd and Beau had never been close. As far as Beau could tell, Norbert Tradd had no close relations with anyone outside his own family. Even so, there had been no trace of hostility or frigidity toward him in the past. Something important had changed in the time Beau had been away.

Obviously, Tradd had lost half his family, along with his prospective son-in-law, a tragedy to chill the warmest heart, and Norbert Tradd's heart had never been better than tepid. If Tradd knew about the baby, perhaps he blamed Beau for some reason, even if it couldn't possibly have been his. He was already in Europe when it was conceived.

And there was the business about his father. For some reason, Norbert Tradd held great enmity toward Gordon Shipley. Perhaps Tradd's rejection of Beau had nothing to do with Victoria at all.

He recalled the troubling figure in the window as he had walked away from the Tradd house. While he hadn't been able to make out her face through the distorted glass, he was certain it was Victoria. He couldn't forget the image of her claw-like fingers rasping against the ancient glass, and couldn't fathom what her hand gesture meant. Resignation? Grief? And who closed the curtains? Victoria? Her father? Had she been signaling him, or simply taking a last look at what might have been?

A car horn behind him broke Beau's concentration. Sophie Wildmon, behind the wheel of a Model T, pulled alongside him. Henry Ford had famously proclaimed you could purchase a Model T in any color you wanted as long as it was black. Sophie had sprung for a jazzy red aftermarket paint job on her car, with yellow piping on the running boards. It looked like a miniature fire truck. She wore a flowing silk dress in a floral print and a large floppy hat with flowers in the band.

"Morning, stranger," she said. "Give you a lift?"

"I'm headed to my house."

"It's on my way. I have a breakfast engagement west of the Ashley. I can drop you off. What are you doing walking the streets this time of day? Stumbling home after a late party?"

Beau showed her his pastel pad and the box with his easel and supplies. "The light doesn't last long, and you have to be there to catch it."

"Ooh, lemme see," Sophie said. Beau handed her the pastel. "Not bad at all. You might have some talent, soldier boy. Hop in. I'll drive you home."

Relenting being the course of least resistance, Beau walked around the car, dropped his gear into the back seat, and climbed in beside her. She readjusted the spark idle and took off.

"Hope the weather holds for the Sullivan's Island outing," she said. "Still coming, right?"

"I'll be there," Beau said.

"And Victoria?"

Beau's face clouded over. Sophie glanced at him.

"Oh," she said. "Want to talk about it?"

"I'm still figuring it all out myself."

"Might help to dump it on some fresh ears. Besides, if Victoria's not coming, you're my date, Sport. Called dibs on you last weekend. Makes me responsible for you."

He chuckled. Sophie had always made him laugh. It was a shame she didn't make his heart flutter. She was insanely attractive, fun-loving, and knew her way blindfolded around the dark side of a duvet. Beau couldn't explain why he found Victoria so much more alluring. A scientist someday might define the ins and outs of attraction, but Beau still found it all a great mystery. He felt as if a treasure of great value had been ripped from his hands by the vagaries of fate.

He described the confrontation with Norbert Tradd. "Please don't spread this around. This is between you and me. Victoria's been through enough. She doesn't need people talking behind their fans about her everywhere she goes."

"She doesn't go *anywhere*," Sophie said, too quickly and far too facilely. Beau glared at her. "Sorry. Okay. This stays between us. And I'm sorry it isn't working out the way you had hoped. I am. I have a soft spot in my head for you, Shipley. I'll try to keep you distracted."

She pulled the car to the curb in front of Beau's house.

"Thanks for the ride." He bent into the back seat to retrieve his stuff.

"Hold on," Sophie said, pointing at the picture. "Can I have this?"

"Why?"

"I don't know. You might be famous someday and selling it will make me rich. A hole in one of my walls needs covering. I like it. Take your pick."

Beau glanced back and forth from the picture to Sophie. He dropped the sheet back into the rear seat. "Sure. Keep it. I'll create more."

He reached for the door handle. She grabbed his face with both hands and planted a wet kiss on his lips. It wasn't aggressive or forceful. It was sweet and soft and warm. They separated and Beau blushed.

"Something for the neighbors to gossip about," Sophie said. "You'd better get inside before someone calls a cop."

Beau stepped out of the car. Sophie put it in gear, but he stopped her by placing his hand on the door sill. "Hey."

"Yes?"

"Want to go out tonight? I found a place in the segregated district last week which is reputed to sell illegal spirits."

"I believe I know the exact place," she said. Her smile dissipated. "Are you sure, Beau? I know you're all busted up about Victoria."

"Might take my mind off...things. So? Are you game?"

Sophie wrapped the loose end of her tasseled silk scarf around her neck and beamed. "Oh, sweetie. I am always game. You know where I live. Call on me at eight."

CHAPTER EIGHTEEN

BEAU QUICKLY BATHED and dressed before joining his family for breakfast. His father, as usual, sat at the head of the table reading the newspaper. Both his mother and Adelaide had finished and gone out for a day of shopping.

"You went out this morning," Gordon said, without lowering the paper.

"Yes. I went to the point to do a drawing of the sunrise over the harbor."

"I see. How did it go?"

"Could you put away the paper, Father? It's hard to talk to the *Morning Post.*"

Beau expected Gordon to be cross with him, but when he lowered the paper, his father looked more curious.

"What does Norbert Tradd have against you?" Beau asked.

"I haven't the slightest idea," Gordon said. "Why? What have you heard?"

"I tried to take Victoria to church on Sunday. Her father refused to let her go. He told me in no uncertain terms she would have nothing to do with me. It was my impression this was entirely his decision, not hers. When I asked him why, one of the reasons he gave was because I am your son."

"He did, did he?"

"He did. What kind of bad blood is there between you two?"

"Again, I have no idea. I barely know the man. You could say we are nodding acquaintances. I'd be shocked if we've passed more than ten words with one another over the last decade. Now I'm curious. From what you've told me, though, it seems the wheels, sadly, have come off the Tradd family. The losses they've sustained have broken them. It's tragic. I consider our family to be extremely fortunate not to have been touched by the influenza, but I also empathize with those on whom luck did not smile."

Beau said, "Nothing makes sense. I went to Europe and came home to a different world."

"It was a traumatic couple of years. There were changes. But as far as this Norbert Tradd business goes, I'm as in the dark as you. Have you considered...I don't wish to sound insensitive, son, but perhaps, under the circumstances—"

"Maybe I dodged a bullet?" Beau finished. "Yeah, Father. It's crossed my mind. I've thought about little else since Sunday. I want the Victoria I left behind. I'm not sure she exists anymore."

"I don't understand."

"There was a fellow in the trenches. Can't recall his first name, but his last name was Morven. His best friend, the guy he walked with to the recruitment station, took a sniper round between the eyes. One thing you can say about the German snipers, they know their business. Morven watched his best buddy in the world check out of it in an instant, just a foot away. He was never the same again. It changed something so deep inside of him, there was no getting back.

He stared off into space twenty hours a day. Didn't eat. Didn't drink. Barely slept, and when he did, he woke every five minutes screaming. This went on for days. We were five minutes from shuttling him off to the aid station for shellshock when he tossed away his pot, dropped his rifle, and climbed over the lip into No Man's Land for a stroll. I think about him a lot, and the awful way he died. Maybe most of him died the same instant as his buddy, and the Germans only finished the job. If there is such a thing as a soul, he lost his. What scrambled over the berm was the empty husk. That's how Victoria looks now."

For the first time in Beau's memory, his father appeared dumbfounded. It was as if he finally saw Beau clearly. Beau saw something in his father's eyes he barely recognized. It looked like respect.

"I'm sorry," Gordon said. "I'm sorry you had to experience that. I'm sorry you enlisted without consulting with me first. I would have tried to spare you that tragedy. I'm sorry about the influenza and about Victoria and I'm sorry we couldn't preserve the world you left behind. I'm sorry you're so troubled. As a father, I should be able to do something, but you're a grown man now. You have to work it out for yourself. I want to help, though. Tell me what I can do."

"When I figure it out, I will," Beau said.

——

The weekly delivery at the café at the nexus of Rue Montmartre and Rue de Turbigo went off exactly as expected. Remy Fousheé left with his articles and Keeby remained with cash in his pocket. It had been a lucrative week. In addition to penning his articles for Fousheé under the pseudonym *Monsieur Cloche,* he had received a contract from a newspaper in Toronto to buy pieces from him on an *a la carte* arrangement. He'd send them his best stuff, they'd select what they wanted to print, and send him a check. The remainders he was welcome to peddle elsewhere. He'd just sold two of them to Fousheé.

Even with the two commissions, maintaining his loft in the Montorgueil was tight. He considered the possibility of moving across the river, to the marginally cheaper Rive Gauche, perhaps into the Latin Quarter. A lot of the artsy crowd had congregated there, driven out of the Place du Tertre in Montmartre by construction of the new Sacré Coeur Cathedral. Keeby knew three different writers who had relocated to St. Germain des Pres, and a couple of painters as well.

It was a cool, crisp spring day, almost a throwback to March. Ever since his conversation with Fousheé at the Pere-Lachaise Cemetery, Keeby had thought about the strange little man. He knew almost nothing about Fousheé. His writing work was largely done for the day—Keeby typically wrote late into the night and slept until noon—and he fancied a stroll.

He caught sight of the back of Fousheé's long sealskin coat as he crossed over the Pont Neuf at the point of the Ile de la Cite into the Left Bank and followed him as he continued ahead south to Rue St. Sulpice. He circumnavigated the Jardins du Luxembourg, by way of rue de Vaugirard, into the Montparnasse neighborhood. Following Fousheé was easy. He was the only man wearing a long coat in sight, and his hunched-over lope was impossible to miss. Keeby was able to stay several hundred feet behind the Frenchman.

Fousheé might have been telling the truth about being a psychiatry student at the Salpêtrière. He was headed toward the Boulevard de l'Hôpital. Keeby knew a little about the hospital from his college studies. It was the location where a mousy little physician named Philippe Pinel—otherwise a failure in life—had revolutionized the treatment of the mentally ill at the end of the eighteenth century. Eighty years later, Jean Martin Charcot trained every important neurologist in Europe there, including Sigmund Freud. It was renowned as a training center for neurologists and psychiatrists from the world over. Perhaps Fousheé had crafted a clever cover story. On the other hand, he could be exactly what he claimed. If Keeby didn't follow him, he might never know. Following Fousheé was silly and foolish, if only because it put his regular income at risk, but it scratched Keeby's curious itch.

Fousheé turned onto the Boulevard Saint Germaine, in the Seventh Arrondissement, away from the Boulevard de l'Hôpital and the Salpêtrière. Pedestrian traffic increased, and Keeby was able to close within fifty or sixty feet without risking detection.

Fousheé turned at the corner of Rue de Rennes, turned again at the Rue de Notre Dame des Champs, and finally onto Rue Montparnasse where he entered a building at number twenty-two. It was a typical Paris apartment building, constructed in the ornate French Provincial style, with an obligatory café on the sidewalk level at the nearby corner. The front door of the building opened into a small lobby with post boxes along one wall for the residents. Keeby gave

Fousheé time to get wherever he was going before he pushed through the door and headed for the post boxes. He scanned all the labels, but never found the name *Fousheé*. He wasn't surprised. The little man had told him it wasn't his actual name at their first meeting.

Keeby spied a young man across the street peddling an armful of broadsheets. He took one of them. The peddler held out a palm for a contribution, but Keeby ignored it. He had contributed plenty already.

It was the first time in Paris he had seen his name in print. Well, not his name, but his alter ego *Monsieur Cloche*. The broadsheet was titled, unimaginatively, *Solidarité*. The lead story was about the formation of the first Communist International in Russia by Lenin and Zinoviev. Fousheé's editorial crew had woven in calls for French solidarity with the International. It was part old news, part recruitment advertisement.

He sat in the café, ordered a glass of wine, and perused the rest of the paper.

Fousheé had honored his pledge to keep Keeby anonymous. The articles were appropriately attributed to the pseudonymous *Monsieur Cloche*, as promised. Fousheé had done precisely as Keeby had predicted—taken his true stories of hardships among the Paris working class and intermixed them with comparisons of the Third Republic to the workers' paradise promised by the Communist International. Keeby's stories were the cautionary tales—the rest claimed, *'Join with us and don't let this happen to you!'*

Fousheé exited the building at 22 Rue Montparnasse, carrying a fresh sheaf of broadsheets, which he deposited with the busker on the sidewalk, and walked away from Keeby in the direction of the Salpêtrière.

Keeby dropped some change onto the table, stowed the broadsheet in his jacket pocket, drained the wine, and followed him.

CHAPTER NINETEEN

SATURDAY MORNING DAWNED to thunder and pouring rain over the Charleston peninsula. Beau awoke, saw a flash outside the window, heard the drops pound against the ancient glass that rattled as the thunder broke, and said, "Guess there's no beach trip today."

Sophie rolled over, opened one eye, observed the inclement weather, and mumbled, "Fucking shame." She threw an arm over Beau's chest and nestled under his arm. "I had such elaborate plans to seduce you today."

"Thank goodness I dodged that bullet."

"Yeah. I'm a genuine vamp. Shut up and let me sleep." Seconds later, she snored softly.

It was too late for Beau. He was already awake. His body still responded as it had in the trenches to any new sound or condition, with spurts of adrenalin preparing him to either fight or run like hell. Neither was a useful option in his current situation. Instead, he stared at the water dripping on the windowpanes, counted the seconds between flashes of lightning and the booming thunder, waited for his heart to slow, and tried to figure out how he had wound up in Sophie's bedroom.

Well, the *how* was obvious. They had gone out, spent the evening drinking and dancing at Chance Howe's blind tiger, had gotten snockered—again—and when he saw her back to her home somewhere between midnight and sunrise, Victoria no longer stood between them.

Sometime around their third round in Howe's bar, he had described the entire conversation with Norbert Tradd, and how it appeared things were over between him and Victoria. He hadn't described the figure he saw in the Tradd house window. He still couldn't be certain it was Victoria, even if he believed it in his deepest heart. Sophie had listened to him, patiently, for far too long as he wallowed in grief for a woman he'd barely touched in two years. When he was finished, she ordered another round.

The streetcars had long since stopped running by the time they left the hotel in the segregated district. He recalled the carriage ride home, the stars twinkling overhead through wisps of clouds, Sophie allowing Beau to help her to the street, and telling him to pay the cabbie. The rest was a blur of skin and sweat and rumpled sheets and a heavy musk of lust which still hung in the air like incense.

Victoria had never been as enthusiastic in bed as Sophie. Beau hated himself immediately for making comparisons, because he knew it meant he was already building barriers between himself and Victoria. Without a public declaration of defeat, he was distancing himself from her, erecting protective comparisons and patting himself on the back over his exceptional luck at having dodged a stunted marriage with the emotionally wilted carapace of his former lover. He marveled in the worst possible way at how fickle he could be, and how quickly he had abandoned his pursuit of Victoria and found solace with Sophie. He was particularly disappointed in himself for not standing up to Norbert Tradd, for all the good it would have done, and for his false vow not to give in.

Victoria and Sophie couldn't have been more different. Victoria represented the past, the stodgy traditions of generations of Charleston aristocracy. Her family had lived on Charleston soil since the first settlers landed on the peninsula in the seventeenth century. They were neck-deep in low country conventions.

Sophie was a modern woman, a representative of the future—self-confident, adventurous, and sensual. Yet, Sophie, as delightful a diversion as she was, had never stirred in Beau's breast the depth of affection and longing Victoria had. He had believed he loved Victoria as he sailed for France. The notion had never entered his mind with Sophie, though he was terribly fond of her and confident he could grow to love her in time, as every other necessary component was in place other than the constant desire to be with her and her alone.

Perhaps he wasn't destined to be with either of them. The perfect woman for him might still be out there, waiting, while he dallied with the redheaded vixen who now lay across his chest snoring like a newborn kitten, and as he pined for a woman whose reason might have already taken wing.

If Victoria was denied to him, Sophie was far from the worst person to pass the time until the right woman came along.

———

Beau was an adult. Sophie was an adult. Logic dictated they were free to act as they pleased, but Charleston society adhered to a different set of standards. Suffrage on the horizon or not, women's most prized possession remained their reputation.

The lingering thunderstorm provided perfect cover for Beau's exit. He carried one of Sophie's umbrellas to avoid ruining Talmadge Shaw's excellent work on his new tweed suit. Before he left, Sophie extracted from him a promise for a rematch in the segregated district later that evening. No self-respecting southern gentleman would ever decline such an invitation. To do otherwise, after placing her reputation in such precarious circumstances, would open one to accusations of being a cad. They agreed Beau would escort Sophie to dinner at eight, and on to whatever illicit delights awaited at Chance Howe's club afterward.

Beau was lucky to catch the streetcar almost immediately, before the cuffs of his trousers were sodden. His home was only ten or twelve blocks away, but he didn't want to take chances with his new clothes.

He arrived as his mother and sister came downstairs for breakfast. Gordon's place at the table was vacant.

"Where's Father?" he asked.

"Business," Mother said. "One of the ships arrives today. He wants to oversee the offloading. Let this be a lesson to you, Adelaide. Marry a banker or some other man who keeps regular hours. Doctors, lawyers, businessmen? You never know when they'll come home. Speaking of which, Beau, did you just come in?"

"Yes," Adelaide said, "Did you leave early this morning to catch the sunrise over White Point Gardens?" Her sly smile betrayed the underlying taunt

"Oh, don't be silly, Adelaide!" Mother said. "It's been stormy all morning. I hate your father is out in it. He'll catch his death of cold one of these days. When it happens, I'll say I told you so!"

Relieved the subject of his nocturnal whereabouts had been safely shuffled into the background, Beau took his seat as their housekeeper brought in the breakfast plates.

The storm blew out to sea by noon. Gordon still hadn't returned home by sunset. Beau dressed for the evening and hired a cabbie to take him to Sophie's place. They had dinner at a restaurant on Meeting Street and Sophie described her preempted devious plan to seduce Beau at the beach, and exactly what he had missed by pulling the trigger the night before. Beau couldn't deny his pleasure at being out with Sophie, which only led to another stinger of guilt. No matter, he decided. He was young, as his father had pointed out. There was plenty of time to find another Victoria, and plenty of candidates to spend it with.

"I was just thinking how much I miss our old friend Vladimir," he said as he placed his fork and knife on the plate.

"We should call on him," Sophie said.

As she spoke, a mob of shouting men dashed past the window of the restaurant.

"Now what do you suppose that's all about?" Beau asked.

CHAPTER TWENTY

DESMOND MIDDLETON and Jerome Downs had been friends since childhood, growing up black and poor on the streets and alleyways of old Charleston. Early in life, both had independently discovered Barnum's dictum about suckers and takers. They had mastered a dozen short cons before they were rightly out of short pants. Desmond's specialty was the shell game, but he could pull any of ten or twelve other routines at the drop of a hat. Since a large portion of the customers in the segregated district were sailors, most on shore leave during relatively brief layovers, and only the most naïve of locals fell for the rackets in the district anymore, the chances of running across a mark later were relatively remote.

For the past week, Jerome had been dodging a gang of sailors from the Navy Yard. He'd run across them moping on the street because none of the illicit blind tiger bars would let them in wearing their uniforms after they had gone riot in one club and smashed the furniture. Recognizing opportunity, Jerome offered to procure a bottle of hooch from a friend who worked in an underground bar. They gave him twenty dollars, and Jerome disappeared into the night.

After a couple of hours, the sailors suspected they had been taken. They took it personally and had been out in the district in growing numbers every night for a week looking for Jerome. As their frustration grew, any brown face would do. They had hassled several black citizens on the streets already, roughing up one or two. Desmond had encouraged Jerome to lie low until the sailors went to sea in a week or so, but Jerome had never strolled past a chance to make a quick buck, and on Saturday night the segregated district was plumpest with cash. He'd keep one eye over his shoulder, Jerome assured Desmond, and everything would be jake.

It wasn't.

On Saturday night, the Navy Yard crew searching for Jerome Downs swelled to twenty-five men. They roamed the district, clotting the sidewalk with their uniformed numbers, intimidating every person of color they ran across.

About a half hour after dark, they ran across Desmond Middleton running a shell game on Princess Street. Desmond saw them round the corner, four wide and six deep on the sidewalk, and he decided it was a good time to close up shop. He gathered his shells, stuffed them in his pocket, tipped his hat to the assembled crowd, and hightailed it up the street toward Beresford Street. He rounded a corner at full tilt, grabbing a streetlight pole to swing himself, and ran directly into another cadre of uniformed Navy Yard sailors searching for Jerome Downs. He collided with one of them, a burly youth named Roscoe Coleman, pushing him off the sidewalk into the street. Coleman stepped into a puddle, soaking his shoes, before jumping back onto the sidewalk. Desmond was getting back to his feet when Coleman grabbed at his shirt sleeve.

"Hey, nigger! What do you mean, pushing me into a puddle?"

"Sorry," Desmond said, weakly. "I didn't see you."

"Who you runnin' from, anyway?" Coleman demanded. "What kinda trouble are you in? Because we're looking for one of your brothers, who's also a troublemaker. Maybe we should take it out on you. What do you say?"

"I'd just as soon you didn't," Desmond said. He stomped on Coleman's toes. Coleman yelped and howled as he jumped around on the sidewalk. He released Desmond's sleeve, and Desmond dashed away with the other sailors in pursuit.

Desmond skidded around the corner at Meeting Street and saw Jerome ahead. "Run!" he yelled, and Jerome fell in step with him. They crossed Beaufain Street, where Charles Street became St. Philip Street, and took refuge inside the rooming house where they resided, only seconds ahead of the crowd.

The rooming house was two stories divided into eight individual apartments with shared baths. The rooms were cheap and clean, and all the rooms were occupied by black men and women who worked in the district. Doors on both floors opened as soon as the sailors surrounded the house, and the residents—ten in all—gathered in the upstairs parlor.

"What's going on?" one of the neighbors asked.

"I don't know," Desmond said. "The sailors out there have gone crazy."

A window in the front room shattered as a rock sailed through it. It was followed by several others, and a brick boomed against the front door.

"We need the police," one resident said.

"You want to run for them?" Desmond asked. "I'll hold the door for you."

"So what do we do?" Jerome asked.

"Find whatever you can to throw back at them. Jars, bottles, maybe grab some rocks from back of the house. Anybody got a gun?"

Everyone shook their heads. Seconds later, they scattered to the corners of the house to gather ammunition. They congregated on the upper veranda, arms laden with junk that would leave a mark if it hit anyone in the mob. Immediately, the sailors on the sidewalk pelted them with rocks and broken bricks. The residents ducked the fusillade and retaliated.

The sailors danced right and left as bottles and jars crashed and shattered at their feet. When the attack stopped, they scrambled to find new projectiles. They were interrupted by gunfire. All the sailors ducked as Jerome appeared on the veranda with a pistol and fired three shots into the air.

"You crackers don't want to get shot and I sure don't want to shoot you, but as God is my witness, I will put a hole in anyone who takes another step toward this house!" He leveled the pistol toward them. "Who's first?"

"Where the hell did you get a gun?" Desmond asked.

"Kinda busy," Jerome said. "We'll talk about it later." He turned back to the crowd of sailors on the sidewalk. "Now would be a good time to get." He emphasized it by firing into the ground near the sidewalk, spewing a geyser of mud. The sailors scattered, regrouped down the street, and headed back to the segregated district.

"Don't worry!" the tall gawky one said to his buddies. "We'll be back. Let's go to the Navy Yard and round up a whole bunch of guys. This is our night. We're gonna take the district down to the studs!"

The sailors returned an hour later, over a thousand strong, and the streets ran red.

The original contingent returned to the barracks with florid claims of wild Negroes running amuck in the streets of the segregated district. Word spread like kudzu, and within minutes hundreds of their fellows gathered to support their insulted and injured brothers. They split into gangs of ten or twenty, each taking a street, and they systematically worked their way from one end of the segregated district to the other, specifically picking black faces to accost.

Violence erupted at a billiard parlor at the corner of King and Charles Streets. A contingent of sailors burst through the front doors and beat several black men they found there. After wrecking the place, they returned to the streets, armed with broken pool cues, to continue their havoc.

Another gang broke through the doors of a barber shop on King, which the owner had bolted when he saw the disturbance. The owner and another employee, both black, were overwhelmed by the crowd and beaten without quarter. Both survived, but with injuries that would revisit pain on them for the rest of their lives. Before they left, the mob broke all the mirrors and slashed the barber chairs. They threw chairs from the waiting area through the front window, scattering broken glass across the sidewalk and street. After finishing with the barber shop, the crowd moved next door to a shoe shop owned by another black man. They robbed the till and destroyed the shop after beating the owner senseless.

The district had two shooting galleries for the non-alcoholic amusement of its patrons. Instead of air guns, the galleries used small-bore .22 rifles, breech loaded with tubes of ten short cartridges each. Navy Yard personnel weren't allowed sidearms on shore leave, so the sailors had invaded the district with little more than their outrage and bravado, and whatever weapons they could steal or improvise. The mob swarmed both galleries. They stole thirteen rifles and every brass tube of cartridges they could locate, before tearing both galleries to the ground.

Trolley cars ran the length of both Meeting and King Streets. In a city that had largely made peace with its former racial hatreds, the streetcars were typically integrated. On Saturday evening they were packed with people coming from all over the city for a taste of the segregated district's renowned illicit pleasures.

The Navy Yard mob flooded into the streets, blocking the tracks, forcing the trolleys to stop. They pulled every black person they saw out of the trolleys and beat them on the sidewalks with makeshift truncheons crafted from broken chair legs and pool cues.

False rumors ran wild among the pack that a black man had shot a sailor, and the mood of the mob turned homicidal. In the mind of every sailor, a black face equaled an armed threat. Five black men would be gunned down by the rampaging horde of bluejackets before midnight.

When the sound of small caliber rifles echoed across to St. Philip Street, Jerome Downs turned to Desmond Middleton. They were still standing on the veranda of their rooming house.

"What's happening?" Desmond said.

"Those white sailor boys gone crazy. They're burning the district. I can't stay here, Des. I gotta go help our people. Are you with me?"

"Just because those bluejackets gone crazy, you have to go with 'em? They're shooting people. Best thing we can do is sit tight."

"You stay if you want. I'm going."

Jerome retreated into the house.

Desmond sighed. He and Jerome had been part of each other's life as long as they could remember. They watched each other's backs. They protected one another. It was essential to their survival working the streets of the most lawless section of Charleston.

"Bad idea," he said, as he followed Jerome down the stairs.

CHAPTER TWENTY-ONE

ALARMED BY THE RUCKUS outside the restaurant, Beau paid the bill and escorted Sophie to the front entrance.

"What is it?" Sophie asked.

"A sound I hoped I'd never hear again. Most of the trouble is downtown. We should go the other way. I'll escort you home."

"Are you crazy?" Sophie asked. "I want to see! Come on."

"There's fighting. People are getting hurt. Maybe killed. There will be blood. Perhaps a great deal of it. You don't want to see that, Sophie. Believe me."

"Don't tell me what I want!" Sophie said, her eyes afire. It wasn't the first time Beau had seen her angry. He knew better than to press the issue.

"If I take you down there, we don't get involved," Beau said. "We can watch from a distance. If you get shot, you agree not to haunt me."

"Deal," Sophie said. She grabbed his hand and dragged him in the direction of the shouts and sound of breaking glass. In the distance, plumes of smoke climbed into the sky, and the smell of burning wood and rubber stung their eyes as they edged closer to the center of the action. Cinders and ashes borne aloft in the flames settled back onto the district like a fall of fine black snow.

A block into the district, they ran across a young black man sitting hunched over against the base of a streetlamp. He was naked from the waist up, his blood-soaked shirt wadded and held against a deep wound in his forehead. He flinched as Beau and Sophie approached, and he raised his free arm to defend himself.

Beau tried to get between Sophie and the young man, to shield her from the blood, but she sidestepped him and knelt in front of the bleeding man.

"What happened?" she said.

"Those sailors came from the Navy Yard and started splitting skulls," the man said. "I was on a trolley, coming home from work. They pulled me off and beat me with chair legs. I don't know why I'm still alive, Miss. I surely don't."

"Do you live near here?" Sophie asked.

"Two blocks over. I was just feeling strong enough to head home when you showed up. I thought you were here to finish the job." Tears welled in his eyes as he shuddered and sobbed.

"You're safe with us. We'll take you home." Sophie took the man's hand and helped him to his feet. "Two streets over, you said?"

He pointed the way. Beau followed directly behind them, keeping an eye over his shoulder. They reached the house and Sophie walked the man to the front door.

"You stay inside for the rest of the night. Keep pressure on that gash. See a doctor about your head tomorrow," she said.

Escorting the man home had placed them closer to the center of the violence than Beau preferred. He was about to steer Sophie away from the loudest fighting when Jamie Norton skidded around the corner and almost bowled them over. His carefully oiled hair hung in shiny strands on either side of his sweaty, smoke-stained face.

"Beau! Sophie! What in hell are you doing here?"

"Just finished dinner," Beau said. "We were headed to Chance Howe's place, but it looks like people had other plans for tonight."

"It's a battle zone in the district. The Navy declared war on Negroes. Why in hell would they do that?"

"I gave up analyzing people's motivations back in the trenches," Beau said. "How bad is it?"

"Bad enough. Stopped being entertaining when the bullets started flying. I'm out of it. Headed home for the night. I suggest you do the same."

"Not yet," Sophie protested. "I want to see it all."

Her eyes nearly glittered with adrenaline. The prospect of danger aroused her, and Sophie would not be denied.

"I warned you," Jamie said. "Stay out of the district. You'll only get hurt."

"You want to stop her?" Beau said. "I can't let her go alone. She'd be safer with both of us."

"She'd be safest if you took her home. I tried, my friend. We've already established I'm no hero. Good luck, but count me out."

Jamie trotted off in the direction of the point. Sophie grabbed Beau's hand and dragged him toward a rising column of smoke somewhere on Beaufain Street.

"Don't worry about Jamie," she pled as they hurried. "He's never had much of a spine. Nice fellow. He'll charm the knickers right off you if you let him. But he's not one you want around when the black flag goes up."

"The black what?" Beau asked, trying to follow.

"Flag. When things go wrong. He's a bit of a coward."

"I'm not feeling all that courageous myself."

"But you're still here, aren't you?"

The rioting grew louder and the smoke thicker as they approached the center of the district. Sophie stopped as soon as she saw multiple store windows smashed, and furniture strewn in the street. Blue-jacketed sailors dashed from building to building, wild-eyed, wielding makeshift cudgels. Some carried the shooting gallery rifles they'd pilfered. They kicked in doors and dragged people onto the sidewalk, where they kicked and beat them unconscious. On Charles Street, gunfire crackled in the night, accented by the tinkling of newly broken glass as the sailors took potshots at second and third floor windows.

"Seen enough?" Beau asked, a hand on Sophie's shoulder. "It will be like this one street over, or two, or three. It's always the same. Let me take you home."

Sophie looked both ways on Princess Street, at the carnage and wreckage of the segregated district, and her eyes widened, her pupils dilated, and her breathing deepened. She grabbed Beau by the lapels and pushed him into the darkness of a recessed shop doorway, backed him against the door, nearly shattering the glass, and she pressed her mouth against his. Her lips parted and her tongue flicked at him, and he opened his lips and accepted her willingly.

"I can't remember when I was this excited," she gasped. "It's the danger. Don't you feel it? Aren't you rock hard already?" She grasped at him and smiled and crushed her mouth against his again. She wrapped her arms around him in the shadows and pulled him to her. "You can absolutely take me home now."

"Fine with me. Let's go."

He took her arm and looked both ways before stepping back to the sidewalk. They were halfway back to King Street when Desmond Middleton and Jerome Downs dashed around the corner, followed by three uniformed sailors. Desmond and Jerome had a fifty-foot lead. They stopped at one set of doors and pulled at them, but they'd been bolted and wouldn't budge. They looked around desperately, searching for another place to hide, as the sailors bore down on them.

Chance Howe strode around the corner from Beaufain. He'd disposed of his fancy tails and white tie and was dressed in his shirt unbuttoned halfway down his chest, the stiff paper collar discarded, and the sleeves rolled to reveal forearms muscled like braided cables. He carried a shotgun, sawed off to a two-inch barrel. He held it aloft and ripped off two shots that reverberated between the buildings like thunder.

The sailors froze long enough for Howe to eject the shells and replace them. He locked the shotgun with a click that pierced the suddenly still night like a scream. Desmond and Jerome huddled behind Howe, and Beau quickly walked Sophie to their side.

"Now, you boys may know what a sawed-off will do to flesh and bone," Howe shouted, his voice echoing off the buildings. "And if you don't, you might think you can imagine it. I'm telling you here and now, you can't. You have no idea. They call this hog leg a street sweeper for a reason. Best thing you can do is head back the way you came, all the way back to the Navy Yard, but for damn sure out of my sight. Is there anything I've said here you don't understand?"

None of the sailors moved. Howe pointed toward Desmond and Jerome. "These boys are under my protection. You want to find out what that means, go ahead and mess with them." He waved the shotgun from man to man. "I'd advise against it. Turn around and walk away."

The sailors looked at one another, waiting for one of them to sound the call to attack, but it never came. They grumbled, trying to save face. The shotgun spoke louder. Slowly, they backed off. Within a minute the street was clear.

Howe turned to Jerome Downs. "Give me the goddamned gun, asshole."

"Gun?" Jerome said.

"Don't fuck with me. Not tonight. I saw you shooting at a man on Charles Street."

"He shot at me first. One of those pop guns from the shooting gallery."

"Hand it over. Guns are ninety percent of the goddamn problem here tonight."

"But Chance—" Jerome whined.

Howe turned the shotgun on him, and Jerome's eyes went wide. He pulled the pistol from his pants and handed it to Howe, who pocketed it and turned to Beau and Sophie.

"Young Shipley, and Miss Wildmon. I must admit I did not expect to see you tonight."

"It wasn't my choice," Beau said.

"Neither of you should be here. It's too dangerous. I've already spoken with Mayor Hyde. He's contacted the Navy Yard. The commandant there is sending Marines and soldiers into the district to haul off the sailors. The police are on the way to clear out everyone else. You need to go home. I'll walk you to the edge of the district, see you get out safely." He turned to Desmond and Jerome. "You two shitheads come with me as well. We need to find a place to hide you for the night, so the cops don't lock you up."

Cradling the sawed-off shotgun in his arms, Howe walked Beau and Sophie across King Street. "I have to get back," he told Beau. "You can catch the northbound trolley two streets over. Take Miss Wildmon straight home. And, if you discuss this evening with your father, please let him know I kept you safe. Tell him we're even. Will you do that?"

"If it comes up," Beau said. "Thanks, Mr. Howe."

"And please, do drop by the club once all this unpleasantness subsides. I anticipate we'll be running a special or two to draw people back into the district."

CHAPTER TWENTY-TWO

DESPITE SOPHIE'S ARDOR—which was undiminished in the time it took to escort her home—Beau didn't stay the entire night. It was better for Sophie's reputation, and the night had left Beau disturbed. He hadn't handed in his best performance.

Sophie didn't act as if she minded when he dressed and let himself out, and Beau used the time walking home in the blue-black hours to ruminate over the Charleston he'd left and the one to which he had returned. They seemed two different entities, as if—sailing across the Atlantic Ocean—he had crossed into a universe where up was down and left was right. He had looked forward to returning home, but now he couldn't find it anywhere. He envied Keeby Styles, living the high life in Paris.

He rose after a few hours' sleep. Only five blocks from the segregated district, the breeze wafting through his window carried the tang of gunpowder and wood smoke. He washed and dressed for breakfast. It was Sunday. Church was a social expectation, but Beau intended to head to the marina on the Ashley River to do some sketches later in the afternoon. Mother and Adelaide had eaten early and were preparing for church. Gordon was finishing his breakfast when Beau took his seat. The newspaper lay folded next to his plate.

"I'm happy to see you are safe," Gordon said. "I take it you were in the district last night?"

"Not willingly. I was at dinner a few blocks away with Sophie Wildmon. We saw people running past in the front window. She insisted on seeing what was happening."

"And you didn't?"

"I recognized the sound. I've seen enough blood. But she wouldn't be denied. We ran across Jamie Norton, headed home for the night."

"Not an unwise decision," Gordon said.

"He might have been right, but he was damned caddish about it. If I hadn't been there, he'd have left Sophie in the lurch."

"Then it's a good thing you were there, and incurious. It made yours the calmest head. Since you are here now, I presume Miss Wildmon's curiosity was satisfied, and you were able to convince her to go home."

"Not...exactly," Beau said. "We were caught between some sailors from the Navy Yard and a couple of Negro boys on Princess Street. I don't believe the sailors would have hurt us, but once fists and bullets start flying, anything can happen. It was about to get ugly when Chance Howe stopped it with a sawed-off shotgun."

"Did he?"

"Yes. I suspect Howe is a much more influential and important man than his first impression suggests."

"What does his first impression suggest?" Gordon asked.

"A washed-up boxer in a fancy suit toadying to customers in a Charleston blind tiger. A glad hander. A bootlegger. On the other hand, before he stopped the ruckus on Princess Street last night, he had already talked to Mayor Hyde. What kind of saloon-keep has that kind of access?"

"Tristian Hyde is no fan of bootleggers, but the folks in the blind tigers vote, and Hyde knows the businessmen in this city put him in office. Hyde won by a razor-thin margin—only fourteen votes—and he knows where they came from. Howe owns three blind tigers. He's the most popular host in town. He's also a shrewd businessman. Shrewd businessmen gain entrance to all sorts of doors, including those at City Hall."

"He asked me to tell you he'd protected me last night."

"Thank you for passing the message along. I'm grateful he did."

"He said it made you two even."

"Ah," Gordon said, and he took a sip of his coffee. "Yes. I suppose it might."

"So he owed you? For what?"

Gordon placed the cup back in its saucer and laid both hands on the tabletop.

"Son, nobody was happier than I when you returned from Europe. I may have acted rashly in allowing you to find your own way in the Army. But you did find your way, and now you're back home. Since you returned, you have been curious about my business. I imagine your conversations with Norbert Tradd and Chance Howe have put ideas in your head. It's possible you fancy me to be something I'm not. Let me be clear. We live at the end of the road on a peninsula surrounded by water. Businessmen in this city are a closed society. We all deal with one another. We all owe one another, to either a greater or lesser extent. This is an insular economy. By protecting you last night, Mr. Howe imagines he has erased a debt to me, and he likely has. After all, what would be more valuable to me than the safety of my son and heir? No debt could be greater."

"I see," Beau said.

"I don't think you do," Gordon said. "You can't, because you're still outside the tent, looking in. I don't want to pressure you. But it is central to my plans that you eventually take over the tobacco import business."

Beau slouched in his chair. "Father, I—"

"Not right away, of course. But a man has to make his way in this world. You need to earn money to put food on the table, not to mention a roof over your head. I am prepared to offer you a management position over our three freighters, give you a few years to learn all the ins and outs before you climb the ladder, and all of it at a salary which will enable you to buy your own home and make a real life."

"I don't know…"

"You have a better offer? I didn't tell you the best part. Once you're in the company, you get the sort of access Chance Howe had last night. You're in the club. We stand behind one another. We're talking about security you can't buy even if you're a millionaire—which you likely will be in a few years."

"I still need time," Beau said quietly. "It's a generous offer, and I've always known it would be there if I decided to take it."

"Mull it over. And, while you do, consider how long it would take you to move from an entry level position to management in another company. Consider how likely it would be you'd own the company someday. I'm cutting ten years off the shitty end of your career, Beau. You'd leap-frog over all the other returning doughboys, an advantage any smart young man would grab with both hands."

CHAPTER TWENTY-THREE

KEEBY STYLES FINALLY had a name for the mysterious Bolshevik publisher who had introduced himself as Remy Fousheé.

When Fousheé first sat next to Keeby in the Montorgueil café, it was apparent the little Frenchman knew a great deal more about Keeby than an average passerby would discern. At a disadvantage, Keeby aimed to level the playing field by learning as much as he could about Fousheé and his accomplices.

It had come at the cost of several days tracking the young man through the streets of the Rive Gauche. The entire time, he should have been writing, but he only had three paying publishers, and a habit of completing his work well before deadline. He was caught up, at least for the moment. His curiosity about Fousheé and his little pack of communards had kept him awake more than once.

He wasn't certain how he'd put the new information to use. There was no indication they intended to exploit or harm him in any way, and Fousheé had honored his promise to provide complete cover for Keeby and to keep him anonymous. As far as Keeby could tell, reading the daily

Solidarité paper, they had also largely kept his work from becoming the message.

It was a warm spring day. Keeby sat in the shadows of the back row at the sidewalk café directly diagonal from 22 Rue Montparnasse. The waiter refreshed his coffee. Keeby dabbed at the remaining crumbs of his breakfast croissant with his finger to get the last bit of buttery goodness and kept an eye on the building across the intersection.

Around eight-thirty, Fousheé exited the building and turned toward the Rue du Rennes, in the direction of the Salpêtrière Hospital, where he purported to be a student of psychiatry.

Keeby dropped in a few hundred feet behind Fousheé and followed him all the way to the hospital, a half hour or so at a leisurely pace. The sidewalks were busy with morning traffic, and Keeby was comfortable Fousheé had no idea he was being tailed.

Things became tricky when they reached the hospital. The Salpêtrière was always a busy place, but the hallways were a much more constricted environment than the boulevards of Paris, and there were fewer places for a man of Keeby's size to hide from Fousheé's sight.

Slouching, Keeby managed to lose himself in the mass of people in the hospital hallways. Fousheé stopped at an information desk and spoke to a young woman standing behind it. Her expression suggested she was familiar with him. She smiled and even laughed at something he said. Keeby strained his neurons trying to recall a moment when Fousheé had seemed the least bit humorous. Nothing came. Apparently, he was more gregarious around the young women in his life. After a moment or two of chit-chat, Fousheé waved at the woman and turned toward the stairs.

Keeby drew a book from his postal bag and walked to the desk where the young woman stood.

"Excuse me," Keeby said in his most formal French.

"Yes?"

Keeby showed her the book. "The young man you were speaking with—" he snapped his fingers a couple of times. "—oh, I'm horrible with names."

"You mean Monsieur Frankl?"

"Yes! Of course. Remy Frankl."

A shadow crossed the woman's face. She had a nice face, moon-round with large brown eyes and bowed lips. He felt a twinge of guilt for exploiting her.

"I'm sorry, but it is Karl Frankl."

"Is that a fact? This book belongs to Remy Frankl. I borrowed it a few weeks back and wanted to return it. I saw your Monsieur Frankl from the end of the hall, and I could have sworn it was him. Do you suppose they're brothers?"

"I could not say. Monsieur Frankl and I only know one another by name. We took a class together."

"Oh. You're a student?"

"I am."

"Good for you. I hope you become a top psychoanalyst. I'm sorry to have bothered you. Obviously, your Monsieur Frankl and my Monsieur Frankl are different people. Amazing resemblance, though. Thanks for your time."

Keeby took a streetcar back to the Rue du Rennes and walked the rest of the way to Rue Montparnasse. In the lobby of Number 22, he again scanned the rows of mailboxes. The label *K. Frankl* was attached to the box for apartment 3F.

"Gotcha," Keeby said with a touch of triumph.

———

Finding Karl Frankl's name provided Keeby with a starting point for identifying the rest of his cell. Keeby knew the faces of the sidewalk buskers who peddled the broadsheet, but they had to be the lowest rung of the organization. It was even possible they were street urchins who hadn't the slightest idea what the paper said, hired for a few francs a week to hand out propaganda on the street corners, and had no connection at all to the core players in Frankl's cell.

Keeby returned to his shadowy café seat each day. He watched for familiar faces coming in and out of 22 Rue Montparnasse. Karl Frankl departed each morning at the same time to make his trek to the Salpêtrière. Keeby recalled Frankl had appeared exactly on schedule at their meetings to exchange stories and money. He had even been early at the cemetery. Frankl was a creature of habit. Keeby didn't know much about psychiatry or how the mind worked, but he recognized signs of rigid adherence to schedules when he saw them. Either Frankl had military training, or his mind demanded inelasticity in scheduling to impose order on his life.

"So, what in hell does that mean?" Keeby asked himself quietly as the waiter refreshed his coffee.

"What does what mean?" a feminine voice said to his right. A woman had taken the seat at the table next to him. She was tall and slim, her skin the color of chestnuts. Her features suggested Asia or the Indies. Her ebony hair was bobbed to the bottom of her ears. She reminded him of paintings of Middle Eastern odalisques, lounging in their harems. She was possibly the second most beautiful woman Keeby had encountered all week, in a city filled with stunning fashion models.

"I'm sorry," Keeby said. "I hope I didn't disturb you. I was wool-gathering."

"*Qu'est-ce que c'est* 'wool-gathering'?"

She spoke articulate French, but with an unidentifiable accent. Malaysia, perhaps? Levantine? He chuckled at the absurdity of a Canadian criticizing another person's French accent.

"Did I say something humorous?" she asked. She said it as if she were mildly insulted, but her eyes suggested she was playing with him.

"No. I did." Keeby tapped the side of his head. "In here."

"How curious," she said. "Do you hear voices in your head frequently?"

"Occupational hazard. I'm a writer."

She pointed to the copy of *Solidarité* at his elbow. "You write this?"

"A boy dropped it on the table a few minutes ago. Why? Have you read it?"

"A passing glance here and there." She held out her hand. "Nathalie Bel."

"Caleb Styles," he said, taking it. "Most people call me Keeby."

"Kee-bee," she repeated. "Odd."

"Long story. It's a nickname. Had it for years."

She removed a cigarette from her purse. He struck a match to light it. She accepted the offer, and her hands cupped his as she pulled the match toward her in the May

147

Paris breeze. Her hands were warm but chapped, even in the middle days of spring. She exhaled a cloud of smoke and waved the cigarette at the broadsheet.

"It's all shit, you know." She had switched to English. Keeby didn't waste time wondering whose benefit it was for.

"Shit?" he asked.

"The basic science is sound. Karl Marx was an economic genius. The problem is human nature."

"Is that so?"

"Theory is one thing. Practice is another. Economics as a cold hard science makes objective sense, but toss human beings into the equation, and it all falls apart. But the biggest insult *Solidarité* commits is not taking a firm position. Are they going to install a society based entirely on nothing but scientific and mathematical principles, or are they going to lose themselves in futile sentimentality?"

"I don't follow," Keeby said.

"Look, read here," she said, grabbing the broadsheet from his table. "Now, here is a perfectly utilitarian account of the formation of the Comintern in Moscow. It is factual, accurate, and—if I were to be brutally honest—a bit pedestrian. Here, the first story under the fold. An interview with a baker in the Montorgueil. It puts a human face on the issue of class struggle. It is sentimental, human, perhaps even a little touching."

"And that's a bad thing?"

"There is no place for sentimentality in a cultural revolution," she said. "These little pieces of fluff serve a purpose, I suppose. They illustrate why the Bolsheviks consider the ills of society can only be eradicated by overthrowing the aristocracy and instituting an entirely new form of government."

"Didn't France already do that only a little over a century ago?"

"And with troublesome consequences. These reactionary Bolshevik agitators miss the point. They reject the individual, but they want to put a human face on their revolutionary zeal by appealing to the emotions of their readers, to make them angry and ready to man the barricades."

"Something tells me you've given this paper more than a passing glance," Keeby said.

"Perhaps I'm a little bit of a revolutionary myself," she said.

"Their greatest failing, in my opinion, is using the Russian revolution as their prototype," Keeby said. "Based on what I've read, their counterparts in Mother Russia appear to be mucking things up magnificently themselves. I suspect running an actual society is a monumentally daunting task for people who have never crafted public policy. The occasional populist uprising may clear the deadwood, but in the end— like cockroaches—it's the career bureaucrats who always survive to climb from the rubble and ride in to save the political day. I've been reading reports coming out of Moscow from correspondents like Jack Reed, and from what I can tell, the new Bolshevik regime is still a few years away from salvation."

"Do you live on the Rive Gauche?" she asked.

"No. I'm across the river. Les Halles."

"And yet I find you on this side of the Seine, lounging in a café, talking to yourself."

"Sun's better on this side. The coffee, too. Conversation's pretty much the same, at least until now."

"But you are a writer. Should you not be in your garret, chained to your desk, frantically scribbling out words?"

"Spoken like an editor. I do come up for air. To be perfectly frank, I am a largely unemployed writer. I only have three paying commissions. It's enough to keep a roof over my head, but not enough to keep me busy every hour of the day. Sitting in this sunny café is considerably more pleasant than lounging across my bed waiting for inspiration. So, what do you do besides sitting in sidewalk cafés interrupting complete strangers talking to themselves?"

"We have never met, it is true. But we are no longer complete strangers, Keeby. You have lit my cigarette, and we have exchanged names and political opinions. At the worst, I would consider us acquaintances. I am a model."

"Of course you are," Keeby said. "Fashion or art?"

"Both, as it suits me—and as jobs are available."

"The war put a kink in your career?"

"The work is not as frequent as I would wish, but like you I keep a roof over my head. Perhaps, after the horrors of the last several years, that is sufficient, *n'est ce pas?*"

"Beats hell out of sleeping in the streets. So, here's the deal, Mademoiselle—it is Mademoiselle?—Nathalie Bel. I have thoroughly enjoyed our brief but engrossing conversation. It also appears my subterfuge is uncovered. But so is yours. Tell Karl I'm done following him. I'm almost certain my error was with the receptionist at the Salpêtrière. She must have described me to Karl, and he recognized me from the description."

"Please do not be offended, Keeby, but I believe you must be a madman," Nathalie said.

"I notice you aren't running away. Karl Frankl. The man who introduced himself to me as Remy Fousheé. You're part of his cell—an enticing part, I might add. He sent you to keep an eye on me."

She settled in the chair, a sly smile crossing her face. "I overplayed the analysis of the newspaper. But you are wrong. I am not in league with Karl Frankl, or any of his misguided friends. I am affiliated with SFIO."

Keeby was familiar with the *Section française de l'Internationale ouvrière*—the French Section of the Workers' International—from the French press. The SFIO had been the backbone of French socialism since before the war.

"The war created a rift within the SFIO," she explained. "The Bolshevik revolution in Russia only intensified it. The acquittal of Faure's assassin enraged the more radical factions within the SFIO. Even as we speak, there is talk of splitting into two separate parties. Karl Frankl is the facilitator for a Bolshevik cell in the Montparnasse, as you are aware. In fact, he is a cell of one. He has no associates or comrades. He is a lonely little man toiling in a shabby apartment, writing revolutionary screeds and pointless manifestos. Between you and me, he is regarded as something of a—what do Americans call it? A cracked pot."

"Crackpot," Keeby corrected.

"*Oui.* The SFIO leadership is concerned about the impact of lone wolves like Monsieur Frankl. I would remind you of the impact such a man, Gavrilo Princip, had on the world over the last several years. We keep an eye on Frankl, to ensure he hasn't gone too far off the rails. I am curious, however, as to why you appear to be spying on him."

"I'm curious as well. He introduced himself with a fake name and told me it was fake. What sort of person does that?"

"I ask you again, Monsieur Styles, do you write for *Solidarité*?

"The little pieces of fluff. Not the polemics. I don't give two shits about his politics. I'm hired to write. I take it you're affiliated with the more traditional wing of the SFIO?"

"We still believe in working within the system. As I noted, the last time France was overrun by a populist rabble, the consequences were not attractive. My faction does not seek revolution. We prefer evolution."

"Horseshit. You both want the same results. Your faction is just more patient."

"A realist would say you are correct."

"Are you a realist, Mademoiselle Bel?"

"I'm a pragmatist. And a socialist. And a feminist. Nobody is only one thing, Monsieur Styles."

"Please. Call me Keeby."

"So we are to be friends?" she asked.

"Remains to be seen," Keeby said. "Tell me more about Karl Frankl."

CHAPTER TWENTY-FOUR

KARL FRANKL, in his guise as Remy Fousheé, arrived precisely at three o'clock on Friday afternoon for his weekly exchange with Keeby. Keeby, already seated, watched him as he approached. The little bespectacled man looked worried. He even glanced over his shoulder before taking a seat.

"Got ants in your pants?" Keeby asked.

"I do not understand this *ants in pants*," Frankl said. "Is this a code?"

"Do I look like the sort to talk in code, Karl? It's an American expression. You look anxious."

"Ah! Yes. As if I had ants in my pants. A most uncomfortable metaphor, but descriptive." He looked past Keeby's shoulder, toward the Rue de Turbigo.

Keeby patted a folder in front of him on the table. "Your stories, Karl. Want to read them quickly?"

"Not necessary, Monsieur. We are, I believe, in a position to mutually trust one another."

"I think you give our relationship far too much credit."

"Our shaky alliance depends on it." He handed Keeby an envelope stuffed with francs.

"One thing I can't figure out, Karl," Keeby said, slipping the envelope into his inside jacket pocket.

Preoccupied with scanning the streets in each direction, Frankl said, "Eh? What is it?"

"You dress like a pauper, but you attend an elite psychiatry institute."

"I am the recipient of various grants and scholarships."

"I love the facile way that answer rolled off your tongue," Keeby said. "It almost sounds rehearsed. Something else. I've called you by the wrong name three times since you arrived, and you haven't corrected me once."

Frankl's head snapped around and his eyes riveted on Keeby. "What? What did you say?"

"Perhaps it wasn't the wrong name after all, Karl? Karl Frankl?"

Frankl appeared to deflate in his chair. He wiped at his face with a handkerchief, and a tortured smile slowly crept in at the corners of his mouth. "That was you? You American cocksucker! I've been terrified the police were coming for me. When Sylvie told me a man had asked after me at the information desk, I knew they were after me. It was only you? Why on earth would you do that?"

"Because I hate living under false pretenses. I like to know who I'm dealing with. You live alone at 22 Rue Montparnasse, Apartment 3F. There is no cell. You have no comrades helping you to publish your newspapers. You pay for everything out of pocket because you can. You pay *me* out of pocket, because you can, and because you need someone who can write from the heart and not from the intellect. You're a self-loathing, card-carrying member of the *bourgeoisie* you claim to detest. You idolize your martyred communard grandparents but gloss over the fact their son—your father— rejected the Paris Commune ideals and embraced good old-fashioned Gilded Age capitalism. Did I say *embraced?* He practically fucked it to death. No wonder you're studying psychiatry. It would take a dozen Freuds to hack through the Gordian knot of your complexes. No charge for the metaphor. Mostly I did it because I was dissatisfied with the lopsided power structure in our relationship. You obviously knew a lot more about me than I knew about you. I decided to level the playing field. And I was bored. It was something to do."

"Something to do," Frankl repeated.

"Oh, and I met a new friend."

Nathalie Bel glided into the café from the Rue du Turbigo. Keeby stood, took her hand, and escorted her to her seat at his table. Frankl's face registered his immediate distaste for the exotic beauty. She smiled warmly as she extended her hand.

"Monsieur Frankl. We meet again," she purred. Frankl reluctantly took her hand with a perfunctory shake and immediately released it.

"Oh, you know one another?" Keeby said. "What are the chances, in a city the size of Paris?"

"Are you enjoying yourself?" Frankl asked.

"Aren't you?"

"I feel as if I have been cuckolded," Frankl said, sourly. Then, as if a cloud lifted, he slowly allowed himself to smile. "Fortunately, it is not the first time. I have experience!"

Keeby was impressed. He turned to Nathalie. "*Savoir-faire?*"

"*Beaucoups!*" She laughed lightly, and in seconds they all chuckled as if nothing had happened, because that was the way things were done in Paris. Karl Frankl ordered another round of wine because he could.

"The SFIO is watching my movements?" Frankl asked Nathalie, as if inquiring whether she had eaten so or a salad at lunch. "So typical. How long?" He waved a finger back and forth at Keeby and Nathalie.

"Only a day or so ago," Nathalie said. "Our paths crossed serendipitously. And don't make it out as if you're under surveillance."

"Feels as if I am."

"We keep an eye on what you're writing. You're still an SFIO member, Karl. When you make public statements, they reflect the party. Or, at least, they should. We have had this conversation before. None of this should be news to you. Some of the inflammatory language you use is dangerous, especially following the revolution in Russia and with the world healing from the war. The instability of the French government offers the SFIO a greater opportunity to seat our members at the next election than we have seen in years. We don't want firebrands confusing the message with calls for insurrection."

"She doesn't want you pissing in the well," Keeby summarized in English.

"You said you were Canadian," Frankl said. "You talk like an American. No consequence. It is good you are here, Nathalie. You can report to your fellows. I will not be a thorn in the side of the SFIO any longer. I am leaving France." Keeby and Nathalie were both surprised. "It seems my revolutionary zeal has interfered with my studies to the extent I am no longer invited to continue them at the Salpêtrière. In a fortnight, I will board the train to Russia. I am too impatient to wait for revolution in France when it has already occurred elsewhere. I can continue my studies in Moscow, freed from the burdens of roiling the proletariat. I hear there are some interesting advances being made in psychiatry there."

"They'll have you digging latrines and slaughtering hogs on a collective farm," Keeby said. "If you aren't starving on line in the city. Intellectual pursuits aren't a priority in Russia. They're too busy staving off a famine."

"Every great culture has its birthing pains," Frankl said.

"You keep telling yourself that," Keeby said. "A fortnight, you say? I suppose this is the end of *Solidarité*."

"Which means you are out of a job," Frankl said. "I would have sacked you in any case for snooping into my business."

"We'll never know. How much do you pay for the apartment on Rue Montparnasse?"

Frankl told him. Keeby whistled.

"Less than half the rent for my rooms in the Montorgueil," he said. "I want to see your apartment, Karl. And you can introduce me to your landlord. I hear the writing and art community on the Rive Gauche is livelier than on this side of the river."

———

Keeby couldn't keep his eyes off Nathalie's skin. Nut-brown, flawless, unmarked by moles or birthmarks, it slipped like silk under his fingers as he softly stroked her spine from neck to tailbone. They lay on his bed in the Montorgueil apartment, sweat drying in the early summer breeze that billowed the window sheers like doves' wings in flight. The aroma of lovemaking mixed with the perfume of Paris in the room, which glowed in the late afternoon light.

"You fuck like an Englishman," she murmured. Her tone made it impossible to determine whether this was a good thing.

"Canadian," he whispered. "Cousins. And, in my defense, it's been a few weeks. I'm out of practice."

She didn't open her eyes. "We need to do something about that. It would be a crime to your next lover if I didn't teach you a thing or two."

"I haven't impressed you into settling down?"

"Dream on, scribbler. I can help you get work, though."

"Tell me more."

"Not with the SFIO. Radicalism is not your strong point. As a model, I meet journalists and editors and publishers. I will arrange for you to meet them."

"In return for—"

"Nothing. Neither of us owes the other a thing, Keeby. We never will. I do it because I like you. I wouldn't be naked in your bed if I didn't. My face and body allow me to be selective. I only fuck men I like, or who can get me what I like. You have nothing I desire beyond yourself, so you know which side you're on."

"I suspect you're the type of woman men write operas about," Keeby whispered.

"Save the poetry for your typewriter. Are you taking the apartment in Montparnasse?"

Keeby rolled over, lit two cigarettes, and handed one to Nathalie. She leaned against the pillows on the brass headrail and didn't bother to cover herself with the sheet. She and Keeby were way past modesty, and it was warm. He blew a cloud of tobacco smoke toward the ceiling fan. It wafted right back at him.

"My friend Beau paid the rent for this place through the end of next month, but I'd be hard pressed to keep it afterward. I make enough from my Canadian press contract to cover the Montparnasse place. If I can scare up some work through your contacts, all the better. Cutting my living expenses by better than half, I can enjoy a much more comfortable life. Moving makes sense."

"It is a shabby little place."

"Only because of the shabby little man who lived there. I see potential. A little paint, some classier furnishings, some art on the walls. Why, with a little elbow grease, I could turn that roach circus into a genuine eyesore."

"An eyesore would be an improvement. Get all your shots before you move in."

———

True to his word, Karl Frankl boarded the eastbound train two weeks later. The landlord at 22 Rue Montparnasse was delighted to turn the flat over so rapidly, and Keeby moved his furniture and other belongings across the river the minute Frankl's train cleared the station.

Nathalie followed through with her promise as well. She either kept her political leanings close to her admirably filled vest, or her artistic friends in Paris didn't care. In the two weeks since they first bedded, he had escorted her to swanky parties where she introduced him to the editors of two local magazines and the publisher of Paris's third most popular newspaper. He met politicians, actors, singers, and at least one accomplished cat burglar—though he only learned about the man's secret life from Nathalie later, when she showed him a pair of earrings he had purloined for her.

Acting on opportunity, Keeby cultivated the contacts, and had already received two commissions for articles. His writing career in Paris was lifting off the ground. Between packing and lugging his belongings across the river, trying to meet his various writing deadlines, and keeping pace with Nathalie's apparently bottomless libido, his leisure time was sliced to almost nothing.

He had not been misinformed. The arts life on the Rive Gauche was everything he had hoped it might be. He had landed in the middle of a Bohemian fantasyland, full of more starving artists, writers, and composers than you could fit into an ocean liner. Nathalie seemed to know all of them and made it her mission to ensure Keeby knew them as well. Each night was a different party, or a mass gathering under the awning of some outdoor café, or dancing, or simply sitting around an apartment drinking wine, smoking dope, and talking about ethereal nothings the way artists frequently do.

He had a three-way one night with Nathalie and a young nightclub dancer recently arrived from New York. Another party devolved into a tangled, undulating carpet of arms, legs, mouths, and torsos. He drank absinthe at La Rotonde and vowed never again to wrestle the Green Fairy. Back in his new apartment—because she never allowed him to visit her own—they wrapped around one another on a bare mattress in a room of unpacked boxes and strewn furniture and clothes, and she taught him new ways to pleasure a woman, always with the promise his next lover would thank her for it.

Until he met Nathalie, Keeby had only been living in Paris. Nathalie was transforming him into a Parisian.

She helped him cover the walls with fresh coats of paint. Together, they wallpapered the private bathroom—the apartment's primary selling point since most buildings only offered shared facilities at the end of the hall—and hung new curtains in the windows. Slowly, the shabby little apartment grew bright and homey.

On July fourth, a date of no particular importance in Paris, but which Keeby knew was being celebrated furiously back home, he was completely moved in. Even though the Montorgueil apartment was paid through the end of the month, it now lay bare and shut, the air stale, dust motes settling to the floor and tables. The landlord would arrive on the first of August to collect the rent, only to discover his tenants had flown the coop. He would shrug and list the apartment for rent again. It happened all the time in Paris.

Keeby set about preparing for his dinner date with Nathalie. Suddenly flush with cash, he had spent the morning in the markets of the Latin Quarter, where he had purchased flowers, a chicken, vegetables, fingerling potatoes, several bottles of wine, and the most perfect baguette he could locate. He had arranged the flowers in a vase which he placed in the middle of the kitchen table and set about making a Provencal chicken with the vegetables and wine. It was the only French dish he knew how to cook, but after several disappointing attempts he had discovered an almost chef-proof recipe.

By eight o'clock, when Nathalie was scheduled to arrive, Keeby was bathed, shaved, and dressed. He lit the two beeswax taper candles he had bought in the market and placed them on either side of the bouquet in the center of the dinner table. He opened one of the bottles of wine, and poured two glasses, so he could offer her one as soon as she arrived. He tasted his, to assure him it wasn't rotgut.

At eight-fifteen, he poured a second glass.

He emptied his third glass at nine o'clock.

At ten o'clock, he snuffed out the candles, ate his ruined dinner in the dark, opened the second bottle of wine, settled into a chair next to the window, stared out into the Parisian night, and drank until he passed out.

Years would pass before he saw Nathalie Bel again.

CHAPTER TWENTY-FIVE

BEAU WAS CONVINCED there was no more humid or miserable place than Charleston in late summer. August of 1919 was no exception.

The riot in the segregated district was an entire season in the past, but the reverberations had rung across the country during the long, hot Red Summer. Each morning, Beau opened the newspaper to read reports of yet another incident of violence against blacks in one part of the country or another.

In July, a mob of angry white men in the Texas town of Longview rioted and killed four black men, destroying most of the black neighborhood in the town.

The madness spread west, and the next day the police in backwater Bisbee, Arizona attacked the all-Negro 10th Cavalry Unit, which had been in existence for almost sixty years.

Two weeks later, in Garfield Park in Indianapolis, hundreds of white teenagers clashed with black citizens, using bricks and clubs to beat senseless any black person they encountered. Shots were fired, houses surrounded, and citizens terrified, but fortunately nobody died.

A week later, however, the violence spread to within shouting distance of the nation's capital. A Washington DC black man named Charles Ralls was accused by the police of assaulting a white woman, Elsie Stephnik, who was married to a Navy sailor. Ralls was released by the police, but rumors spread quickly around the mostly white Navy yard, as it had in Charleston two months earlier. On Saturday evening, July nineteenth, a band of sailors discovered Ralls walking with his wife and attacked them. They escaped to the safety of their home, but the mob—now enraged by its failure to adequately avenge the fictitious assault on Elsie Stephnik—launched into a frenzy of violence and destruction that endured for four days.

On the second night, rioters prepared a black man for hanging, but found the process too laborious and instead simply shot him. The dean of students at Howard University hid in the shadows for days, documenting the atrocities he observed. On the second night, Sunday, the *Washington Post* printed instructions for able-bodied seamen and soldiers to congregate on Pennsylvania Avenue—whether to confront the rioters or join them was never explicitly spelled out. The black community responded by arming themselves with guns and ammunition, which only inflamed the conflict further.

By the end of four days of violence, thirty-nine people— white and black—had died, and several people were charged with murder and manslaughter. Entire blocks of the seat of American democracy were scarred by scorched timber and broken glass.

Tensions remained high, and resurfaced several days later in Norfolk, where a celebration for black soldiers returning from the Great War's battlefields was invaded by white gangs who shot six people before the local police and Marines could quell the disturbance.

Across the country, the rosters of Ku Klux Klan klaverns swelled to the breaking point as mostly working-class white men, frightened by the emerging black power in communities and emboldened by D.W. Griffith's *Birth of a Nation*, banded together to preserve their centuries-old unearned white privilege.

Each new day brought news of a different clash somewhere in the nation.

In Charleston, tensions remained in the segregated district, though most of the rest of the city appeared to conveniently disregard the May riot as a blip in their otherwise genteel existence. Chance Howe's blind tiger had reopened, as had many of the other businesses, but crowds were smaller. Most clubs and restaurants in the district had banned sailors, which partly explained the reduced numbers of people prowling its streets in the evenings, but there was another factor as well. The good feelings and exuberance accompanying the end of four years of bloody European war, which had buoyed business in the mostly black district, had been tempered by caution. The segregated district was still regarded by many former Charleston patrons as a risky place to visit after dark.

Reports of the most recent episode, in Chicago, with thirty-eight people dead, over four hundred injured, and thousands left homeless, weighed heavily on Beau's mind as he set up his easel and canvas and arranged his tubes of oil paints and brushes on a steamy August morning that portended heavy thunderstorms in the late afternoon. He had claimed a few square feet of shade on a sidewalk across from the Circular Church on Meeting Street, mostly out of the way of passers-by, to work on his latest piece.

It had been a turbulent summer in more than the social and racial sense.

Sophie, predictably, had grown weary of him by the middle of July. She had never demonstrated a robust attention span in the best of times, so it was inevitable her interest might wane with time and familiarity.

He noticed it slowly. He would ask her out, and she'd make some obscure excuse. An unnamed sick friend—which was entirely possible, since the influenza epidemic, while quelled, had not been entirely quenched. A previous social engagement. Washing her hair—which, ignoring Beau's hearty objections, she had bobbed exactly as she had threatened. Beau knew he was self-absorbed, but he was not impervious to reason, and with time he recognized the signs of the impending end of an affair.

They still met once or twice a week, and their dates still frequently ended in Sophie's bedroom, but she no longer protested when he rose in the blue-black hours of the night to dress and skulk home under the cover of darkness, and she was more likely now to doze off after sex rather than talk. Their lovemaking, perhaps due to the lack of *love* in it, had become perfunctory, the satisfaction shorter-lived with each encounter. They were each other's temporary respite from loneliness. It was a matter of time. Sophie's eye would turn to some new and exciting quarry, and that would be the end.

He would miss Sophie's bed, but he knew she wasn't the one. *My match is still out there*, he thought as he squeezed paint from tubes onto his palette. He enjoyed pastels, but any budding creator must also master oils if he planned to lay any claim to an artistic legacy.

Beau chuckled quietly at the idea he might have an artistic legacy. Like a Quixotic duffer, he tilted at painting without ever challenging it. He imagined the great artists he had encountered in Paris staring at themselves in the mirror and accusing their reflections of fraud. Van Gogh must have. There must be other tragic examples, but none came to mind as the meridian sun roasted the street in the muggy old quarter of Charleston.

Beau attacked painting with the same battle plan he had with pastels. *Ignore the structure*, he reminded himself. *Paint the colors.*

He had found an old pair of eyeglasses in a second-hand market on King Street a few weeks earlier. Beau had perfect vision, but he had found acuity to be a hindrance in his painting. When he put the glasses on, the world resolved into a soft blur of color and amorphous form, almost like a Monet painting. It was far less uncomfortable than squinting, even if both strategies eventually left him with a headache.

Ah, well, Beau thought as sweat dripped from his hairline and across his cheek. *All great art arises from suffering.*

He set about his work, mixing pigments on his palette, and daubing the paint at the canvas as if stabbing for its heart. His first strokes were always bold, aggressive, and decisive, almost impulsive, smearing gobs of paint across the canvas to represent the larger components of the scene. Later, with a wide soft brush, he would blend the gross assemblage of blotches into a cohesive kaleidoscope of color depicting the soot and ivy-covered walls of the church and the solemn, shaded churchyard with its gardens of headstones. He mentally stripped the landscape into layers, which he would stack one on another in paint from background to foreground until he captured the idea of the wrought-iron fence separating the churchyard from the Meeting Street sidewalk.

Over the course of minutes, the world collapsed into only three entities—the church, the light, and the paint. Beau's consciousness faded and dissolved. The blurred and fuzzy images in his second-hand eyeglasses translated automatically into patterns of rainbow hues and traveled directly from eye to paintbrush with no deliberation or mediation. He became trancelike, his head bobbing from church to canvas. The heat was meaningless. The sweat was unimportant. If his hunched back ached, he ignored it. Passers-by stopped and watched as he smeared paint across the canvas, but he was oblivious to them. He had experienced this ecstasy before, this sense of flow and immersion in the act of creation. His fingers stabbed at globs of paint on the palette, mixed with a frenzy, and attacked with the fraying bristles again and again, as the impression of the church and graveyard gradually emerged from the chaos of the early strokes.

He could sense it, the intensity of becoming one with his work. It was as satisfying as the immediate moments following sex, a cascade of peace and relaxation flooding through his body, the abandonment of pain and ego. Sophie's distance, his father's pressures, his wartime trauma, the frightening fractures in racial relations across the country— none of them existed. There was the church, the light, and the paint. There was no longer intent, only the transformation of a brick-and-mortar church to pigments and canvas.

His concentration shattered as a voice behind him said, "It's good."

His hand froze, the brush suspended between the palette and the easel. A droplet of paint flew off the tip and arced in space, splattering on the tray. He recognized the voice. Slowly, he turned, hoping it hadn't been a hallucination spurred by his artistic reverie.

Victoria still dressed entirely in black. Her face appeared nearly bloodless. Her cheekbones threw shadows. Her hands were clawlike. "I had no idea," she said. "You never painted before."

"No." The shock of her sudden appearance had left him speechless. "Surprised me as well. Something I learned in the hospital in Paris."

"Paris. Yes," she said. "Was it lovely? I've never been."

"There is no other city like Paris," he said, reflexively, and he meant it. He looked at the painting, back at Victoria, and an idea struck him. He pointed toward the canvas. "Would...would you like to be in it?"

"The painting?" she asked.

"Sure. Wouldn't take five minutes. All you do is—" He took her hand and led her across the street to the wrought iron fence of the Circular Church graveyard. "I'd like you to stand like this, as if you're looking through the fence at a particular headstone." He posed her with one hand gripping the fence as if trying to keep her balance, and the other stretched out toward the churchyard.

"Should I do anything with my face?" she asked.

"Let your eyes follow the line of your arm. It doesn't matter. It's impressionism. There are no subtle facial expressions, only broad strokes. Now, don't move."

"How long?" she asked.

"A couple of minutes."

169

He dashed across the street, quickly added some paint to his palette, and rapidly slashed eight or ten quick swipes across the canvas.

"That's it," he said.

"Already?"

"I said it would be quick."

He crossed the street and escorted Victoria to his artist roost.

"Can I see?" she asked.

"Who has a better right?"

She gazed at the painting. With only a handful of strokes, Beau had created the impression of a mourning woman yearning for a lost love. The emotion in the scene was unmistakable.

"You took a simple architectural painting and turned it into art," he told her. "Now it tells a story."

"It's beautiful," she said. "I'm so happy I came along and saw you."

"Well, you made my day." He packed his supplies, and she hovered over him as he secured the easel.

"You told my father you wouldn't stop trying," she said.

The tone of her voice had changed. There was a keen edge to it, now, a metallic glint of resentment.

"I know," he said. "Was that you in the window?"

"Yes."

"I've visited your home twice since I returned from the war. Neither time did I receive even the slightest hint of welcome. Your father nearly ran me off with the shotgun, and all I wanted to do was take you to church. What would he do if he caught me making love to you?"

"Lower your voice," she snapped. "We're in public. Perhaps Father was right. I don't suppose there is much I can offer compared to Sophie Wildmon."

"Sophie?" he said, only momentarily surprised. Why wouldn't Victoria know? Nothing stayed secret long in Charleston society.

"Just because I spend most of my time in my house doesn't mean I don't hear things. I still have friends who visit. You didn't waste any time finding a place to lie your head after Father turned you away. Maybe all you were interested in was—"

"Stop it, Victoria. You know why I'm not in Paris right now? I came home to stop you from marrying Alton. I didn't know he was dead until the night I arrived. I didn't know you'd lost your mother and had become a recluse. When I was in the trenches, the chances were real that I might not live to see the next sunrise, but I'd have traded every sunrise for the rest of my life to see your face one more time. Then I came home and you were different and Charleston was different and every goddamn thing was different and I didn't belong anywhere."

She cast her eyes toward the sidewalk. "I'm sorry," she said.

"Well, it goes for both of us. I've had a lot of time to think over the summer. There's no future for us. There never was, after I went across the water. The war and the damned epidemic drove us in different directions, and there's no getting back to where we were. What I said to your father, I said out of pride. Later, after I had the chance to think, I agreed with him. But that doesn't mean I don't care. And I'm worried about you. You don't look well."

"No," she said. "I don't suppose I do."

"I'm not saying this as a lover. Now I'm your friend. Let me help you. You're twenty-two years old. Maybe, a thousand years ago, you might have had one foot in the grave, but nowadays you're only at the end of the first quarter. There's a lot of living in front of you. I can't imagine you want to spend it in a dark room in your house, staring out at the world. Before I left, the world was a much brighter place with you in it."

"What's broken can't be unbroken," she said.

"Damn it, Victoria. I don't care about the epidemic. I don't care about your father. I don't give a damn about Alton or the letter or the baby or any of it. I only want you to be happy and healthy again, as your friend."

He couldn't register the expression on her face. He thought he had seen horror, but this time he didn't recognize it.

"The...*baby,*" she mumbled. "What do you know?"

"I..." he couldn't find the words.

"What...*baby?*" she demanded. "Who told you this? Who told you about a baby?"

Beau took her arm and walked her toward a nearby bench. He helped her sit and ran back to gather his art supplies.

"Who else knows?" she asked as he sat again.

"I have no idea," he said. "A lot of people."

Her skeletal hands trembled in her lap. Her head bobbed in disbelief. A tear plopped against the bodice of her dress.

"I know where it started," she said. "I only told one person. Sally Porter. You say you want to be my friend. I can see what friends are worth now. I can't be here right now, Beau."

She stood to leave. Beau grabbed her arm as gently as he could to restrain her. "Wait. Let's talk."

"What is there to talk about?" she said, her eyes empty again. "My life here is over. Every respectable man in town knows. Who will have me? Sally Porter might as well have stabbed me in my sleep."

With remarkable vigor, she yanked her arm from his grasp and ran across the street into the church.

————

1919 was an uncommonly calm year for hurricanes, but the low country did see three or four tropical storms. As Beau sadly gathered his painting gear and trudged toward Wentworth Street, and as Victoria took refuge with Jesus in the Circular Church, and as Gordon Shipley oversaw the unloading of a fresh shipment from Cuba, and as the segregated district prepared for another night of semi-legal debauchery, a strong tropical system skirted the empty ocean between the Bahamas and Bermuda, button-hooked, and bore due east toward the Charleston peninsula. It was a tight, fast-moving maelstrom, and it had gathered millions of gallons of water in its last day of life.

The storm struck after midnight. Observers along the battery near White Point Gardens first saw the anvil-colored clouds and lightning in the distance but disregarded them. Storms in the low country typically moved west to east, and this one was well out to sea beyond the harbor. Surely, it would continue moving away as the evening wore on.

It didn't. Instead, as it approached the mainland, it grew in strength and fury. Frying-pan billows collected over the peninsula, spitting brilliant white-yellow bolts of lightning thirty times a minute. Thunder rolled over Charleston in a constant rumble accented by artillery-like explosions that made Beau's heart race. Some people reported waterspouts beyond Fort Sumter, seen only in eerie frozen glimpses of lightning.

By the time the storm surge breached the seawalls along lower Bay Street, most people in the peninsula had been warned, and had time to close the shutters and prepare to ride it out. It slammed into Cooper River side of the harbor, driving sheets of rain and surging waves over the stone breakwaters. Flashes of lightning illuminated the skies. The storm drains were overwhelmed, and water rose over the curbing in the lower streets near the point and ran down the sidewalks to flood courtyards and gardens.

Hetty Oliver lived in one of the houses on Bay Street closest to White Point Garden. Around two in the morning, a shutter came loose on one of her harbor-facing windows. It banged against the sill and threatened to shatter the glass, which had stood in the window since before the Civil War. Hetty was seventy-eight years old and remembered when it was installed. It had survived the war and the great earthquake, and she was damned if it wouldn't survive a tropical storm. She had seen more than her share of low country squalls in her life, and she could tell the difference between a real hurricane and what deluged Charleston that evening. She decided it was safe enough to run out and refasten the shutter.

She finished the chore and turned toward the seawall. At first, she thought the storm was playing tricks with her eyes. It looked as if someone was dancing along the top of the wall, which was perhaps ten feet wide. It was a short enough drop on the street side—the worst you could do was snap an ankle. Fall the other way, though, and it was a twenty-five-foot drop at low tide.

The storm had hit at high tide, the worst possible time for storm surges. There was no big drop on the other side. Fall over, and you'd be swept away by the current before anyone could save you. Only a fool would walk along the battery on a night like this.

Or someone who doesn't care if they live or die, Hetty thought.

Braving the two inches of rushing water in the gutters, Hetty crossed Bay Street toward the seawall. There *was* a person there, dressed entirely in black, pacing back and forth on the walkway, gazing out at the storm.

"Hey!" Hetty yelled. "Are you crazy? Get off there!"

The figure turned toward Hetty as twin forks of lightning blazed over White Point Gardens. The light reflected off a shock white face as gaunt as a skull, framed by sodden, straight black hair. The figure raised one bony hand and waved. It stepped backward and disappeared over the edge into the torrent of the harbor.

At almost the same moment, Norbert Tradd checked on his daughter Victoria, and found her bed perfectly made. An envelope rested on her pillow, addressed to *Father*. With shaking fingers, Norbert opened it and held it to the candle.

Even over the roar of thunder and the driving rain, neighbors heard his anguished scream.

CHAPTER TWENTY-SIX

THE MOST EXPENSIVE possession Prince Grigorii Yurievitch Romanov owned was something he could neither sell nor give away—his royal title.

Maintaining appearances was important, even if his princely title was worth roughly the proverbial hill of beans by 1919. The Bolsheviks had seen to that. It was a good thing for them, he mused, that he was vacationing in the south of France when revolutionaries charged the Winter Palace. Considering the recently revealed fate of the royal Romanov family, it wasn't such a bad thing for Prince Grigorii either.

He now lived in Paris, safe from the Bolsheviks and their bloodthirsty vengeance against Russia's former ruling class, but burdened by his title and bereft of the funds to keep it polished.

It wasn't as if he had ever had a great deal of money, at least compared to most European royalty. Princes were, sadly, not uncommon in imperial Russia. Pundits had claimed Russia was without peer at producing vodka, depression, boring endless literature, beautiful music, and princes. After three hundred years of Romanov rule, the family tree had grown broad, with dozens of branches and thousands of leaves. Prince Grigorii had once calculated he was either sixty-third or sixty-sixth in line for the Tsar's throne. It was a social distinction barely worth mentioning, especially since the throne itself was probably firewood by now, but the word *prince* was all most people needed to hear. The tawdry details were irrelevant. Despite being the supposedly enlightened and egalitarian twentieth century, nobility still carried its share of gravitas in the better social circles, deserved or not.

And Grigorii had friends. Hundreds of friends. He was an extrovert of the most notable accomplishments. He had two sterling qualities—he never met a stranger, and he was personally charming and handsome. Combined, they enabled him to mingle effortlessly among captains and kings, and to be accepted almost immediately into any crowd to which he was introduced. Once accepted, he became a catalyst for bringing people together. *"Oh,"* one of his friends would say to a new acquaintance, *"have you met my close friend, Prince Grigorii Romanov?"* Being in his presence elevated the status of his friends, and they kept him in good stead to maintain the advantage.

Prince Grigorii was of slightly more than average height, his posture ramrod straight thanks to the military education provided by his parents in Russia. His hair was dark brown, combed straight back, and accented by sideburns trimmed to a razor-sharp point. The bridge of his nose was as straight as a ruler, ending in an almost geometric vertex above a pencil-thin mustache, full lips, and a prominent chin. His eyes were his best feature, he knew. Women had described them as sultry. He had been born with double rows of dark eyelashes, and his eyes themselves were brown bordering on ebony. The contrast gave him the face of a kohl-rimmed matinee idol.

Prince Grigorii had been aware of his attractiveness to women for years. A shrewd observer of human nature, he had determined the most attractive people he knew—at least by his personal standards—were also the most socially desired. They were the women whose dance cards were already filled before their feet touched the floor. They were the men who were never declined for a job or—more frequently—a loan. He had also observed that he fit this exact description, and therefore he must be an immensely attractive man in his own right.

An early bloomer, he had lost his virginity at thirteen to a housemaid who lured him into her cellar room late one night after finding him sitting by the fireplace stairs long after the rest of the family had gone to bed. She was only sixteen herself, but clearly well-versed already in things people did in the dark. She taught him, patiently, over dozens of secretive late-night visits, and he was an eager student. As he matured into a man, he continued his matriculation in the sexual arts at every opportunity across Europe until, at age twenty-five, he had achieved near master status.

Prince Grigorii's awareness of his attractiveness, his cultivated European manners and personal charm, his wide knowledge of cuisine, art, music, and wine, and his persistence had made him almost predatorially confident in any social situation. There was no feminine—or masculine— conquest beyond his grasp if he decided to pursue it. He adapted to each new social situation as if bred to it.

It was inevitable that Prince Grigorii Yurievitch Romanov would become a gigolo.

Postwar Paris was crawling with them. Displaced Russian princes, financially embarrassed German dukes, and lackland

Italian counts roamed the parties and cafés and the opera, trolling for potentially lucrative companions. It was the most remarkable economy. The children of the former crowned heads of Europe preened and cajoled and ingratiated themselves with *nouveau riche* women—and sometimes men— who showed the slightest interest. There was never a negotiation, or even discussion of the actual nature of the transaction, because talking about it would be *so* tacky.

Frequently, there wasn't even a transaction beyond Grigorii providing a lonely woman with attentive companionship for an evening on the town, with her picking up the checks. At least he did not go hungry on those evenings, and there was always sex afterward. Once Prince Grigorii identified a woman of interest, he charmed her incessantly, made his availability abundantly evident, and thanked her for her company.

Predictably, he'd receive a telephone call in a few days asking if he might be free to accept an unexpectedly available ticket to the opera or to a new symphony. Women in Paris talked, and Grigorii's reputation preceded him. Prince Grigorii always accepted the unspoken invitation to more carnal entertainments later in the evening.

There were always presents, if never acknowledged openly. Sometimes it was cash. Other times watches or jewelry. One woman had given him a Monet sketch, which still hung in his apartment. It was simple and not polished at all, but it was an original, and Prince Grigorii found it too beautiful to sell, at least yet. He simply wasn't hungry enough yet to part with it.

He kept some of the jewelry, and one or two of the better watches, but all things come to an end, and once a paramour's brief dalliance with him concluded he was no longer obligated to hang on to physical mementoes of the affair. He had cultivated a network of men who claimed to be pawnbrokers. A fancy watch could keep him for a month or two. A diamond ring, three or four months. There were benefits to living in a depressed postwar economy. He especially liked the cash, as tawdry as it was to take it, because he didn't have to give a cut to anyone. Ready cash made it easier to maintain his snappy wardrobe and daily attention to his hair and mustache. His apartment in the Montparnasse neighborhood was nothing to brag about, but it was clean and tidy and even a little fashionable, the rent was paid without fail each month, and—after all—every prince had to start *somewhere*.

It was a warm evening in July. Prince Grigorii held the door to a cab open for Baroness Giuliana Moretz, a dowager in her fifties who had taken a shine to him. Her late husband had the foresight to relocate to Switzerland before the Great War and to provide her with a generous inheritance which she in turn lavished on people she liked. She liked Prince Grigorii. Giuliana herself was Dutch, with deep blue eyes and probably blonde hair framing a perfectly creamy complexion. Despite her years, she remained uncommonly attractive and unexpectedly limber, which made Prince Grigorii's job all the more fun.

Traffic on the Rue du Rivoli streamed past in the early evening. There were rumors of a general strike in response to the government's limiting of work hours, and people wanted to stuff as much of Parisian nightlife in as possible before the lights of the city faded. Grigorii took the baroness's arm and escorted her toward the building occupied by Misia Edwards.

The Tuileries Palace loomed ahead of them. To their left the Seine ran higher than normal thanks to a thunderstorm earlier in the afternoon which had swept the air of dust and soot, leaving the evening sky clear as a picture window opening on heaven.

Misia Edwards had emerged as a powerful force in Parisian society. Like Prince Grigorii, she was a Russian expatriate, born Maria Zofia Olga Zenajda Godebska in St. Petersburg to a cheating sculptor father and musician mother who died in childbirth. While gifted as a pianist, trained by family friends Franz Liszt and Gabriel Fauré, she had never risen to the apex of the concert world. Instead, she achieved artistic gratification by surrounding herself with the finest painters, composers, writers, and intellectuals Paris had to offer. It was considered a social coup to receive an invitation to one of her soirees, where one might encounter Marcel Proust, Serge Diaghilev, Maurice Ravel, Pablo Picasso, Erik Satie, Coco Chanel, Pierre Auguste Renoir, and any number of other notables. On a truly fortunate evening, guests might be serenaded by Enrico Caruso, accompanied expertly on the piano by Misia herself.

As Paris braced for a seemingly inevitable labor shutdown, Misia had gathered seven or eight dozen of her closest friends to a party celebrating Bastille Day and Ida Rubinstein, a former Ballets Russes star who had broken with Serge Diaghilev before the war to form her own company. Now, in postwar Paris, she was launching her career as a stage actress while the arts scene recovered from years of bellicose distraction. Misia Edwards was sponsoring her sendoff.

Misia's apartment on the Rue du Rivoli was expansive, befitting the settlement from her divorced second husband Alfred. Even so, it was packed with partiers as Prince Grigorii and the baroness entered. A small gypsy jazz band—a guitar and violin and clarinet—played in a far corner, their music competing with fifty different conversations, laughter, and the clinking of glassware. A bar had been erected at each end of the apartment, so nobody had to walk far to replenish their glass. It was difficult to see from one end of the living room to the other through the thick fog of cigarette smoke.

The crowd was dense, making it tricky to mingle. It was more advantageous to take a neutral position in some quiet corner and wait for the party to come your way. Grigorii and the baroness made a game out of identifying the famous faces in the room, and Grigorii provided her with the most salacious gossip about each of them, which left her giggling and red-faced. Making the baroness laugh warmed Prince Grigorii's heart, as he knew she would be generously grateful later.

Eventually, it was necessary for Grigorii to make his way to one of the bars for drinks. Waiting in line for the bartender, he found himself behind the poet Ezra Pound and a man he didn't recognize. Pound was long faced, with an unruly thatch of hair, thin mustache and goatee, and a perpetual scowl. The other man was tall and dark, and apparently a fellow American, as both spoke in English with similar accents.

"No," Pound told the man, "I am disillusioned with London. They are so fucking stodgy and provincial. They have no idea what to do with a man of my talent, so they instead attempt to destroy my work. Piss on them. I'm scouting about for a place to land here in Paris."

"It shouldn't be difficult," the other man said. "You might look on the other side of the river. Plenty of empty apartments, thanks to the war. I moved from the Right Bank myself a few weeks ago."

"You're a writer?" Pound asked.

"Not of your caliber, naturally, but I like to think so."

"What do you write?"

"Whatever pays best."

They both chuckled, but Pound's scowl rapidly returned.

"All well and good," he said. "Sooner or later, though, they'll ask you to write something you detest, and you'll hate yourself for doing it. Art first, money second, my friend. You'll starve, but you'll sleep better."

"Not to mention you'll become better traveled, escaping to another city every time the critics peel away your skin," the man said.

"Give in to the money-grubbers, and you'll peel away your own skin," Pound said. "Are you comfortable describing what you're writing now?"

"Sure," the man said. "It's not terribly interesting. I recently signed on as a correspondent to a syndicate in the states, covering the talks at Versailles."

"Straight reporting?"

"Not at all. Someone else writes the hard news. I provide the...well, I suppose you'd call it the color. The sidebar human interest pieces. How the peace process affects the average guy in the streets."

"I see. And how *does* the peace process affect the average guy in the streets?"

"There'll be a general strike later this week. That should tell you everything you need to know."

"It could be worse," Pound said. "We could live in Moscow."

"True enough. The fellow in my apartment before me was a Bolshie. He took off for Russia. Can't for the life of me imagine why."

"He must love borscht," Pound said, as he noticed Prince Grigorii for the first time. "How about you?" he asked.

"Please allow me to introduce myself." Grigorii extracted exactly two calling cards, which he held out splayed between his fingers, resembling the fork in a snake's tongue. "I am Prince Grigorii Yurievitch Romanov."

"Another refugee gigolo," the tall dark man said, as he examined the card. "Don't get me wrong. More power to you, friend. A title can be a real commodity. You work with whatever you have these days."

"How irritatingly colloquial," Grigorii said, but his smile betrayed his amusement.

The man held out his hand, "Caleb Styles. My friends call me Keeby. This is Ezra Pound."

"Mr. Pound, I recognize, of course," Grigorii said, taking the poet's hand. "It is pleasure to make your acquaintance, sir. I enjoy your work."

"Thanks. Sorry I don't have a calling card for you, kid," Pound said. "I mean, they're all so…irritatingly colloquial, aren't they?"

"I suspect the twentieth century is not going to be pleasant for nobility or good manners," Keeby observed. "But I'm certain Prince Grigorii here has a much better perspective on it."

"Indeed," Grigorii said. "If first couple of decades are any indication. I could not help but overhear your conversation as we stood in line."

"About writing?" Pound asked after ordering. They had finally reached the bar.

"About Russia," Grigorii said. "I, of course, have strong interest in events in my mother country, so your comments intrigued me. Especially yours—" he gestured toward Keeby. "If you are writing about hardships placed on Paris citizens, perhaps you might be interested in perspective of man displaced by Russian revolution as well. I would be pleased to discuss these matters with you."

"And I'd be interested to hear what you have to say."

"As it happens, it is my great fortune this evening to accompany delightful woman who demands my attention. However, I would be pleased to meet with you for drink some other time, Monsieur Styles."

"Call me Keeby. I live on Rue Montparnasse. Café La Rotonde near the Boulevard Raspail is a short walk, and easy enough to find. Perhaps we could meet there some afternoon this week."

"I know exact place. I live in Montparnasse as well. And you are right. It is only short walk. Would Wednesday at two work for you?"

CHAPTER TWENTY-SEVEN

WHEN PRINCE GRIGORII gravitated away to attend to his companion the baroness, Keeby discovered Ezra Pound had disappeared as well, no doubt off to rip the hide from some unsuspecting dilettante.

No matter. It was a crowded room. On a pair of facing sofas near him, Tsuguharu Foujita, a popular artist who lived near Keeby in Montparnasse, and his wife and model Fernande Barrey chatted with Amedeo Modigliani and his young bride, the model Jeanne Hébuterne. Keeby overheard them discussing the time they'd spent in Cagnes-sur-Mer. Jeanne was visibly pregnant.

Everywhere Keeby glanced, he found a famous face. He marveled, starving only two months earlier, that he was even invited to one of Misia Edwards' lavish parties. He had Nathalie Bel to thank. Before disappearing, she had introduced him to dozens of Paris's most illustrious figures and in arts and letters. He believed she was preparing to leave him without warning, so in her absence he might still find success and fame as a writer. She had told him several times that in the business of art, a person's contacts made all the difference.

"A curious position for a socialist who believes everyone should be the same," Keeby had jibed.

"That isn't socialism, and you know it," she had responded. "And, besides, as I have always told you, I am a pragmatist first. You work with what works."

He even owed his syndication contract in America to one of her friends, a publisher she had obviously seduced at some point, and on whom she foisted Keeby as if he were the next Sherwood Anderson. Acknowledging her enhancement of his career only made Keeby miss Nathalie more among all the glittering lights of Paris.

"Excuse me. Do you have a light?" a woman next to Keeby asked. He automatically pulled out his box of matches as he turned toward her but stopped when he saw her face. She was tall and lithe, with prematurely silver hair and blue eyes and the most perfect mouth Keeby had ever seen. She wore a shimmery silk dress with a textured oriental silk shawl, and a turban with a multicolored ostrich feather.

Keeby thought he must have stared at her for ten minutes, but it was only seconds before he fumbled for a match and held the flame to the tip of her cigarette. She turned her head and exhaled a cloud of smoke to the side, then held out her hand, palm down, in the continental style.

"Lady Alexandra Twining, but you can call me Bish. Everyone does."

She said it as if it were already a *fait accompli* they were to be the closest of friends. As she had offered her hand, Keeby responded in kind, lifting her hand and air kissing the tops of her fingers.

"Bish? How uncommon. Why do they call you that?"

"Beats the hell out of me."

188

"Caleb Styles. Everyone calls me Keeby."

"How uncommon. Why do they call you that?"

"I'm sort of multinational. American father, Canadian mother. I was born in Montreal but raised in the states. I still identify as Quebecois, so some of the guys shortened it to Keeby, and I don't know why I'm telling you all of this."

"Men tell me things. Like Mata Hari," Lady Bish said, smiling.

"I hope you won't share her fate."

"Better not to speak of it. People still hold a grudge. She and I are both Swiss. Well, she *was*. I still am. Why haven't I seen you at other parties?"

"Nobody invited me. New to the party scene."

"What do you do?"

"Writer," Keeby said.

"Published anything?"

"Some. I'm getting my feet under me."

"Have I read anything you've written?"

"Only if you subscribe to American newspapers. But I hope for better."

"Don't we all, darling," Bish said. She pointed at Foujita and Modigliani and their spouses on the couch, "Caught you eavesdropping. Anything scandalous?"

"I wasn't eavesdropping. I was lingering. They talked about a trip to Cagnes-sur-Mer."

"Ah. The musical beds tour."

Keeby glanced at her. "You know things."

"I do," she said. "But I'm far too sober to divulge them. Be a darling and see if the bartender can find another glass of wine. Any color will suit."

As Keeby waited for the bartender, Prince Grigorii sidled next to him.

"I saw you talking with Lady Twining," he said.

"Bish? We're old buddies. Grabbing her a drink. Why?"

"You may be next."

"Had a feeling I'd missed my shot at being first."

"By about quarter century, I would say."

"Count her rings, did you?"

"Bish and I were acquaintances some months back. I envy you, my new friend. Play your cards right, and you could be in for several delicious weeks. Maybe months. Her parting gifts can be extravagant."

"Is that a fact?" Keeby said.

"She has been around. She knows...things."

"Nothing beats experience. I take it you and she..." Keeby rotated his index finger in the air.

"A gentleman never kisses and tells."

"He just insinuates."

"He advises. Cultivate this friendship, Monsieur Styles. You will find it rewarding. She not only knows things; she knows people. All of them. She can open doors."

Keeby took two glasses of wine and said, "I think you've jumped several chapters ahead. I lied. We met a few minutes ago. I'm only bringing her a drink."

"That is how it starts," Prince Grigorii said. "Have lovely evening, sir. I look forward even more to our conversation later this week. Perhaps we both have story to tell."

"You were talking about the musical beds tour," Keeby said, as Bish accepted the glass of wine.

"Good lord, was that tonight? You have an amazing memory, Keeby. Or are you a shameless gossip?"

"I'm a writer. Same thing, I suppose. I collect stories. Everything I see, hear, touch, smell, or taste is grist for the mill. Stories ride on three things—irony, conflict, and violation of expectation, and I bet you're full of all three."

"Good God," Bish said. "You are *so* young."

"In years, maybe. Someday I'll show you the hole a two-by-four blew through my side in the Argonne. Nobody's innocence survived the battlefield, Lady Twinings. You mentioned the musical beds tour. That's a story title if I ever heard one."

"You're cheeky," Bish said.

"It's a cultural thing. I was raised in America."

"That explains a lot. What the hell. I've already decided I like you, which means we will be fast buddies, you and I. Buddies share confidences, do they not?"

"It's one of the expectations. I should warn you. Writers have no scruples whatsoever about blabbing everything we hear. We do occasionally change names.

"Are all Americans such blatant opportunists?"

"It's called the Land of Opportunity for a good reason. I bet somewhere in your head is a trunk full of interesting stories to share."

Bish pouted. "You only want me for my stories."

"I'm American, but I'm also a gentleman. I like to take things slow."

She placed a hand on his chest. "I want to read your writing."

"Trade you a story for a story," he said. "The musical beds tour."

"You...are...relentless," she said. It sounded like an ecstatic moan.

She hadn't removed her hand from his chest, and he could feel it there, almost vibrating. He harbored no illusions as to which of them was in control. Keeby was a gazelle pinned under a lioness's paw.

"Oh, what the hell," she said again. She removed her hand and surreptitiously pointed toward the chatting couples. "Look at Jeanne. How would you describe her?"

"Modigliani's wife? She's beautiful, but she looks...I don't know. Sad. Worried."

"Do the math, darling. She's dreading the day her water breaks. She goes to bed each night praying the kid comes out with curly hair and round eyes."

Keeby's eyes widened. "I see. Musical beds. Then, Modigliani and..."

"Fernande? But of course, darling. Fernande sleeps with *everybody*. I mean, she was a child prostitute, for Christ's sake. It was a free-for-all. Fernande with Amedeo. Tsuguharu with Jeanne. Tsuguharu with Amedeo. Fernande with Jeanne, and I don't doubt for a second they all tossed in together in one big pile from time to time. I swear, I think about all the permutations and get dizzy. But, I mean, who can blame her? Or him? Or any of them? Look at Amedeo. That face. My God. Makes me want to crawl up his body and sit on it."

"Is any of that true?"

"What reason would I have to lie?"

"You sound jealous," Keeby said.

"Oh, God, not at all. Orgies are highly overrated. So many goddamn thank-you notes to write."

Alcohol had blown out all of Lady Bish's inhibitions. But it was Paris, and it was a party at the Rue Rivoli home of the great arts patroness Misia Edwards, and nobody gave a damn what anyone said because they were all the most perfect Bohemians in the most enlightened city in the world, and the receding and fading memory of war almost mandated a never-ending party. As Bish draped herself against Keeby's body, he recognized with amazing clarity that this was only the beginning of what he would later recount as a most fascinating and eye-opening night.

CHAPTER TWENTY-EIGHT

THE STORM TOPPLED several trees on Wentworth Street, including one several doors down from the Shipley home. Palmetto fronds, broken tree limbs, and storm detritus littered their yard. Gordon and Beau were outside collecting the garbage when Norbert Tradd stopped in front of the house in a valve-chattering Monroe Coupe. Gordon walked out to the street to greet him.

"Sorry, Norbert. Can't go any farther. Street's blocked by a tree."

"Not passing through," Norbert said. His face was sallow and his eyes glowed crimson from a night of sobbing. "Want to see your son."

"Are you all right?"

"Call your son."

"Beau? Got a minute?" Gordon called over his shoulder.

Reluctantly, Beau joined them at the street.

Norbert jumped from the front seat of his car, grabbed Beau by the collar of his shirt and swung him around against the engine cover. "Demon! Heathen! What did you say to her?"

Gordon grappled Norbert and pulled him off Beau, who pushed Norbert away. Beau pulled his fists up in the boxing stance he'd been taught in school.

"What in hell, Norbert?" Gordon asked.

"She's dead!" Norbert cried out, and the tears ed again. "This apostate drove my daughter to kill herself."

"What?" Gordon gasped.

Beau dropped his hands. "When?"

"Last night. During the storm. She threw herself off the battery into the harbor."

"Oh my God." Beau sat on the low stone wall next to the sidewalk. "I can't believe it. I know she was upset."

"Because you drove her to it!" Norbert wailed again, lunging at Beau. Gordon held him back, which was easy since Norbert had wasted away to nearly skin and bones. Beau gathered himself.

"Maybe I did," Beau said, quietly, tears in his eyes. "But I swear it, Mr. Tradd, it wasn't intentional."

Gordon let go of Norbert, who collapsed on the running board of the coupe. He pulled an envelope from his inside jacket pocket and tossed it at Beau, who opened it and read the note inside.

There wasn't a word about him. Victoria blamed nobody for her decision. She merely told her father she saw no other options, and she had no one left to turn to for help. She outlined her plan to throw herself into the harbor at the height of the tropical storm, to a certain and welcome death. She asked him to forgive her.

Gordon and Norbert watched as he read. When he was finished, Beau folded the paper, placed it back in the envelope, and handed it to Norbert. Norbert held it to his chest, his head drooping, his tears watering the azaleas.

"As soon as I found the note, I dashed out into the night. I ran all the way to the battery. A woman named Hetty Oliver saw her jump. I ran to the seawall myself, climbed on top, ignoring any danger to myself. The water...it was as black as tar, and it rolled and crashed against the stones like a furious living thing. Several men dragged me away. I never saw her. I'll never see her again."

"What do you mean, it wasn't intentional?" Gordon asked.

"Maybe we should take this inside," Beau suggested.

Later, in Gordon's study, after Norbert had calmed, marginally, a profoundly somber Beau tried to explain.

"Victoria told one of her closest friends a secret, something she couldn't tell anyone else, something that could ruin her. Her friend...betrayed her trust. The secret got out. Jamie Norton repeated it to me my first night back in town. I chose to...to let it go. It didn't matter. It didn't change how I felt about Victoria in the least."

"What secret?" Norbert demanded.

"Maybe later, after you know everything. I'll tell you the same thing I told her. The only reason I returned from Paris was to win her back from Alton. But after she and I met, and after you refused to let me see her, I had time to work things through. I decided you were right. There was no future for me and Victoria. Our lives had taken different paths, and there was no going back."

Beau crossed to the window and gazed out at the street, afraid to look Norbert Tradd directly in the eye.

"I talked to her yesterday. I was painting the Circular Church from across the street. I didn't expect to see her. I hadn't seen her in months. It wasn't planned. We met by chance. On a whim, I painted her into the picture. I told her I had come around to your point of view, and there was no future for us. I told her I wanted to be her friend, and to help her any way I could. I...I said the wrong thing. She realized she had been betrayed by her friend. She was ashamed, terrified. She said nobody would want her now. She ran into the church, the last I saw of her. Yeah. Maybe I was responsible. Maybe I should have been the only person in town to keep her secret. If we hadn't met, she might still be alive."

"What was the secret?" Norbert said, quietly.

Beau turned away from the window. "Does it matter, Mr. Tradd? Will repeating it help her now? Will it help you? Either you already know it, or you don't. If you do, it doesn't matter. If you don't, it might break your heart. I'm out of the heart-breaking business. She wanted it to be a secret. I figure I'll keep it that way. Hold on."

Beau left the room. Gordon crossed to the bar and poured a snifter of brandy. "Don't know about you, Norbert, but I could use a snort. I know you've taken the pledge, but you might want to consider this a medical emergency. You've had a hell of a shock."

Norbert sat grimly. Gordon handed him a glass and returned to his chair.

"My son tells me you rejected him as a suitor for Victoria partly because of me."

"He's right," Norbert said.

"For the love of God, why? What have I ever done to you?"

"Nothing," Norbert said, as he sipped at the brandy.

"Then what is it?"

Norbert told him.

"Ah," Gordon said. "That."

Beau carried a canvas into the study and placed it on the floor against her father's desk.

"The painting from yesterday. Victoria posed for it."

"My goodness," Gordon said. "I had no idea. This is...well, I had no idea."

Norbert lifted the painting and held it at arm's length. He raised his hand toward the hastily painted figure in black grasping at the wrought iron fence and gesturing yearningly toward the cemetery.

"Careful," Beau warned. "It's still drying."

"This is Victoria?"

"When she saw it, she seemed happy," Beau said. "Take it."

"Why? I haven't been kind to you."

"It doesn't matter now. It's Victoria's last happy moment. You should have it."

Norbert carried the painting to his car and cranked the engine. He mouthed something at Beau before pulling away from the curb. It was hard to hear over the wheezing and coughing motor, but Beau thought he said, "Sorry."

CHAPTER TWENTY-NINE

LIFE HAD CHANGED for Keeby since Beau returned to Charleston, and especially since meeting Lady Twinings. While Nathalie Bel had introduced him to important people in the publishing industry, becoming the personal project of Lady Bish had been like awakening in an entirely new world.

His education hadn't been confined to the arts and letters, either. As Nathalie had predicted, Bish deeply appreciated the erotic skills she had taught Keeby, but she also found herself obligated to instruct him in many of the finer—and in some cases esoteric—bedroom exercises Nathalie might have considered too advanced for such a young student, even a large man who had played college football without a helmet. Keeby quickly discovered he was using muscles he had never even dreamed he possessed.

Despite Bish's marital status, she was disinterested in maintaining any pretense of fidelity in public. It would have been impossible in any case, since word quickly spread about Lady Twinings' new squire about town.

Keeby arrived at Bish's *pied a terre* on the Rue du Raspail one afternoon for a tennis date and found Lieutenant Colonel Lord Ross Twinings mixing a tall scotch and water at the dry bar in the living room.

He was a compactly athletic gentleman in his middle fifties, with short pewter hair, cat-like movements, eyes that missed nothing, and an empty right sleeve.

"Boer War. Sniper. Damned annoying business," he explained without prompting as he handed Keeby the glass. "Hardly notice it anymore. Murdered my golf swing, though."

Being in Paris and familiar with the *savoir faire* with which the French handled personal relationships, and ignoring the fact that Bish and Ross Twinings were Swiss and British and therefore born with no *savoir faire* at all, Keeby tried not to look as if he intended to lie and introduce himself as Bish's tennis instructor.

"Relax." Twinings sat on the sofa. "Bish is changing into her tennis outfit. Gives us a chance to chat. I promise, I only kill one out of every five of her lovers, and only if they bore me. I let the last four off the hook so, for the love of Christ, be interesting."

"You're being open-minded about the situation," Keeby offered.

"What situation? I've shared Bish's bed for almost a quarter century, off and on. More off, I suppose. The military will have its way. I'm away on assignment far too much of the time for a woman like Bish. It would be selfish and rude to suggest she ignore her—I'm sure you will agree—prodigious needs. I was foolish to marry her in the first place, but wouldn't you, given the chance? I lost count of all her young escorts somewhere around my second pinky. You're the flavor of the month boy. *Slainte.*"

They clinked glasses fraternally, and settled back into the discomfort of the moment, at least for Keeby.

"What is it you do again?" Twinings asked, after a heavy silence.

"Writer," Keeby said.

"Academic?"

"Hardly. I write puff pieces for newspapers back in the United States and Canada. Everyday life stories, mini-tragedies, stories about irony."

"Ever written a novel?" Twinings asked.

"I'm working on one at the moment."

"Damned waste of time, novels. Oh, they're fine for people who have nothing else to do, I suppose, or whose lives aren't filled with enough romance or adventure. What's your novel about?"

"This and that. The theme is rebuilding a life from shreds. The war turned people's lives sideways. I write about how they cope."

"Why?"

It was the one question Keeby hadn't expected. Everyone seemed satisfied to know *what* he did for a living, but never got around to asking *why* he did it. Keeby had noticed people avoided questions when the answers might lead to a conversation far deeper than they intended. Simple facts were easier to digest, and far less likely to lead to unintended introspection. Keeby suspected most people were terrified of learning exactly who they were, and so avoided examining the lives of others too closely.

Ross Twinings was different. He acted genuinely intrigued by the fact Keeby spent the majority of his time producing a product Twinings found superfluous and wasteful.

"I suppose you haven't read Dickens, since you don't like novels."

"Never said I didn't read them. Just find it a waste of time is all. No offense, old bean, but it isn't everyone's cuppa, if you know what I mean. Of course I read Dickens. And Chaucer, and Wilkie Collins, and Conan Doyle, and Sherwood Anderson, and many more. I believe I know why they write what they do. I want to know if you know why *you* write what *you* do."

Keeby drained the glass and placed it back on the table, vamping for time. How long did it take Bish to put on her tennis togs anyway? Keeby smiled, imagining her with her ear to the door, loving every minute of his trial. It would be like her.

He pulled the tail of his shirt from his tennis slacks. He yanked away the side to expose the puckered scar tissue covering several inches of his right torso. "Meuse-Argonne. I was a hundred feet from the brigadier headquarters when a German shell turned it into toothpicks. One large flitch did this."

"So you've seen battle," Twinings said.

"Enough for a lifetime. It occurs to me, someday, people are going to want to know more about the war, from the perspective of someone who was there but wasn't an historian, someone who left actual skin on the field of battle. Facts and figures are one thing, but the death of a single innocent can rend hearts into ribbons. Except for Charles Darnay, nobody gives a damn about the thousands of aristocrats whose heads roll in *A Tale of Two Cities*. A hundred thousand Belgian orphans starve, and the world shrugs, but Hans Christian Anderson's little match girl freezes to death and melts our hearts. It's the little stories about courage and determination and pluck, even in the face of certain failure, about how people muster on even when hope is almost but not entirely flickered out, that make us want to be better people and not allow the horrors to happen again."

"I see," Twinings said. "Well, damn. I was looking forward to killing you, young Keeby. But you didn't bore me, so I suppose you live. I look forward to further conversations with you when I return."

"Return?"

"Shuffling off again tonight, I'm afraid. Popped by for dinner and a quick one with the missus. Short leave. Duty calls. Soon as you two run off for your tennis date, I'll hop into my uniform and head for the airfield to shuttle back across the pond."

Bish opened the study door, wearing her tennis outfit. "I see you've met. Thank you for not killing him, Ross."

"My pleasure, m'dear. He's smarter than your usual protégés. I approve of this one. Don't knock her up, Keeby. Bad form. Run along, you two, before you lose your court."

CHAPTER THIRTY

BEAU WAS DISAPPOINTED and angry when he spied Sally Porter in the churchyard following Victoria's memorial service. He started to say something to her, but Jamie Norton restrained him and pointed him toward home as soon as the service concluded, and before Norbert Tradd could kill him with the daggers in his eyes.

"It wouldn't have served any purpose," he said to Beau, who ignored the world around him as he stared at his shoes slapping the sidewalk.

"What?"

"Taking Sally to task at the funeral. Besides, if you want to dress her down, you might as well take a swing at me as well. I passed on what she'd told me, which makes me as bad."

"You weren't the only one she told. And I dragged it out of you. You refused to tell me at first. That's not all of it."

"I know. Victoria deserved a bigger turnout."

"This city," Beau said. "This goddamned inbred, stick-up-the-ass city. As soon as the rumor spread that Victoria killed herself, nobody in *polite* society wanted to be associated with her. Appearances were more important than celebrating her short, sad life."

Beau moped around the house for days, trying to figure out when precisely he had lost control of his life. He started three different novels from his father's library, but within ten pages the print flowed together until he might as well be reading Urdu. His mind took off on its own tangent, leaving him staring emptily at the page for minutes at a time without comprehending a single word. Food was tasteless. He considered going to the segregated district to drown his sorrows, but each time he rose from the sofa he lost every shred of motivation.

The only activity that still consumed him was painting. When he finally mustered the energy to leave the house, he ventured out to James Island to paint a brackish saltmarsh, home to a flock of nesting herons. For a brief time, as he fell into his artistic fervor and lost himself in translating the blurred image in his second-hand glasses into splotches of paint on the canvas, he forgot about Victoria and Sophie and his father's pressures, and his own crushing guilt. Then, as the reverie lifted, his chest constricted again, and he wept as he put away his brushes and tubes of paint and folded his easel for the trip home.

Two weeks after the somber, ill-attended memorial, and after the Charleston gossips had nearly sated themselves on Victoria's suicide, Beau and Jamie ventured at last into the segregated district on a Saturday night to pickle their troubles at Chance Howe's blind tiger bar.

Howe, who apparently knew everything about everybody in Charleston, greeted Beau with a warm smile and a comforting handshake instead of his usual over-the-top bonhomie. He personally escorted Jamie and Beau to a prime table far enough from the band that they could hear each other talk, and he assigned his most trusted employee, Miss Lovely, as their personal attendant for the evening.

She might have been twenty. Her skin was the color of strong tea, without a mark or blemish to be seen. Her eyes were bright, her face narrow and chiseled. She looked like an umber Nefertiti.

Miss Lovely arrived with a tray bearing a bottle of scotch, two glasses, and an ice bucket.

"I don't suppose either of you gentlemen are interested in water?"

"The ice melts," Jamie said. "It'll do. Do you have a first name, Miss Lovely?"

"It's Bernita, Mr. Norton. Can I get anything else for you?"

"We're fine for the moment," Beau said.

"If you need anything, I'll be here." She smiled again and returned to her station to wait for their signal.

Jamie poured some liquor and added ice with silver tongs. They lifted their glasses.

"To Victoria," Beau said.

Jamie clinked and took a sip. Immediately, his eyes widened. "Holy smokes. This is scotch? What have I been drinking until now?"

"Mighty fine," Beau agreed. "Are you flirting with Miss Lovely?"

"Why? Do you think I shouldn't?"

"At least wait until she's off duty. Upset her, and she might cut us off from the good stuff."

They sipped again. Jamie said, "Hey. You ever been with...you know. One of them?"

"In Paris. A model."

"Hot damn, Jackson. A model?"

"Don't make a federal case out of it," Beau said. "Every fifth woman in Paris is a model. She was nice, we enjoyed a pleasant dinner, and afterward we found ourselves at her pension. It was a one-time deal. Happens all the time over there."

"So? What was it like?"

Beau, for reasons he couldn't fathom, was irritated by the question. "What are you? Fifteen? You've been with a woman. It's like that."

"Okay. Don't get sore. I was just asking."

Bernita Lovely appeared by the table. "Is everything all right?" she asked.

"Perfect," Jamie said.

"What he said," Beau added. "We're fine. It's been a tough couple of weeks. We're blowing off a little steam."

"No," Jamie said, and turned back to Miss Lovely. "I mean, yes. Everything's fine. But that's not what I was referring to," he told Beau. "Look who walked in."

Beau glanced over his shoulder. Sally Porter stood at the door with Chance Howe and one of Beau's high school fellows, Darryl Horlbeck. Horlbeck had been a studious, serious youth, and he hadn't changed, judging by his heavy dark horn rim glasses, the conservative cut of his suit, and his frizzy, unkempt ginger hair.

"Horlbeck stayed home too?" Beau asked.

"He tried to volunteer. Rejected. His eyesight. Kid bumps into stuff all the time if he isn't wearing his specs."

"Yet he tried, and you didn't."

"Are we going down that road again?"

"What's Darryl doing these days?"

207

"Banking," Jamie said. "He's an assistant manager. Word is he's going places."

"Everywhere except under Sally's skirt," Beau said.

"Don't be so certain, old fellow. Pillow talk, remember? Sally has an avaricious streak. She has an acute sense of the side on which her bread is buttered, if you know what I mean."

"I know."

"She'll probably latch onto old Horlbeck for security and string along a lover or two for the yucks," Jamie suggested.

"Bet she can't pull it off," Beau said. "She's lousy at keeping secrets."

They watched as Chance Howe seated the couple, first holding out the seat for Sally, and placed a hand on Horlbeck's shoulder for considerably longer than one might expect in a casual social encounter. He even squeezed once or twice.

"I don't know," Jamie said. "Maybe they're both better at keeping secrets than you think."

Sally caught Beau watching her and returned his gaze. She smiled and blew him a kiss when Darryl turned away. Beau held up his glass as if toasting and turned back to Jamie.

"She's measuring you for Lover Number One," Jamie said.

Beau ignored her. "Fat chance."

"You could do worse. I speak from experience."

"Might as well tell you. I'm about ninety percent settled on returning to Paris."

"You just came home!"

"Did I? Funny. Haven't seen it yet. Point it out to me as we walk by."

"I know it's been a tough homecoming—"

"You reckon?"

"Knock off with the guilting. I didn't go over for a reason."

"Sure. You're a coward."

"And damned proud of it. Let other people have grand adventures. I intend to live to see dirt shoveled over every brave face in Charleston and die at the age of a hundred, shot by a jealous husband."

"Without the adventure, what are you living for?" Beau asked.

"So it's about doing something…else?"

"That's part of it. Father's putting pressure on me to take my position at the cigar import. He plans to take me to Havana in October."

"There's an adventure for you. The land of rum and rhumba. Of course, you may need a shot of Dr. Ehrlich's magic bullet once you get back. One of the hazards of being born with the right genes, old sod. The ladies can't resist that kisser of yours."

"I don't want to go. Havana is lovely. Been there twice, but not since high school. I can't stop dreaming about Paris, though. Did I tell you about my buddy Keeby?"

"The boy you saved in the trenches? Only five or ten times."

"We lived together in Paris until April, when I came to Charleston. He gave up our apartment in Les Halles. Moved to the Left Bank."

"Wasted on me, I'm afraid. Never made the crossing, and I'm rotten at geography."

"The south side of the Seine. They call it the Rive Gauche in French. The Left Bank. It's become a chic artists' colony. The apartment has two bedrooms and a bath. He wrote me last week. The room's mine if I want it."

"How in hell will you support yourself?"

"There's work if you want it. I plan to paint, though, whatever else I do."

"Well, if you get famous, remember your old buddy and send me a painting to tide me over in my dotage."

The band played again, a woeful minor blues number. Darryl Horlbeck escorted Sally Porter onto the small dance floor, where they swayed to the music. Each time they spun around, Beau caught Sally glancing at him.

"Keeby's become the protégé of a married woman of title," Beau said, as he watched Darryl and Sally. "Her husband knows about it. It's all terribly sophisticated and cosmopolitan and modern. The French way. An older acquaintance died while I lived there earlier this year. His wife and mistress rode to the funeral in the same carriage and comforted one another throughout the burial. Can you imagine that in stodgy old Charleston?"

"I'm willing to give it a shot."

"According to his letter, his paramour has introduced Keeby to artistic and literary luminaries all over town. He's building an impressive list of connections. He's promised to get me into the club."

Jamie freshened each of their glasses and tossed in a couple of ice cubes. "Sounds to me like you're a lot farther than ninety percent determined to leave."

Darryl swung Sally around again, and this time she was left facing Beau's table. Her eyes caught his. She winked.

"Excuse me," Beau told Jamie as he tossed his napkin to the table.

"Take it easy. Don't cause a scene," Jamie said.

"Wouldn't think of it." Beau crossed the dance floor and tapped Darryl on the shoulder. The young man whirled around. He blinked once or twice until he recognized the face.

"Beau! Beau Shipley! When did you get back to town?" He grasped Beau's palm and gave him his heartiest loan underwriter handshake. "You know Sally Porter?"

"Of course. Sally and I go way back," Beau said, turning on the charm. "Mind if I cut in? I'd like to catch up with Sally for a moment."

"Of course. Good to see you back."

"Sure it is." Beau took Sally in his arms and swung her back out onto the dance floor.

"I'm sorry we didn't talk at the service," Sally said. "I almost didn't recognize you. You could be your older brother."

"It was kind of a rough war."

"I heard. I'm so happy you returned. I knew you were in town, of course. Sophie and I talk."

"Sophie's a gem," Beau said.

"It's terrible about Victoria. I was her maid of honor, you know."

"Is that so?"

"Oh yes. Then poor Alton got the flu and died. I had it also, but nobody in our house died. Not like with poor Victoria."

"It was tragic," Beau said.

"And then she…well, I can't bring myself to say it. I've lain awake in bed until the darkest hours of the night trying to figure it all out. Why did she do that to herself?"

"You'd truly like to know?"

"It would be a great comfort. She was such a dear."

"You know what, Sally?" Beau said. "I'm going to ease your mind. I know why she did it."

"You do?" Her eyes widened.

"Yes. I'm going to tell you. But first, I want you to know what happens afterward."

"I don't understand," she said.

"You won't make a scene. You won't burst into tears and have a conniption. You will return to your table and tell Darryl you've taken a sudden headache. You'll have him walk you home."

"None of what you're saying makes any sense," she said, her face concerned. "Are you all right? You don't have that awful shell shock, do you?"

"Victoria lost more than her mother and fiancé to the influenza." He was careful not to make it sound like a question. "She confided in you, Sally. You were her closest confidante. Victoria told you everything. Her deepest, mostly closely held secrets."

"She did," Sally said, mechanically.

"She told you about losing the baby when she had the flu."

"She swore me to secrecy."

"And you betrayed her. Jamie told me you blabbed about it in bed with him."

She glanced at Jamie. She had flames in her eyes, but he simply shrugged. He knew precisely what they were talking about. He and Sally had parted ways long ago. No skin off his nose.

"And you didn't only tell Jamie."

"No," she said. "I...I want to leave."

"Dance is almost over," Beau said. "I talked with Victoria the day she died. In my passion to help her, I forgot what I wasn't supposed to know. I made a slip of the tongue. As soon as I mentioned the baby, she saw it all. She had told only one person, and that person betrayed her. That's why she killed herself, Sally. She tossed herself into the harbor because you couldn't keep your fucking mouth shut."

A tear landed on the shoulder of his jacket. If it weren't so maudlin, he might have smiled.

"And neither could I. I have to find a way to live with that. But nobody would have known had you been a true friend to her. Remember what I said. No scenes. No tantrums. Your social standing is hanging by a spider's thread. Go home. I have a secret now, and I don't owe you a damned thing. I can spill my guts any time I want. You need to work on your personality and figure out the meaning of the word *loyalty*. Oh, and I approve of your designs on Darryl. He's kind of a congenial milquetoast, but he's steady and decent. You could do a lot worse. If you wind up marrying him, you'll be comfortable. Only one thing. If I ever hear even a whisper that you've stepped out and had an affair, I'll blow up your entire life. Do you need any of this repeated?"

She shook her head.

"Good. Get your life in order, Sally. Darryl's waiting."

The song ended, and the crowd of dancers clapped before returning to their tables. Beau and Sally went their

213

separate ways, and seconds later Darryl held Sally's shawl for her, and they made a quick exit through the restaurant stairs.

"What did you do?" Jamie asked.

"I showed her a glimpse of her future."

"Hot damn," Jamie said, as he uncorked the whisky bottle, "I'm gonna miss you around here."

———

Jamie and Beau managed to leave Chance Howe's blind tiger before they were reduced to staggering. Jamie was about to take a left turn toward his home south of Broad when they both heard shouting up the street.

"Oh, hell, not again," Jamie groaned. "Those damned Navy squids."

"No," Beau said. "I know that voice."

They followed it to the top of the block. Around the corner, they found a wizened, dilapidated man in a formerly fashionable suit railing at a tiny assembly of street people and curious tourists, slapping a Bible with his palm. His pewter hair fell in limp, sodden strands. His face was scarlet with exertion, his voice raspy. He was unshaven, and he smelled. He quoted random verses with no apparent context, spittle flying from his lips as he spluttered the gospel at his unreceptive flock. His eyes were reddened and rheumy, and there was something haunting in their depths.

"Dear God," Beau gasped. "It's Norbert Tradd."

Victoria's father had gone insane. In his abject grief, he had given himself over so completely to his faith—the only possession not ripped from him—that he now trekked the

214

handful of blocks from his rapidly decaying home to the seediest, most evil part of town where he exhorted the denizens of the segregated district to abandon their wanton paths and follow in the footsteps of the saints. He rose in the morning, ate bread and water, and began his futile ministry at the crack of dawn. He returned in the evening after a simple, frequently deficient supper, and continued his nonstop tirade until the streets emptied, and often for some time thereafter unless someone threw an old shoe to shut him up.

Beau recalled the dapper, urbane, reserved man he'd known before the war, and he couldn't find his face in the human wreckage shouting at the heavens from his soapbox perch. It was a pathetic end for a once-respectable gentleman.

"I have to get the fuck out of this town," Beau said.

CHAPTER THIRTY-ONE

HIS FATHER HAD ALREADY left for the warehouse when Beau sat for breakfast on Monday morning. That was fine with him.

Beau had spent most of Sunday deliberating how to tell his father he planned to sail for Paris with no job waiting and no idea when he might return. Each time he rehearsed the conversation in his imagination, he sounded ungrateful—which he decidedly wasn't—or merely petulant, which was worse. His only reason for fleeing the country was that Charleston no longer felt like home.

He also imagined his father's arguments for staying. Even before he'd arrived at the shipyards in May, one of the most popular songs of the year had been Arthur Fields' *How Ya Gonna Keep 'Em Down On The Farm (After They've Seen Paree)*. Yearning for the bright lights and sophistication of Europe had become epidemic once the doughboys flowed back into the states. His father would probably think he was only responding to a romantic notion, with no practical plans for survival once he arrived.

"Where's Father?" he asked his mother, who was finishing her breakfast.

"You missed him by five minutes," she said. "Or maybe it was ten. I'm not certain. He was here only a short time ago, I know. He can't have been gone long. You haven't seen him, have you?"

"No, Mother. That's why I...Do you know where he went?" Beau asked.

"Why, to the warehouse, of course. Where else would he be? It's a workday, after all."

Beau ate a leisurely breakfast and dressed to go out for the day. Typically, he'd be painting. Not today. There was a much more urgent task at hand, one which he dreaded.

The Shipley Company warehouse sat at the north end of Bay Street, a block back from the offloading cranes for the shipping docks. The building was faded red brick, with huge top-hinged windows that opened out in the summer with massive iron cranks. The floor was heart pine, originally gleaming, but scuffed and dulled over years of foot and barrow traffic. Most of the Shipley employees worked in an office off Calhoun Street, several blocks west. The warehouse typically was staffed by two or three young men employed more for their strong backs than their agile minds.

When he walked in through the shipping dock doors, Beau saw Kow Musgrave lug a crate off one of the barrows they used to move stock from storage to the loading bay. He was one of Shipley's oldest employees, easily in his late fifties or perhaps older. After a brief career in the merchant marine, during which he discovered his unfortunate propensity for seasickness, he had signed on to work at the Shipley warehouse and had remained there ever since. Nobody remembered why his name was Kow, but his pirate accent was not uncommon in the peninsula.

217

Kow was from James Island, a marshy patch in the floodplain of the Wapoo Creek and Ashley and Stono Rivers. The island had been separated from the Charleston mainland ever since it was founded long before there was a United States, and the settlers—mostly English and Scots Irish immigrants—simply never lost their original speech patterns. Family trees on the island looked like French braids. It was only after a bridge connected the mainland and the island that the James Islanders started to assimilate into the Charleston community, but many still spoke in the same way their great grandparents had in their mother countries.

To make matters worse, Kow had taken a punch or two to the throat over the years and was a heavy smoker. His voice was graveled and coarse.

"Kow, have you seen my father?" Beau asked.

"Waal, now, he was here a while back. Seems I recall he had to step around to the bank for a spell," Kow growled. "I reckon he'll return momentarily."

"Where are the other boys?"

"One's off with the influenza, but word is he'll recover, thank the Lord. The other didn't come back from the war, and we ain't replaced him yet. Don't see the need, don't ya see."

Beau didn't see, but he waited for Kow to elaborate. Kow appeared disinterested in pursuing the subject further, and he turned back to lift the crate.

"Need a hand with that?" Beau asked.

"Wouldn't refuse it," Kow said without looking back. Beau took the other end of the crate and hefted it.

"Cigars have gotten heavier," Beau said.

"Waal, I reckon they have, don't ya know." Kow winked at him and turned the barrow to return to the receiving dock.

Beau tried to lift one end of the crate. It was only two feet square, and it should have weighed only a few pounds. This box weighed forty pounds at least. Kow whistled merrily around the corner at the receiving dock. Nobody else was watching. Beau grabbed a nearby pry bar, rapidly broke the seal on the crate, and pulled away the insulating straw.

At first glance, it looked like exactly what it was supposed to be—hand-rolled Havana cigars in sturdy cedar boxes printed with garish colors and tropical paintings. Each box carried a glued paper seal, and all the seals were intact. Each layer of sealed boxes was cushioned by another layer of straw. It seemed impossible that straw and cured tobacco and Spanish cedar wood boxes could weigh as much as it did. He dug through the second layer of cigar boxes, and his fingers rapped on a solid wood false floor, only halfway down the inside of the crate. A hole had been drilled in the center of the floorboard. He inserted a finger and pulled, and the false bottom of the crate pulled away with a brief wooden squeak.

Underneath were two softwood cases, cushioned inside and out with fine straw. He didn't have to open them to know what was inside, but he did anyway. He extracted a bottle of fine light Cuban rum and held it to the light. It was one of the expensive brands, almost impossible to find with national prohibition looming.

"Finally figured it out?" Gordon Shipley said behind him.

Beau whirled around, mindful not to drop the bottle. He held it by the neck.

"Took you long enough," Gordon said. "Perhaps we should adjourn to my office. Bring the bottle."

Gordon took the bottle from Beau as they entered his upstairs office. It was a cramped space, used sparingly and never for more than a few hours, and it was nothing like Gordon's walnut-lined testament to robber barony in the Calhoun Street building. It had comfortable chairs and a utilitarian desk and two glasses, and for the moment that was all that was necessary. Gordon poured a finger of rum into one of the glasses and handed it to Beau. He poured another for himself.

"I'm sure you have questions," he said, as he settled into his chair.

"You're a bootlegger," Beau said.

"Weeeeellll…" Gordon drawled, waving a hand in the air and shaking his head slightly, but he took a sip of the rum and said, "Yeah. That's about it."

"And here I thought it was Chance Howe."

"He's a bootlegger too," Gordon said, and took another sip. "Only on the demand side of the equation. I handle supply. Damned fine, isn't it?"

Beau sipped his rum for the first time. "It is. But you'd expect it to be. It's the best. So, how long?"

"Bootlegging? Only since before the war. No need for it until then, of course. You could buy a drink anywhere."

"I suppose that's some kind of relief," Beau said.

"*Smuggling*, now…well, the Shipley family has been in that business for almost sixty years."

Beau stared at this father, waiting for the punchline. Nothing came, and after an awkward silence he said. "You're serious."

"It's time you knew, Beau."

"The business between you and Chance Howe. You supply his illegal liquor."

"His and three or four other blind tiger owners. I have a special relationship with Mr. Howe, though."

Beau almost dropped his glass. "Aw, geez, Father. Don't tell me!"

"What?"

"The first night home, Jamie told me Chance Howe was a…well, a…"

"A poof?" Gordon said.

"Yeah!"

Gordon let his head fall back, and he laughed uproariously. "No, son. That's not what I'm talking about," he said after regaining his composure. "No. It's a bit more complicated, and a little awkward. You see, son, your grandfather owned Chance's grandfather."

Only sixty years after the Recent Unpleasantness, as many Charlestonians still referred to the Civil War, it wasn't unusual for a newly introduced black man and white man to discover, with some discomfort, that their recent ancestors lived on different ends of the property continuum on a nearby plantation. Slavery was a reality in the memories of many people still living in the city, both black and white. The upper-class white people in Charleston, ever conscious of appearing socially correct, had adjusted to the changes in their lives wrought by the War of Northern Aggression and Lincoln's Emancipation Proclamation, and had politely decided to embrace the new southern order. Integration in Charleston had been enhanced by the relative equal strength of numbers on both sides of the racial divide, and the uneasy peace was typically only broken by outsiders like the Navy Yard sailors.

"Chance and I grew up together," Gordon said. "We played together as boys. You never seemed curious why the Shipleys went into the import business."

"I figured it was what we did. A family business. We'd always done it and always will."

"Not at all. Your grandfather sailed with Joseph Donovan himself, as a blockade runner in the Civil War."

"Chance Howe's grandfather sailed with Donovan."

"Not because he had a choice. This is, well, a little unsavory. Your great-grandfather Daniel gave Chance's grandfather to Silas Shipley for his eighteenth birthday. War broke out shortly after. Silas Shipley ran off to sea to join Donovan's blockade runners, dragging his birthday present with him. Donovan had three ships, all running different routes and schedules, so if one of them was captured he'd still be in business."

"I know the Joseph Donovan story. Every kid in Charleston does."

"What you don't know is Joseph Donovan taught Silas Shipley how to smuggle. Hell, son, the blockade runners were nothing but smugglers anyway. They hid bales of cotton all over the ship in Charleston, traded them in Havana for tobacco and cheap bolts of cloth and guns and powder and such, and tried not to get famous as they sailed back home through waters churning with Union gunboats. By the time the war was over, Chance's grandfather, Charlie, was a free man. Silas Shipley offered him a choice. He could walk away clean and make his own way in the world, or they could put their intensive training under Joseph Donovan to good use and become wealthy men. Silas and Charlie went into the smuggling business together. They passed it to their sons, and now I'm passing it to you. Tell you the truth, I'm glad to finally get it off my chest. Freshen your glass, Beau?"

"No. Thanks. I need to keep my head clear for this. I've had quite a shock today. Everything I know is a lie."

"I can sympathize," Gordon said. "I was sitting right where you are thirty years ago when my father dropped it on me."

"I'm going back to Paris."

Gordon stared at him and took another sip. "Well," he said. "This is a day for surprises. That complicates matters."

"I can't live in Charleston. If I stay here, I'll go as crazy as Norbert Tradd. Nothing has been right since I came home from the war. Now I discover I come from a family of gangsters. How am I supposed to react? My buddy Keeby Styles invited me to move into his apartment on the Left Bank. I'm going."

"How will you live?" Gordon asked.

"I won't be fucking smuggling, that's for sure." Beau slugged back the rest of his glass. "Hit me."

Gordon poured another two fingers into Beau's glass and settled back in his seat.

"I'm sorry," Beau said. "I'm not stupid. I know what you do has given us a top-shelf life. I never... I always thought—"

"The Shipleys were the good guys?" Gordon said. "You and me both, son. It was a little different for me. A little easier, maybe. It was the Gilded Age. Being a robber baron was a badge of honor. Ruthlessness was a virtue. It was an ugly, violent, lawless time. But it gave us a railroad that

223

stretched unbroken from New York to San Francisco, and it conquered the west, and it built great concrete skyscrapers and electrical cables that let you talk to an Eskimo in Alaska as if he were in the same room, and it gave you opportunities and privileges few other young men can even dream of."

"You sound like you miss it."

"Here's the straight and narrow of it, Beau. You come from three generations of businessmen who also happened to be criminals. We don't kill people or rob them or burn their houses. We give people a little snort to make their hard lives easier at the end of a long workday. But however we sugarcoat it, we make a great deal of money from illegal activity, and if you come into this business, that will fall on your shoulders. I have five different public officials on the take. I have a senator in my back pocket. All of that takes money and a lot of secrets and tons of grudging trust. It's a headache on top of a toothache, son. It's also the key to your fortune."

Beau leaned forward, rubbing his face. "I don't know, Father."

"But I don't want that for you," Gordon said.

Beau looked up. "What?"

"I remember this exact moment when I was in your seat. My anger. My disappointment. Confusion. Maybe a little shame. The business was nowhere near as large, thanks to the temperance idiots in the state house. I made a great deal of money during the war, and with national prohibition I expect to make a lot more. There's enough to go in another direction."

"What direction?"

"Aviation. I've read the newspapers. I saw how the aeroplane brought an entirely new dimension to the war. I've seen a few of them fly over the city, and I see the future. Imagine breakfasting in Charleston and enjoying dinner in a fine New York restaurant, all on the same day. It's coming, son. All those pilots the military trained in the war are looking for work, and they have a rare skill to sell. Aeroplanes will be the railroads of the twentieth century. Ten years from now, perhaps sooner, you'll see aircraft carrying fifteen or twenty passengers at a time and traveling two hundred miles per hour. The smart cookies who get in early will make a killing, and you won't have to smuggle a single bottle of booze."

"You don't know anything about aviation. You've never even been in a plane. Hell, *I've* never been in a plane," Beau said.

"Neither had the Wright brothers, but they created a tidy little business. I can hire the brains, Beau. I can't find another son to build it for me. Flight is going to be a young man's game. I'm offering you the shot to get rich without breaking the law. My illicit money can give you a clean and immensely prosperous life."

"You don't know what you're asking."

"What's in Paris?" Gordon asked.

"Peace of mind. Maybe."

"How will you feed yourself? Pay for your apartment? You never said."

"I'll find a way. I want to paint as well."

Gordon pulled a cigar from a thermidor on his desk and held it out.

"No thanks," Beau said.

225

Gordon clipped and lighted the cigar and blew a cloud of blue smoke toward the ceiling.

"When I saw the painting you gave Norbert Tradd, I was shocked. I had no idea of your talent. I'm not trying to flatter you. I wouldn't do that, not about something this important to you. I don't know a thing about painting, but I know what's good and what isn't, and your stuff is good."

"It came as something of a surprise for me as well."

"I wanted to write," Gordon said.

"Come again?"

"Thirty years ago. When I sat where you are now. I wanted to be a writer. I read every dime novel I could find. I devoured libraries. I loved words and stories. I wanted to do that with my life. Your grandfather dropped the bomb on me. It was the time, son. Acquisition was everything. It wasn't just the money. It was bloodsport. Nothing was more satisfying than stepping over the body of a fallen competitor to deposit a fat check. We kept score back then, and the most vulnerable person was always the man out front."

"I didn't know—" Beau said.

"No. Writing was frivolous. Money was the only thing that mattered. I made a choice. I haven't written a paragraph of prose since before you were born. I made my decision."

"Do you regret it?"

"Yes and no. Mostly no. The rewards were significant. My talent might not have been, in hindsight. I probably made the right decision."

"But you'll never know."

Gordon poured from the bottle again.

"And neither will you," Gordon said. "Unless you try."

Beau sat up. "Say that again."

"The aviation company can wait. Prohibition can't last forever, but as long as it does, I'll stockpile more seed cash. No business ever died of excess capital. Go to Paris. Paint. Find out if that's where your fortune lies. I'll...oh, hell. I'll reinstate the allowance through Alphonse Rimbaud. There's no point in having you slave away in some fish market to avoid starving. While you explore that life, I'll have time to investigate the aviation business, pick a few brains, and find out who knows what. By the time America craves a shot and Prohibition ends in a year or so, we should be ready to hit the ground running, and perhaps you will know which life you want to pursue."

"You mean it? I can go?"

"I only have one condition."

"What?" Beau asked.

"You break it to your mother. She just isn't going to understand at all."

CHAPTER THIRTY-TWO

KEEBY WAS INTO HIS second glass of wine at La Rotonde before Prince Grigorii showed, almost a half hour late, still dressed in his evening clothes from the night before. He wore a white-tie tuxedo, a white cashmere scarf, a top hat, and dark glasses. He wobbled a bit as he approached the café. He sat and lowered his glasses to show Keeby his eyes.

"How do they look?" he asked.

Keeby winced. "Like Bram Stoker's vampire."

"*Dermo*," Grigorii swore. "The bitch gave me pinkeye. I'll be out of commission for days."

"How'd she—?" The warning scowl on Grigorii's face stopped him. "This was the baroness?"

"*Oh, bozhe moy, nyet.* The baroness and I part ways, extremely amicably. And profitably. At least I won't starve before I can show face in public again."

"You're in public now."

"Don't tell anyone."

"Why are you dressed like this? You look like a choleric penguin."

"Opera last night."

"One of the good ones?"

"*La Boheme.*"

"Aw, shit. Art imitates life. Good angle for a story, though. Who called with tickets at the last minute?"

"Do you want to hear about escape from Russia or what?" Grigorii asked.

"It's all I've thought about for the last three seconds."

"Buy me drink. Bordeaux, preferably prewar. I hate to think what might be fertilizing French grapes this season. And croissant."

"Have you eaten today?"

"Only madame's *petit chat*."

"Ah, yes," Keeby said. "Pinkeye." He moved his seat several inches farther from the prince. "Sure you don't want a sandwich? A crepe, perhaps."

"You are generous. I will not insult you by refusing." The waiter appeared next to him, and Grigorii ordered the wine and a *croque monsieur*. "It's on him," he said, pointing toward Keeby. The waiter glanced his way, and Keeby nodded.

"It had better be a good story," Keeby said, as the waiter disappeared back inside.

"I was traveling in Russian countryside when word arrived of overthrow of czar and czarina in St. Petersburg and storming of Winter Palace. I am educated man, *monsieur*, well-schooled in languages and history. Knowing in all too horrible detail events that took place in Paris at end of eighteenth century, I recognized history about to repeat itself in my own country. There was no point in riding to defense of royal family. The war was lost already. I saw no profit in adding my body to bonfire. My other option was to leave Mother Russia in my wake and flee to neutral country where Bolsheviks could not touch me."

"With you so far. You snatched survival from the jaws of honor."

"We will discuss tone of article later. I made logical, pragmatic decision. Live or die. Any man would do same if there was no prize for dying."

Keeby recalled his relief when Beau tapped him to run the trenches instead of going over the top, and he knew Prince Grigorii was right. He had never once considered refusing the order and joining Wally Smith in the evening assault. He still remembered with some pain the resignation in Wally's eyes, knowing he had drawn the worst short straw ever.

"My problem is obvious. I am thousand miles from the Russian border, a vast wilderness separating me from safety. I dare not appear in bank to fund my journey. I'd be revealed as aristocrat in an instant, and that would be end of me. I have clothes on my back, a few pieces of jewelry, and money in my wallet. Only thousand rubles or so. I have to make it all the way to eastern boundaries and across into Poland.

"I travel mostly at night, using stars and moon to guide me ever eastward. I avoid villages, sometimes walking miles out of my way to not be caught. My feet blistered. Walking became torture. It nearly drove me mad, so during day I try to find stream or spring in which to rest throbbing feet. I stay well out of sight of other people.

"One night, I venture on farm. It is freezing, and I fear I am at end of rope. Poland still several hundred miles away. Russia is remarkably large country. My exhaustion overcame my better judgment. I broke into barn and fell asleep in pile of filthy hay, covered with mildewed horse blanket.

"I was discovered next morning. A young woman, attractive for someone who works with hands, came across me when she arrived to milk cow. I am still dead to world, snoring exhausted in my straw bower. When she poke at me with pitchfork, I awake fearing worst. I see short future ending against pockmarked wall.

"But luck is with me. She is alone. Her father, a Bolshevik, is in St. Petersburg tending to revolution. Her name is Sofia. She is serf, but local landlord, a nobleman, was fair and generous to her on many occasions, so she is kindly disposed toward me. I offer her everything I have for peasants' clothes and help to cross border. She said her father will not return for several weeks, and she'll help me if I assist her with some things that need doing on farm.

"So you stayed," Keeby said.

"For week or so. My feet healed, and I ate well, so my strength returned. Within a few days, I felt like old self. Sofia and I talked every evening. I never told her I was prince, but she suspected I was of noble birth."

"Breeding will tell," Keeby said.

"She fell in love with me," Grigorii continued, after ordering a second glass of wine. Keeby ordered a third. "She was so *strong*, too. Perhaps you have discerned we became lovers."

"Goes without saying," Keeby said.

"Now I am presented with dilemma. The girl is smitten. She will follow me to ends of earth, which I cannot allow. What if I am caught? She might be executed for helping me. What kind of cad would allow that to happen to her?"

"The kind of cad who'd steal her father's clothes and run away in the middle of the night."

"Have I told story before, *monsieur*?"

"No. I saw it coming. Please, continue."

"I left her letter. Deserting her would break my heart, but I could not risk her life over someone like me. Over time I was on road, my hair had grown shaggy, and my beard thick. In Sofia's father's clothes, I look like peasant. After day or two, I smell like one. I no longer travel at night. I make Polish border in little over a week. I sneak over during night, and slowly sidestep ruined parts of Europe to make my way to Paris."

"Why Paris?"

"Why not? What better place to live than Paris?"

Keeby had jotted notes as Grigorii recited his daring story. He placed the pencil down, drained the glass of wine, and waggled a finger at his guest. "You, Prince Grigorii Yurievitch Romanov, are *so* full of shit."

"*Monsieur!*"

"We both slept with Bish Twinings, remember? The woman talks. A lot. I know you were vacationing in Nice during the revolution. The only trek you made to Paris was in a sleeper car on Train Bleu to Gare du Lyon."

The waiter delivered their drinks. Grigorii took a sip of his.

"But you met with me anyway?"

"I wanted to see what sort of tall tale you'd spin."

"It was good one, *non?*"

Keeby raised his glass. "It was a good one, *oui.*"

Grigorii saluted him with his glass. "You will write it?"

"And make you famous?"

"Would it be such bad thing? Being prince might give me advantage in attraction of generous women, but as you have noted, there are so damned *many* of us in city. Prince who is also tragically romantic hero, on other hand…"

"I write about real life, Grigorii. Real tragedies. Real triumphs. You're looking for an advertising agency."

"It was worth try," he said, smiling as he lifted his glass. "And for only cost of a few lies, I walk away with full belly and slightly inebriated disposition."

"Don't forget pinkeye," Keeby said. "You should see a doctor about that."

CHAPTER THIRTY-THREE

"LADY TWININGS TELLS ME you're an up-and-coming writer," Armitage Knox wheezed to Keeby, sitting across from his desk. Knox was in his mid-forties but looked older thanks to pattern baldness and corpulent obesity. An American expatriate who escaped to Paris as a youth and never returned, Knox was the French acquisitions agent for a large publisher in New York. Knox was also one of Bish Twinings' oldest friends, and a good man to know if you were, indeed, an up-and-coming writer. "So, tell me, what have you written?"

Keeby, intimidated but confident, handed him a paper-clipped sheaf of papers, cut sheets from articles he had sold to Canadian and American newspapers and magazines. Knox grunted as he accepted it and allowed Keeby to stew while he deliberately examined each story. He chuckled once or twice, clucked a few times more, and smiled enough to be encouraging.

"So you know how to arrange words," Knox said, handing the samples back. "But can you tell a story?"

"It's my strong suit," Keeby said, unapologetically proud of his work. "Straight reporting isn't my thing. I prefer to tell the stories behind the story."

"The mundane, boring stuff," Knox challenged.

"Not to me, and so far not to my readers."

"Yes," Knox said, and settled back in his chair, which groaned and squeaked in protest. "Magazines and newspapers are fine, young man, and a great place for a writer to hone his skills. My company in New York does not publish newspapers and magazines. They publish books. Novels, specifically. I'll be honest. I reject a hundred eager young authors each month. Some of them can write, but they can't write what I want. I only took this meeting because Lady Twinings requested it. It's up to you to do the rest. Give me your pitch."

"For a novel?" Keeby asked.

"It's what we publish."

"I have a work in progress. It's built on the back of many of my magazine articles. They follow a common theme— ordinary people forced into extraordinary circumstances, and how they adapt and survive."

"So far, so good. How do you like John Buchan?"

"He's a popular writer," Keeby said.

"He writes about ordinary people in extraordinary circumstances, does he not?"

Keeby fidgeted in his seat, trying to find a comfortable position under Knox's withering gaze.

"I believe he has. But Buchan and I are different writers. He writes to thrill. I write to inspire."

"Inspire what?"

"Inspire people to be better people. I want my readers to identify with my characters, and to learn how to believe in their own abilities. I want them to see other people have had it as bad or worse than they have, and there's hope."

"I see," Knox said. He opened a thermidor on his desk and extracted a cigar. He didn't offer to share, which Keeby immediately recognized as Knox establishing dominance. More intimidation. "So, this *inspirational* story you're working on?"

"I took four of the real people I wrote about, people whose personal tragedies are directly related to the war. Each one lost nearly everything. Some of them were ruined permanently and couldn't regain their footing. Others had to scratch their way back from the shambles of their lives, though determination and persistence. Their empty hearts are filled with loss, and at night they cry themselves to sleep, but to the outside world they present a face of confidence and triumph. I wanted to tell the stories of four different reactions to tragedy, let readers know they have choices. They can give in or dig in."

"This is a novel about the war," Knox said.

"Not exactly. I can insert a battlefield scene of course, if required. Lord knows I know what it's like. But this novel is about the people left behind, those who never came within a hundred miles of the trenches and the bombardment, but whose lives are nonetheless altered forever by the conflict they only experienced abstractly from a distance."

"I see." Knox finished preparing his cigar and lit it, blowing a cloud of smoke almost as large as he was into the air. "I'm already bored with the war. People in the States are bored with it as well."

"Again, it's not *about* the war," Keeby said, more impatiently than he intended. He throttled his emotions back and added, "It's about the people left behind."

236

"Sounds depressing," Knox said. "People don't like depressing books. You know who I like?"

"No, sir. Please tell me."

"I like John Buchan. Your analysis was spot on, boy. He writes a ripping yarn. Literary books are fine, Mr. Styles. They keep library shelves from flying away willy-nilly. Inspirational books are fine as well. I love a good message once in a while. But—and this is important—my company in New York is not in the inspiration business. They are in the bookselling business. I want people to think, but I'd prefer they buy one of our books to spur their rumination. People are tired of being frightened and worried. They want escape. They want a sympathetic hero, someone forced into misfortune and peril. They want someone to root for."

"An innocent man running for his life," Keeby suggested.

"Now you're talking!" Knox said. "Got one of those in you?"

"Maybe." Keeby stared out the window, wrestling with his emotions. He had a story. Maybe it was the ripping yarn Knox wanted. He could write it. He could write anything he set his mind to, but did he *want* to write it? Would it ring true if it were based on lies?

Keeby's stomach grumbled. He recalled he'd skipped breakfast, and lunch was still an hour away. His body reminded him of the nutritional value of pride.

"How about a hero who is a man of noble birth?" Keeby ventured. "A…a prince perhaps. A…ah, Russian prince. He's on vacation, relaxing in solitude at his dacha deep in a forest, when word arrives. Bolsheviks have stormed the Winter Palace and have overthrown the government."

"Bolsheviks," Knox said, his eyes already brighter. "Nasty, uncultured brutes. Great villains."

"The prince, a pleasant and well-meaning fellow who bears nobody ill will, is a student of history, and knows what happens to aristocrats in any populist revolution. His only hope—"

"—Is to flee to another country!" Knox finished. "You may be onto something here. American readers are tired of that damned kaiser and his silly hats, but by golly they are fascinated by all the folderol in Russia. The papers are full of the Red Scare. You write *that* novel, and I may persuade my fellows in New York to publish it."

They discussed it for an hour. Knox became even more excited with each new plot point. He loved the Russian peasant girl and suggested Keeby take great pains to describe every lush curve and to include scenes with lots of implied sex, which was about all the sex puritanical American audiences could handle.

When he left, Keeby was queasy and conflicted. It wasn't as if he were betraying a trust. Grigorii had told him the story—as mendacious and fanciful and self-aggrandizing as it was—with the specific intent that he write and publish it.

It was a lie, though. None of it ever happened. Keeby was cynical enough to predict, as soon as the book was published, Prince Grigorii would emerge from the shadows and proclaim it as his own story, thereby enhancing his social standing. Keeby had prided himself on telling true stories, stories which arrived with gravitas simply because they *were* true.

Writing Grigorii's story felt like fraud.

Keeby sincerely hoped it would pay well.

22 Rue Montparnasse

CHAPTER THIRTY-FOUR

1921

KEEBY WAS ALREADY hard at work on his novel in October 1919 when Beau Shipley arrived at the Saint-Germain-des-Prés station following the hundred-mile train trip from Le Havre. Alphonse Rimbaud, his father's agent in Paris, met Beau at the station and drove him directly to the apartment building at 22 Rue Montparnasse. Rimbaud was trim and athletic, even for a man in his late fifties, and constantly dressed immaculately. He wore round eyeglasses and a meticulously trimmed goatee.

As soon as Keeby had described the flat to him, Beau knew it wouldn't be adequate. His added—and more importantly, guaranteed—income would allow them to move into a larger apartment.

They were in luck. The landlord had exactly the space Beau described, on the fifth floor, and since the rent was considerably higher than what Keeby was paying, he was delighted to transfer the lease.

Beau settled in, turning his bedroom into a combination sleeping quarters and painting studio. The room, by any standard of sanitary housekeeping, was a lost cause. At any time, you might find jars filled with turpentine and brushes sitting on every available surface, or tattered swatches of muslin rags drying on racks, or a half dozen paintings leaning against the wall to cure. But, within a month, Beau had found his place, and he cheerfully ignored the mess in his room in return for living the life of a Parisian painter. Each morning, he ventured from the apartment to a different part of the city. He discovered almost any place the Metro dropped him provided a subject for a painting far greater than he had ever found in Charleston.

He ventured frequently to Place du Tertre, a quaint fork in a bricked road in the shadow of the new Sacré-Coeur Basilica, built around a small park in which painters traditionally fought over real estate, and lined with shops, cafés, and apartments. It was a small piece of ancient Paris that had been preserved almost by accident. At one time, a visitor might have run across Manet and Renoir chatting over a glass of wine in one of the cafés. Now, it had become popular with tourists, and like most such places, the established artists had long since deserted, leaving it to the newcomers and ardent amateurs. Beau liked painting it in each of the seasons—the verdant springs, dusty summers, golden autumns, and snowy winters.

By the time Keeby finished the first draft of his novel in March 1920, he had also introduced Beau to many of his artistic contacts in Paris. They attended several parties at the home of Misia Edwards, who had finally decided to make things legal with her longtime lover, the muralist José-Maria Sert. As Misia Sert, she still reigned nearly unchallenged among the arts patrons in the greatest arts city in the world. Misia made a larcenous offer and purchased two of Beau's first Paris paintings, in what she called speculation. If Beau managed to rise to the top of the art world, as some people occasionally and inexplicably did, it would prove to be a wise investment. If not, there was always another bathroom or dressing room to decorate. Beau might have been insulted by the offer she made for the works, but she added an incentive—the opportunity to hobnob with the greatest artists in Paris, or indeed the world. She offered him access to the ground floor. What he did with it was up to him.

————

After interminable rewrites, editing, cutting, expanding, and recutting his manuscript, Keeby believed he was polishing the polish, and he presented it to Armitage Knox in September of 1920, nearly a year after he was recruited to write it. Knox responded in November, with a list of changes, and by March of 1921, Keeby finally cleared the first hurdle. Armitage Knox agreed to present the book to the boys on Madison Avenue in Manhattan.

Keeby continued to work on other projects, including articles for a magazine in Montreal. There were fat months and lean months, but between his writing for hire and Beau's allowance, they lived comfortably. Some might even have accused them of bourgeoisie extravagance, since they were observed almost every night either in one of the Latin Quarter's best nightclubs, or simply lounging at a sidewalk table at La Rotonde or Les Deux Magots or La Closerie des Lilas. And, for once, thanks to his almost regular payments from America and Canada, Keeby was able to keep pace when it came to grabbing the checks.

It was at the Closerie des Lilas that Keeby and Beau met Hemingway, a fledgling writer recently turned twenty-one and newly arrived from the States with his bride Hadley. Keeby enjoyed conversing with the deadly serious young man, as they mostly bandied war stories, including how both had nearly been blown to bits by artillery fire. Beau found him overbearing and pompous, at least until Hemingway made an offer to introduce him to Gertrude Stein.

"If Gertrude accepts you," Hemingway told him, poking at Beau's chest with his finger. "Your career is halfway there. I can tell you she's been a huge help to me. Hadley and I asked her to be godmother to our baby."

"You and she are that familiar?" Beau asked.

"Not yet, but we plan to be. The woman is ridiculously rich and inclined to spread it around. She knows what's good and what isn't, except when it comes to her own stuff. Some faulty sixth sense. At the least, she'll buy one or two of your pieces."

"I sold two to Misia Sert a few months back," Beau said.

"For God's sake, don't mention Misia to Gertrude. They're on the outs. Something about Picasso. Damned if I know what."

———

Keeby heard back from New York in June of 1921, on the same day Beau responded to an invitation to an audience with Gertrude Stein in her salon at 27 Rue de Fleurus.

The letter was ebullient and congratulatory, and contained a contract with the New York company to publish Keeby's book the following spring. The advance was generous. In fact, it was almost embarrassing, enough to support him for several years.

Beau had a similar emotional response to his meeting with Gertrude Stein, who was generous with her criticism, and the afternoon was embarrassing for Beau.

He brought along three pieces he had worked over the most in the previous two months. Alice Toklas met him at the door when he rang. Toklas was a tiny woman with a beaked nose and severely bobbed dark hair who greeted Beau warmly and escorted him into Gertrude Stein's salon. The ceiling was tall, perhaps twenty feet, which left an immense amount of wall space Stein and Toklas had filled with dozens of paintings, some of which Beau recognized immediately. The portrait of Stein by Picasso. Several delightful Cézannes. Several artists he didn't recognize, but he knew were gifted at first glance. No doubt, they would be famous enough shortly.

Stein was shorter than he had expected. Given Hemingway's larger-than-life descriptions, he had expected to find her six feet tall with flames shooting out of her nostrils. She was a hefty woman, with unnaturally raven hair styled in what looked like a monk's bowl cut, sans tonsure, and combed straight forward high on her forehead like a Roman senator. She had a penetrating gaze, but as soon as he saw her Beau relaxed, her presence less intimidating than he had imagined.

At her request, he arranged the paintings for her to examine.

"With whom did you study?" she asked after looking them over.

"Self-taught," Beau said. "An art therapist worked with me on the basics when I was in the recovery hospital here in Paris."

"Recovering from what?"

"Shrapnel. Grazed my head. I was blown out of a trench by an artillery round, and it took a while for all the parts of my body to fit together correctly afterward, but the furrow in my head was the main thing. Not to worry. It healed some time ago. I took to painting as part of my therapy."

"I see. Yes. It shows. You know the problem with bad habits, Mr. Chipley?"

"Um, it's Shipley, Miss Stein. What's the problem with bad habits?"

"Unlearning them. On the other hand, I can name five top-shelf painters whose technique is utter shit, and they have no interest whatsoever in changing, and never should. Sometimes, it is not necessary to learn to walk before one can run if the native ability is inborn. So bad habits can be overcome. Why did you decide to mimic Monet?"

"I like the impressionist experience," Beau said. "I enjoy looking at the paintings, so I want to emulate them."

"Yes. Like the painters of every canvas hanging in every hotel room in Paris. There's nothing wrong with that. They're painted on a factory floor by men who paint for a respectable salary and go home at night and eat a hearty dinner with their families. They may be the happiest of creatures, because they paint landscapes and rain-drenched street scenes all day long instead of walls and ceilings and woodwork, but in the end, they are no more artists than their craftsmen house painter brothers. If you'd like, I can arrange a job for you beginning tomorrow, and you can Monet your balls off for a weekly paycheck. There are worse ways to survive in postwar Paris."

"I apologize," Beau said. "Perhaps you can tell from my accent I'm from the southern part of the States. We are careful not to engage in direct confrontation with new acquaintances. I am unused to your candor, and therefore at a loss as how to respond."

"And now you're being overly polite. There's no place for manners in the art world, young Shipley. The quicker you abandon manners, the sooner you'll be on your way."

"On my way?"

"Are you an artist or a craftsman?" she asked.

"To be honest, until I was blown out of a trench in the Meuse-Argonne, I expected to be a tobacco importer. Art is something I've only recently discovered. To learn, I studied the paintings I saw in museums. I wanted to understand how they were completed, what kind of broad or fine brushstrokes the artists employed. I tried to imagine how they thought as they painted, what life events inspired them to paint that image on that day."

"Oh, dear God. Why don't you just become one of those tedious art historians?" Stein said. Something behind the razored words sounded almost empathetic. Beau was certain of it, if only because he wanted to hear it.

"Too old to start college over," Beau said. "Time to do something."

"And for you, doing something means painting. Which leads us again to the question—"

"I like to believe I am an artist."

"But you aren't certain."

"I know I'll do what I have to, to be an artist."

"Then burn this crap," she said, pointing at his canvasses. "Or sell them to a hotel."

"You don't like them?"

"They're excellent facsimiles of a style only *au courant* among people who know nothing whatsoever about art. The cigar import thing. It isn't off the table?"

"Why? Do you think I should go home?"

"You wouldn't be the first," Stein said. "And what does it matter what I think? Well, it matters a great deal, of course. When you have my sort of money and influence, it matters. But, in this case, only you can decide definitively whether you are an artist or a craftsman, and whether you should ditch the art world for what I can only imagine would be a lucrative life as a cigar importer. Or, I can make a telephone call right now, and you will begin your new career as an assembly line artist tomorrow morning. It would be a perfectly acceptable compromise for some people, the type who'd be grateful I did so. Shall I make a call for you?"

"What other telephone calls can you make?" Beau asked.

"Are you an artist or a craftsman?" she replied.

"I'm an artist." He felt the icy flow of adrenalin course across his chest, as it was the first time he had ever declared it openly.

She shook her head sadly. "No. You aren't. Not yet. This—" she pointed again at his paintings. "—is workmanlike. It is a fine impression of a true impressionist painting. It looks like something painted while squinting your eyes."

"Prescription eyeglasses," he said. "Bought them at a local store. They blur everything."

"Impressionism isn't about blurring," she said. "It's about feeling. You're going about it all wrong, boy."

"So it's home, then," Beau said.

"You have some native artistic talent, but you don't understand being an artist. Not yet. You're still painting with your eyes, and you've developed some alarming habits that are unlikely to change, so you'll have to incorporate them as your style. What you're painting would have been entirely serviceable thirty years ago. You have some catching up to do, and the only way you'll do is if you decide it's the right path for you. Painting isn't about chasing the most successful current style. Any craftsman can do that. Painting is about transforming your soul onto the canvas. Sometimes people have messy souls. You asked if I could make any other telephone calls. I can. At least, I could. I could pave your way right into the fucking Louvre if I wanted. That isn't what I do, young Shipley, except for craftsmen. Hotels need paintings, and I am happy to spare the serious art world the contamination of craftsmen."

"What do you suggest?"

"Learn. Study. Stop imitating and start innovating. You are only at the start of your artistic journey. Right now, you are a duffer. You are raw meat. I'm having a party this Saturday evening. Come. There will be people willing to help you, but you'll have to seek them out. I'll keep your three paintings here in case you wish to impress one of them. I would suggest not doing so, but I may purchase one or two of these for my private storage collection in any case. You never know. Might be worth something someday."

"May I bring a friend?"

"Is he an artist, or a craftsman?"

"He's a writer," Beau said.

"Even better. What's his name?"

"Caleb Styles. Everyone calls him Keeby."

"Ah! Bish Twinings' protégé. I would like to meet the young man. By all means, extend my invitation to him."

CHAPTER THIRTY-FIVE

BEAU AND KEEBY ARRIVED at 27 Rue de Fleurus fashionably late on Saturday evening, after a lovely dinner at Les Deux Magots. They walked into the salon shortly after ten, to find it packed. The room rumbled with the shrill din of three dozen conversations at once. Everyone drank and smoked.

Bish was in London, savoring a rare weekend with Sir Ross. She had left Keeby with explicit instructions to enjoy the evening at Stein's salon and to get laid if there was any remotely possible way, preferably with someone famous who knew what they were doing. She relished hearing the details later.

Keeby discovered Armitage Knox among the crowd. The rotund agent spotted him across the room and gestured for Keeby to join his small gathering in the corner. Keeby excused himself, leaving Beau to look for a ready supply of alcohol.

He rounded the corner, glanced up at the wall, and stopped, horrified. Gertrude Stein had hung all three of his paintings, the ones she had derided several days earlier. They were clustered in a row underneath Picasso's portrait of her, as if to draw a stark contrast between the genius and the duffer. Beau's heart hammered inside his chest, and the room seemed to spin, his vision dimming at the edges, and he knew his face must be cherry red from humiliation and embarrassment. His impulse was to make a quick exit to the safety and anonymity of the street. His stomach was knotted, his skin dry and tight.

He jumped when someone laid a hand on his shoulder, and he whirled around, wild-eyed, to find a stocky man with thick black wavy hair and a firm jaw facing him.

"Are you all right?" the man asked in English, with a French accent. "You look panic-stricken."

"I apologize," Beau said French. "I had a bit of a shock."

"You did not expect to see these on the wall tonight?" the man said.

"Not at all."

"They are yours, then?"

"I painted them," Beau said, as if confessing to a murder.

"And you don't feel worthy."

"You seem to know a lot about it."

"Inside joke," the man said. "Our hostess has a mean streak. She does this on occasion. She did it to me." He extended his hand. "Georges Braque."

"Oh, dear God," Beau said. "I need a drink."

"An excellent idea. First, though, your name?"

"Beau Shipley."

"Please, come with me, Beau Shipley."

Beau thought Braque was leading him to the bar. Instead, they located Gertrude Stein in one of the rooms. She sipped wine and talked at anyone who'd listen. Braque caught her eye, and they gravitated toward one another. Braque took her hand and shook it the way he would a man's.

"So lovely to see you tonight, Gertrude! I have made the acquaintance of young Beau Shipley here, and he graciously showed me the samples of his work you hung on the wall outside."

"Is that a fact?" Stein said.

"Indeed. I am impressed, both with Mr. Shipley's nascent grasp of the esthetics of art, and by your sharp eye for a new talent. Did you purchase the paintings yet?"

"Why? Do you want them?" Stein asked.

"So you haven't. My advice? Buy them. Pay what he asks—" Braque glanced at Beau. "—within reason, of course. It might be a wise investment."

"You think so?" Stein asked. "How intriguing."

"I will introduce your young discovery to some people. Perhaps we can find a few moments to chat later?"

"*Absolutement!*" Stein said, as Braque and Beau drifted toward the door to the next room.

When they arrived at the bar, Braque reached across, grabbed a bottle of wine from the surprised server, and handed Beau a glass. He poured six or seven ounces into the glass and drank the rest from the bottle.

"The bitch bought it," Braque said, wiping his mouth with his sleeve. "I suggest you decide quickly how much you want for that crap on the wall. She'll write you a check tomorrow."

"Wait. You don't like it?"

"I like it fine. It's still crap. I mean, I'm sure someone will buy it, but they'll also buy flypaper and hemorrhoid cream. It's surprising what some people would rather have than money."

"I see. You were putting one over on Gertrude Stein."

"Oh, don't take it hard," Braque said. "I've been where you are now, and my shit she hung on the wall makes your shit look like Rembrandt. It's a rite of passage. A...what do they call it in American colleges?"

"Hazing," Beau said.

"Yes. Congratulations. You have survived your trial by fire. After the way she humiliated you, isn't it fun to stick it right back to her? She's going to pay you for the privilege of humiliating you. That's the Paris art world, my new friend. A thousand backs, but only one knife, so we pass it around. Let's grab another bottle and we'll make a tour of the room."

"Why are you doing this?" Beau asked as Braque liberated another bottle and filled his glass nearly to the brim.

"Drinking? Occupational hazard. You'll find out."

"Introducing me to people," Beau said.

"Would you prefer I didn't? Fine with me, but..." Braque scratched at his chin. "All right. Your paintings are for shit, but only because they're derivative. There is no worse crime in the art world than being derivative. The underlying technique is workmanlike and shows promise. Mine was the same way until I met Matisse and Derain. From them, I learned that representative art is dead. Now we paint our hearts and souls. We translate reality into our warped perspectives. This is the age of psychoanalysis. The artist's unconscious mind is now the subject, not bridges and lily ponds and seascapes. We splatter the canvas with our conflicts and fears and desperation. We reflect the mechanization of man and society with sharp angles and fever-dream colors. Impressionism is a dying language in the art world, my friend. We've advanced three or four

253

civilizations since. You need to learn a new dialectic. Are you in a workshop?"

"No," Beau said. "Don't even know what it is."

"It's a collective of artists who support and learn from one another."

"So far, I've worked pretty much alone."

"Ah. The suffering solitary artist in his garret. A romantic stereotype," Braque said. "This will not do. How do you know you are painting shit if nobody tells you? Hold on."

Braque waded into the crowd, returning after a while with man about Beau's age. He was short and muscular, and had shaved his head to the scalp, but not within the last several days, so his stubble resembled a field of newly scythed wheat. His eyes were narrow and darted about the room as if he were searching for prey. He wore a pretentious little whisk broom mustache that covered the middle third of his upper lip. Braque introduced him as Helmut.

"Helmut what?" Beau asked.

"That is all. Helmut," the man said, with a stout Germanic accent.

"Is Helmut your first or your last name?"

"I am Helmut," he said again, without elaborating. Neither did he appear irritated at having to repeatedly explain.

"Beau Shipley." They shook hands. Helmut's hand was rough and callused. Beau's hand was like a baby's in comparison.

"This is yours?" Helmut pointed at the three paintings on the wall.

"Our hostess is playing a joke on me."

"For what they are, they are acceptable work."

"And what are they?"

"Well, of course, they are garbage, but well-done garbage. I particularly like this one." He pointed to a painting of a church cemetery shaded by ancient trees, and a lone distraught figure grasping at the wrought-iron fence and gesturing longingly toward the graveyard. Beau had returned to Paris haunted by the painting he had given to Norbert Tradd and had reproduced it from memory. "It has an unusual kinetic energy."

"I don't know what that means," Beau said.

"At least you are willing to admit it. Acknowledging you know nothing is the first step on the road to wisdom."

"You've made this journey already?"

"It is a work in progress, but I am far enough along to see potential even in—" He gesticulated at the painting with his index finger. "—failed attempts. Are you in a workshop?"

"You're the second person who's asked me tonight," Beau said.

"You will join mine."

"You seem confident."

"You will join mine," he repeated. "It is small, and you have never heard of any of us, and likely never would have without my offer. Even so, working in a collective provides advantages. We paint together. We show together. Braque was total shit before he found his workshop with Matisse. Now, you have found your workshop with Helmut."

"Are you German?" Beau asked.

"Does it matter?"

"Not so long ago, Germans were shooting at me. This feels familiar."

Helmut laughed so loudly several of the other attendees stopped their conversations to glance at him.

"Good. You tell your jokes. It will lighten things in the studio. I am Danish. We sat the war out."

"And what are you painting?" Beau asked.

"We aren't only painting," Helmut said as he grabbed a glass from the tray carried by a passing server. "We have a sculptor, and a photographer, and several painters. We even have a motion picture photographer. We each learn from one another. Please. You will join us tomorrow evening. Our film photographer is going to show a new picture from Germany. Extremely artistic, I hear. You are familiar with the German expressionist movement?"

"I've seen some artwork."

"Wait until you see what they are doing with film. Do you have a card?"

Beau took a calling card from his jacket pocket and handed it over. Helmut already had a sharpened charcoal crayon in his hand, as if carrying one everywhere he went was the most natural of behaviors. He wrote something on the back of the card and handed it back. It was an address.

"Tomorrow evening, seven sharp. Bring wine."

———

The address was a brisk walk from Beau's apartment on Rue Montparnasse. The building turned out to be an old horse stable, converted into a studio of sorts. The stalls remained in place, the ancient white oak beams and pillars long since fumed a rich, deep, golden umber by the ammonia-rich atmosphere. While the building hadn't housed livestock for decades, Beau still occasionally caught a whiff of the Ghost of Urine Past.

Each stall now housed a separate artist, and was large enough for a desk and chair, a couple of easels, and of course wall space to hang works in progress.

On his walk over, Beau had purchased a bottle of Montrachet and another of pinot noir. He had no idea what sort of wine Helmut's companions preferred, so he chose a white and a red.

Helmut saw Beau walk through the door, and shouted, "Huzzah!" Besides Helmut, there were four other men in the room. All the conversation stopped, and everyone looked in his direction. "Please, my fellows, welcome our new workshop member, Monsieur Boo Shipton."

"Ah, that's Beau Shipley," Beau said. He forgave the Dane, since the man hadn't kept his calling card.

"Of course, Beau Shipley. Please forgive the error. In my defense, I have been drinking a great deal, and for a good part of the day." The crowd laughed heartily.

Beau had dressed casually for the evening, in a pullover knit polo shirt with a merino wool sweater and dark trousers. He was far and away the best dressed man in the studio. Most of them wore sleeveless undershirts or paint-stained collarless linen shirts that might have been stylish before the war. One wore a tattered pair of American farm overalls and nothing underneath. They all smelled almost as rank as soldiers in the trenches.

Helmut took the bottles from Beau. "And it appears we shall continue drinking into the evening. Please forgive the informality, Shipley. We have been working all day, and now we are—how you say—blowing off steam. When we are attending to our creations, we are solemn as monks."

"No doubt," Beau said.

"So," Helmut said, his breath stinking of alcohol and tobacco. "Allow me to introduce you to your new artistic family." He went around the room and named each man there. Two painters, a sculptor, and a photographer. He could see why Helmut was the self-appointed leader of the pack. They were all young. Beau was only twenty-five himself and might have been the oldest man in the room except for Helmut.

Next came a tour of the various stalls. Helmut was working on a Cubist canvas, which looked as if it had been traced with a yardstick and a French curve. One of the other two painters also dabbled in surrealist images. The third was painting in a gaudy and hallucinatory style Van Gogh might have achieved had he lived long enough and become insane enough. Beau questioned the painter's mental state.

The door swung open, and a lean, graceful, blond man stuck his head in. "A little help?" he said, in a thick German accent.

"Our entertainment has arrived!" Helmut said. "Come along, Shipley. We can use a strong back."

Helmut and Beau joined the newcomer outside, where they found him standing next to a dilapidated pre-war Renault with a large wooden box in the back seat. "Help me get this inside," the man said. "It isn't heavy, but it's clumsy for one person."

After unloading the box, Beau greeted the man. "Beau Shipley. I'm new here."

"I can tell," the man said, looking over Beau's outfit. "Dietrich Heyder, but people call me Dieter."

"You're the fellow who makes the motion pictures?"

"Well, I intend to. I arrived in Paris only this past month. I did motion picture work in Berlin at UFA after the war." He opened the box and gestured for Beau to help him lift out a heavy cast-iron projector, which they placed on a table Helmut and the sculptor had set in the middle of the studio.

"You were in the war?" Beau asked.

"You are perhaps concerned I might have been shooting at you?" Dieter asked, bluntly. "Do not be. I spent the war in Berlin, as a civilian office clerk. I am not political. I am an artist. That is all that truly matters."

The two other painters strung a large blank canvas from the rafters using twine, to fashion a projection screen. Dieter retrieved another smaller box from the Renault and brought it into the studio. He opened it and took out a reel of film.

"What have you brought us tonight, Dieter?" Helmut asked. "Some fresh pornography from München, perhaps?"

The other members of the collective laughed and slapped each other on the back. Dieter smiled and shook his head. "Sadly, no. What I have tonight is something entirely new. Do you remember when I screened *Der Golem* a few weeks back?"

"Of course," Helmut said.

"This is in the same vein. A new film by Robert Wiene. It came out only last year."

"Not another horrible film about a monster," the sculptor said.

"A horrible film, perhaps," Dieter said. "The monster is not who you might think it is. But that is beside the point. I

259

want you to see what they are doing in Germany with film design." He turned to Beau. "You are a painter?"

"I'm trying to be," Beau said.

"This may intrigue you. You know Picasso and Braque, do you not?" He threaded the film into the projector.

"I met Braque only last night. Never met Picasso."

"But you know their work?"

"Sure," Beau said.

Dieter winked at him. "So do the Germans, especially Wiene."

Helmut killed the lights, and Dieter turned on the lamp in the crank-driven projector. Beau watched as Dieter turned the crank and the first frames jumped onto the makeshift screen.

"Isn't that tiring?" Beau asked.

"Good practice," Dieter said. "To show the film correctly, one must maintain twenty-four frames per second. Five less, and the film jumps. Five more, and the people race around like ants. The same goes for shooting the film. Watch now, painter."

The film was *The Cabinet of Doctor Caligari*. Within seconds of the opening credits, Beau saw what Dieter meant. Accustomed to naturalistic settings in American and even French films, the design Wiene conceived for his monstrous tale was artificial, composed of weird angles and jarring transitions from light to shadow. It looked like an avant-garde stage play filmed in performance.

"I see what you mean," Beau said. "It's surrealism translated to film. Fascinating."

"You paint this surrealism?" Dieter asked, without taking his eyes from the screen.

260

"I haven't," Beau said.

One of the other painters seated in front of them raised his hand. "I do."

"But you paint surrealist shit, Marcel," Helmut said.

The other painter piped up. "They called Picasso's early attempts shit, you know. Perhaps Marcel is in the vanguard."

"You only defend him because he sucks your cock," Helmut said.

Marcel said, "He's right, you know. It is shit, and you'd agree in an instant if I stopped sucking your cock."

Dieter and Beau glanced at one another and returned to digesting the images on the screen.

———

After the film, Beau helped Dieter pack the boxes and return them to the Renault.

"I'm having a glass at La Rotonde," Dieter said. "Would you care to join me?"

Minutes later, over wine and olives, Dieter asked, "What did you think of the film?"

"I'm still working it out. I've never seen a movie like it before."

"You will see many more soon, I believe. I hear Murnau is doing a horror film now. Rumor has it he is using Bram Stoker's vampire story as the basis for his screenplay. I believe the Cubist and surrealist movements lend themselves well to the screen."

"It sets an eerie mood. I'll be honest. Most of my works so far have been more…conventional."

"Analyze and imitate," Dieter said.

"Come again?"

"The artistic process. We analyze the works of those we admire, and we attempt to imitate them. If I made a movie tonight, it would look much like Herr Wiene's *Cabinet of Doctor Caligari*. I worked with him briefly at UFA, you know."

"Of course I didn't," Beau said. "We only met tonight."

"Oh, I knew all of them. Wiene, Lang, Murnau, Lubitsch. Most of them weren't directors yet. We all started out rigging the sets. That's how you learn. You watch those who already know, and you copy them. Innovation comes later. As time goes by, you develop your own style, your own artistic voice. First you copy, then you invent."

"Well, that's where I've been for the last three years. Copying."

"Perhaps you are ready to find your own expression."

"With all the exciting things happening at UFA in Berlin, why did you leave and come to Paris?"

Dieter chuckled and ate an olive. "Followed love," he said.

"I see," Beau said. "As is often the case in stories like this, there is a woman involved."

"Not at all," Dieter said, and let it hang in the air between them.

"Oh," Beau said. "I see."

"His name was Rolf, and he was the most magnificent human being I had ever seen, and that's all there is to say about it. It's over. And don't worry. It isn't contagious. I'm not trying to seduce you. I know you aren't interested."

"Do you?"

"Oh, hell yes," Dieter said. "You didn't know the secret handshake. In any case, love brought me to Paris and then abandoned me, but Paris has decided to embrace me, and here I am. So, if you don't paint surrealism, what do you paint?"

Beau drained his glass and waved for the server. "The wrong things, by all accounts."

"There is a lid for every pot," Dieter said. "Someone will like whatever you paint."

"I'm still learning. Everyone seems to consider my stuff derivative."

"Of whom?"

"Monet. Renoir. Sargent."

"Ah," Dieter said. "The dinosaurs. Don't take me the wrong way. There is a market for that sort of art."

"On hotel walls," Beau said.

"Hotel walls keep many a painter from starvation. What did you think of the workshop?"

Beau's refill arrived. "Not for me," he said, after sipping.

"I am much the same. They are a herd of imbeciles, are they not?"

They both laughed, and Beau said, "I wasn't going to mention it."

"I suppose each endeavor has its share of dilletantes. The art world appears to tolerate them, though."

"They'll become richer and more famous than either of us," Beau said.

"That, young Herr Shipley, is the essence of irony. So, I suppose we are both in search of a new workshop."

CHAPTER THIRTY-SIX

1922

KEEBY'S NOVEL was a flop.

It came off the presses in March 1922, and flew immediately to the bottom of the sales charts, where it languished for some brief moments, gasping for breath, before disappearing altogether.

Armitage Knox broke the horrible news to him in early July. There would be no second printing.

"It's a mystery, my boy," Knox told him as they commiserated in his office over a hearty pour of brandy to soften the impact. "Who can explain it? Between you and me and the wainscoting, nobody knows shit in this business. Everyone knows what they like, and some people know what they can sell, but in the end it's all a flip of the coin. The book hits or it misses, for no easily defined reason. This one missed."

"Any idea at all why?"

Knox shook his head and his three chins wobbled. "The reviews weren't awful. They weren't ebullient, but they weren't awful. There weren't many of them, though. Maybe somebody in the marketing department dropped the ball.

These things happen. If people don't hear about a title, it falls through the cracks. Sometimes, bad things happen to good books."

"What can I do now?"

"Yes," Knox said. "I was getting to that. Your contract states they have the right to see your next novel first, and the right to make an offer on it before anyone else."

"That's comforting."

Knox cleared his throat. "They have, ah, waived that right."

"They're dumping me?" Keeby said.

"In essence, yes. The publishing company has decided not to exercise its first refusal option. Their business philosophy discourages throwing good money after bad."

"I see," Keeby said. He straightened his back, which had ached of late. Tension, he figured. The ruined muscles in his side didn't help. Sometimes, it was less painful to stand. He crossed the office floor and stared at a painting on the wall for what seemed a long time.

"You have a lot to think about," Knox suggested.

"Can you help in any way?" Keeby asked.

"Not directly. I'm not your literary representative. I work for the publisher, and that bed is made, I fear. The fraternity of publishing company agents in Paris is small, though, and we all know one another. A few of them owe me favors. If you write another novel, I can ask around, see if anyone is interested. Are you writing another novel?"

Keeby didn't look at Knox. "I...I am. I may have a story."

What's it about?"

"It takes place right after the war."

"Oh, shit, Keeby. Not another one."

"This is different. It isn't a thriller. It's a serious novel. A soldier returns to his hometown after the war and discovers everything has changed, and none of it for the better. The war and the influenza epidemic not only changed him, but they also changed everyone back home. He keeps trying to find the life he left behind, but it has disappeared, and what he finds in its place troubles him greatly."

"I'm intrigued," Knox said. "How does it end?"

"I don't know. It's a work in progress."

"Finish it. I can't send it to my superiors in New York, but I'd like to hear how it turns out, and I may know someone who will be interested. In the meantime, I have one positive bit of news. The publisher has no intention of authorizing a second printing, as I mentioned, but they also haven't found any takers for the corpse with the smaller reprint houses. Rather than carry the financial liability and costs of maintaining the copyright, they have decided to relinquish all rights to the book to you, with the proviso they can sell the remaining first printing stock to reduce their losses."

"I'm not an attorney, Mr. Knox," Keeby said.

"It means you own the book. Lock, stock, and barrel. Perhaps you can find a French publisher who will print a translation of it. Or you can publish it yourself privately. In any case, it's yours to do with as you wish."

———

After the first halting experiment with Helmut's band of misfit artists a year earlier, Dieter and Beau decided to be more selective in forming their own collective workshop. Their first objective was to find a space. The horse barn Helmut used was esthetically repugnant, but the concept was spot on—a place with individual workspaces for the artists, but also space to meet collaboratively and critique their work.

While it would also be nice if this dream space were cheap, money was no particular problem, given Beau's generous monthly allowance delivered by Alphonse Rimbaud. Dieter also seemed to have some family money, though he seldom discussed it. He never lacked for ready cash, and Beau presumed he was adequately financed.

A month or so after the screening of *The Cabinet of Doctor Caligari*, they found their space, a former dance studio on the second floor of a commercial building in Le Marais, across the river on the Rive Droit. It was a fifteen-minute walk from the apartment on Rue Montparnasse, and even closer to Dieter's apartment in the Quartier Latin. The rent was right, and the owner was open to negotiation regarding the lease period. Beau arranged for an increase on his allowance through Rimbaud to cover the first several months, after which they planned for the artists to contribute their shares. Rimbaud consulted with Gordon Shipley in Charleston, who approved the increase. Gordon also suggested that art had better pay off for Beau soon, or it might be time to discuss returning to America to import cigars and illegal booze. With the entire country in the grips of Prohibition, demand for Cuban and Jamaican rum had jumped exponentially. Funding Beau's collective studio was easy, because Gordon was raking in cash hand over fist.

Beau moved all his art supplies from his room at the apartment into his space at the studio. The bedding and walls and furniture were already ruined by stray paint and splashes of turpentine, so Beau tossed it all into the alley. He spent a weekend painting the walls, and he purchased a new dresser and bed and a comfortable reading chair designed by an American named Stickley but manufactured in England. He transformed the room from an abused ad hoc studio into a bright and cheery bedroom within several days. Keeby expressed his appreciation to be liberated at last from solvent and linseed fumes.

Within six months, after trolling parties at Misia Sert's Rivoli digs, and at Gertrude Stein's salon, and at various galleries around town, Beau and Dieter assembled their artistic commune. Unlike Helmut's ragtag pack of drunken partiers, *The Salle*, as they had elected to call their collective, had become the work home of several serious young painters with genuine potential. Also unlike Helmut's collection of bumblers, artists at The Salle were required to wear clean white cotton smocks over their street clothes. No overalls or stained sleeveless shirts allowed. Beau and Dieter stressed from the beginning that—allowing liberal margins for artistic expression—members of The Salle should behave professionally.

Beau took Dieter's advice about innovating, and he experimented with applying impressionistic techniques within a Cubist/surrealistic framework. The results, so far, had failed to fan a flame in his breast, but some of the other Salle artists thought he might be on to something, at least half the time.

Even so, Beau was grateful for his allowance, as his sales were lackluster at best.

One of the painters, a young lion named Cesare, who had dropped out of the Ecole de Beaux-Arts de Paris, had initiated a weekly life painting session for The Salle's artists. Everyone enthusiastically approved, partly because rendering the human form in modern art presented something of an esthetic challenge, walking the tightrope between desirable abstraction and *outré* representation, but also because it provided the opportunity to look at naked women once a week. For about three-quarters of their cadre, that was a perk. For the rest, it was educational, as they rarely encountered the nude female form in other settings.

On a particular evening in July, Beau arrived at The Salle to find most of the other painters already there, arranging their easels around a small, velvet-covered platform in the middle of the room. Cesare, a short, solid, athletic youth with a thick mustache and a pretentious inch-wide goatee, stood next to the platform with their model for the evening, who smiled as they chatted. She wore only a thin satin robe which clung to the curve of her hip and telegraphed her shape so transparently, she might as well already be naked. She was tall, her sable hair fashionably bobbed by someone who knew how to do it. She reminded Beau of the film star Pola Negri, but darker-skinned, like some mixed-race women he had happened across in Charleston's segregated district. Her eyes were the color of milk chocolate. Beau felt the sadness in them from across the room.

Cesare frequently recruited their models on life painting nights from the readily available corps of prostitutes who roamed Le Marais. Beau recognized immediately that this was not one of them. The way she moved suggested experience and grace. It would take a lot more than a few sous to open this woman's legs.

Beau moved his easel from his workspace into the circle, and assembled his brushes, charcoal, and paints. Cesare met him at his easel.

"Eh?" he said, pointing at the model.

"You've outdone yourself," Beau said. "Who is she?"

"An actress. A real one, not one of those whores who claim to be actresses. She used to be a model. Dieter found her. She said she's done a lot of nude sessions, and so I invited her to pose for us tonight."

"How much?"

"The same as the others."

Each artist at the life painting sessions pitched in to pay for the model. Beau had expected this one to charge twice as much as usual. Times were tough, though. Maybe she needed the work. He made a mental note to ask Dieter about her later.

Cesare finished setting the spotlights to illuminate the pedestal and turned off the surrounding lights so only the model and easels were left in the bright spill. Beau sat on a stool in front of his canvas, a piece of charcoal ready to make the rough sketch.

The goal of the life painting session each week was simple. Complete one painting in one two-hour evening session. It was an exercise in the transcription of a visual model into a kinetic image on the canvas, and in doing it quickly.

The model stepped onto the platform, casually undid the sash to her robe, and dropped it to the ground.

She was stunning. Her nutmeg skin was flawless, not a mole or a freckle to blemish it. Under the unblinking spotlights, she seemed to shimmer.

"How would you like me to pose?" she asked, with a hint of an unfamiliar accent. Her voice was throaty and sultry, but not at all seductive. She might as well have been asking which shoes she should wear to dinner.

Cesare directed her into a relaxed but contemplative pose, like a Greek statue of a recumbent muse. Beau allowed his eyes to drink her in for a moment or two, to preserve her shape and pose, and he frantically sketched her on the canvas.

————

The model was back in her robe, and the artists were stowing their canvases and supplies at their workstations, when Dieter Heyder strolled into The Salle. He located the model as he walked through the door and crossed directly to her. He took her hand and kissed it, and led her to a small storage closet where she would dress.

Seconds later, he appeared at Beau's side. "So. What do you think?"

"The model? She's great. Where'd you find her?"

"She's an actress in a film I'm shooting across town for Pathé. It's a small role. A servant. I saw her and was reminded about the life painting sessions. I'm running the camera on the film, and what I saw in the eyepiece nearly drove me mad, which as you might imagine is quite an accomplishment for a woman. She is a natural, don't you think?"

"A real step up from our usual models. Thanks."

The woman exited the storage room, carrying the robe over her arm. She had changed into a white blouse with black piping and puffy sleeves, black slacks, and heeled shoes. She wore a black cloche hat. She spied Dieter and Beau and smiled.

Dieter said, "We're going out for drinks. Lilas. Why don't you come? It'll be fun."

"Sure," Beau said, unable to take her eyes off the model. "Sounds good. First round's on me."

"Why did you think I invited you?"

She arrived and kissed Dieter on the cheek.

Dieter said, "Please, allow me to introduce my co-founder of The Salle, Beau Shipley."

The woman kissed Beau on both cheeks in the traditional Parisian fashion, and said, "Monsieur Shipley. A pleasure to meet you. My name is Nathalie Bel."

CHAPTER THIRTY-SEVEN

NATHALIE BEL'S APARTMENT was tiny but neat. A studio off the Rue des Saints Pères, its two greatest features were a private—if microscopic—*en-suite* bathroom and her massive Louis XVI bed which dominated the space.

Nathalie sat at a small circular table in the corner next to the window and daubed black cherry preserves on a croissant Beau had bought minutes earlier in a patisserie on the next corner. A signed Picasso sketch hung in a frame over the table. Silk sheers billowed in the window that opened onto a central courtyard.

Across the courtyard, a man played a bassoon. Beau had always considered it the loneliest sounding of wind instruments. The bassoonist played the same passage again and again. Beau imagined he might be in an orchestra and was ironing out some difficulty with a specific musical phrase. Beau wished him luck.

In the center of the circular table at which Nathalie sat was a vase with fresh-cut flowers. Daisies. Nathalie had picked them up as she and Beau strolled in a street market the day before. The florist threw in a sprig of baby's breath for accent.

Nathalie, as was frequently the case in her apartment, was naked. The sun streaming through the window splashed against her perfect skin and spread like cream over the surface of her body. Satisfied the croissant was smeared immaculately with the preserves, she raised it toward her mouth, and froze in space.

"Perfect," Beau said from across the room. He sketched furiously with the charcoal. "Oh, my God. Trying to capture this moment before it vanishes is a chore. I wish I was a photographer."

"There's a camera in the closet," she said, without moving.

"Who would develop the pictures?"

"I know people."

"Hush. Drawing."

He finished the charcoal sketch and examined it one more time. In times past, he would have tried to capture her likeness on the canvas. This time, he tried to capture her essence and the geometry of her figure against the plane of the table and the angles of the framed drawing. He focused on the interaction of the yellow-white sunlight and her cinnamon skin, the lines and shadows and curves. He had posed her so the lines of her body melded into those of the chair in which she sat and the table in front of her, and even with the Picasso on the wall and the croissant in her hand. He worked for almost fifteen minutes, blending pigments on his palette, to capture her exact skin tones and her hypnotic eyes, which he portrayed as enormous milk chocolate orbs.

When he was finished, he cleaned his brushes and let them soak in a large, capped jar of turpentine, and he stripped of his painter's smock and took Nathalie in his arms and carried her to the Louis XVI bed where they alternately made love and held one another and joked and giggled until the shadows lengthened, and the bassoonist across the courtyard played his clumsy phrase into twilight.

———

Beau and Dieter sat at an outside table in the corner café across the street from 22 Rue Montparnasse, sipped wine with some bread and a saucer of herbed olive oil, and talked about dinner plans.

"Thank you for the introduction to Nathalie," Beau said.

"*Bitte,*" Dieter said. "She is a fine model, is she not?"

"She's a fine everything."

"Ah. So the artist and the model, I think? Is this not a cliché?"

"Pretty damned fine one," Beau said, and raised his glass. "To clichés." They toasted, and Beau dragged a chunk of the bread through the olive oil. "I don't think for a second there's anything permanent there," he said, after swallowing. "But, by golly, we're making memories I'll recall fondly for decades to come."

"I suspect Nathalie Bel will never be possessed by any man but will be shared by a grateful many."

Keeby rounded the corner, his shoulders slumped, his eyes fixed on the sidewalk, and headed toward the apartment entrance. Beau whistled loudly to get his attention.

"Keeb! Over here!"

Keeby spied Beau and Dieter and changed direction. He took a seat next to them, and a waiter appeared almost instantaneously. Keeby ordered a Danish beer. The waiter sniffed and hustled away.

"Bad news, boys," he said. "My publisher's dumping me."

"What?" Beau said. "How can they do that?"

"As cruelly as possible," Keeby said, and explained what Armitage Knox had told him.

"I do not believe it!" Dieter said. "I love your book. The images leap from the page. What happened?"

"Bad roll of the dice," Keeby said. "It happens. The law of averages. Some books die on the vine."

"What will you do now?" Beau asked.

"Write another one, I suppose. Still have to eat. I have my correspondent contracts in Montreal and Detroit. I can put together another two or three of those if things get tight. I've decided to look at this as a bump in the road."

"Please," Dieter said. "Did you say the publisher relinquished all the rights to you?"

"That's right."

"Intriguing. Would it be inappropriate for me to ask whether you have considered allowing your book to be made into a motion picture?"

"Are you serious?" Keeby asked.

"I told you already. I loved your book. You write vivid images. I saw many film possibilities for it. With your permission, I would like to film your novel."

The waiter arrived with Keeby's beer. Keeby took a sip and placed the glass back on the table. "I never thought about it."

"I have access to all the necessary equipment," Dieter said. "I know actors who would work for little money. Being a contemporary piece, costumes should be easy to procure. The greatest expense would be the film stock."

"How much do you figure it would take?" Beau asked.

Dieter told him.

"Still a pretty big chunk of coin," Keeby said.

"I can raise it," Beau said. Dieter and Keeby looked at him, surprised.

"You could?" Dieter asked.

"It's an investment, right?" Beau said. "For a percentage of the profits, I could talk my father into investing. I can meet with Alphonse Rimbaud today and set things in motion."

"There may be no profits," Dieter said. "This will not be a studio production."

"I'd want a percentage myself," Keeby said. "Unless you want to pay me up front for the rights to the book."

"We can work that all out," Dieter said. "That is all—how do the Americans say it?—nuts and bolts. Are you saying you would like to see it filmed?"

"And how," Keeby said. "If the film becomes popular, I can find a publisher to re-release the book. In fact, I might have your leading man already. Have I ever introduced you to my acquaintance, Prince Grigorii Yurievitch Romanov?"

———

"Your father has declined to invest in this motion picture project," Rimbaud advised Beau. "He was most adamant. He is happy to bankroll your pursuits, but he has no intention of supporting every artist in Paris."

"But this *is* one of my pursuits," Beau argued.

"I fear you are pleading to the wrong court," Rimbaud said. "Motion pictures are new. Whether they will last is still in question. Compared to stage plays, they are inherently inferior in visual quality and—being silent—not as intellectually engaging."

"I never took you for an artistic snob, Monsieur Rimbaud."

"I am merely stating economic facts. Investment in any new form of entertainment entails significant risk. Perhaps you should write your father directly, and personally outline not only your plans but the prospects for the film to be successful enough to repay his investment. He might relent."

"Or he'll say to come home and work in the cigar business," Beau said.

"That option has always been on the table."

"I know. Do you have an account of my financial statements handy?"

"Of course." Rimbaud crossed the office to a filing cabinet and extracted a folder. "It's right here. Would you like to examine it?"

"Thanks."

Since returning to Paris, Beau had been acutely aware of the privilege he enjoyed as the wealthy heir to a highly successful American business. His allowance, even before the increase to pay for The Salle, had been more than generous. From the moment he stepped off the boat at Le Havre, he knew his lifeline could be cut off at any time. While he had lived extremely comfortably in Paris, and in a relatively lavish fashion compared to his companions, he had been careful to put a significant chunk of his monthly allowance into the care of Alphonse Rimbaud, charged with investing the money prudently but profitably.

As he had encountered no need to access it, Beau had largely ignored the growth in his investment account for several years. Now, examining the balance sheets, he was impressed. His savings had increased exponentially in the postwar boom in France and the United States. The American stock market particularly had gathered tremendous steam, and unlimited growth seemed possible.

Unfortunately, while his personal financial state was stable and growing, there wasn't enough expendable money to risk on Dieter's film, and wouldn't be for some time.

"Perhaps you're right," Beau said, handing the folder back to Rimbaud. "I may write to my father tonight. Thank you for managing my accounts so ably, Monsieur Rimbaud."

"It is my privilege," Rimbaud said.

———

"Well, that's a kick in the pants," Keeby said as Beau related Rimbaud's news over dinner at La Coupole.

"Dieter took it pretty hard," Beau said. "I should have checked with my father before suggesting he might finance the film."

"Seems you have a habit of making decisions before consulting him."

"I don't suppose you can ask Bish—"

"Good God, no," Keeby said. "She's already done far too much. She won't be back in Paris until September in any case.

She likes the autumn here but prefers to summer in Scotland."

"Who wouldn't?"

"What about you? I've noticed you haven't come home at all a few nights recently."

Beau smiled as the waiter delivered their steaks frites and freshened their glasses. "An actress in a film Dieter's shooting. I'm painting her as well. We've done a few sessions at her apartment. She's not the one, but things could change."

"Congratulations," Keeby said, raising his glass. "Peace on Earth, and good tall women."

"Hear hear," Beau said.

"Prince Grigorii is going to be disappointed as well. He was looking forward to being a movie star."

"I've seen the test footage Dieter shot of him. Strange thing. Some people look amazing in person, but the camera can't seem to capture them. Others are plain enough in real life, but blossom on the screen. Grigorii is the latter. He's good looking enough in person, but the camera loves his face. He shoots like a Russian John Gilbert."

"Dieter said something similar when he showed me the footage. Something to the effect he would love to crawl all over Grigorii's cinematic face."

"Not out of the question. Grigorii's closet has a revolving door."

"Bish mentioned the same thing."

"Ah, well. It's Paris," Beau said.

"A handy excuse for any debauchery. Speaking of Grigorii, he's arranging an outing to the Cote d'Azur for the month of August. Sounds like fun.

"Why not? Paris empties out in August anyway. Where would we stay?"

"Baroness Moretz, one of his cyclical clients, owns a villa overlooking the Med. She's letting him have it for the month at a discount because she's going to India on some damned spiritual pilgrimage or something."

"I could get out of the city for a month. Change of scenery. Paint some beach landscapes."

"You should invite your actress," Keeby said.

"You know what? I just might."

CHAPTER THIRTY-EIGHT

BEAU WAS AT HIS WORKSTATION in The Salle, putting the final touches on a painting, trying to ignore the din outside the studio windows. It was Bastille Day, and Paris had gone wild celebrating the liberation of the prison and the birth of the revolution against the Bourbons thirteen decades earlier. Car horns honked on the boulevard outside, crowds cheered, and firecrackers rattled somewhere in the distance.

Though he had lived in Paris for almost three years, Beau still found it difficult to become excited over the holiday, though he did plan to meet people later in the evening for dinner and, presumably, copious drinking. In the heat of the day, he had decided to steal a few hours to work unmolested in the studio.

He had worked feverishly over the past week, completing his outstanding canvases ahead of his trip to the south of France for August. The high cranked windows in The Salle were wide open, but the air outside was still and sodden, and sweat rolled down Beau's cheek as he slashed paint at the easel with a palette knife.

The courier was beside him before Beau noticed his presence. Beau was startled. He hadn't expected to find anyone working on France's biggest national holiday. Only bad news could warrant sending a messenger on this of all days. Beau's pulse quickened as he thought of his mother and father.

"What is it?" Beau said.

The courier handed him the message. Beau ripped it open. Rimbaud had an urgent matter to discuss with him.

Curious. Rimbaud, while being his father's agent, was French. Of all his acquaintances in Paris, Rimbaud would be most likely to have taken the day off. Instead, he had summoned Beau to his office. Perhaps his father had relented on funding Dieter's film. Relieved that the courier hadn't borne a black-bordered envelope, Beau handed him a franc and told him to inform Rimbaud he would be by shortly.

Beau freshened himself in The Salle's washroom and combed his hair neatly before trotting out the door toward Rimbaud's office.

———

"I...I don't understand," Beau said, his face slack as he sat across from Rimbaud. "Tell me again."

"Your father has been indicted and arrested in the United States," Rimbaud repeated.

"Yeah, yeah. I heard that the first time, but what does it mean?"

"Mr. Shipley has been charged with violating the Volstead Act by smuggling alcohol from the Caribbean."

"But he has connections to protect him from this sort of thing. The mayor. The governor. A senator."

"The United States government is less inclined to look the other way in cases of violation of federal law, compared to the government of South Carolina."

"I need to take care of my mother and sister," Beau said. "Can you help me find quick passage home?"

"Your father's instructions are direct and explicit. You are to remain abroad for the duration."

"The duration of what?"

"Your father was arrested, as I said, but he is not in prison. He has been released for now. There will be a trial. It will be difficult on the family. By remaining in Paris, and never having been employed by your father's business, you are insulated from suspicion. If you return and try to keep the import business afloat, you may be implicated. You would have federal agents looking over your shoulder every waking moment, waiting for you to make a mistake. He's protecting you, Beau."

"I feel awful, cooling my heels over here while he's going through—"

"I'm afraid there's more," Rimbaud interrupted. "Your father's bank accounts in the States have been impounded. He isn't ruined. Your father has been in his particular...ah, line of work for many years, and was careful to maintain sizable accounts in many offshore banks, especially in the Caribbean. However, accessing money at this time is...well, problematic, and will be for the practical future."

"What about my mother and sister?" Beau asked.

"It will be difficult for them as well. The house was paid for before your father was born, and isn't impounded, nor the furnishings or other possessions, so they have a roof over their heads. Arrangements are being made to transfer some funds from an offshore account into a…well, you don't want to know the details. They will be comfortable if they are frugal. In your case, however, I'm afraid the situation is different."

"How do you mean?"

"Your father is an optimist, Beau. He expects to rise above this and prevail. Failing that, he expects you to eventually pick up the pieces of his shattered business and revive it. That has been his plan all along. You can't fulfil his wishes if you have any taint of this smuggling scandal on you. At the moment, you do not. However, your allowance…"

"I see where you're going," Beau said. "I can't be seen taking dirty money. I'm cut off."

"I would not phrase it so strongly," Rimbaud said. "It's more as if the spigot is temporarily clogged, but we have no idea when the plumber will arrive."

"At least I have my accounts here in Paris," Beau said.

"That is another matter. You have accumulated a healthy savings account, but with your current…ah, rate of spending, it would not last long. No more than a year, and we have no idea how long you will be stranded in France. I can turn those accounts into a dependable monthly income to tide you over."

"How?"

"I can purchase a contract to pay an annuity for, say, the next twenty years. It would require me to liquidate your savings."

"It's irrevocable?"

"Unfortunately. You will not be able to recover your savings, but you will have enough to live."

"How much?"

Rimbaud told him. Beau was shocked.

"Well," he said. "I really am a starving artist now."

CHAPTER THIRTY-NINE

BEAU WAS SWAMPED by Bastille Day revelers as he strolled back to his apartment on Rue Montparnasse from his meeting with Alphonse Rimbaud, but he barely noticed all the hoopla. He had far too much on his mind, and no real inclination toward revelry. Two problems loomed immediately.

The first was obvious. The good news was, he wouldn't starve. The money from the annuity Rimbaud would purchase for him would pay his living expenses—barely. On the other hand, his now-limited funds wouldn't leave a great deal for leisure spending. For better or worse, Beau found himself among the legions of working artists in Paris. Whereas he had been afforded the privilege of living the life of a talented dilettante, and to pat himself on the back over the comparative success of The Salle, his artwork so far hadn't brought in a great deal of cash. That needed to change.

There would be no money for Dieter's film, at least in the short term. He'd already handed Dieter one parcel of bad news when Gordon Shipley refused to back the project, but he'd softened the blow by offering to help with some of his savings, under the presumption his allowance would last forever and allow him to rebuild the account rapidly. Now, there was no allowance, and there were no savings, which meant no film, at least for a while. He'd have to take Dieter out and get the German good and drunk before dropping the other shoe.

Then there was the trip to the Cote d'Azur. He'd already promised Prince Grigorii he'd go and had pledged his share of the cost of the villa for the month. It wasn't a fortune, but it was more than he had readily available, and more than he expected to see anytime soon.

He had one thing going for him. He had made a sizable withdrawal from his account several days earlier, before the news of his father's indictment. It was a nice wad of cash, stowed safely in his room at the apartment. He wouldn't suffer financial embarrassment for a few weeks, but he'd have to think more carefully before picking up any checks.

The solution was simple. He was an artist, and he had a collection of completed or nearly completed canvases. He had to sell them. *That's what artists do*, he reasoned. Without poverty staring him in the face, he'd been allowed to concentrate on the creative side of his career. Now it was time to put on his salesman's hat.

———

Beau counted two of Paris's greatest arts patrons among his acquaintances—Misia Sert and Gertrude Stein. The thought of going to Stein's salon, hat in hand, turned his stomach. He still resented the way she had humiliated him years earlier. She had purchased the three paintings, though, and at his asking price.

While Misia Sert had always been direct with him, she had never abused him, so he went to her first.

He found her lounging in her Rue Rivoli apartment after lunch with Coco Chanel. Misa and Coco had been the closest of friends ever since the death of Chanel's lover, Arthur Capel, and were known to spend much of their leisure time together. Beau had met Chanel once or twice in the years he had resided in Paris, usually at one of Misia's society affairs, but they knew one another only by name. Beau made a perfunctory bow to both as he entered the music room, where a young pianist he didn't recognize played nocturnes on the piano.

He would have preferred to speak with Misia alone, but Coco was disinclined to allow them privacy, and Misia did not ask for it. He explained, avoiding as much detail as possible, that after experimenting with his new painting style, he had decided to take the next step and offer the best examples for sale. He had brought along two canvases, including the one he had painted of Nathalie Bel at her breakfast table. It was titled, simply, *Nude with Croissant*, though any untrained eye would be hard pressed to suss out the nude or the croissant in Beau's new abstract expressionist style.

"What do you think?" Misia asked Coco. Coco examined each of the paintings as closely as a half second afforded her.

"They are workmanlike," she said. "I see no great faults, nor any thrilling genius. Very commercial. They should sell, though Mr. Shipley would be ill-served to dream of a hanging in The Louvre. Thank God at least they aren't more of those atrocious Renoir copies you see all over town."

"I agree," Misia said. "I don't believe I am in the market for any of these today, Mr. Shipley, but you do not care who buys your paintings, do you? I'll spread the word that you are eager to part with your children, and you can be located at The Salle."

"I would be greatly appreciative," Beau said, before making his exit.

———

Gertrude Stein welcomed Beau into her salon two hours later. She sat in an overstuffed chair underneath the Picasso portrait and sipped tea as Beau delivered the same spiel he had at Misia Sert's apartment.

"I would love to help," she said when he finished. "But I cannot afford to buy them myself. I recently purchased two of Matisse's works, which leaves me cash-strapped for a month or two."

"My...my situation may be temporary," Beau said. "Several years ago, you said you could make a telephone call and I'd work the next day—"

"You? Painting hotel pictures?" Stein laughed out loud. It was one of the few times he had seen her laugh, and it was mildly disconcerting. "That door is closed and sealed, young Shipley. You made your decision to be an artist, not a craftsman. In this salon, that decision is irrevocable. It's time to sink or swim, and I will help if I can, but I cannot throw you a life preserver in the form of buying your paintings. I will spread the word, however. Have you considered hosting a showing at The Salle? Toss some *hors d'oeuvres* out, open a few bottles of wine, and hang every canvas in the studio. People will come if you lay out a spread."

"I suppose that would be an option," Beau said.

"Don't be discouraged. I'll ask around. Consider the show idea. Maybe I can get you a couple of gallery hangings, but we both know that's all hit or miss. Feed them, and they'll come to you. Fish in a barrel."

CHAPTER FORTY

BEAU FED THEM, and they did not come.

After his meeting with Gertrude Stein, Beau hustled back to The Salle, where everyone but Dieter was present, working on their projects. He called a quick meeting, and they gathered around the platform on which Nathalie Bel had posed. He explained Stein's proposal and asked who had works ready to sell. All but Cesare raised their hands.

They agreed to put on a show and sale of The Salle's cadre of painters a week later. Beau met Alphonse Rimbaud and told him of the plans. The sticking point was money. While The Salle's members were highly talented and productive, none of them had come from wealthy families except Beau, who had absorbed the early costs of establishing the studio. He asked whether Rimbaud could find some money among his father's far-flung bank accounts to pay for the food for the exposition. Beau and the team could take care of the rest—setting display boards for the various artists and sprucing up the studio for visitors. Rimbaud was enthusiastic about the idea, but skeptical about finding money to pay for it. He promised to get back with Beau within twenty-four hours.

Later in the evening, in Nathalie's apartment, Beau began to experience doubt.

"What is it?" she asked, awakened after he rose from bed and paced the floor for the fifth time since midnight.

"I might have bitten off too much," he said, sitting on the side of the bed.

"The show?"

"The show is easy. I've been making lists in my head. Invitations to print and mail—which I'd have to do tomorrow if they are to arrive in time. And if Rimbaud can't come up with money for the *hors d'oeuvres*, we're truly sunk."

"You're trying to solve too many problems at once. Of course you're overwhelmed. Focus on what you can do tomorrow." She glanced at the clock next to the bed. "Today, that is. And you don't need formal invitations. Word of mouth works so much faster and cheaper. You should spend tomorrow visiting galleries all over the city with flyers about the show. Let them tell their customers about it."

"All I have to do is print the flyers."

Nathalie tossed the sheets aside, padded naked across the small studio apartment, and took a pad and pencil from the table next to the window. She sat on the chair and crossed her perfect legs.

"What do you want the flyer to say?" she asked.

"We can do this in the morning," he said.

"In the morning, I get them printed. By mid-morning, you should be wearing out shoe leather visiting galleries."

"You can get them printed?"

"I have access to a press. The owner owes me a favor. So tell me when the show is to be held."

"The twenty-third."

"All day?"

"Let's say all afternoon into the evening. Oh, hell. We'll need wine, too."

"I can help with wine."

"A vintner owes you a favor as well?" Beau asked.

"No questions. We promised, remember?"

And, indeed, they had promised. Their first night together, Nathalie had sensed Beau was tortured by events in his past, either in the war or in Charleston, and he wasn't interested in discussing them. Nathalie preferred to maintain personal privacy as well, so they came to an arrangement in which neither of them were compelled to reveal their pasts to the other.

"What about the food?" Beau said.

"We have already exceeded our quota for problems to solve today. We'll work on the food tomorrow. Give me the names of the artists on display."

Beau recited the names of The Salle's painters.

"You do plan to sell your paintings, right?" Nathalie asked. "After all, the immediate problem is your own finances, is it not?"

Beau had forgotten to include his own name. "I must be exhausted."

"Let's go back to bed. I have to wake early to print the flyers."

She trotted back around the bed to her side and slid between the covers. He fell in beside her.

"I owe you for this," he said.

"Yes," she said. "You do."

The food issue solved itself. Cesare knew a culinary student at Le Cordon Bleu who planned to go into the catering business on graduation and jumped at the opportunity to prepare the various platters for the showing. All The Salle had to do was provide the money for the groceries, which, as it turned out, weren't as expensive as Beau had expected. Since he wasn't showing his own paintings, Cesare volunteered to tend the bar.

Nathalie arrived at The Salle with a box full of flyers around ten the next morning.

"That was quick," Beau said. "And they look beautiful."

"They should. They cost me a favor," Nathalie said.

"Now I owe you instead."

"And what do you have of value, poor starving artist boy?"

"Want a painting? I'm lousy with them."

"I might take one at that."

"Don't hang it on the same wall as your Picasso. I'm kind of sensitive about that. Want to ride around town? Dieter loaned me his Renault, so I don't have to hoof it."

She kissed him on the lips and wiped away the lipstick with her thumb. "Alas, I am filming this afternoon. It's my last day. Perhaps I can meet you for dinner, say around eight?"

"I'll be done by then. Let's meet at the café across from my apartment. I can introduce you to my roommate."

"Do you find my bed so uncomfortable?"

"I find your bed a good distance from my bed. I've remodeled my place. I'd like to show it off."

"If you insist. Give me the address."

"Twenty-two Rue Montparnasse."

For a second, he thought he had said something wrong. A worried look crossed her face, but it disappeared as quickly. Nathalie, if nothing else, was a master at controlling her emotions. Even a great shock would barely faze her.

"How curious," she said. "I knew someone who lived there once. Third floor."

"We're on the fifth. A two-bedroom with a private bath."

Nathalie relaxed and placed her hands on Beau's shoulders. "Paris is a city where a hundred coincidences can coexist at once. I know exactly where you live, and I'm familiar with the café. We'll meet there at eight tonight."

———

Paris was a cultural adjustment for Beau in many ways, but one of the things that surprised him most on his return in 1919 had been the sheer volume of motorcars in the streets and boulevards. Automobiles were common enough in Charleston, but not ubiquitous. Sometimes it seemed as if every Parisian owned a car, and they had all decided to go for a spin simultaneously.

Traffic snarled his path all day long as he drove from gallery to gallery, distributing the flyers. The owners were mostly enthusiastic and willing to spread the word, which made the work easier. He had feared he might walk headlong into opposition or professional rivalry. He was reassured by the reception he received throughout the day, and slowly harbored some faint hope he might pull the entire deal off. When he dropped a flyer by Gertrude Stein's salon at 27 Rue du Fleurus, she scanned it and smiled, thanking him for making her day.

He parked Dieter's car in the small gravel lot behind The Salle shortly after seven o'clock, which left him less than an hour to dash back over the bridge to Montparnasse, wash the road dust off and change clothes, and meet Nathalie at the café across the street.

Keeby wasn't in the apartment when Beau arrived. Beau scribbled a note asking his roommate to join him in the café when he arrived home. He washed, changed clothes, and was at a table in the café two minutes before eight, only slightly winded by the exertion.

Nathalie arrived minutes later, carrying a shopping bag. It was summer in Paris, and she had dressed lightly in silk and cotton, a white dress that ended daringly close to her knees, and a royal blue jacket. She wore a smart beret in the same blue, which had become the fashion in the Paris, slowly replacing the cloche hat for women. He stood as she approached, air-kissed her on both cheeks to prevent smearing her immaculate lipstick, and held her chair as she sat.

"The bag?" Beau asked.

"I bought a new outfit for the showing. You did want me to host, didn't you?"

"It was the first item checked off my list. I...I really do owe you. You've been terrific with this show. I couldn't have made it happen without you."

"Certainly not as quickly. Will your roommate join us?"

"He wasn't in when I left. I wrote him a note."

They ordered wine and bread and asked the server for the dinner menus. The café's culinary range was limited, but all the selections within it were excellent. Beau asked the server to bring a charcuterie board as well, and some olive oil for the bread. The server briefly sneered at the olive oil notion but had long since adjusted to the outlandish behaviors among the new crowd in Paris since the war, and immediately forced his mouth into a smile, congratulating Beau on his excellent selection.

The sidewalks were crowded with summer evening strollers on their way to dinner or a show, or simply enjoying the cooling breeze as the sun settled over the trees of the Montparnasse. They ranged from old-school Parisians dressed in fancy wardrobe and reeking of perfume and ancient money; to Bohemian young lions from Vienna or Chicago or Berlin choking the sidewalk wearing clothes passed through two or three previous owners, slipping a bottle back and forth and singing bawdy songs filled with double entendres; to romantic young couples starting out in life, still cocooned in the undeniable delusion that dominates the first blossom of infatuation. Dining *al fresco* at a sidewalk café in the City of Lights was like strolling through a constantly evolving human zoo.

They sampled the variety on the charcuterie plate and talked about the show, until Beau drained his wine glass.

"We might as well order a bottle," he said. "Might be splitting it three ways, and even if it does end with only you and me, we weren't planning to travel far anyway."

He pointed at the apartment building with his chin.

"Good thing I packed a toothbrush," Nathalie said.

"That's all you packed?"

"What else will we need? Do you fancy a Bordeaux?"

Beau raised his hand to get the server's attention as Keeby rounded the corner, walking with his head and shoulders hunched. Beau recognized it as his deliberative posture, the stance he took when he was struggling with a plot point or a tricky exchange of dialogue and walking the streets of Paris in deliberation was infinitely preferable to staring at a blank sheet of paper.

"Keeby!" Beau called out. He turned to Nathalie. "That's my roommate."

"*Mon Dieu,*" Nathalie exhaled, slightly louder than a whisper. "Oh, *merde.*"

Her face frightened him. "Nathalie? What's the matter?"

She looked past him at Keeby's face, who gazed back at her the way a Doberman watches a ceiling fan, his head cocked to one side, his eyes registering disbelief.

Beau turned to him and saw the expression as well, and he was confused.

"Uh," he said. "Keeby Styles, this is my...well, my..." There was no polite word in his vocabulary to accurately describe what he and Nathalie were to one another.

Nathalie saved him. She stood and held out her hands. "Hello, again, Keeby," she said, and kissed him on both cheeks as composed as if she encountered this situation every day.

"You know each other?" Beau asked.

Keeby ignored Beau and looked into Nathalie's eyes. He took her hand and kissed it in the chivalric style. "*Savoir faire?*" he said.

"*Savoir faire,*" she repeated. They both turned to Beau, who was more confused than ever.

299

"Well," Keeby said as he escorted Nathalie back to her seat. "This promises to be an incredibly awkward evening."

"I ordered a bottle of wine," Beau said.

"Order two," Keeby replied.

"I feel like I walked in on the second act of a play here," Beau said.

"A French bedroom farce, perhaps?" Keeby asked.

The waiter returned with the bottle. Beau held up three fingers, pointing to the two glasses. The waiter sneered again—he appeared to enjoy sneering—and turned about face.

"Short version?" Keeby said. "Natalie and I...um, dated a few years back, while you were in Charleston. We drifted apart quite suddenly."

"Oh, now you are being poetic," Nathalie said, barely concealing her amusement.

She's enjoying the situation, Beau thought.

"Like I said, it was years ago," Keeby continued. "It was fun, and I enjoy the memories, but there have been others since. Tell me, Nat, are you still a socialist?"

"A socialist?" Beau asked.

"You always got it wrong," Nathalie said, pulling a cigarette from her clutch. Beau reached into his jacket pocket, but Keeby whipped out his matches and lit it as she said, "I am a pragmatist. Socialism was a means to an end in a previous decade. I have evolved since. I'm an actress now."

"And a model," Beau said. "Don't forget."

"She was a model three years ago," Keeby said.

"And a socialist," Beau added.

"We've moved on, buddy," Keeby said. "Try to keep pace."

"I read your book," she said.

"Thank you. Not many people did. And in English, yet."

"What a shame it was not popular enough to be printed in French," Nathalie teased.

"Ouch. You're an actress? Want to star in the movie we're making of it?"

The waiter returned with the bottle and another glass for Keeby.

"Could you make it two bottles?" Beau asked.

The waiter held up the bottle, pointing to it.

"Yes," Beau said. "Two bottles, though."

"Oui, Monsieur," the waiter said. "I was concerned you might decide in the fullness of time you would prefer a red and a white, and I wanted to save myself yet another trip to the cellar."

"Sounds like a personal problem to me, Pierre," Keeby said.

Pierre bristled for a second but couldn't hold it any longer and giggled. "I am sorry, Monsieur Keeby. You win again. I will return with two bottles." He held up a V with his fingers.

"Little game we play," Keeby said, after Pierre hustled off. "He lives to taunt Americans, but he enjoys himself so much he can't keep a straight face. The longer he holds out, the better I tip him. So—" He turned back to Nathalie. "You were telling me how much you loved my novel."

She blew a cloud of cigarette smoke toward the awning over their heads, where a fog had already accumulated from all the smokers in the café. "I *wanted* to love it. Does that count?"

"Did you pay for the book?"

"Of course."

"It counts. I don't do this for adoration, you know."

"I know. I always found cynicism one of your most endearing traits."

Beau said, "And, on that note, I believe we should be drinking. Would anyone like to split the chicken?"

Keeby said to Nathalie, "*Savoir faire?*"

"He did much better than I expected," she said. She raised her glass. "*To savoir faire.*"

"You are being terribly civilized about all this," Keeby said to Beau.

"It's Paris," Beau said. "What else is there to say? Besides—and please forgive me for being indiscreet, Nathalie—you aren't the first woman we've both dated at one point or another. Once I was over the surprise, I found it humorous."

"Hey, Nat," Keeby said. "Do you have any money?"

"Why do you ask?"

"You know Prince Grigorii? He's hosting a bunch of us at a villa on the Mediterranean, but we have to pay our cut. Interested in getting out of the city for August?"

"August on the Cote d'Azur?" Nathalie asked. "Sounds delightful."

"It will be a working holiday," Beau said. "I'll be painting, and I'm sure Keeby will work on his next book. What's it about, Keeb?"

A shadow passed across Keeby's face. "I, um, I'm toying with several ideas," he said. "Still not sure which direction I want to take."

"Well, no doubt you'll be inspired by the crystal waters of the Med and spend every waking hour scribbling away on your notepads. So we'll be working a lot, but we'll also relax.

The point of getting away in August is to relax. It's a vacation, after all."

"I can model," Nathalie said. "But Beau is right. More than anything else, I wish to relax and read and drink every bottle of wine in the south of France and make love three times a day. If there is room, count me in."

Beau refreshed their glasses, and simultaneously calculated how many paintings he needed to sell if he had any chance of seeing the Cote d'Azur himself.

———

Beau had made a singular fatal miscalculation.

The morning of July twenty-third dawned with clear skies and fair temperatures, considering it was Paris in the dead of summer. Everything was ready. Beau arrived at The Salle before eleven in the morning. Cesare's chef friend prepared trays of *hors d'oeuvres,* and Cesare himself stood at a makeshift bar in the corner, looking properly servile in a brocade vest and black tie, ready to pour wine for the showing guests.

Each artist had prepared a display in front of his divided workspace. They were all dressed in new spotless white work jackets, ready to answer questions from any interested patrons.

In a just world, it should have been a huge success. But this was Paris, the ficklest of cities, where dreams often throw themselves into the muddy Seine out of frustration and seemingly overwhelming fate.

In another part of the city, Belgian rider Fermin Lambot, who wore the yellow jersey but had never won a single stage, led the field furiously from Dunkirk into Paris and circled the Arc de Triomph to seize victory in the Tour de France. Enormous throngs of French citizens lined the streets and sidewalks and hung from streetlights and precarious tree limbs to watch the spectacle of the amazing athletes who had left Paris exactly four weeks earlier and had raced over three thousand miles around the perimeter of France to return. Many among the masses of spectators may have received flyers inviting them to attend The Salle's showing. On this day, the final stage of the Tour de France was a bigger draw, nearly emptying the outer arrondisements.

Beau was unconcerned when they had received only two or three casual strollers by one in the afternoon. The French were notoriously relaxed when it came to punctuality. Being fashionably late was an expectation.

By two in the afternoon, doubt took station on his shoulder and began to whisper in his ear. He stepped to the front door, where Nathalie had positioned herself to greet visitors. The dress she had purchased for the event was stunning, an emerald and jade green beaded affair with a peacock chevron that started at her shoulders and converged at the same point where her legs converged. She'd accented it with an inconceivably long string of pearls that drooped almost to her thighs, and a beautiful green silk headband adorned with a peacock feather matched to the chevron on her dress. She had been waiting patiently at the door for patrons to arrive and to provide them with a tour of The Salle.

"What in hell is going on?" he asked, quietly enough so the others couldn't hear.

"We should be patient," she advised.

By four o'clock, Beau knew the awful truth. The Salle's showing was a failure.

At five o'clock, he discovered why, when clusters of pedestrians trickled back into Le Marais, having walked the Champs Elysees and through the Tuileries and the Montorguiel. Within minutes, the clusters of revelers turned into a parade. When he saw the flags waving over their heads, Beau had a heartbreaking revelation.

"Oh my God," he said. "The race. I forgot about it."

All the artists looked stricken, as they had forgotten as well. Nathalie stood at the door, her hand over her mouth, her sympathy for Beau a palpable thing. Beau crossed to the bar and told Cesare to open several bottles of wine and to keep the corkscrew handy.

"My compatriots!" Beau said, hefting a glass. "We are undone by bad luck, poor timing, and the pathetic fact that none of us are bicycling fans. But what the fuck? There's food and drink. Tomorrow we may live on the streets, but tonight we feast!"

The inertia of shock slowed them, but within minutes all the artists embraced the fatalistic momentum in the room. They filled glasses with delicious wine and gobbled at the food platters and got ungodly drunk and told awful jokes that were little more than gallows humor and imagined what fish market they'd work at next week. Their fondly anticipated showing had become a suicide party. Each of them feared The Salle had parked a bullet in its brain. None of them had money, least of all their previous primary benefactor Beau. All of them had contributed to the pot to pay for the showing, and now they were eating and drinking their investment. Not one of them had made the first sale all day.

Beau sat in the stairwell with a plate of food and a full glass of wine and stared at the wall, trying to figure out what to do next. Inside The Salle, the French artists had discovered a Belgian had won the Tour de France. Despite having little interest in the race itself, they were fervent French nationalists, insulted that a Belgian had won *their* race, and were making inebriated plans to invade Brussels. One of them launched into a wildly off-key rendition of *Le Marseillaise*, and the others joined in. Glass broke somewhere. Beau thought he should do something about it, then decided it wasn't his problem until he made it his problem, and he had enough problems for one day.

Nathalie appeared at the top of the stairwell. Beau looked up when her shadow fell across his face. She held a half-full glass in one hand and a bottle in the other.

"Have a seat," Beau said.

Nathalie shook her head. "In this dress? On the stairs? *Non.*" She leaned against the handrail a couple of steps down instead and faced him. "What will you do now?"

"Beats the hell out of me," Beau said. "I'm running out of options."

"I'm so sorry."

"Oh, I'll get by. I have enough coming in to put a roof over my head and food on the table and to pay for my share of The Salle, but only barely. I'm stuck in Paris, though. I can't go home until my father's trial is over, and maybe not even then. Selling my paintings today was supposed to pay for some of the extras, like Dieter's film and the trip to the Med next month. I suppose I'll be in the city this August."

"The south of France is *so* overrated," she said, and he couldn't help smiling. "Think how easy it will be to get a good table."

"But how will I pay for the meal?" Beau mimed breaking a stick. "*Casse.*"

"How do you feel about washing dishes? I mean, a *lot* of dishes?"

He chuckled. "You're cheering me up. Keep doing it."

"Have you considered going Prince Grigorii's route?"

"Become a gigolo?"

"If he's away at the coast for the month, the field is wide open."

"I lack a title."

"You're a southern American gentleman from a wealthy family. Most people in Paris think everyone lives on a plantation where you come from. It's a romantic notion. It's almost as good. And your father is under indictment as an American gangster, which makes you dangerously attractive. Your backstory alone will open half the dowager legs in Paris."

"You're serious."

"Show me a woman who hasn't slept with a man to get something she wanted, and I'll show you a virgin. You're a cute boy, Beau, and terribly sweet, but you have seen so little of the world. I suspect you have even seen little of *your* world. You sneer at Prince Grigorii. You believe he has debased himself."

"Hasn't he?"

"Imagine what it is to be Grigorii Yurievitch Romanov. Born to nobility. Educated in the finest schools. Deferred to by commoners. He lived a life of privilege and wealth. He could go where he pleased and do what he wanted and if anybody fucked with him, they would answer to the Tsar. Then, while he was abroad, a band of thugs took possession of his country and placed him on a list of people to toss against a wall."

"I read Keeby's book."

"You cannot go home right now? He can *never* go home. He can never see his family again. Most of them are dead or withering away in Siberia. Every possession he ever had was ripped from him, and he has no Alphonse Rimbaud to whom he can turn in Paris. You are not so different, but you look down on Prince Grigorii because he has found a way to live the only life he knows? And don't forget how *we* met. Do you think less of me because I take off my clothes so boy artists can draw my *petit chat?* Grow up, Beau. Sometimes life is all about the least worst choice."

"How serious was it between you and Keeby?" Beau asked.

"I will presume the wine is asking, and I will save you future embarrassment by forgetting it asked. We said no questions, remember?"

"Did he tell you how I saved his life?"

"I know about his scars. He told me his friend carried him to the aid station after a shell exploded in the trenches."

"I was the friend. Carry a guy a few hundred yards under bombardment after a bullet bounces off your pan, and you grow attached to him. He wasn't happy to see you the other night. How badly did you hurt him?"

She drained her glass and refilled it. "Badly enough, I suppose."

"Are you going to hurt me the same way?"

"Given the opportunity, history suggests it is my nature."

"Thanks for the warning. Why did you hurt him?"

"He developed domestic inclinations. That is a hard line for me. I am happy to share my bed, but in the end, it is *my* bed. The same goes for my flat, my body, and my life."

"Dieter was right. He said no man would ever possess you."

"Why would any person want to possess another? One life is plenty to manage. Allow me to give you the short version. I like you. I enjoy being around you. I have a good time with you in bed. But do not love me, Beau. If you do, I will find your weakest point and destroy you with it. Keep it fun and casual, and I won't feel cornered. I only strike when I'm cornered."

"I want to be alone tonight," Beau said.

"We agree on something. But tomorrow night may be different."

"Time will tell."

"I will go home now. You know my telephone exchange."

"Yes," Beau said. "I do."

CHAPTER FORTY-ONE

LONG AFTER NATHALIE LEFT, and long after the shadows turned to darkness outside, and after Cesare threatened the other artists with a grisly death if they didn't collect all the mess, and after the mess was collected and disposed and all the artists had disappeared into an uncertain future, Beau cut the lights—reminding him the electricity bill would be due soon—and retreated to his workstation with the last bottle of wine and a glass. He switched on a small, green-shaded desk lamp, sat in the oak swivel chair, and poured another glass. He tried to remember how many he had already imbibed. The fact he couldn't recall suggested he had already drunk too much. He decided to mull it over with another glass.

He had been naïve to believe he had any future as a serious artist. Maybe he should have taken Gertrude Stein's first offer and gone to work in a production studio, happily glopping paint onto canvases for a weekly wage, recreating impressionist street scene after boring impressionist street scene. At least he would be paid for his work.

Footsteps echoed on the stairwell. Beau ignored them. His was the only illuminated station, and easy enough to find. The way his life had gone recently, it was probably some critic come to assassinate him for being an insult to the art world. *Bring them on*, he thought. *Being bludgeoned to death doesn't sound at all bad right now.*

Dieter manifested out of the studio darkness at the door to Beau's workstation.

"We forgot about the Tour de France," he said.

"No shit," Beau said. "You figured that out?"

"I am so sorry, Beau. I can only imagine what a disappointment this is."

"Grab a glass."

Dieter reappeared seconds later with a glass, and Beau filled it before hoisting his own glass. "To glorious failure."

Dieter and Beau drank a lot quickly and Beau emptied the bottle.

"That's it," he said. "The last bottle. Each of the boys took some home, and we drank the rest."

"What will you do?" Dieter asked.

"Looks like I'll take a pass on the trip in August. I hate to miss the coast, but I can work as easily here. Keep trying to sell some stuff. It'll give me time to make some hard decisions. I'm sorry as I can be about the movie, Dieter."

"That is life," Dieter said. "One kick in the nuts after another." They both laughed, Beau so hard his ribs hurt. "Besides, I may have found a solution. The picture I am working as cameraman is produced by a serious studio. Big money operation. They go through film like it is free. Shooting a movie always produces waste. The unused film can be spliced together and sold cheaply in reels. They are called short ends, and the studio is practically giving them away. I believe I can obtain enough stock to shoot the movie while we are in the Riviera."

"The book took place in Russia and Poland," Beau reminded him.

"It is in a forest. They have trees on the Cote d'Azur. There are farms there as well. In fact, we can use the villa as a stand-in for both the farm *and* the dacha from which the hero escapes. It is motion pictures, my friend. Lighting and angles and set dressing and point of view. Nothing is what it pretends to be."

"How much for the short ends?"

Dieter told him.

"Still more than I can put together," Beau said. "I'm on rations for the duration. How much does Prince Grigorii want to play the fictitious vision of himself?"

"We came to an arrangement," Dieter said. He blushed enough for Beau to get the idea.

"The man is nothing if not versatile," Beau said.

"I am thinking about casting Nathalie Bel as the farm girl."

"It's your movie."

"Is there a problem?" Dieter asked.

"With putting her in the film? Be my guest. I have no hold on her at all. Nobody does. Trying to rein her in is like hugging smoke."

Dieter drained his glass and placed a hand on Beau's shoulder. "Find a way to come to the coast," he said. "We would miss you." He squeezed once and walked back out into the darkness.

———

An hour later, exhausted from racking his brain and rendered nearly cross-eyed by the wine, Beau finally locked the door to The Salle—he dearly hoped not for the last time—and ventured out into the streets. He crossed the Seine at the Pont Marie, pausing for the briefest moment to consider throwing himself in, and then strolled with only the occasional misstep toward the Rue Montparnasse.

It was deep into the night. The streets were empty. The ubiquitous motor traffic had stilled for a few precious hours of silence. Most windows were dark. Beau imagined hundreds, maybe thousands of people sleeping soundly in their beds as he shambled by. He wondered how many were still awake, how many hundreds of couples he passed were making love mere feet away, and he felt a brief ache for Nathalie and a little ashamed of the way he had behaved toward her. If she wanted to know his greatest weakness, she'd learn it soon enough, because she brought out the worst in him.

A fog rolled in off the river, blanketing the streets and creating wreath-like halos around the streetlights. Beau walked for blocks without seeing another soul, wending through the mist which muffled sounds as effectively as if he had wrapped his head in a woolen scarf. In the distance, two cats fought in the night, yowls of pain and fury breaking the silence. As quickly as it rose, the battle ended, and Beau was again wrapped in a quiet dense fog.

He turned onto Rue Montparnasse, a block from his apartment building, when a late model Peugeot cabriolet careened around the corner, twin cones of yellow headlights piercing the mist. The tires skittered as they lost rear traction on the dampened cobbles, and the car spun into a streetlight post. It rocked on the springs and rolled onto its convertible top, which collapsed under the weight of the undercarriage. It happened in only seconds, thirty yards away, but even through the pea soup Beau couldn't imagine anyone might survive it.

Remarkably, the accident had taken place nearly unnoticed. No lights appeared in the windows of the apartments nearby. No people streamed from doorways to help any possible survivors. The car lay upside down, half on the sidewalk and half off, smoke and steam rising from the ruined hood, the front wheels still spinning silently.

Beau stumbled to the car and knelt beside the crumpled and torn coachwork to see if he could help. It looked as if there were two people inside. A woman was closest to him. She was in her forties, with the sort of red hair no human is born with, her face painted with kohl and rouge. She wore an expensive dress and a feathered turban that had fallen off during the wreck and now lay under her head like a pillow. Her neck was twisted at an improbable angle, her eyes wide open, the pupils dilated all the way to the perimeter of the irises. She wore a diamond choker and a long string of pearls, with a jewel-encrusted bracelet and four exquisite diamond rings. The car looked as if it had been bought only that afternoon, and it was an expensive model. In the faulty spill of light from the overhead streetlamps, Beau could see the man on the other side of the car, pinned to the gutter under the wooden steering wheel. He was dressed in evening clothes, the expensive kind you can't buy off the rack. He looked older, perhaps in his late fifties or early sixties, with a full head of hair now streaked with blood and street grime.

He lay on his back, his head resting on the concrete as if he were merely taking a catnap.

They were affluent. They looked as if they might have attended a night at the opera followed by a late supper at Maxim's and maybe dancing until almost dawn, and they capped off the night by joining the Choir Eternal.

For years to come, Beau would beg sleep to take him as he stared at the ceiling, trying to understand why he didn't run for help. He rationalized it, saying his reason was impaired by the massive amount of alcohol he had drunk. It loosed his basest instincts, made him act out of character. In any case, who could he call at the darkest hour of the night? Who could do anything useful? The people were already dead. They were destined for crypts or urns. They had no need for ambulances or hospitals or surgeons or—well, anything.

He saw the future of the two unfortunates on the ground, and he saw his own, and he acted without allowing his conscience to intervene, at an enormous price.

As he removed the jeweled bracelet from the dead woman's wrist and stuffed it in his jacket pocket, Beau reminded himself it was no use to her anymore. *You can't take it with you,* he whispered as he slipped each of the rings off her fingers. Removing the choker proved to be particularly grisly, and he ghoulishly slipped the pearls over her obscenely cocked head, but he reminded himself she would never know they were gone, along with her diamond earrings. The diamond brooch was a cinch, because by that point he had become adept at grave-robbing.

He crossed to the other side of the car and reached around the steering wheel into the man's jacket pocket for his wallet, which he found stuffed with bills. After stowing the bills in his jacket and returning the wallet, he removed the man's watch as well. He left the gold wedding ring on the man's left hand, as he had with the woman. He had enough presence of mind to know if he stole the wedding rings, the future punishment he would rain on himself would make the darkest circle of hell an attractive leisure destination.

There was nothing left to take. He whispered apologies to the couple for the tenth or twelfth time and made off into the fog toward his apartment.

The man's head rolled to one side, and his eyes opened in time to see Beau's legs retreat into the mist. He sighed, and he closed his eyes again, laboring to breathe under the weight of the steering wheel nearly crushing his chest, saved from certain death by the gutter in which he lay. He didn't wake again when headlights fell across his face, or when a car parked next to the overturned Peugeot, or when the fire brigade and the ambulance arrived. He didn't wake again for several days.

When he did wake, he remembered.

CHAPTER FORTY-TWO

BEAU WOKE THE NEXT MORNING to a thunderclap inside his head, Bacchus collecting his tribute for the night before. He was on the floor, half inside and half outside his room, naked. He was face-down in a pool of saliva, and when he rolled over his head exploded again and he closed his eyes tight to ward off the throbbing pain. Trying to keep his balance as the apartment spun around him, he crawled to the bathroom, vomited into the toilet, and dashed cold water on his face. He soaked a hand towel and lay on his back on the floor, breathing through the sodden towel to moisten his enraged membranes. He needed aspirin, but the empty tin of Bayer had been in the trash since his last bender, and the chemist was too far to crawl.

He thought at first he might have contracted the dregs of the Spanish influenza and chuckled wryly at the irony he might succumb to a virus after all the other close calls he had survived. He winced as he caught a whiff of the odor rising from his body and he remembered the drinking. The other memories flooded back, and he remembered why he had drunk so much, and he remembered—

He flung the hand towel into the sink and stumbled back to his bedroom. His suit from the night before was tossed carelessly into the corner, and for an instant Beau was proud he'd had the presence of mind not to pass out in it. He grabbed the trousers and immediately felt the lumps in the pockets. He drew out jeweled earrings and a diamond bracelet. The morning sun streaming through the window caught the bracelet and projected rainbowed refractions against the wall. The watch and a wad of cash in his jacket pocket confirmed it. It hadn't been a dream.

He had only a fractured recollection of stumbling to his building, lurching upstairs to his room and stripping off his clothes before falling over and passing out in the doorway. He'd snored through the commotion on the Rue Montparnasse as the fire brigade and an ambulance and a dozen gendarmes swarmed the accident scene, and when a truck pulled the Peugeot back over onto its wheels and towed it away. By the time Beau's hangover blew him out of the middle of a pleasant dream and back into his bizarre, horrific reality, the only remnants of the accident the night before were a few shards of glass in the gutter and the gut-wrenching guilt Beau harbored over playing the ghoul.

Beau checked through his window. It looked like any other morning in the Rive Gauche. Patrons sat at the café across the street and drank morning coffee and nibbled on pastries from the patisserie next door. They had no idea, not even a clue, that two people had died in an instant only yards away from their breakfast tables, mere hours earlier. Beau envied them and their appetites and their ignorance. It was possible he would never be hungry again.

The door to Keeby's room was open, and his bed was made. He hadn't come home the night before. That was convenient.

Beau returned to his room and fished through all his pockets again, laying the contents on his bedspread. There was a lot of sparkle there. The watch was a Bell and Ross, terribly expensive but common enough among the wealthy that it wouldn't be lonely in almost any pawnshop case, and he disappointed himself with his relief when he discovered it had not been engraved. He checked all the jewelry, especially the inside of the rings. No engravings anywhere. That was good.

He returned to the bathroom and splashed water in his face and soaked his hair, trying to clear his head. He was thinking like a thief, and it scared the hell out of him. The last thing he had stolen was a pack of Faggot Donnie's cigarettes in the trenches of the Meuse-Argonne, almost five years earlier, and Donnie was dead by then as well. Before that, maybe some candy at the apothecary in Charleston when he was a kid. He had no genetic faculty for larceny. It wasn't in his nature. He'd never had the need to steal, which had made it easy for him to adopt the moral position that pilfering was wrong under every circumstance. That he had stooped to it sickened him.

Taking the jewelry and the money had been a poorly conceived impulse. He'd known it was wrong even as he pried the rings off the woman's limp, lifeless fingers. He'd told himself he'd regret this act of disrespect for the rest of his days. The alcohol and his desperate circumstances told him to ram it, and now he had a bedspread covered with baubles he couldn't explain, and no clue in the world what to do with them.

Lacking both criminal personality and experience, he found the entire problem overwhelming. His brain was still drying out from his fatalistic revels the night before. Rational deliberation would have to wait. He stuffed all the jewels and bills into a sock, hid the bundle in the back of his underwear drawer, vomited again on general principles, and slid between the sheets for a few hours of real sleep.

————

Though her primary residence was in London, Lady Bish Twinings kept a small *pied a terre* in the First Arrondissement to live in when visiting the city. It wasn't far from Keeby and Beau's first apartment in the Montorguiel. During a period of especially conspiratorial intimacy between them, Bish had slipped Keeby a key and had told him he could use the place any time he needed to get away from his roommate for a night. She also preferred he not abuse the privilege, which Keeby was most likely doing with Monique, the actress he had met at a post-Tour de France party on the Rue Rivoli.

It had started as a simple pickup. Keeby noticed Monique from across the room at about the instant she spotted him. They met in the center, dodging two or three conversations en route. She was small, almost tiny, not an inch over five feet, and appeared to be in her late thirties, which—having squired Bish around Paris for a couple of years—Keeby didn't mind at all. Her hair was short and blonde, her eyes emerald. Keeby had never seen eyes her shade, the iris almost uniform in color.

"Caleb Styles," he said, taking her hand. "Most folks call me Keeby."

"Who doesn't call you Keeby?" Her voice was surprisingly deep and resonant for her size.

"Mostly my mom."

"Monique Rothe," she said. "One of us is trying to pick up the other."

"Let's grab a drink at the bar and figure out which is which," Keeby said. "Rothe. French?"

"Austrian. You are American?"

"Sometimes."

He ordered their drinks and pointed toward a couch in a relatively quiet corner of the apartment. They retreated to it so they could talk.

"Canadian by birth, raised in the States," Keeby said. "College, the war, writer, correspondent, temporarily failed novelist, single. There. My autobiography."

"You are young," she said. "There is still time to grow a life. Austrian, through and through. Austrian mother. Austrian father. Austrian ancestors in every churchyard in Salzburg dating back as far as you can read the stones. Widow. Actress."

"Widow?"

"Fucking war, right? He died at Meuse-Argonne."

"I was there," he said.

"Don't tell me about it. I already have horrid nightmares about how he died. I don't need details. I hope you didn't shoot him."

"I never shot anyone. He might have killed a couple of friends of mine, though."

"Unlikely. He was in a rear position, clerking for a colonel."

"So, that's not hanging between us. Actress? A lot of those in Paris right now. Are you working?"

She searched his eyes for artifice or guile, and slowly a smile formed at the corners of her mouth.

"What?" he asked.

"Yeah, Keeby. I'm working. A play. We're dark tonight, of course, because the end of the Tour is almost a national holiday. Who would come out to a play tonight?"

"The opera's on tonight."

"Dueling institutions," Monique said. "The unstoppable force meets the immovable object."

"What's the play about?" Keeby asked.

"It's a tragedy with comic overtones. About a thief who falls in love."

"Falling in love is tragic?"

"It is for the woman who loves him. From the moment they meet, she is as doomed as he. Their fates are melded by their intertwined souls."

"Sounds kind of ham-handed to me," Keeby said.

"Oh, it's utter sentimental crap. But it sells a lot of tickets."

"So young, and yet so jaded," Keeby said.

"Not so young," she said. "Lie to me some more. Tell me about your failed novel."

They finished their glasses and two or three more, until their conversation turned into loose associations and meandering blather and veiled innuendo. Monique laughed at something Keeby said that wasn't funny at all, and she zeroed in on his eyes, raised herself from the couch and pressed her lips against his. He wasn't surprised. He'd expected it for several minutes and was ready and accepting when she pounced.

She was acting, playing the role of the seductress. It was painfully obvious, the way she nibbled at his lower lip as if chewing the scenery. *Well, what the hell*, he thought.

"Sure," he said. "Why not?"

"Why not what?"

"You were about to ask if I want to get out of here. Do you know any of these people?"

She made a quick scan of the room. "Not a soul. Where in hell are we anyway? Let's blow this joint."

They hit the sidewalk laughing. It was a warm night, a lowering cloud layer holding in most of the heat and humidity of the day. In the distance, heat lightning glowed every several seconds.

"You really don't know, do you?" she asked, as she snaked her arm inside his.

"Entire encyclopedias are written about stuff I really don't know. Can you narrow it down?"

"It doesn't matter. Would you like to see the play? I can get you a ticket."

"A trustworthy review says it's utter sentimental crap."

"Damn. Good memory."

"I remember stuff. This is the part where I warn you anything you say and do can wind up in a novel someday."

"But it will be a failed novel, so I needn't fear."

"Ouch."

"You mine your memories for stories?"

"I mine other people's memories. I collect stories, Madame Rothe. I retell them."

"Oh, God. *Madame?* Call me Monique, or this may be a short evening."

"Speaking of short," he said, looking down on her. "How do people see you onstage?"

"You'd be surprised. Most actors are short as well. I can stand closer to the audience. There are tricks. And there are advantages to being small."

"Dare I ask?" Keeby said.

"Portability, for one."

"Now you've piqued my curiosity."

"Call me *Madame* one more time, and you'll never satisfy it."

They were dozens of blocks from Rue Montparnasse, and on the wrong side of the river. Taking Monique to his apartment meant dealing with Beau and privacy. Bish's *pied a terre* was nearby, and she was in Scotland, inspecting kilts or eating haggis or whatnot for the summer. He had a key. He knew the bar was stocked. This might constitute abusing his privilege and he thought hard about it for the four or five seconds it took to throw caution entirely to the winds. Scotland was half of France, a channel, and an entire other country away. Even if Bish started out that second, it would take her a day and a half to arrive. He'd have the sheets cleaned and back on the bed by Tuesday. A week later, he'd be in the south of France, basking in the Mediterranean sun, with nobody the wiser. Why distress Bish and bother her with the formality of permission?

Hey, he thought, *rationalizing is fun.*

Monique was right. There were advantages to being small. Keeby woke the next morning in Bish's place next to Monique's tiny snoring figure, and he smiled. He rolled over on his back and stared at the ornate plaster ceiling, and he sighed contentedly.

He wasn't surprised Monique had been so masterful in the dark. He had expected it. Every actress he had ever known had put on a performance in bed and expected applause afterward. They were never *not* performing, which was fun, at least for a while. What surprised him was that he *liked* Monique. She wasn't only physically attractive. She was witty and intelligent. He enjoyed talking to her. He liked the way she laughed, part silly chortle and part blood-chilling cackle. He liked the way she spoke dramatically, as if the world were hanging on each syllable. He liked her eyes, the deepest green he had ever seen, and how they managed to look both seductive and angry at the same time.

Everything was perfect. The room was the perfect temperature. The weight of his skin against the mattress. Monique's contented purr of a snore. The light streaming in through the sheer curtains. The weight of the bedclothes. Bish leaning against the bedroom door jamb.

Bish leaning against the bedroom door jamb.

"Morning, love," she said.

"Oh, fuck," Keeby gasped. "How long have you been there?"

"A bit. I was musing on how innocent you look when you're asleep," she said, as she peeled off her gloves. "I'd planned to arrive before the end of the race yesterday, but the damned trains weren't running from Le Havre. Checked out this morning and took the first train to the city. I did have the most amazing bouillabaisse last night in a quaint restaurant by the water, near my hotel, so it wasn't a total waste of time. Looks like you picked up a nice dish yourself."

"Ah, Bish, I can—"

"Explain? Don't bother, not on my account." She dropped her jacket on the wing chair next to the window. "You're the man with whom I cheat on my husband, darling. Neither of us is exactly an aggrieved party. I said you could use the place if you needed it, and for exactly this circumstance. Roommates get in the way. You do plan to wash the sheets?"

"Of course."

"Carry on, then. I'll check into the George Cinq and come back when you're gone. Tomorrow okay?"

"Bish, I—"

"Relax, scribbler. Who is she? Anyone I know?"

She circled the bed to take a peek as Monique awoke, pulled the sheet from over her face, and squinted at Bish standing over her.

"The fuck?" she slurred. "Bishy?"

"Nickie?" Bish said. "Oh, Keeby, you caught a tiger by the tail. You know who this is?"

"Monique Rothe," Keeby said. "At least, that's who she says she is."

"Did she say what she does for a living?"

"Yeah. She's an actress. Half the women in Paris are actresses."

"I'm *the* actress!" Nickie squealed, raising both hands toward the ceiling.

"She isn't wrong by much," Bish said. "You bedded one of the most popular stage actresses in Paris, and a dear friend of mine. She's starring in the hottest play in town. Has been for over a year. How can you not recognize her?"

"I'm not a theater guy," he said.

"Writers," Nickie said.

"Tell me about it," Bish said. "So, as I see it, we can either have a *menage a' trois*, or you two can get dressed and we all go to breakfast, or I can take a taxi to the George Cinq alone."

"I could eat," Monique said in the middle of a yawn.

Keeby was hungry as well. He hadn't eaten dinner before attending the party.

"Sounds like it's breakfast," he said. "We can discuss that first option over coffee."

CHAPTER FORTY-THREE

POUNDING ON THE DOOR of his apartment jerked Beau from a deep, dreamless sleep. Immediately, his heart bounded as he imagined the gendarmes on the other side of the jamb, waiting with manacles to drag him off to the Bastille, or wherever the most desperate criminals were lodged in modern Paris. Wearing only his boxers, he jumped from the bed and padded to the door.

He listened, trying to discern how many people were outside. He waited for the creak of a floorboard, or a stifled cough. Hearing nothing, he leaned his ear close in toward the door. He heard nothing at all. Perhaps they had gone away.

He jumped and gasped when someone banged the door three more times. He fell back onto the floor and expelled the air from his lungs with an *oof* sound they heard on the sidewalk five floors below. Stealth was out of the question now.

Three more pounds. "Beau? Are you in there? Are you all right?"

It was Nathalie Bel. Beau had never been happier to hear a voice in his life. He threw the dead bolt and door lock and pulled her inside the apartment. He slammed the door and locked it again.

"Are you alone?" he asked.

"Are you drunk?" she asked. "I'm the only other one here. Yes. I'm alone. How many of me do you see?"

"I mean, did you come alone?"

"No. My legion of spies lines the street outside. What are you talking about, Beau? Oh, my God, you smell."

"I'm sorry," he said. "I haven't bathed today."

"It's…it's like someone vomited in a tannery bathroom after running a marathon."

"I get it. I smell. I can fix it."

"Oh. Your breath is worse. What in hell is wrong with you, Beau?"

"Man. Is that a great question. It's the question of the day, isn't it? What is wrong with Beau?"

"You're still asleep," she said. "Go take a bath. We'll talk when you are conscious."

Half an hour later, Beau wiped the dregs of shaving soap from his cheeks, stowed his razor, and dragged a comb through his hair. He wrapped a towel around his waist and found Nathalie sitting in the common room between his and Keeby's bedrooms. He smelled fresh coffee percolating on the hotplate. A box of warm buttery croissants from the nearby patisserie sat on the table, with fresh Normandy butter and French black cherry preserves.

"You cooked," he said, as he poured coffee. "How sweet."

"I borrowed your keys and bought a few things across the street. Beau, what I said last night—"

"Stop. It was a bad day. The worst day I've had since coming to Paris. We both said things. And you weren't entirely wrong."

"Oh?" She cocked her head.

"You weren't entirely right either."

"I know."

"You know?"

"I gave it a lot of thought last night, when I was at home." She paused and said, "Alone."

"Not necessary but thank you. Here's what it comes to. I said stuff I regret, and I'd take back if I could."

"As did I."

"But neither of us was entirely wrong, either. I *am* stuck here, Nathalie."

"Thank you."

"For what?"

"Calling me Nathalie, instead of Nat. Keeby calls me Nat. It would be confusing."

"Confusing you would be a hefty chore," Beau said.

"And you are right. You are stuck here. The difference between you and Grigorii is there is light at the end of your tunnel. Even so, you must navigate the tunnel, and there is no way to know how long it is. I neglected to consider that last night. I came this morning to say I am sorry."

"What's the worst thing you ever did?" Beau asked.

"I killed a man," she said without hesitation.

Beau opened his mouth, but nothing came out. He knew Nathalie was a woman with a past. He could imagine any number of possible felonies she might have committed in her short life. He had been prepared for almost anything except murder.

"You are shocked?" she asked.

"Are you serious?"

"I never lie, Beau, except to protect someone else. I have no reason to. I find it easier to remember the truth."

"And you come right out and tell me?"

"I trust you. I won't give you any details, though. Those are my memories, not to be shared. That is my hell. What about you?"

The entire time he was in the bath, Beau had wrestled with the same exact question. His life over the previous four years had been a series of bad decisions. Enlisting in the Army. Returning to a Charleston he no longer recognized. Blurting out a secret which led Victoria Tradd to throw herself into Charleston Harbor in the wailing winds of a tropical storm. He recognized the way he carelessly tossed about his privilege and wealth. And he couldn't forget taking a fortune in jewelry and money off a dead couple under an overturned Peugeot.

"I want to go to the Cote d'Azur," he said. "What if I wanted to sell something of value to earn the money to pay for it? How would I go about it?"

"There are pawn shops—"

"Not to pawn. To sell, for a decent price. Like, a nice watch, or jewelry."

"You could take them to a jeweler. They buy gold and stones all the time."

"What if I couldn't explain how I came across them?"

She buttered another croissant and dabbed on a small spoonful of the preserves. "That is easy. You go to Prince Grigorii." She bit into the croissant. A speck of preserves dripped onto corner of her mouth. A flick of her tongue, and it disappeared.

"The part about not being able to explain how I acquired what I'm selling doesn't bother you?"

"I killed a man. Morality is fluid for a pragmatist," she said. "Women give Prince Grigorii expensive gifts in lieu of direct payments. It makes the whole arrangement less...commercial. Grigorii can't buy food or pay his rent with baubles, so he converts them to cash. I can assure you he gets the top dollar."

"You are a surprising woman," Beau said, reaching for a croissant.

"Would you believe those were the exact words the man said when I killed him?" she said.

"Yes," Beau said. "Yes, I would."

He looked past her, and the room dissolved into a swirling abyss, a yawning maw into which he could feel himself being drawn against his will. He was about to cross a line he was powerless to avoid, and once across, there would be no turning back. He was about to become a different person.

CHAPTER FORTY-FOUR

BISH INVITED KEEBY and Monique for galettes and caviar at Dejeuner au Caneton. She waited in the living room for them to bathe and dress. Even so, wearing their clothes from the night before, nobody would be fooled. It didn't matter, because this was Paris and half the patrons at the restaurant still wore their clothes from the night before.

"I'm ordering drinks," Bish said. "Have you tried Buck's Fizz?"

"Of course not. Those rumors about Buck and me were blown all out of proportion," Monique said, and tried to hold a straight face, but quickly collapsed into giggles.

Bish smirked and ordered the drinks.

"You told me you were working," Keeby said to Monique, as the waiter left to fill their order. "You didn't tell me everything."

"I was enjoying a moment," Monique said. "I saw you at the party, and you were so young and attractive, and my first thought was, *Oh, another stage door Johnny.* Then I discovered you had no idea who I was, and we could talk like real people. People don't understand how rare that is for me, or how difficult even limited fame can be. Now, of course, you know, and—"

"Nothing changes," Keeby said. "I liked you before I knew you were a star and before I took you to bed. We had fun. No reason we can't keep having fun if you like."

"I work nights," she said.

"I'm a nightowl. Sometimes I don't get to bed before sunrise. I love midnight dinners. This is Paris. It's always open."

Bish cleared her throat. Monique and Keeby glanced her way.

"Oh," Keeby said.

"*Merde,*" Monique said.

"Yes," Bish said. "Whatever are we to do with Bishy?"

Keeby turned to Monique. "That was the first option, right?"

Monique said, "The *menage a' trois?*"

"I distinctly heard her propose it."

"Bastards," Bish said, but she smiled as she said it, an expression more promise than protest.

The waiter returned with three large flutes. "Three Buck's Fizzes," he said, distributing the glasses.

Keeby sipped from the glass. "Champagne and orange juice," he said. "But mostly champagne."

"They're all the rage in London," Bish said. "Perfect eye-opener. But watch out. They'll sneak up on you."

"You didn't tell me you were coming to Paris," Keeby said. "I wouldn't have used the key if I'd known."

"I planned to surprise you for the celebration following the Tour de France," Bish said. "I didn't know the train was canceled at Le Havre."

"Was there a problem in Scotland?" Monique asked.

"Only too many readings of *Wuthering Heights* in my youth. The moors are every bit as desolate and depressing in real life as they were in Miss Bronte's imagination. At first, the solitude energized me, allowed me time to relax and contemplate. I fantasized about my brooding Heathcliff riding into the courtyard to sweep me away. Over the weeks, he didn't show, and I became melancholy. I yearned for the lights and excitement of the city, if only for a few days, before plunging myself back into the summer wilderness in the Highlands."

"I spoiled your surprise," Monique said.

The waiter arrived with the breakfast menus.

"The train spoiled the surprise. I arrived to find a different surprise. My lover and my friend brought together in my bed by fate."

"Your lover and your friend? Which is which?" Monique asked. "I'm confused."

They ordered breakfast, and all had another Buck's Fizz, because it seemed like a perfect idea at the time, and a third with their food, fluffy buckwheat galettes folded over a heavy spoon of caviar and *crème fraiche*. They finished breakfast and relaxed in an alcoholic haze over coffee.

"Can the lieutenant colonel spare you for the month of August?" Keeby asked Bish.

"The lieutenant colonel is presently on assignment in an undisclosed location, for an indeterminate time. Terribly hush hush. Another reason I made the trip. Why?"

He told her about Prince Grigorii organizing the vacation to the Cote d'Azur. "It doesn't have the resplendent glamour of Heathcliff's moors," Keeby told her. "But there are the

335

Mediterranean waves for contemplation, and people and noise around when you crave it."

"And what of Nickie?" Bish asked.

"It hasn't come up yet. Apparently, neither of us divulged all our secrets last night," Keeby said.

"It's not a problem," Monique said. "I'm committed to the play through the end of October and might sign on for another six months if the money's right. It sounds like a ball, but I can't get away. You two kids have a blast."

"I hope I can see you when I get back in September," Keeby told her.

"As do I," said Bish. "We should plan a memorable reunion."

———

Nathalie and Beau found Grigorii at Dieter's apartment—the second place Beau checked. Dieter brought Grigorii to the telephone without the slightest hint of self-consciousness.

"I need to see you," Beau said. "Nathalie is with me. Can you meet us at The Salle?"

"I have only now awakened. I haven't eaten or bathed or shaved. I cannot see you for at least three hours."

"Make it two and I'll make it worth your while."

"You intrigue me," Grigorii said. "I am now curious. I will meet you in two hours."

He arrived at The Salle shortly after one in the afternoon, predictably nearly an hour late. He was dressed in a casual open-necked shirt, cream slacks, and a light summer weight linen jacket. He wore a cream fedora and arrived smoking a cigarette. Nathalie and Beau were waiting when he walked into the studio. The sock full of valuables lay on Beau's desk in his workstation. Beau was loathe to touch it. Nathalie escorted Grigorii to Beau's station, and strategically left the room.

"I need money," Beau said.

"A universal predicament," Grigorii said.

"I wish to sell some items to raise cash. I hear you know people who buy…things."

Grigorii loomed over Beau menacingly. For an instant, Beau thought he had offended the prince and was about to be attacked. Instead, a second later, Grigorii burst out laughing.

"So melodramatic!" Grigorii said, beaming. "Meeting in deserted studio. Cryptic references to consorting with men who buy stolen property. You are funny man, Beau. Now, we have had fun. Tell me what you want to fence."

"Fence?"

"Sell," Grigorii said impatiently.

Beau turned the sock inside out and dumped the contents onto his desktop. Grigorii pulled the green-shaded lamp closer to examine the earrings and bracelet and brooch, before straightening.

"You steal these?" he said.

"No questions asked," Beau said. "For ten percent."

"Ten percent?" Grigorii asked.

"You know these people. They know you, and they know they can't bullshit you. If I went, they'd cheat me blind. I want you to sell these, take ten percent plus whatever I owe you for my piece of the Mediterranean trip, and I take the rest."

"I could cheat you."

"We're spending the entire month of August in the same villa. A lot of time for you to worry I might find you out. Who can enjoy themselves under that sort of stress?"

Beau watched Grigorii's face as he deliberated. The prince might be charming, but he would have made a horrible poker player. *The jewels must be worth a lot. He's calculating his split, and he likes the numbers.*

Grigorii hefted the bracelet and the brooch in his palm again and took another look under the lamp.

"Fifteen percent," he said at last.

"All right, then," Beau said. "Fifteen."

"You want receipt for these?" he asked.

"You're joking, right?" Beau said.

"Of course I am joking. You are too tense. This is nothing. I bring you money tomorrow."

"So soon?"

"You prefer, I can make it day after tomorrow. I presume you are in hurry."

Beau said, "I am. In a hurry, that is. We leave for the coast next week."

"Yes," Grigorii said. "Piece of advice?"

"What?"

"This life is not for you. Do not steal again."

"I said no—"

"No questions asked. Yes. Of course. And I have not asked. I am making statement. Some people can steal. Some cannot. I sympathize with your predicament but find another way. I like you, *meilchik*. I don't want you to have stroke. Shall I come to your apartment tomorrow with money? It is closer than your studio."

"Yes," Beau said. "The apartment is fine."

Grigorii replaced his hat, stowed the jewelry in his jacket, and he was gone. Nathalie appeared in Beau's doorway seconds later.

"Did he agree?" she asked.

"He'll bring my cut of the money to the apartment tomorrow."

She sat in the second chair. "So it is finished."

"You think?" Beau said. "I think it's just beginning."

"You don't want to tell me where the jewelry came from?"

"I didn't want to involve you at all. You said your memories of killing a man were your private hell? Meet your new neighbor."

"Oh, Beau. What did you do?"

"I didn't hurt anyone. But what I did was wrong, and it's all I can think about now, like an endless nightmare loop of movie film in my head. I don't know how to make it stop. Grigorii was right. I'm not cut out for this."

She placed her hand over his. "I remember. It will get better, but you need to know it will never go away. Look on the bright side. As you say, nobody died."

That's not what I said, Beau thought. "I'm tired. Still hung over, I suppose. I'm going to my apartment to sleep for three or four days."

"I'll go with you," she said.

"You don't have to."

"Maybe, but you will find sleep difficult if you are alone. And, once you manage to slip away, your dreams will not comfort you. You do not want to face this ordeal alone. If someone had stayed with me, my life might have turned out differently. Nobody was by my side at the worst time of my life. I don't want that for you."

"You're getting sentimental on me," he said.

"Don't misinterpret it. I'm not the one, Beau. But I'm here for you right now. Next week? Time will tell."

"This should be an interesting vacation," Beau said.

"No doubt."

———

They dropped by Nathalie's studio, where she packed clothes and toiletries in a small bag, and they returned to 22 Rue Montparnasse. On the way, they purchased two bottles of red to nurture Morpheus and a baguette and some charcuterie to stave off the wolf.

Nathalie stayed with Beau through the night, as he woke again and again, sweating feverishly and with lemur-like eyes, tortured by the dream that wouldn't go away. Each time, she wrapped him in her arms and rocked him back and forth until his shaking settled and she could detect individual heartbeats pulse through his breastbone instead of a constant thrum like hummingbird wings. She had no idea what demons danced on his soul, but she recognized their hoofprints and their handiwork.

She rose at sunrise, but he slept on until almost noon, finally in the embrace of exhaustion so deep no dream could penetrate it. She passed the morning reading on the chaise in the living room. She was hungry, but she didn't dare leave the apartment until either Grigorii arrived or Beau was conscious enough to answer the door.

Finally, Beau raised himself from the sheets and looked around the room as if he didn't recognize it. Nathalie walked him to the bathroom and filled a tub. Half an hour later, he was washed, shaven, dressed, and still woozy from the wine and the long dark night of psychic trials, each of which featured him as the already condemned prisoner.

He guaranteed her he would remain awake. She slipped out to find food for lunch.

Prince Grigorii arrived five minutes later. He rapped out a complicated rhythm on the door, sadistically playing into Beau's paranoid need for melodrama. Beau opened the door immediately and ushered him inside.

"I didn't get to use password," Grigorii complained, pouting.

"Is it done?" Beau asked.

Grigorii, eager to amuse himself at Beau's expense, sighed and extracted an envelope from his jacket pocket. Beau broke the seal and looked inside. Color slowly drained from his face.

"My...God," he gasped.

"I think, perhaps, you steal crown jewels, Monsieur Beau."

"I...this is...*so* much money."

"They were highest quality gems, all authentic. And, you have already discerned, I sold them at substantial discount from actual value. As we agreed, I already extract fifteen percent and your contribution toward villa. I look forward to your company in south of France, and I expect to sleep like baby, for I have not cheated at all. There was no need. My percentage was generous. I do not know if you stole them or they were gifts, but if you are now gigolo and these jewels were kiss-off, I would appreciate introduction to your friend."

CHAPTER FORTY-FIVE

THE DOCTOR WAS GLUM as Henri Carosel slipped his undershirt back over his head and reached for his dress shirt. Carosel, a keen observer of human behavior, suspected bad news. Doctors never smiled when they were about to invoke the name of the disease destined to kill you.

Something taught in medical school, Carosel thought, keenly aware he was distracting himself. He imagined a classroom of students registered for a symposium on Stoic Objectification and Emotional Distancing early in their training.

On the other hand, in Henri Carosel's experience, the doctor *always* looked glum. He probably looked glum at a football match, or when his wife sucked his cock once each year on his birthday. He had been cursed with a naturally glum face. There was nothing at all he could read into the doctor's demeanor as he dressed and followed him to his office.

The doctor closed the door and gestured for Carosel to have a seat. Carosel expected the doctor to sit behind his desk, but instead he took the chair next to him, as you might with a friend.

"Oh, *merde*," Carosel whispered.

"The X-rays are not conclusive," the doctor said. "But there are new lesions in the pulmonary tract, compared to your pictures six months ago. We have no way of knowing for certain without opening you up and looking around, but I want to assure you this does not mean you have cancer. Your current symptoms are more consistent with emphysema or chronic bronchitis. We have had this discussion before. You were gassed. There was damage to your lungs. This damage will never heal, and with time it will get worse. It may become cancer someday. Nobody knows for certain. For now, though, I don't think so."

"And you are saying it has gotten worse in the last six months?" Carosel asked.

"I am saying there are more lesions, but we expect this in a chronic and progressive disorder. Do you feel worse?"

"I cough when I wake in the morning. I cough if I walk too quickly. I cough after sex. Is it worse than six months ago? Who can say? I have been more fatigued lately."

"You may be getting less oxygen due to the compromised lung tissue. It would result in fatigue."

"So," Carosel said, leaning in. "Tell me the truth. What's the endgame?"

"The same as all of us. You die," the doctor said. "But not for a while, and perhaps not of this. I'm not a fortune teller, Monsieur Carosel. How long? To be honest, we don't know. I would be happier if your lesions were stable, but nobody has any real idea. We were never trained in school to deal with monstrosities like mustard gas, and we only have a few years of data to work with. It does appear the severity of exposure is directly related to the severity of symptoms."

"Shoot a man with enough bullets, and he will eventually die," Carosel said.

"An apt analogy," the doctor said. "If a troubling one. You inhaled a small amount through a gap in your mask. Had you taken a deeper breath, or if you hadn't worn the mask at all, you'd have died long ago. For a while, we only divided soldiers exposed to sulfur mustard into those who lived and those who didn't. With time, we discovered those who did survive seldom improve, though it is possible they may live a normal life span, however compromised by breathing problems. The degree of exposure might predict long-term survival, but we don't know for certain. Ten years from now? There may even be a cure by then."

"Will I be around in ten years?" Carosel asked.

"I hope so, my friend," the doctor said. "We need the data so we can figure out how to fight this before some damned fool starts another war."

———

Henri Carosel left the doctor's office and strolled at a snail pace toward his own office on a side street off the Champs-Elysees a dozen blocks from the Arc de Triomph. He didn't hurry, because even walking briskly frequently left him gasping for breath or coughing himself nearly unconscious.

Forty-two years old, and he had the lungs of a geriatric coal miner. He had been a policeman when the war broke out, embarked on a fine career in the gendarmerie. Was on track to make inspector someday. Bloody fucking anarchists had to kill an otherwise superfluous archduke and spoil everything.

Gas was a horrible weapon. You could dodge a bullet, duck a mortar shell, or take cover behind sandbags and mud walls when the aerial bombs dropped, but gas was insidious. It was the manmade cohort to the Mosaic angel of death. It wafted on the wind and enveloped unprotected soldiers in a lethal cloud, peeled their skin and clouded their eyes, and blistered their lungs, leaving them gasping blood in utter agony as their vision narrowed to foggy pinpricks before winking out forever.

Carosel had been protected, or so he thought. The mask was defective. It gapped at the jawline, just enough and at precisely the wrong time.

The line of blisters running from his ear to the side of his chin had healed long ago, leaving only a slight discoloration following the ridge of his jaw. You would have to know it was there to notice it, though to Carosel it looked like a port-wine stain and felt like coarse sandpaper. He had the presence of mind at the instant he sensed the gas inside his mask to shut his eyes tightly, but he had to breathe. His reflex was to rip off the mask to remove the poison inside it, but he knew that would be the end, and he restrained himself as the whiff of gas seared his skin and burned his lungs and he gasped for oxygen. At the instant the lethal combination of mustard and sulfur were sucked into his lungs, he believed he was dead. Over the next five minutes, he wished he were. Only his instinct for self-preservation stopped him from tearing the mask from his face and ending it all.

His mask eventually sealed, but the damage had been done. He fell unconscious in the trench and woke in the hospital where they told him he was lucky he hadn't taken in any more than he had.

"Sure," he muttered to himself as he took another tortured step. "Lucky me." He accented it by coughing into his handkerchief. As he always did, he checked it before placing it back into his pocket. Blood was bad. No blood was good. Today was a good day.

There was no place for him in the gendarmerie when he was discharged from the military in the closing days of the war. French police officers, being an extension of the military, had to be fit and healthy. Henri Carosel could barely walk from his apartment to his office without entertaining thoughts of a nap. Fortunately, most of his work entailed sitting around and waiting.

He had parlayed his police training into a similar—if less stimulating—career. Henri Carosel was a private investigator who specialized in civil cases. Divorce work was easy. Following a philandering spouse took little effort. The lack of security was a concern, but only a small one. There would be no mustering out after two decades, no gold watch or hearty congratulations, and no civil pension. All his plans for his future security evaporated the second the gas invaded his mask. It didn't matter. Financing his dotage didn't worry Carosel. He didn't expect to have one.

He had lied to the doctor. The new lesions in his chest X-rays confirmed what his own body had already told him. His lungs were dying. He had placed several books under each of the headboard legs on his bed, so he could sleep on an incline, because lying flat left him gasping for air in the darkest hours of the night. He now had to stop to rest on the second landing on the way to his fourth-floor apartment, and he knew the day would come when he couldn't make it there at all and would have to seek a ground floor flat, or worse.

At least he didn't also have to worry about a pension.

He arrived at his office. There was no glass on his solid office door. His landlord was a cheap bastard and glass was expensive and it broke and had to be replaced. Instead of writing on the nonexistent glass, a small plate next to the door said, with no embellishment, *H. Carosel.* There was no suggestion of his profession, no engraved magnifying glass or crossed pistols or handcuffs. Anyone seeking his office already knew what he did for a living. Maintaining some degree of anonymity made his work infinitely easier. They couldn't see you coming if they didn't know who you were.

Henri Carosel was a man in the prime of middle age, made prematurely geriatric by trauma and his chronic affliction, but most people would agree he had a pleasant enough face. He wasn't handsome in the classical sense, but neither was he trollish. He looked like a thousand other mildly attractive but otherwise forgettable men you run across each day. He was of average height, average weight, average build, and average coloring. He didn't stand out in a crowd, which was also beneficial in his work. He could fade into the background in a police lineup of one. Henri Carosel was a shadow walking among humanity. He liked it that way.

August was a dry month for private investigators, as it was for most professions in Paris. Anyone who could afford his daily rates was at the coast or languishing in the shadow of the Matterhorn or on the beaches of Tuscany for the month, flushing all the city's toxins from their bodies with hourly internal alcohol rubs. If he was lucky, frustrated Parisian spouses all over the Riviera and the Swiss Alps were already tossing the sheets with newfound paramours and launching illicit affairs that would provide him with a tidy income for the next year.

That presumed, of course, that he would still be around to investigate them.

Carosel arrived at his office and opened the door to find a young woman sitting in the unattended waiting area. Carosel couldn't afford a receptionist, and he hadn't hurried back from his medical examination because he hadn't any appointments scheduled for the afternoon. He would have been reluctant to admit it to anyone else, but the tests and the doctor visit had fatigued him, and he was looking forward to napping on the chaise in his office for an hour or so.

So much for a nap. At some level, Carosel resented the young woman's interruption of his afternoon plans to doze until dinner. On the other hand, it was the slow month, and income was income. If he wanted to sleep, he should have gone home.

She looked to be in her early twenties. Contrary to Parisian fashion, she wore her auburn hair long and piled onto the top of her head. *An old-fashioned girl,* he reasoned. *Sweet face. Clear skin. Straight nose and teeth. She smells like soap instead of perfume. Not Parisian, judging by her clothes and shoes. She is from the country. On the chair next to her, a carpet-cloth handbag, bound with a leather strap. Her traveling clothes. Perhaps enough for two or three nights. She must have arrived in Paris on the noon train, since she hasn't had time to check in to a hotel yet. She doesn't intend to remain in Paris long, which suggests she traveled to the city specifically to see me, or for a short list of errands including requesting my services.*

Whatever her reason, he wasn't interested. There were cases he simply didn't take—especially those which might entail physical exertion. The girl didn't wear a wedding ring, and her finger didn't display a tan line, so a philandering spouse wasn't the issue. Couldn't hurt to hear her story, though, as long as it wasn't too terribly long. Carosel's chaise beckoned.

"May I help you?" Carosel asked as he slipped a key into his office door lock.

"I am waiting for Monsieur Carosel," the girl said. Her accent suggested the south of France, perhaps Monegasque.

"I am Henri Carosel," he said, opening the door. "Please, step inside my office."

Once they were situated and Carosel had a pencil and pad to take notes, the girl said, "My name is Lisette Seydoux."

"How can I help, Madame—"

She shook her head.

"—*Mademoiselle* Seydoux. What can I do for you?"

"I need you to find some lost objects."

"What sort of objects?"

"Jewelry. Four rings, a diamond bracelet, diamond earrings, a brooch. A diamond choker and a pearl necklace. Mostly, though, I want a watch."

"A watch."

"Yes. A Bell and Ross watch. Here is a picture of the model." She slid a newspaper advertisement for the watch across his desktop.

Carosel let it lie there, because picking it up might encourage young Mademoiselle Seydoux to think he was interested in taking her case. It was perfunctory to at least hear her out. "Perhaps this is a story you should tell from the beginning."

"I'm sorry," she said, her eyes watering. "I'm so frustrated. It's been two weeks, and the police have been of no help whatsoever. I live in Cagnes-sur-Mer. So far, I've had to handle everything from a distance."

"I remain confused," Carosel said. "Perhaps you could try an earlier beginning."

"Of course," she said. "Two weeks ago, my father and my stepmother were in an automobile accident on the Rive Gauche, in the Montparnasse. My stepmother died, the police say instantly. Broken neck. My father had severe injuries. He's paralyzed from the chest down, but he might survive as an invalid. I work in Cagnes-sur-Mer, in a stationery store. The local constable informed me of the accident. I couldn't leave immediately, until I could arrange for someone to look after the store. I run it alone, you see. My stepmother hasn't been buried yet. We're attending to it shortly in Monaco."

"I am still not certain how I can be of service," Carosel said. "What does this automobile accident have to do with missing valuables?"

"The automobile accident occurred late at night. The streets were deserted. My father was rendered unconscious when the car rolled onto its roof, but he awoke to see a man's feet running away from the car. It was minutes before anyone came to his assistance. He passed out again and woke in the hospital days later. I still had not arrived from Cagnes-sur-Mer, but they informed him my stepmother was killed. He asked for her belongings, and they brought him an empty clutch purse. Her rings, bracelet, earrings, necklace, choker, and brooch were missing. Only their wedding rings were left behind."

"The stolen items. They were of great value?"

"They were extremely expensive. When he saw they were gone, he asked for his own effects. His wallet was in his jacket pocket, but it had been rifled and the money was missing. His Bell and Ross watch was also missing. My father is a wealthy man, Monsieur Carosel. Terribly wealthy. Embarrassingly wealthy. We are Monegasque but moved to Paris some years ago when my father expanded his business. I own a stationery store selling art supplies a thousand kilometers from here, as far as you can go from Paris and remain in France, to escape the umbrella of his wealth. We bear no animosity toward one another, and in fact I love him dearly, but we see the world differently. There are things he cannot buy, however, at any price. The watch belonged to my brother. Father gave it to him the day he graduated from university. Philippe was killed in the war. The watch is all my father has left of him. It is irreplaceable. I wish you to locate it."

"Mademoiselle, this is a case of theft," Carosel said. "It is a matter for the police."

"I told you! The police have been useless. According to them, whoever took the jewels and the watch happened on the accident and seized an opportunity for a quick profit. The officer in charge of the case told me the rings and brooch and bracelet would be dismantled and the settings smelted into ingots once sold. The jewels would be sold individually, and recovery is unlikely. He said there was a chance the watch might make it to a second-hand store, because it was more valuable intact, but there were a hundred places it could land in the city alone, and the gendarmerie doesn't have the manpower to inspect each and every one for something as trivial as an old watch, regardless of how expensive it is. My father lost his wife and his legs. His son's watch is gone. I want to return it to him. It would mean the world for his recovery."

"I see," Carosel said. "I must admit, your story is compelling, but the type of investigation you request is outside the scope of my office. I handle mostly civil disputes, divorce complaints and the like. Criminal cases are outside my area of expertise."

"I don't want you to arrest the bastard who ripped jewelry from my dead stepmother's fingers. This isn't about revenge. This is about restoring an important memento to my father. I don't want the thief. I want the watch."

"Yes," Carosel said. "And were it in my power, I would restore it to you this instant. Undoubtedly a great crime was committed, at least from your perspective, and you deserve justice. However, I am not certain I am the right man to obtain it for you."

"I don't—"

"Please allow me to explain. There are three ways a person might dispose of such a watch. Well, four now that I think about it, since keeping the watch for one's personal use would be an option. However, if the intent was to convert the watch into ready cash, the thief could take it to a pawnshop, sell it to a second-hand jeweler, or find a fence."

"A fence?"

"Another criminal who specializes in buying and selling stolen goods. A middleman."

"You know such people?"

"Many of them. This is what I am trying to explain, Mademoiselle Seydoux. In a city the size of Paris, there are hundreds of registered pawnbrokers. The number of second-hand jewelers might be even higher. This is the problem the police face regarding your search. There are simply more places to search than inspectors to search them. To search the pawnshops and jewelers all over the city would take inspectors away from solving much more extreme crimes—murders, kidnappings, and the like."

"What can be done?"

"Perhaps nothing. Please, I do not wish to sound pedantic, but I am often accused of it, so I warn you in advance. Let us examine your story a little more closely, and perhaps we can narrow our options. Where precisely did this automobile accident take place?"

"At the corner of the Rue Montparnasse and Boulevard Raspail, on the Rive Gauche."

"And the time of day?"

"Around four in the morning."

Carosel raised his eyebrows as he wrote. Lisette caught it.

"They had been out celebrating. It was the night of the Tour de France final leg. They attended a party with friends, had a late dinner, and they left their friends' apartment late. My father had been drinking. He should not have driven. He has talked of nothing else since I arrived from Cagnes-sur-Mer. He is riddled with guilt that he drove in such a state, and it resulted in the death of my stepmother."

"So there were no other vehicles involved in the accident?"

"No. It was terribly foggy, and the streets were wet. My father lost control of the car. The front tires hooked the curb at the intersection and rolled the car over."

"Your father has no idea how long he was unconscious?"

"He doesn't believe it was long. He said he could hear the front tires still spinning on their bearings, so it couldn't have been more than a couple of minutes."

"He awoke to the sound of shoes running away."

"He saw them as well, but only a glimpse. He was certain it was a man."

"And your stepmother was killed instantly?"

"Yes."

"So the thief removed her jewelry first, before he took your father's belongings."

"Is it important?"

"Everything is important, Mademoiselle. Anything overlooked might be the key to everything. In order to solve the crime, we must first reenact it."

He quickly drew his handkerchief from his breast pocket and coughed into it heavily. When he pulled the cloth away, he checked it surreptitiously. Still a good day.

"Are you all right?" she asked.

Carosel knew how he looked after a racking cough fit—red and swollen eyes, blotchy skin, wheezing—and had dealt with the question more frequently than he preferred.

"Pardon, Mademoiselle. It is nothing. A chronic condition. Please do not concern yourself."

"But how can you know he robbed her first?"

"The car was overturned, and your mother was on the passenger side. She would have blocked his view if he were running away after stealing her jewels. Instead, the man was running away from the driver's side, and the jewels were already missing, so he took them first, before he stepped around the car and rifled your father's wallet and stole his watch. Afterward, there would be no reason to remain, *ne c'est pas?* He ran as soon as he finished taking your father's items. It is possible the act of stripping him of his valuables roused your father into consciousness. So we have established he robbed your stepmother first and father second, before running away. Do you know in which direction the thief ran?"

"Presuming you're right, it would have been toward the Boulevard du Montparnasse."

"What was he doing there at four in the morning?" Carosel asked.

"I beg your pardon?"

"I am looking at this now from a different direction. We have established your father and stepmother were out at four in the morning because they were attending a party. The crash occurred, and the thief had more than adequate time to rob your family of their valuables and run off into the night without being detected. At four in the morning, almost everyone in the block was fast asleep. Why was the thief not among them?"

"He is a thief. Do they not work at night?"

"Was he a thief, though?" Carosel asked. "We only consider him a thief because he stole your stepmother's jewelry and your father's watch. I have known many professional thieves in my time, Mademoiselle. I can assure you they do not loiter in the streets at four in the morning waiting for automobile accidents. I do not believe your parents were victims of a professional villain. It is likely the man was another reveler, wandering home himself after a night of celebration, in his cups as your father was. He was alone in the streets, and there was an automobile wreck. He went to check on the victims and believed them both to be dead. He was drunk, and the temptation was too great. He woke the next morning with valuables that proved he had committed a felony, and no idea what to do with them."

"You surmised all that from the little I told you?"

"And much more. Why was this individual walking around in the Montparnasse at four in the morning? Why, he was going home, where he should have been hours earlier. He lives nearby, perhaps off the Boulevard du Montparnasse, since that was the direction he was running."

"Is that helpful?"

"Only if I'm right, and the man is a rank amateur. But I believe that is the case. He left the wedding rings after all. A professional thief would never give in to such blatant sentimentality. An amateur, however, acting on uncontrollable impulse, might experience enough guilt to leave the wedding rings. Some things to our subject are still sacred. Now he is in a tight spot. Put yourself in his place. He desperately wants to get rid of the incriminating evidence, but he can't simply throw it into the Seine. What a waste! Potential wealth is intoxicating, seductive. He might consider dumping it, and a professional thief would in the absence of other options, because they know when to cut their losses and move on to the next score. An amateur, though? Some ordinary man who made a bad decision in a moment of weakness, and now sees an opportunity to profit by it? He will do something stupid. I like it when criminals do stupid things."

"What are you suggesting?" Lisette asked.

"We operate on the supposition the thief lives near the Boulevard du Montparnasse. The sheer volume of sources a professional thief might employ to dispose of stolen goods is immense across the breadth of the entire city, but if we can narrow it to a single arrondissement, or even a specific neighborhood, we have a manageable list of buyers to canvas."

"Are you saying you can help?"

Henri Carosel considered the question carefully. "You should prepare yourself for failure. I can identify all the pawnbrokers and jewelry dealers within the Sixth Arrondissement. I know several fences who operate on the Rive Gauche. I can inspect the pawnbrokers and the jewelers for the watch. I can try to contact the fences. They may not wish to cooperate. Even if they do, if the thief decided to keep the watch, you may never see it again. With the fences, I can ask to see if anyone has recently dumped a large quantity of jewels and bullion. If they wish to be honest with me, perhaps we shall find out something we can use. But the greater likelihood is you will spend your money for nothing."

"I have enough. I won't miss it," she said.

"Please do not allow yourself to be falsely encouraged. I have already advised you I do not typically take this sort of case. It is possible we are dealing with a clever amateur, smart enough to sell the goods far from where he lives. Any success we enjoy will be entirely due to good fortune. I will canvas the Sixth only," Carosel said. "I will not drag through the entire city looking for a watch. If I find something useful, we will consider it a success. If not, at least you tried."

CHAPTER FORTY-SIX

HENRI CAROSEL HAD NOT been entirely candid with Lisette Seydoux. The physical impairment imposed by his injuries had limited him to the sedate pursuit of errant spouses, which mostly involved sitting on a bench outside a hotel or watching a couple from across a restaurant dining room. He could engage in this work without exerting himself into a coughing fit or passing out from lack of oxygen.

He was not without experience in criminal investigations, however. His brief career with the Paris gendarmerie, before the war tossed his life into the hopper, had involved mostly walking a beat and maintaining the peace. By a stroke of luck, his beat had been in the St. Germain on the Rive Gauche, within shouting distance of Montparnasse. Walking a beat had provided him with ample opportunity and time to learn how to make educated guesses about people based on ridiculously inadequate information.

His educated guess that Mademoiselle Seydoux's thief lived in the neighborhood and was simply a drunk person with poor impulse control was one hypothesis, but not the only one. There was no reason, for instance, why he couldn't also be a professional thief who happened to wander to his nearby home after a night of partying. Two things could be true at the same time, and if that were the case, his investigation was likely doomed before it began. He was counting on this particular thief making bad decisions.

He reminded himself that the goal of an investigation isn't success. The goal is to get paid, and it appeared Lisette Seydoux was amply prepared to pay. He would do the legwork, of course, and he would earn his money, but he doubted he had even a scant chance of finding her father's missing watch, or any of the other valuables.

During his prewar days in a cape and a kepi, patrolling the sedate streets of St. Germain, he had not encountered great volumes of overt crime. There was a flourishing underground economy in place, of course, but the local constabulary ignored it as long as it remained underground. To do so, they had to know *who* to ignore.

At one time, Carosel knew every dip, every murphy artist, every illegal fence, every pimp and every prostitute—some better than others—every two-bit con, and every pornographer in the district. The war had changed things. A lot of the players he knew in 1914 had died in the trenches after being conscripted. Some had perished in the influenza epidemic. Some had stumbled improbably into a legitimate life. Undoubtedly, the underworld of the Sixth Arrondissement had new faces, people he didn't know, yet.

But enough of the old guard were still in the game. One of Carosel's superiors in the gendarmerie had said it often about petty criminals. *Take any two of them, shave their heads, dress them in tuxedos, and place them into a football arena full of tuxedo-clad people with shaved heads, and they will find one another in five minutes.* The criminal element, even nonpredatory ones, tended to flock together, attracted by some magnetic force only they recognized. While it was a bit of a stroll from the Montparnasse, his old contacts in St. Germaine would undoubtedly know the new kids in the neighborhood.

Carosel avoided the Metro whenever possible. The confined spaces and the greasy air in the tunnels aggravated his lungs. He preferred to travel above the ground, usually in streetcars. He didn't own a car. There was no place to park it at his apartment building. Most of the people he knew who owned cars spent half their time pushing them, and Carosel was in no physical shape for such strenuous activity. Walking from one Arrondissement to another was out of the question. He might make it twelve blocks before collapsing. Streetcars proved the most dependable and accommodating transport he could find.

He hopped off the streetcar half a block from La Rotonde and strolled to the outdoor café, where he took a seat next to a man with a beaked nose and strong chin. Blond hair spilled out from under a red beret. He wore a linen suit and smoked glasses. He was absorbed in the newspaper on the table in front of him.

"Jean Messier, you are under arrest for being an insult to humanity," Carosel wheezed.

Messier didn't twitch a muscle or take his eyes from the paper. Almost without moving his mouth, he said, "Fuck you, Carosel. You couldn't arrest a sloth, even when you had a badge."

"I see I need no introduction."

"I smelled you when you hopped off the streetcar."

A waiter appeared, and Carosel ordered a glass of wine. The waiter left a bowl of olives. Carosel popped one in his mouth.

"A diamond bracelet and earrings, several rings with precious gems, a gold and diamond brooch, diamond choker, a pearl necklace, and a Bell and Ross watch," he said.

"Is this your list for *Père Noël?*"

"Someone has either tried to sell these items, or they will soon. They're stolen, but I don't think he's a pro."

"I'll keep an eye out. I hope he is desperate. It is easy to cheat desperate people."

"In my opinion, he'll approach someone in Montparnasse."

Messier dropped the paper and held out his hands, palms up, and moved them like the arms on a set of scales. "These days, the entire Rive Gauche is one big happy family. Progress, my friend. Turns out killing half of Europe was excellent for business."

"That is the purpose of war," Carosel said. "And where did you serve?"

"Don't be an asshole," Messier said, rapping his knuckles on his wooden leg. "What is your interest in this?"

"Mostly the watch. Recovering the baubles would be a bonus."

"And the man who stole them?"

"Nobody gives a shit about him," Carosel said.

"I know nothing about it," Messier said. "But I am not the only person on this side of the river who might be interested in purchasing such things. I'm sure you will find someone who knows something about them."

Carosel folded a bill and slipped it onto Messier's table. Messier rested his index finger on it, the way a chess player might on a bishop while deciding whether to complete a move. Carosel folded another bill, and Messier scratched the one under his hand with his fingernail. Carosel slid the second bill on top of the first one. What did he care? It was Lisette Seydoux's money, after all. Part of his expenses. He'd double it on the final bill anyway. Wartime gas victims had notoriously lousy memories for details.

"I can ask around," Messier said. "Hell, we all know one another in this business. Like any business, I imagine. Don't you know every private investigator in Paris?"

"No," Carosel said. "I have several other old friends to visit today. Between you and your network of acquaintances, we should be able to locate the missing items. Please advise your acquaintances my client is willing to pay for information that leads to their recovery, especially the watch. You might remember yourself."

"What is so special about this watch, Carosel?" Messier asked.

"Sentimental value."

"One might pay a great deal for sentiment in this case. A fence's customers are his lifeblood. Asking him to betray one of them—"

"I don't know how many times I have to say it. I don't care about the thief. Nobody is being betrayed here. We want to recover the watch, and the other items if they're available." The emotion in Carosel's outburst prompted a fresh spasm of coughing. He covered his mouth with his handkerchief and waited for the paroxysm to pass. Messier stared at him throughout the episode, and when the waiter arrived with his wine. Carosel slipped the handkerchief back into this pocket and sipped at the wine to soothe his throat.

"You need a sanitarium," Messier said.

"Tuberculosis can be cured," Carosel said. He slipped his card with his telephone number onto Messier's table. "No sanitarium will help me, I'm afraid. Call me if you hear anything. It will be worth your while."

"Always happy to help a friend," Messier said.

———

Messier didn't call the next day. Neither did any of Carosel's other contacts. Carosel arrived at his office to find Lisette Seydoux waiting in the outer alcove. Her carpet bag sat on the seat beside her. She was returning to Cagnes-Sur-Mer.

"We bury my stepmother tomorrow in Monaco," she said. "I stayed longer to be with my father, but this must be done."

"I wish I had better news," Carosel told her in his office. "I have spread the word among those in the Sixth Arrondissement who traffic in stolen items. It is an undependable network, and any hope of success rides heavily on our naïve thief attempting to dispose of your family valuables locally, and a person who makes an illicit living being willing to expose a customer. I have visited half of the second-hand jewelers in the Arrondissement, and none had a Bell and Ross watch matching the description. They all know to contact me should someone approach them with one for sale."

"I suppose it was always a long shot," Lisette said. "I must return to Cagnes-sur-Mer. The foolish girl I hired to run the stationery store will burn it to the ground if I don't go back immediately."

"Things could change at any time. However, I should also inform you, should one of my contacts pay off, it may cost a considerable amount of money."

"But it is my father's property. It was stolen!"

"And, by the time we recover it, somebody will likely have already paid a great deal of money for it. They will not relinquish it for free and take a loss. If you wish to return your brother's watch to your father, you will be forced to buy it back. Having you a hundred miles away could make negotiations difficult."

"I'll leave money," she said. "If it runs out, let me know and I will wire more."

She lifted an envelope from her carpet bag and handed it to him. He opened it and examined the thick sheaf of bills inside.

"I believe this would be more than sufficient, Mademoiselle. I shall write you a receipt."

He handed the receipt to her moments later, and she stowed it in her purse. "I take the Train Bleu to Nice. You have my telephone number in Cagnes-sur-Mer. Please call me any time if you receive news."

———

Messier called on the third day. It was late afternoon. Carosel had finished his tour of all the second-hand jewelers in the Arrondissement, without success, but had secured promises from all of them to call should a Bell and Ross watch appear in their cases at some point. Exhausted, Carosel returned to his office and was asleep on the chaise when his telephone rang.

"This is Messier," the man on the other end said when Carosel answered.

"Good afternoon, Monsieur Messier. Do you have news for me?"

"I found your man."

"How much will an introduction cost?"

Messier told him.

"That is reasonable," Carosel said.

"I am a reasonable man, Carosel. Reasonable people will do reasonable things. Besides, if I perform this service for you at a discount, you will be in my debt."

"You had better be quick collecting," Carosel said. "I may not be around much longer."

"I will keep it in mind. The place where we met? La Rotonde?"

"Yes."

"Eight o'clock tonight. Bring my fee, and I will make the proper introductions."

———

Carosel arrived at La Rotonde precisely at eight, only slightly winded from his travel across Arrondissements. It was like any other night in Paris, and the outdoor café was packed with people enjoying a drink and a light meal. It took Carosel several seconds to locate Jean Messier, who sat next to a corpulent man of indeterminate age. Messier spotted Carosel at the same instant and waved him over.

Skipping pleasantries, Messier said, "Henri Carosel, this is Sandoval."

Sandoval had been put together with genes swept from the floor at the end of the day. His skin was sallow and acne scarred. His face looked like someone had punched a pillow, all puffy bits with indentations containing eyes and a nose and a mouth. If Sandoval had a chin, it would take a day to find it. He had numerous cowlicks in his scalp, so his greasy hair took off at odd angles.

"I will leave you two to discuss your business. My fee, Henri?" Carosel handed Messier an envelope. Messier slipped it into his inside jacket pocket. In an instant, Messier disappeared into the human parade on the boulevard. Carosel ordered drinks and the waiter hustled away as well.

"Is Sandoval your first or last name?" Carosel asked.

"It is the only name I will give you, Monsieur," Sandoval said. His voice was muted, as if someone had stuffed a scarf into his throat. "Forgive me, but I do not know you. I am taking a chance meeting with you this evening."

"I hope I can make it worth your risk," Carosel said. "I suppose Messier has told you what I'm looking for?"

"He described a list of items, including four jeweled rings, a diamond and gold brooch, a set of diamond earrings and pearl necklace, a diamond choker, a diamond bracelet, and a Bell and Ross watch," Sandoval said.

"The watch is of particular interest to my client," Carosel said.

"That is a pity, Monsieur," Sandoval said. "Recently, a gentleman of my acquaintance approached me with a desire to sell some items that sound exactly like your list."

"Did you purchase them?"

"I did, with the exception of the watch."

"What was wrong with it?"

"Nothing. It was exquisite. A fine example, marred only by a barely detectable scuff on one corner of the bezel, as if it had been dropped at some point."

"Why didn't you purchase it?"

"The gentleman was suddenly reluctant to part with it. To be honest, I could not blame him. He had no use for the other items, but the watch was a prize."

The waiter arrived with their drinks. "Do you still have the rest?"

"I do."

"Are they intact?"

"They are."

"What do you want for the lot?"

Sandoval told him.

Carosel sipped at his wine. "And how much for the name of the man who sold them to you?"

"Messier told me you were not interested in the man. Only in the items."

"I am only interested in the watch. He has it. I still have no interest in the man, but I cannot purchase the watch from him if I do not know his name."

"You do not wish to arrest him for the theft?"

"Monsieur, *nobody* wants to arrest him for the theft. The gendarmerie is completely disinterested in this case."

"Even so, you ask a great deal. The man in question—I have known him for some time. We have done a great deal of business together."

"In stolen goods?"

"Not until now. In fact, I did not know these items were stolen until Messier contacted me. If I tell you the man's name, he will figure out where you learned it, and he may stop doing business with me."

"Telling me his name is going to cost you," Carosel said.

"This is the truth."

"How much?"

Messier named his figure.

"Where can I receive the jewelry?" Carosel asked.

Sandoval slipped a candy box from inside his jacket and placed it on the table. He tapped it with his index finger. "If you have the money, we can do the transaction right here."

"In the café?"

"Nobody pays attention to anyone here except themselves."

"True enough." Carosel removed a second envelope from his jacket pocket and placed it on the table. "I would like to purchase some candy and a name, please."

The envelope contained slightly more than Sandoval had asked. Lisette Seydoux didn't need to know, though. If his information was good, it was worth the cost. There was another envelope in Carosel's office safe with the remainder of her cash should he need more. By overpaying Sandoval, he was building good will among the new criminal element in the Rive Gauche that might provide benefits later. It never hurt to build trust with people who could do you favors, especially if you could do it on someone else's franc.

Sandoval unselfconsciously riffled through the bills, counting with his lips as he did. If he recognized the overpayment, he said nothing about, it. He stuffed the envelope into his pocket and drained his glass of wine. He placed the candy box on Carosel's table and leaned over.

"The man you want is Prince Grigorii Yurievitch Romanov. He was a big Russian muckety-muck before the revolution, but now he's a gigolo. Mostly, he brings me baubles given to him by women he has pleased. I had no reason to believe the contents of this box were stolen. No matter. I deal in stolen articles all the time. The only reason they are in your possession now is because your client is more generous than my buyers. I do request that you not mention my name to Romanov. I should regret losing him as a supplier. *Merci, Monsieur.* Do have a pleasant evening."

Seconds later, he had disappeared as quickly and facilely as Messier.

CHAPTER FORTY-SEVEN

ON THE MORNING before he left for the Cote d'Azur, Beau woke with an idea he couldn't shake. He lay in bed thinking about it for almost an hour before he rose, bathed and shaved, dressed, and made his way to Alphonse Rimbaud's office. Rimbaud was brewing a cup of tea in his office when Beau walked in without introduction.

"Did they impound my father's ships?" he asked before he even said hello.

Rimbaud scattered a spoonful of sugar all over his coffee table. "*Mon dieu*, boy, you nearly scared five years off my life. Wear a bell or something next time."

"The ships. Are they still in operation?"

"Two are at anchor in Charleston, and one in Guantanamo, Cuba."

"Why Guantanamo?"

"It's cheaper than Havana. And it belongs to the United States since the Spanish-American War. Why do you ask?"

"What about the crews?"

"The ships are not in operation. The crews are furloughed. I suspect many have signed on elsewhere in the interim. Your father has far more to worry about than running his business, and in any case, he is not at liberty to do so."

"You act as my father's agent in Paris. What percentage of his business is conducted here?"

"I thought you wanted to be a painter. Why this sudden interest in the family business?"

"I might have a way to save it. How much business does my father do in Paris?"

"A considerable amount, taken by itself. As a percentage of your father's overall enterprises, it falls in the high single digits."

"All tobacco, or does he also import alcohol?"

"At the present time, our business in France is based on cigar sales. They are immensely popular here, as I am certain you know."

"Why not booze?"

"Why booze? There is no prohibition in France. We make the finest wine in the world. Admittedly, our beer leaves something to be desired, but Germany is nearby and our proximity to Russia and the British Islands gives us ready access to it and gin, whiskey, and vodka."

"But not rum."

"Rum is not as popular in France as it is in America," Rimbaud said.

"So it's not in ready supply."

"There are some importers bringing it in as a side trade."

"Every bar in Paris has rum on the shelf, at least every bar I've seen. Even if it isn't popular, there's a market," Beau said. "How are my father's cigars brought into France?"

"They arrive at the port of Marseilles. As I said, France provides only a small percentage of the Shipley trade. Any surplus your father has in cigars is crated and shipped by commercial freighter. It would not be cost-effective to use your own ships."

"Unless they're already sitting around drawing water, rusting at the Charleston Harbor docks," Beau said.

"What are you suggesting?" Rimbaud asked.

"We have the ships. We have some crewmen—between the three ships we should be able to scrounge one entire crew together. Get our feet wet, as it were."

"I appreciate the pun, Beau, but I'm not certain this is what your father envisioned."

"He didn't envision his ships sitting idle either. Is the federal government allowing Father to engage in any business at all?"

"Any that does not involve trade in alcohol in the United States. However, you can be certain any Shipley vessel entering United States waters will be torn down to the keel. The government is in the mood to make examples out of smugglers, and the Coast Guard will harass your boats every chance they get."

"The French Coast Guard doesn't give a damn about the Shipleys, do they?" Beau asked.

"Not yet, but we have only operated here for a few years. There is time."

"And, between now and then, we can make enough money to ensure my mother and sister don't suffer financially while Father stands trial. We have a ship in Cuba. Is it loaded?"

"With both rum and cigars, but it can't leave port. Nowhere to go."

"Let's bring it here. You already have contacts among the tobacconists. Surely you could push more stock on them or expand our territory to a larger number of shops. You said it yourself—Parisians are nuts about fine cigars. We might not be able to saturate this market, but let's give it a try."

"And the rum?"

"Marseilles is a shipping town. Sailors arrive from all over the world, and rum's their poison of choice. There's a much higher demand in Marseilles. We import the finest Cuban and Jamaican rums. We may not need to go any farther than the port of Marseilles to dump them. If we need to move the rest, there's always Le Havre or Calais."

Rimbaud crossed the office to his desk and extracted a file from the side drawer. He stroked his chin as he looked over the contents.

"Your father would have to approve this plan," he said. "The logistics will be difficult. We have no relationship with the local dockworkers and stevedores. The stock we currently import into France comes, as I said, by commercial freighter. It is delivered by rail to our warehouse from there. It would take me…let us say two weeks to make the logistical arrangements."

"There's no rush. I'm out of the city for the month of August anyway, like everyone else. The rum only gets better with age."

"In addition, if we are to import a greater volume of goods, we may need enhanced storage facilities."

"We have to look for a larger warehouse," Beau said. "I expected that. But what about the rest? Can you put together a customer base in only a few short weeks?"

"That is precisely why your father pays me. He wants me to keep the warehouse empty. What? Did you think I existed in Paris for the sole purpose of doling out your allowance?"

"I know why you're here," Beau said. "That's why I came to you first, as soon as I had the idea. I'm a Shipley, but *you* know the family business inside and out. I need you running this if it's going to work. I'm just the idea guy. Wire Father today. Tell him what I want to do. Trust me, he'll jump at the opportunity. He's always wanted me in the family business."

"But, Monsieur Beau, what about your painting career? Are you abandoning it?"

"Not at all. You're doing the heavy lifting. And, if we succeed, you may find yourself a much more valuable employee to my father than you are now, and I can assure you he already values your work greatly. You could be the man who saves the Shipley Company."

CHAPTER FORTY-EIGHT

BEAU, NATHALIE, KEEBY, AND BISH took the overnight Train Bleu from the Gare de Lyon station to Cagne-sur-Mer for the summer retreat.

While automobiles might have been ubiquitous in Paris, the highways to the south became narrower and less traveled as the city disappeared in the rearview mirror. Traveling by motorcar would take over ten driving hours, some of it along dusty washboard dirt roads. Better to relax in the lounge car of the train, and to retreat to their luxurious private cabins when they became fatigued.

They were sitting together in the lounge car, enjoying an aperitif before heading to the dining car for a fashionably late dinner.

"So, let me get this right," Keeby said to Beau. "You're going into the shipping and import business after all?"

"I suppose I've always been in it, one way or another. Where do you think the allowance came from?" Beau said. "I will be making some decisions, but the bulk of the work will be handled by Rimbaud. I'm afraid I placed a lot on his shoulders during the August break. He assured me he had already intended to remain in Paris for the month, though. As for me, I plan to relax and eat and drink and paint and swim in the ocean and get brown as a nut while Rimbaud toils in the city. There will be plenty for me to do when we return in September. What do we know about this villa of Prince Grigorii's anyway?"

"It belongs to the baroness he sometimes squires around town. She isn't using it for the month, but she still charged him for it—at a discount, of course. Makes me wonder just how good a gigolo he is."

"And what's the name of the town?"

"Cagnes-sur-Mer," Keeby said. "Site of the musical beds tour."

"I never should have told you that," Bish said.

"Everything is fair game, my dear," Keeby said. "I believe that was part of my introduction. And, in your defense, you had been drinking."

"The *what* tour?" Beau asked from the back.

"A thing between Modigliani and Foujita and their wives a few years back. Apparently, they all spent the summer together in Cagnes-sur-Mer and it was a free-for-all. Jeanne Hébuterne became pregnant, and it was kind of a toss-up who shot the magic bullet."

"Ah, I see."

"And you bring this up for what reason?" Nathalie asked.

"Yes," Bish said. "Don't get your hopes up, scribbler. Besides, it's tacky to talk about it now."

She was right. Modigliani and Hébuterne were long gone. The consumption behind Modigliani's sickly appearance at the party three years earlier had finally overwhelmed him the following January. Overwhelmed by grief, still-pregnant Jeanne threw herself from a window two days later in a tragic act that that had already entered the realm of artistic legend.

Keeby tactfully changed the subject. "I'm glad you decided to come along after all, buddy. So the show at the Salle was a success? You sold some paintings?"

Beau glanced across at Nathalie. "I made a couple of sales. I was able to plow some money into Dieter's film of your book. He plans to shoot while we're there."

"Did he cast the farm girl yet?" Keeby asked.

"He did," Nathalie said.

"Who is it? Wait." Keeby peered at her. "*You're* playing her?"

"Dieter asked me yesterday."

"No. You're all wrong. You aren't her at all!"

"Dieter thinks I am."

"But the farm girl needs to be rustic and athletic. Muscular, from all the work in the fields. Strong hands. And it is Russia, dear. You don't run into many people with your complexion in the forests of eastern Europe. No, you aren't the way I envisioned her at all. Please, don't get me wrong. You are beautiful, and I've seen how the camera captures your beauty, but…no. You aren't her."

"Sorry you feel that way," Nathalie said. "Makeup will deal with my complexion. Dieter can put me in padded clothes."

"Nobody is going to buy it," Keeby said.

"It's the movies," Beau said. "It's all about the suspension of disbelief anyway. The audiences will take one look and fall in love with this farm girl."

"It's Dieter's movie," Keeby said. "I can't tell him who to cast. I don't have to approve, though."

"Is this about your book or is it about me?" Nathalie asked, the bristles in her voice unmistakable.

"What is she talking about?" Bish asked.

"I should have told you," Keeby said. "Nathalie and I had a fling before you and I met. Beau knows about it."

"So," Bish said, apparently unfazed by the news, "Is this about your book, or is it about Nathalie?"

"Are you ganging up on me?" Keeby said.

"It's a fair question," Beau said.

"Jesus! I'm surrounded!" Keeby yelped. "Of course it's about Nathalie. But not because we used to sleep together. Beau would stab me through the heart with a palette knife if I walked into his studio and told him which color to use in a painting. I paint with words."

"I can't write a grocery list, but even *I'm* embarrassed by that sentence," Beau said.

"You know what I mean. Words and mental images are my medium. Paint and canvas are yours. I have a certain internalized vision for what I write. Nathalie is not that vision. She might be one of the Parisian women the hero meets on his arrival, or perhaps a member of the Russian aristocracy before the revolution. But the farm girl? No sale."

"Get over it," Nathalie said.

"I agree," Bish said. "Get over it, Keeby. If this is the worst thing that happens to you all summer, consider yourself fortunate."

———

The villa was an Italianate manor, three stories high on a fifty-foot cliff overlooking a small private beach on the crystal waters of the Mediterranean. The rear of the house featured a travertine semicircular patio designed to give the illusion of jutting over the water. Eight bedrooms, as many baths, and a housekeeper to keep everything ticking over nicely was a bonus.

They arrived shortly before sunset, and the light cast over the Mediterranean was nearly pink and vaguely ethereal.

Grigorii and Dieter greeted them as they parked a rented car on the gravel and shell drive at the front door. Grigorii looked ghostly in white facial makeup and mascara to accentuate his mustache and goatee and slicked back hair. He was dressed as a Russian aristocrat before the revolution, in a fine evening suit. Tufts of tissue paper stuck out from under his shirt collar, to prevent makeup from soiling his clothes.

"Ah! You have arrived! We have already begun shooting!" Dieter said as he took Keeby's hand.

"I heard you cast the farm girl," Keeby said.

"We can discuss it later," Dieter said. "Please, let us help you with your bags."

Dieter, Grigorii, and Cesare had arrived the day before to open the house, which also provided them the opportunity to determine the distribution of bedrooms. Keeby and Bish would stay together, as would Beau and Nathalie. Grigorii was shacked up with Dieter, at least for the moment. Cesare had brought a woman named Amelie with him.

"This was a great idea," Beau said as Dieter led them into the villa. Part of the main salon had been transformed into a film studio, a depiction of the smoking room in a Russian country dacha. Dieter and Cesare, who had assumed assistant director duties on the film, had dragged in the most opulent rugs in the house and had distributed them on the floor and across a fainting couch next to the fireplace. Despite the blistering August temperatures of the Cote d'Azur outside, a blaze crackled in the fireplace. Grigorii wore a quilted satin smoking jacket and an evening suit underneath. He carried a footlong cigarette holder as a prop. His hair was slicked back with what looked like a quart of motor oil. Cesare was dressed in what was supposed to pass for Russian peasant clothing—coarse cotton and wool shirt and pants, well-worn leather boots, a heavy vest, and a flat cap. He had smeared dirt from the flower bed on his arms and hands to simulate his poverty. Both had half the makeup in France on their faces, giving them a spectral quality, like the long-dead spirits floating outside Ebenezer Scrooge's lodgings.

"You're in time for the shot," Dieter said. "Last one of the day before we lose the light. This is the part of the book where Prince Grigorii is informed of the revolution in St. Petersburg."

"Wait," Keeby said. "Prince Grigorii? In the book he was Prince Sergei."

"A minor change," Dieter said. "It was Grigorii's idea. By stating the actor Prince Grigorii is portraying his own story, he immediately becomes both a heroic and sympathetic character to the audience. It will become part of his personal history, and perhaps lead to a long career playing such heroic characters on film. Not only that, but we can trot him out to theaters for personal appearances."

"Aw, fuck it," Keeby said. "It's all bullshit anyway, but it was his bullshit before it was my bullshit. Do whatever you want as long as the check clears. Hey, Bish, want to unpack and take a walk on the beach before dinner?"

"Of course, dear," Bish said. "In a bit. I'm fascinated by this film business. I've never seen one made before."

"All right," Keeby said. He retreated to a corner to pout.

"*Pauvre petite chose*," Nathalie said quietly to Beau.

Beau looked over his shoulder at Keeby. "He'll find something else to gripe about soon enough."

"Ready?" Dieter called out. He flipped a switch, and all the lights came on at once, increasing the radiant temperature in the room several degrees at once. He stood behind the camera and called "Places!"

Grigorii arranged himself on the chaise near the fireplace, lounging as luxuriously as possible. He puffed on the cigarette holder as he held a book.

Dieter cranked the camera. "Action!"

Grigorii pretended to be deeply engaged in his reading, the fire roaring and popping next to him, the picture of Russian aristocracy. Cesare crashed into the room, a cloud of dust rising from his filthy clothes. He made a show of handing Grigorii a tattered envelope before backing out of the frame, leaving Grigorii alone to rip the seal on the letter. He read the note inside, and his face contorted into a mixture of anger and grief. He tossed the cigarette holder across the room, rose from the chaise, ripped the smoking jacket off and tossed it onto a chair, and crossed his arm over his eyes, head bent backward, in the universal silent film posture for abject grief.

"Cut!" Dieter called out, as he stopped cranking the camera. He slapped at the switch, and the lights went dark, leaving the room in twilight gloom. Grigorii relaxed and picked up the smoking jacket.

"*Bozhe moy*, this thing is hot!" Grigorii complained.

"That's it?" Bish asked.

"It's one shot," Dieter said. "We shoot the film out of sequence and reassemble it in the order the story dictates."

"Oh," Bish said, the disappointment in her voice unmistakable. "I suppose I presumed you shot it like a play, continuously."

"I'm sorry, Lady Bish," Dieter said. "That would be impractical."

"So it's a lot of short shots," Bish said.

"This is the case."

"And they don't even have to memorize lines?"

"This is also true. Movies, at least for now, are silent."

"My. Seems to me the stage actors have it all over movie actors. Keeby? How about that walk?"

Beau waited until they were out of distance before saying to Dieter, "I don't think she was impressed."

"Fortunately, she is not an investor," Dieter said.

"So, you purchased the short end film stock?" Beau asked.

"No, in fact. I found an amazing deal on fresh stock at the same price."

"Hope you didn't trade away anything important," Beau said. "One thing my father always told me. Many a man has lost his shirt on a great deal. How many more scenes are you shooting today?"

"We are finished with daylight scenes. There are former servants' quarters off the side of the house, little stone cottages surrounded by a garden. It will be the perfect location for the farm scenes. I believe we can shoot seventy percent of the film without ever leaving the villa!"

For the first several days, Beau thought a life of leisure was a pretty good idea. After a week of nonstop lounging, sunning, swimming, dining, screwing, and drinking, he became restless.

A week into the August respite, a telegram arrived from Alphonse Rimbaud. The news was excellent. Gordon Shipley had approved diverting the Cuba-docked ship to Marseilles, and if it worked, he was prepared to remove the two other ships from the Charleston docks as quickly as he could assemble a dependable crew and put them into service on the same routes.

Sensing his return to Paris would entail a great deal more responsibility than he had expected, Beau realized his time to devote entirely to art was ending. The idea saddened him.

The art supplies he had brought with him sat accusingly in the corner of his bedroom, still wrapped in burlap and canvas and tied with twine. It was shortly after ten in the morning, and too stuffy to stay under the covers. Nathalie snoozed naked on her stomach next to him, snoring softly, her bangs falling across her face. A fine sheen of sweat covered her back and buttocks and legs.

Nathalie had filmed her first scenes the day before. Dieter and Cesare had transformed the former servants' quarters beside the villa into a representation of a Russian farm. At Keeby's suggestion, he had devised a bulky layered wardrobe to cover Nathalie's svelte figure, to make her look a bit more as if she had labored in the Russian fields for years. The day before, Dieter had filmed the scene in which the farm girl discovers Prince Grigorii in the barn. It was a combination of twelve shots, including closeups, and took the entire day to shoot. It would likely make up half a minute of screen time. Beau learned that was the nature of filmmaking. Next to novelists, he imagined filmmakers must be the most patient of artists.

Grigorii relished his role as the star of the movie. He enjoyed strutting around the set in costume and makeup, putting on airs and pretending the entire enterprise revolved entirely around him. When he became too insufferable, Dieter would shoot him a cryptic glance, enough to bring the Russian back into line.

Several doors away, Beau could hear Keeby's typewriter. He always heard Keeby's typewriter. His buddy would never admit it, but the failure of his first novel had cut him deeply. He had been working overtime on something new. When pressed, he refused to talk about it. Bish tried to drag him away from his work for a week before deciding she'd much rather return to Paris.

Beau walked around the corner as her car arrived, and Bish kissed Keeby goodbye.

"You're leaving?" Beau asked.

Bish gave Beau a hug. "Can't compete with his muse, I'm afraid. I might pop back into Paris and see what Nickie is doing. I'll be back in a couple of weeks, once his creative frenzy wanes"

"I'm sorry again," Keeby said.

"Oh, posh, darling. What's the point in having an artistically tortured protégé if he isn't obsessed with his craft? You're lovely company when your nose isn't stuck to the grindstone. This isn't one of those times. We'll see each other again in a few weeks. In the meantime, Nickie and I will violate some morals laws and try to get our names in the newspapers."

"Guess I'm a pretty lousy boyfriend," Keeby said, as they watched Bish's car pull away.

"Look on the bright side. Her husband likes you," Beau said.

"Hey, gotta write that down."

"Take a break," Beau said. "Come to the village with Nathalie and me. Have a drink. You're wound tighter than a cheap wristwatch."

"Maybe later this evening," Keeby said. "I'm on a roll right now. Knock on my door around eight."

———

"Oh, hell," Beau said, as he unpacked his painting gear.

"What is it?" Nathalie asked from across the bedroom.

"I left behind a bundle of brushes. All the rest of them are here, but one bundle is missing."

"You are going to paint?"

"Thought I might desecrate a few canvases."

"So you've grown tired of me?"

"Not at all. Want to pose?"

"I always want to pose for you. Once, though, I wish you would paint me as I truly look."

"Representation is dead," Beau said.

"Nicely recited. I will pose for you if you paint me as I am."

"Sure," Beau said. "Why not?"

"And you will paint me nude?"

"As you wish. I'm sure a bordello somewhere needs a painting over the bar. I can't paint anything if I don't replace the missing brushes, though."

"Are they necessary?"

"Not until they are, and then it's too late. Saw a stationer in the village on the way in. I might drop by tomorrow and see if they have some in stock."

"Oh, sounds like fun. We can have lunch while we're there."

"It's a date," Beau said.

————

Before leaving for the village the next morning, Beau peeked in on Keeby and found him sprawled across his bed, snoring like a foghorn. A half-finished sheet of paper poked from the typewriter. Scribbled bits of scrap paper were pinned to the wooden window molding. Even with the double windows open to the Mediterranean, the room smelled like old socks, stale cigarettes, and neglect. Keeby had taken two hours off the previous evening to stroll into the village and have dinner with Beau and Nathalie. He was distracted and prepossessed the entire time. Beau recalled hearing the typewriter as late as two in the morning, but he also heard Keeby pacing the floors later. *Better to let him sleep,* Beau thought as he quietly closed the door.

Cagne-sur-Mer was built right up to the blue waters of the Med. Behind the beach was a medieval village of stone and brick, with cobbled streets and tiled rooftops and the slightest aroma of decay common to European towns that predated the Magna Carta.

Beau and Nathalie enjoyed a lovely brunch of galettes and cheese, with a delicious Rose d'Anjou Nathalie found immature and unsophisticated, but Beau thought was light and refreshing. They finished with fresh fruit and watched the waves of the Med crash gently onto the rocky beach of Cagne-sur-Mer.

After lunch, they strolled through the ancient narrow lanes of the old town, dropping in on some small shops to browse, until they came across the stationer Beau had mentioned the day before. Nathalie spied a modiste several doors away, and passed on the musty shelves of the stationers, suggesting Beau find her in a few minutes.

"Bonjour," Beau said to the shopkeeper as he walked in. It was considered rude not to greet your host, or for the host to ignore a new customer.

"Bonjour, Monsieur," the girl said back. As far as Beau could tell, they were alone in the shop. *"Comment puis-je vous aider aujourd'hui?"*

"Mon français est pauvre. Par hasard, parlez-vous anglais?" Keeby asked.

"Oui—yes, Monsieur. I speak English well. And, please, do not be offended, but I believe I will find this easier in English. You are American, I believe?"

"Yes," Beau said. "I am American."

"How strange what America did to the English language," the girl said. "But what they do to French is another matter entirely."

"You know, there's probably another stationer in town," Beau said, smiling.

"*Non, Monsieur.* This is the only one."

"In that case, I am condemned to endure abuse in order to satisfy my need for brushes."

"What brushes would those be?"

He told her.

"With regrets, Monsieur, we do not carry this specific brand. However, I do stock a suitable substitute, if you are interested in substitutes. Follow me, please." She wended her way through shelves filled with papers and pads and inks and paints. "Where did you live in America?" she asked.

"Charleston. It's in South Carolina. The lower part."

"Ah, yes. The Confederate States. I saw it in a movie. *The Birthing of the Nation.*"

"Close enough. That was decades ago. Before my time."

"Here are the brushes I mentioned, Monsieur. Would you like to inspect them?"

She had selected a canvas bundle from the shelf and unrolled it on the countertop. The brushes were stored in individual pockets, varying lengths and thicknesses of stiff horsehair and softer sable.

Beau was distracted by the shopgirl. He was used to Parisian girls with bobbed hair and the latest fashions and the faint hint of superiority. The shopgirl had left her thick auburn hair long. She'd pulled part of it back and tied it with a ribbon, leaving a chestnut waterfall to course over her ears and caress her shoulder. Her eyes were blue, and a single strip of freckles flowed across her pert nose and cheeks before blending with her skin. She had the slightest overbite. She wore a businesslike black dress and sensible shoes to cope with hours on her feet. Her hands were pale and slim, the nails cropped short. She wore no rings, and in fact Beau noted she wore no jewelry of any kind. Her smile made him feel five degrees warmer.

"These will do perfectly," Beau said. "Thank you."

"And what is Monsieur painting?" the girl asked as she escorted him to the checkout desk.

"Some landscapes. Maybe a nude or two."

She didn't flinch. "Are you a professional painter, Monsieur?"

"Let's stop the *Monsieur* thing, all right?" Beau said. "I'm American, after all. We don't stand on ceremony. My name is Beau Shipley. Call me Beau."

"All right, Beau. I am Lisette Seydoux."

"You own this shop?"

"I do."

"Congratulations. It's neat and tidy. The answer to your question is not so cut and dried. I moved to Paris several years ago with the aim of becoming a painter. My success so far has been limited. But I persevere."

"And you are painting now in Cagne-sur-Mer?" she asked.

"For the month. Some friends and I have taken a villa nearby for August."

"The Baroness?" she asked. "She is a lovely person. I look forward to seeing her again."

"Not this time, I'm afraid. She's off getting her soul laundered in India. We're renting the villa from her for the month. Then it's back to Paris. It's nice to know you, Lisette Seydoux. If I stay as busy as I expect over the next several weeks, I will drop in on you frequently."

"I will look forward to it, Mon…Beau."

He extended his hand. She took it. Her skin was cool and soft against his. He decided he liked Lisette Seydoux.

He found Nathalie waiting for him on a bench outside. She looked at him curiously as he walked out of the stationer shop.

"What?" Beau said, when he saw the look on her face.

"I don't know," she said. "You looked different."

"Can't imagine why," Beau said. "Got the brushes."

"And now we paint?" Nathalie said.

"And now we paint. Dieter has other plans for you, though. You're filming later this afternoon?"

"Every day. I will finish soon, though, and I will be yours to paint until the end of the month."

"Sounds like a plan," Beau said.

CHAPTER FORTY-NINE

KNOCKING ON GRIGORII ROMANOV'S apartment door proved fruitless. Henri Carosel fingered the mail slot open. He could see a pile of envelopes on the floor behind the door.

"August," he whispered to himself.

The idea of lazing on a sun-drenched beach somewhere was appealing. *Must be nice to afford it*, Carosel thought. Messier had told him Romanov was a Russian prince and a gigolo. In any other place or time, it might have seemed an odd combination. In postwar Paris, it garnered no more than a passing glance.

Grigorii's apartment was in a shabby building, and yet he was spending August on vacation. *Perhaps he is in the company of a consort*, he reasoned. *Someone else is paying the bills.*

Then he recalled that the prince had recently come into a frightfully large amount of money. He found it curious that he hadn't thought of the proceeds of the robbery first.

The building superintendent lived on the ground floor. He was a pleasant Italian gentleman of indeterminate years. He wore a stained apron, and the smell of garlic and basil and fennel rolled into the hallway when he opened the door.

Carosel introduced himself and handed the superintendent his business card.

"I have not seen him in a while," the man told Carosel. "I do not keep track of my tenants, *Signore*. Romanov pays his rent on time each month. That is about all I can tell you."

"Is he close to anyone in the building?" Carosel asked.

"What has he done?"

"As far as I know, nothing of importance. I am not a policeman, and I seldom deal with criminals of any sort. The prince possesses an object my client wishes to purchase. I am only acting as a mediator."

"A private investigator as a mediator," the superintendent said. "That is a new one on me."

"Life does take interesting turns," Carosel said. "Romanov's friends?"

"He was dating a woman on the third floor for a while. Babette Froeschle. She's in room three-twelve. Maybe she's in, maybe she isn't. I don't keep track of my tenants, *Signore*."

Babette Froeschle was a German woman with obviously bleached hair and too much rouge by half. She might have been thirty. She might have been fifty. Her apartment smelled like mildew and sex. She wore a silk kimono and, judging by the way the fabric rode her curves, little else. She was disappointed when Carosel handed her his business card.

"I was napping. When you rang my bell, I thought I had forgotten an assignation."

"A what?" Carosel asked.

"An assignation. I read it in a book. It sounds so much less tawdry than *customer.*"

"Does the superintendent know you are whoring out of your apartment?" Carosel asked.

"He turns a blind eye except at the first of each month. I pay half what anybody else in this building pays, if you know what I mean. You met the superintendent?"

"I did," Carosel said.

"Then you know maybe I'm not getting such a bargain. If you are not here for an assignation, why are you here?"

"I'm looking for Prince Grigorii Romanov. You and he are friends."

"Why do you want him? What's he done?"

"I am aware of no legal difficulties on Prince Grigorii's behalf, and my client wishes him no ill will. This is about recovering an object which the prince should not have."

"Oh. I get it. He pinched one of his escort customers' baubles. If her husband finds it missing, it would be extremely embarrassing. The wife wants her pretty pretty back."

"Something like that," Carosel lied. "My client is in a rush and would like to complete the transaction as quickly as possible. There's a handsome profit in it for Prince Grigorii."

"I can imagine. I'm not sure I can help. The prince has been in and out lately. More out. I thought he had found a new lady friend, but he told me a week or so ago right here in the hallway that he is spending most nights with a film director. A man. The things you learn about your friends, am I right?"

"Did he mention the film director's name?"

"I couldn't shut him up. It was *Dieter Heyder* this and *Dieter Heyder* that. From what he told me, this Dieter Heyder is putting him in a new movie. I fell for that one once or twice myself, but Grigorii seems to believe it's genuine. Sure hope he's right. The kid's had it tough. You know he had to escape to Poland through the snowy forests after the Bolsheviks took over Russia? It's a real story. Get him to tell it to you when you find him."

———

Carosel had a contact in the nascent film industry in Paris at Pathé Studios, a cameraman who had served with him during the war. It took a couple of telephone calls to pin Michel Manziel down, but when he finally connected, Manziel was eager to get together. They met at Closerie de Lilas over glasses of wine.

"Dieter Heyder? A director?" Michel Manziel said. "That is a new one on me. I worked with him last month on a film, and he was only a second unit cameraman. Don't get me wrong. He did a fine job, and I could easily see him becoming a lead cameraman in time. But a director? *Non*, Henri. Someone is jerking you off."

"Maybe he is making a movie outside the studio. An independent film."

"It is possible. I suppose if you are paying the bills, you can call yourself whatever you want."

"Do you know how to contact him?"

"Come with me to the main office when we get back to the studio. I'll find his address for you."

———

Carosel was tiring of unanswered doors. He was fatigued in general. Chasing Prince Grigorii all over Paris, he had tried to do too much too quickly. As he dragged his aching legs and burning lungs up two flights of stairs to Dieter Heyder's flat, all he wanted was to sleep on the streetcar all the way back to his office and sleep on his office sofa for another day or so before heading home to sleep in his bed for a week. He paused on the landing to cough into his handkerchief and catch his breath. He checked the handkerchief. Still a good day.

When nobody answered the door at Heyder's apartment, Carosel decided to go off the clock, and maybe take the rest of the week off as well. The only thing that kept him going was the knowledge that Lisette Seydoux's money ensured he wouldn't starve before business picked up again in the fall.

He turned and faced the staircase, trying to generate the energy to trudge back to the street to find a streetcar. He felt a familiar sensation in his chest, and he grabbed for his handkerchief as his entire body was racked with a coughing fit. He pressed the handkerchief to his mouth to stifle the explosive uncontrollable hacking. Something was different. He doubled over, trying to catch his breath. Crinkly metallic tendrils stole into his field of vision from the sides, and his ears were filled with a waterfall roar. He found himself sitting on the hallway floor with no memory of collapsing, his back against the wall, gasping for breath. A door opened, but his vision was too fuzzy for him to see who opened it. The darkness closed in, and the world disappeared in a blink.

"Are you all right?" someone asked. "Should I call a doctor?"

Slowly, the light returned. Carosel felt as if he were underwater. Sounds were distorted and distant. His head pounded. A face swam into view.

"Can you hear me?" she asked. Carosel was only half-conscious, but his policeman's mind immediately and reflexively evaluated her. She was young, no older than thirty. Round face. Bobbed blonde hair. Soft blue eyes. Warm, comforting voice. British accent. Round and buxom in a not displeasing way. He raised the handkerchief and looked at it. Still a good day.

My God, he thought. *If this is a good day, what will the bad ones be like?*

"I do not understand," the woman said. "What about good days and bad days?"

"I said that aloud?" Carosel said. "How long was I out?"

"Only a few seconds. Perhaps you should come inside and sit. You have taken a bump on the head or something."

"If you will allow me to catch my breath," he said. "I will be only a moment."

He tried to stand, bracing his back against the hallway wall, and he got about halfway upright before his eyes rolled in his head and he settled back to the floor.

He woke again, lying on a sofa. His jacket had been removed, along with his hat, and his tie was loosened, the top two buttons of his shirt undone. He must have groaned as he awoke, because an instant later the woman from the hallway appeared in front of him, carrying a tray with a kettle in a quilted cozy and two cups and saucers.

"Don't try to sit," she said. "I've made tea."

She's British, or perhaps Welsh, Carosel thought.

"Welsh," she said.

"Are you a mind reader, or am I saying everything out loud?" Carosel asked.

"You're saying everything out loud," she said. "I'm Gwynna. Gwynna Tudor."

"Like the British monarchs."

"Well, we didn't all become royalty. A few of us lesser cousins stayed behind to keep the Welsh home fires burning. Can you sit, Mr. Carosel?"

"You know my name?"

"I took one of the cards from your jacket pocket, in case I needed to call someone for help."

Carosel rose to a sitting position. Gwynna Tudor poured a cup of tea.

"Thank you," Carosel said. "I do not wish to alarm you. I was gassed during the war. It affected my lungs. All the stairs. My head is clearing now."

"Maybe you should be home in bed," Gwynna said.

"An excellent suggestion. And I shall be, shortly."

"If you don't mind me saying so, being a private investigator might be too strenuous for a man in your condition."

Henri started to argue that he only took the least strenuous cases, but the fact he had fallen out in her hallway only refuted it.

"Why were you banging on Mr. Heyder's door?"

Carosel sipped at the tea, wishing it were wine. "You know Monsieur Heyder?"

"I'm feeding his fish."

"I apologize, Madame—"

"It's mademoiselle," she said. "But you can call me Gwynna if you like."

"I apologize, but some British idioms do not translate well to French. What is this *feeding his fish?*"

"I'm feeding his fish. He has fish. You know. In a tank. He couldn't run off and leave them for the entire month of August. He'd come back and there would be just one enormous, hungry fish. So I go in each day and feed them, and everyone's happy."

"I see. So Monsieur Heyder is out of the city for the month."

"Yes."

"And did Prince Grigorii Romanov accompany him?"

"You know the prince?" Gwynna asked.

"I have yet to make his physical acquaintance. It is him, in fact, whom I am pursuing, not Monsieur Heyder."

"Oh, my. Is the prince in trouble?"

"Everyone presumes he is, so I would not be surprised. He has nothing to worry about from me, however. I merely wish to purchase something from him. Did he travel with Monsieur Heyder?"

"Sure. They're thick as thieves lately."

"Is that a fact?"

"If I didn't know better, I'd say they were a couple of poofs."

"And why do you know better?"

"The prince made a pass at me. Grabbed my arse, he did. Then he caught me in the butler pantry and felt me up proper."

"Did you resist him?"

"Lord, no. Ain't every day you get groped by a real prince. But that was it. It's all he did. Anyway, he and Dieter's thick as thieves, so I guess the prince is with him."

"Do you know where they went?"

"Someplace on the Riviera. Hold on. He left a note."

She crossed to a small writing desk in the corner and rifled through some papers before finding a scribbled scrap. She handed it to Carosel.

"Mademoiselle," Carosel said as he examined the slip. "Has it ever occurred to you that the entire universe is having a jape at your expense?"

"Constantly," she said.

"I tend to be more skeptical," he said. "But some days…"

The slip of paper read: *Villa Ciel, Cagne-sur-Mer,* and a telephone number.

Carosel couldn't stifle the chuckle that rose in his chest. Here he had put so much effort into recovering the watch for his client, and the thief had brought it almost to her doorstep.

"What does it mean?" she asked.

"It means I am taking a journey by rail," Carosel said.

CHAPTER FIFTY

IT WAS A PERFECT day for painting.

Beau and Nathalie rose early, roused by the nonstop clatter of Keeby's typewriter two doors away. After Bish returned to Paris, Keeby had made no effort to curb his work on the new novel, and no pretense that it wasn't his primary goal for the month—to take a manuscript back to Paris and land himself a new publisher.

He had bullyragged Dieter regarding the screenplay's departures from his book, until the German finally relented and put him charge of the shooting script, which only added work to his already crowded schedule. Beau and Nathalie saw him at dinner every other day, or sometimes pacing the hallway trying out dialogue, but for the most part Keeby had become a recluse.

After breakfast, Beau and Nathalie hiked down the hill to the beach at Cagne-sur-Mer. The August sun pierced the whitecaps out in the Mediterranean. It was a hot but breezy day, and Beau had to clip his canvas to the easel to keep it from flying away. Nathalie took the opportunity to lie out in a bathing suit that would have been scandalous back in Charleston—a white knit tank top suit with a black bottom that left her shoulders and upper arms practically bare. If she immersed herself entirely in the water, the clingy knit fabric would cause her to emerge, for all practical purposes, naked. She brought along a huge woven grass sun hat to protect her face from the elements.

Beau worked until noon, when he and Nathalie broke for lunch in the café next to the beach. They returned to the rocky strand around one. A few minutes later, Nathalie rose from her towel.

"Walking the beach," she announced, and didn't wait for his acknowledgement. He didn't mind. He was used to it. Nathalie did what Nathalie did, and woe unto any person who stood in her way.

He was absorbed in his painting several minutes later when someone said, "You're better than I expected."

Lisette Seydoux was looking over his shoulder. She was still dressed in black, so presumably she had been working.

"Thank you," he said. "The market demands cubism and surrealism, but my first love is impressionism. I'm on vacation and painting for myself. Nice to know someone thinks I still have the chops. Shouldn't you be running your shop?"

"I close between noon and two. Most the shops around here do. People want a nap after lunch instead of shopping, and it's cost-effective to close during the hottest part of the day."

"You're quite the businesswoman, I take it," he said.

"Does that bother you?"

"Not at all. I like modern women. You remind me of someone I know back home."

"In Charleston, where your Civil War started?"

"You're fixated on the Civil War. There's been some history since then, you know."

"Do you live on a plantation?"

He laughed. "Nobody lives on plantations anymore. Are you French still guillotining people in Place de la Concorde?"

"I would not know. I am Monegasque."

"I don't know what that means."

"I was born in Monaco. Not far from here. We are tangentially French, but we also are not."

"Has Monaco joined the twentieth century yet?"

"I think you make fun of me, Monsieur."

She smiled at him. He searched her face for any indication of guile or derision but found only warmth and amusement. He liked her smile.

"Well, maybe a little," he said.

"And now you live in Paris?"

"On the Rive Gauche. But my studio is on the other side of the river."

"Your studio."

"It's a collective. One of the fellows staying in the villa and I started it some time back. If you're in Paris, you should drop by. It's a talented bunch of guys."

"No women?"

"We're open to it, but nobody has applied, and we're currently full. If an opening comes up and a woman applies, she'd get the same shake as anyone else."

"Really."

"I'd see to it."

"You make a living with this?" she asked, pointing toward the canvas.

"Not yet. But I live in hope. Have you ever modeled?"

"For a painter? *Non!* Why would you ask such a thing?"

"Because I'd like to paint you," Beau said. "I didn't think about it until this moment, but there's something about your coloring—your eyes, your hair, your skin. I don't want to embarrass you, but you'd be a wonderful subject. Are you familiar with Jeanne Samary?"

"I do not know this name."

"She was one of Renoir's models. In the art world, her name is as well-known as his. Pose for me, and you may become famous."

She laughed. "Oh, thank you. I don't think I have laughed so much in weeks."

"Being famous is funny?"

"My chances of becoming famous are dependent on *your* chances of becoming famous, and I know how many artists in Paris are trying to become famous."

"How many?"

"All of them, Monsieur."

"I asked you before to call me Beau."

"Beau? That is your name?"

"Well, my full name is Beauregard, but only my mother calls me that, and only when I'm in big trouble. And, to tell you the truth, it's kind of a clumsy name to carry around. I'm Beau."

"Well, Monsieur Beau, I think your invitation is a clever way of getting me out of my clothes."

"I wouldn't object, but I don't see the connection."

"In the shop the other day, you said you intended to paint landscapes and nudes. I would be insulted if you wanted to do a landscape of me."

"Let's expand our horizons. I plan now to paint landscapes, nudes, and enchanting faces. Clothing in your case is entirely optional. I want to capture your eyes and the thousand different shades of auburn in your hair, and the crooked corner of your mouth."

"You are charming, Beau."

"It's bred into us in the Low Country. I also know the Cotillion."

"This is how things are, charming Beau. I believe you are trying to seduce me. Normally, I would not object, because in addition to being charming, you are also an attractive man, and as we have already established, I am a modern woman. However, I am not wearing black as a fashion statement. I am in mourning, and it would not be respectful or decent to embark on an affair."

"I had no idea. Was it someone close?"

"My stepmother. She was kind to me, and I cared for her deeply. I recently buried her in Monaco."

"How terrible. I am sorry. I didn't know. I thought you were wearing black to look professional in the shop. I've only seen you there and here."

"I appreciate your sympathy."

"I meant what I said. I am fascinated for some reason with your face. I would like to paint you. We'll leave seduction on the back burner. There's always next August."

Nathalie returned, dripping from her wade in the sea, her suit clinging to her like wet paint, and picked up a towel. She eyed Lisette. Lisette eyed her back.

"This is Lisette," Beau said, pointing with his brush. "We met in the stationer's shop when I bought the brushes. Lisette, Nathalie Bel, my model and close friend."

Lisette surveyed Nathalie closely, which the wet bathing suit made easy. "A Paris model?" she said.

"*Oui,*" Nathalie said.

"I thought so," Lisette said. "You do all have a certain look."

"Fashion dictates, dear. And, I should say, you've captured this whole convent motif masterfully."

"Oops," Beau said.

"What, darling?" Nathalie asked.

"She's in mourning. Stepmother."

"Oh," Nathalie said. "That is tragic. My apologies, Lisette. Won't you join us for a glass of wine? We have some cheese and bread as well."

"No. Thank you. I must return to my shop. It was nice to meet you, Nathalie." Lisette's tone made it blatantly obvious it had not been nice at all. "Monsieur Beau, I enjoyed our conversation. I will give your offer some thought. I'm certain we will meet again soon. Cagne-sur-Mar is a small place."

Beau tipped his hat as she walked away. Nathalie watched her until she disappeared around the corner.

"You're going to paint her?" Nathalie said.

"I'd like to," Beau said, without looking away from the canvas.

"You plan to fuck her as well?"

"If she wants to. Would you mind?"

"Of course not. We place no demands on one another, Beau."

"No, we don't. Though, now isn't a good time."

"God, Beau. I've had some of my best fucks at funerals. Grief can be an aphrodisiac."

"Doctor Freud would have a field day with you, darling."

She lay back on the blanket and shaded her face with the huge sun hat.

"He did," she said.

CHAPTER FIFTY-ONE

HENRI CAROSEL WAS DOZING on his office sofa when someone knocked on the door. With difficulty, he rose and shuffled across the floor to open it.

"Why do you want to see Grigorii in Cagne-sur-Mer?" Gwynna Tudor said, without greeting him.

"What?" Carosel asked. "How did you find—" Then he remembered the card she had taken from his jacket pocket.

"I was a nurse in the war," she said.

"Apropos of what?" Carosel said. He poured water from a carafe into the cup on his desk. He held up the bottle, but Gwynna waved it away.

"I've seen victims of mustard gas. Plenty of them."

Carosel sipped from the glass, but immediately broke into a coughing fit that forced him to sit to catch his breath. He checked his handkerchief. A good day so far.

"You've got it bad," she said.

"Thank you for your professional medical opinion," he said.

"You have no business trotting around the country. You should be in a hospital bed."

"I have become like the shark. To survive another day, I must keep moving."

"Bollocks."

"Each day I work is another day I eat and sleep in my own apartment and don't check into the veterans' hospital where I will be dead of pneumonia and in an unmarked grave within a week. But what concern is this for you?"

"I dragged you out of the hallway and onto my sofa. I'm invested."

"Your investment will pay poor dividends."

"I'll ask again. Why do you want to see Grigorii?"

"This is not your business, Mademoiselle. It is not the custom in my line of work to openly discuss the affairs of one's clients."

"If you get on the train to Nice alone, you'll never come home," she said. "That's how sick you are."

"There are worse places to end one's life."

"You need a nurse."

Carosel burst into laughter which quickly turned into a wheezing fit that momentarily strangled him and turned his lips blue. He coughed into his handkerchief until his vision filled with sparkling stars and faded in from the edges.

"What I need is a new pair of lungs. You wish to come along?" he gasped when he could breathe again. "Out of the question."

"Why?"

"I cannot afford you, for one thing. This is a slow season in my business."

"I'll pay my own way. I was thinking of getting out of the city for the month anyway. This opportunity tipped the scales."

"What opportunity?" he asked. "What do you expect from accompanying me to the Riviera? If you want a vacation, go on a vacation. There will be little sightseeing or sunbathing on this trip, I can assure you. I will arrive in Cagne-sur-Mer, locate Prince Grigorii, conduct my business with him, satisfy my client, and return to Paris. I am afraid you would find it all horribly tedious."

"And how will you locate Grigorii?"

"You gave me his address. Villa Ciel."

"You've never met either Dieter or Grigorii. I know both of them. For God's sake, Grigorii's had his hand up my dress. I can make the introductions, smooth the transaction."

"Mademoiselle Tudor, I believe you have a far more romantic idea of how this will work than reality dictates."

"And if you go alone, you may fail your client by dying before you can purchase whatever you need to purchase. Face it, Monsieur Carosel. You need assistance on this mission. I'm volunteering to help."

"Why?"

"I'm recently unemployed and have no entangling social ties to the city. The city is boring in August, and I need stimulation. I hear the anchovies in Cagne-sur-Mer are delicious this time of year. Take your pick."

Carosel felt himself yielding. He knew she was right. This was quite possibly his last case. "None of these reasons, I suspect, are genuine."

"I'll go for my own reasons then. You're dying, Monsieur Carosel. Do you have a better offer?"

"Your own reasons, yes," he said. "You are lonely. You are Welsh, living in Paris, a vastly different culture. Your French is passable, if you are talking to a ten-year-old, but I suspect you are uncomfortable in large crowds. You are what the psychoanalysts would call an introvert, naturally disinclined toward social interaction. You like people well enough, but they exhaust you. You do not enjoy small talk or frittering conversations and prefer to get directly to the point. You have been recently disappointed in love. Now, also unemployed, and facing four walls day in and day out in the dog days of August, you see an opportunity to serve another person and experience an adventure of sorts. You expect intrigue, which beats boredom every time. More than anything else, you wish something *good* would happen, and you believe this may be the door to it."

"Well, if you knew all that already, why did you try to dig it out of me?" she said, without blinking.

"All of that aside, you must remain in Paris if only because Heyder's fish depend on you."

"Already covered. Me girlfriend will feed them whilst I'm away."

"Mademoiselle Tudor, I suspect you may be a most unusual woman."

"All of which means I would be fascinating company on your journey."

"You might at that. You are determined to come along, I take it?"

"I am."

"At your own expense?"

"If need be."

"Let us leave it at this. I will welcome your company and any required medical attention as I trek to Cagne-sur-Mer to conduct my business. I cannot pay you for your services, but should I perish in the course of my duties, you are welcome to the remainder of my fees due for this job."

"That isn't necessary."

"Oh, you would earn it. If I should pass away before the job is completed, you will need to complete it in my stead."

"Me?"

"Why not? There is no danger involved. No risk to you of any kind. Grigorii will either sell you the object or he won't. You get paid either way."

"If I am to complete this job, I will need to know exactly what it is you plan to obtain from Grigorii."

"I can divulge that only to someone sworn to maintain absolute confidentiality for the client—say, someone working for my detective agency."

"That's going to make things difficult should you suddenly join the Parade of Saints on the Train Bleu," she said.

"Not at all." Carosel crossed to this desk and extracted a small box of calling cards from his drawer. He handed the box to her. "Congratulations, Mademoiselle Gwynna Tudor. You are now an investigator intern in the firm of *H. Carosel*. It is an uncompensated position, but it does enable me to discuss cases with you. I will fill you in on all the details on the train."

———

Lisette Seydoux locked the front door of her shop and found Beau leaning on a nearby doorway. He wore white cotton trousers and a seersucker jacket with a chrysanthemum in his lapel, and a jaunty straw skimmer with a print silk band.

"Going to dinner?" she asked.

"I hope so. Thought I'd see if you'd join me."

412

"Where?"

"Where do the locals go?"

"It depends on who is buying."

"I'm buying," Beau said.

"You are still trying to get me out of my clothes, I think," Lisette said.

"It's dinner. If you take your clothes off, they'll kick us both out, and I'll go hungry. I shall restrain you should you suddenly spontaneously disrobe. I saw a place on the way here. Chez Marcel. Is it any good?"

"It is expensive, Monsieur," she said without looking at him.

"Beau. Remember?"

"I remember, Monsieur."

"Let's do this Charleston style. Mademoiselle Seydoux, would you do me the honor of accompanying me to dinner this evening at Chez Marcel?"

"It is the high season. You need a reservation."

"Then it's a good thing I made one this afternoon."

She stopped and turned to him. "You are very certain of yourself."

"To tell you the truth, I'm scared to death you'll say no. I slipped the *maître d'* a tenner to get the reservation. I'd hate it to be wasted."

"I will not sleep with you, Beau."

"But you've stopped calling me *Monsieur*. We're making progress."

"You are breaking down my defenses. Besides, I am hungry also, and I haven't eaten at Chez Marcel in ages. I will have dinner with you, but I will not sleep with you."

"I also notice we're no longer arguing about the clothes," he said.

"Do not press your luck, Monsieur."

"Two steps forward, and one back," Beau said. "This may be the most tedious seduction in history."

They were seated immediately on arrival, and agreed on a bottle of the local red, which was surprisingly tasty, with hints of berries and smoke and gunpowder. Beau ordered duck confit and Lisette had lamb cassoulet. The server left a bowl of bread and took their orders to the kitchen.

"So, where is your model and close friend tonight?" Lisette asked.

"Nathalie?"

"That is how you introduced her. As your *model and close friend*. Are you lovers?"

"Sometimes. Nathalie isn't enthusiastic about labels."

"She is the subject of your nudes?"

"Some of them. Most of them, lately. But we've already established I'm open to variety."

"She is beautiful."

"She is."

"I suspect you lead an unusual life, Beau."

"There have been a few twists and turns. If my father had his way, I'd be in Charleston right now, directing the family import business."

"Imports?"

"Cigars from Cuba and Jamaica. With prohibition on, my father became a rum smuggler. He was caught. So, our ships have been sitting idle. I suppose it's a good thing I came to Paris after the war and didn't take over the business the way he wanted me to. If I had, I'd be facing federal prison time now."

"This is a romantic story."

"So I've been told. You should see it from my side. My father is facing a federal trial, and I'm stuck in France because if I go home to take over the business I'll be under investigation as well. Before I came to Cagne-sur-Mer, I authorized my father's agent in Paris to import cigars and rum to France instead. France doesn't care if we bring in booze, as long as all the proper palms are greased. So, as hard as I tried to stay out of the family business, it looks like I'll be running it after all. Luck of the draw, I suppose. This might be my last chance to paint fulltime for a while."

"So you are rich," she said.

"No," he said. "I mean, yes. I suppose I am, but I don't feel like it, and money is tight right now. Because of the federal investigation, my allowance is cut off, and most of our family's money is tied up in foreign bank accounts. My mother and sister are living in Charleston on a meager stipend pending the end of the trial, and I don't have one here at all."

"And yet you can afford Chez Marcel, and to bribe the *maître d'*."

"I sold some stuff," he said. "And the family agent in Paris put me on an annuity. I have enough to get by. Once our first ship arrives in Marseilles later this month, I'll be in great shape again and I can take some of the pressure off my mother and sister."

"It would be easier for you to have stayed in Charleston living in wealth," she said.

"Except for the whole smuggling aspect. I'm not comfortable living the rich life," he said. "I like having enough that I don't have to worry about paying a restaurant tab or making the rent each month. Beyond that, it all starts to look like keeping score, and I'm not that competitive."

"This is probably a good time to say my family has money as well," she said.

"A chain of stationer shops?" he asked.

She laughed. "No. The shop is mine alone. My family is in wine. We're drinking one of my father's labels."

"Should have told me when we ordered. We might have gotten a discount," he said.

"Like you, I may soon find myself drawn back into the family business."

"Why?"

"As you know, my stepmother recently died. My father is not well. He will not get better, I fear. If he is unable to run the vineyards, someone will need to take over."

"You could sell the vineyards and wineries and retire," he said.

"You could sell your import business and retire," she said.

"Maybe we're too young to retire."

"The vineyards and wineries have been in my family for five generations."

"Three for me. You were expected to take over from the beginning."

"I've told you this story?"

"I've lived this story. It's like being born into royalty. From the instant you pop out of your mother, you know what your future will be. You know what kind of work you'll do, and you know you'll be immensely wealthy and never

416

want for anything, but you'll detest every minute of it and loathe yourself for caving in for money, and if you have a passion for anything else you can let it go because the family business comes first. Your first conscious memory is walls closing in. You know you should be grateful, because so many other poor slobs are living in hunger and poverty, but your spirit yearns for freedom and soaring and charting your own course among the stars. It kills your soul. Escape looks pretty darned sweet. I paint. You open a stationer shop. We're both fooling ourselves. We can run, but eventually destiny will have its way with us."

"I had finally decided not to slit my wrists tonight," she said. "But when you put it that way..." She sipped at her wine, and the server delivered their dishes. She lifted her glass as if toasting, and he clinked with her, drained the glass, and refreshed both of them from the bottle.

"We're doomed, aren't we?" she said after a few quiet sips.

"Might as well live it up while we can."

"I'm not going to sleep with you," she said.

"But you'll let me paint you," he said.

"I'll let you paint me."

"An acceptable victory," he said. "A war is won only after many skirmishes. So far, you're in retreat. Shall we order a second bottle?"

———

Nathalie Bel filled her wine glass for the fourth—no, wait—fifth time that evening and lounged in a chaise at the edge of the terrace overlooking the Mediterranean at Villa Ciel. The sun had set, and the full moon reflected on the water and cast a dull glow on the entire Cote d'Azur coastline. Shooting on the movie had finished for the day. Dieter and Grigorii had walked into the village to find dinner. Cesare and his girlfriend were upstairs screwing. She could hear them through the latticed window fifty feet away.

She felt the warm glow of the wine flow through her muscles and skin like slipping into a steaming tub. She liked drinking. She liked the body flush after the first glass, and how her head became thick and slow, and her constant rush of brittle memories slowed to a crawl. She only knew peace when drinking. Sometimes opium worked, but she was wary of indulging in it on a regular basis. She had known people who were bucked by the addictions horse and never recovered. When warranted, though, a few glasses of wine or a bowl of black tar could take the edge off life's spiky ride.

The typewriter had been silent for several hours. Nathalie closed her eyes and listened to the sounds of the Mediterranean night, occasionally interrupted by a lengthy moan or cry of pleasure or a naughty giggle from Cesare's window.

She didn't hear Keeby walk up, and she jumped a little when he said, "Someone's having fun tonight."

He glanced at Cesare's window.

"They have been at it for a while," she said. "I like to listen to people fuck. I remember sex during the war. It was always so goddamned life-affirming and earnest and compulsory. We had to fuck, if only to reassure ourselves the world wasn't coming apart at the seams. It was how we clung to our humanity. Now the war is over, and sex has been stripped of all its social responsibility. It's fun again. I listen to couples fuck and I get wet."

"You're about a bottle ahead of me on philosophy," he said.

"I'm a few baths ahead of you as well. You smell."

"I know. I haven't done much more than work lately. I reached a stopping point. Have to make some decisions about where to go next with the book. Taking some air before drawing a bath."

"Clean the tub yourself when you're finished. The housekeeper never did anything to you."

Keeby grasped the wine bottle and swished it around. There was about an inch and a half left. He drank it directly from the bottle and set it back on the table. "You're in rare form tonight. Where's Beau?"

"Seducing some shopgirl in the village."

"Oh. How do we feel about that?"

"We place no demands on one another."

"Yeah. I recall." He lit a cigarette and held it out to her. She waved it away. He took a long drag and blew a cloud of smoke out over the waters of the Med. "And yet, I also recall that kick in the balls when you disappeared without so much as a goodbye. Until I ran across you and Beau in the café, I frequently entertained the notion you might be dead. The fantasy afforded me some brief moments of comfort."

"I have heard that men deal with the end of relationships with more difficulty than women," she said. "Pity."

"So you didn't regret walking away at all?"

"Give me that cigarette. And go find another bottle of wine. If we are going to discuss this, I need both."

He returned minutes later with an open bottle and another glass. "So, there I was, a perfect roast chicken drying in the oven, half a bottle down, and my dick in my hand."

"A vivid image. You must be a writer," she said.

"My only explanation was you must have been run down in the street. Nothing else made sense. There were no signs. No suggestions. No premonitions of doom. You were just…gone. Days turned to weeks, and weeks to months. You had taken me on as some sort of project, and you had carried me as far as you could, and it was on to the next chump."

"It was nothing like that, Keeby," she said. "Nothing at all."

"It's not as if I'm an uninterested bystander. I had some skin in this game. I would appreciate some explanation."

"I was scared," she said. "I am not intended for long love affairs. I do not see myself as a married woman. I have no desire for children. I find domestic life confining and threatening. Why do you think I kept my own apartment? True, I moved as soon as I deserted you, but I always left my options open. You wanted too much from me, Keeby. I can't give that much of myself to anyone."

"You could have left a note."

"I didn't decide until late in the evening. I walked in the direction of Rue Montparnasse a dozen times. I never got more than a block before returning to my apartment. In the end, I sat at La Rotonde and drank until late in the evening, and I went home and took my telephone off the hook and went to sleep. When I woke the next day, I had made the break. By then, we both knew everything had changed forever. What else was there to discuss? I found a different apartment, moved, and set up life in another arrondissement."

"I can see how that made it easier on you," he said, the bile in his voice unmistakable.

"You are justifiably resentful. But we were not married. I never made any promises at all. In the end, I owed you nothing but an explanation, and now even that debt is satisfied. The scales between us are balanced. We accept that one part of our life is over, and a new one has begun, and we avoid recriminations at all costs. That is how we do things in Paris. That is *savoir-faire*."

"As is sitting alone on a terrace overlooking the beautiful moonlit Mediterranean and drinking half the wine in France while your current lover is seducing some shopgirl in the village?"

"And our conversation has come full circle. May I suggest, on behalf of everyone else in the villa, that you take your bath now?"

A sharp feminine cry burst from Cesare's third floor window.

"Hey, Cesare!" Keeby shouted. "Leave some for the rest of us!"

"Go fuck your hand, Keeby!" Cesare shouted through the window.

"The boy does have stamina," Keeby told Nathalie. "You have to give him that."

"Come on," she said. "I'll draw your bath. I don't want to smell you anymore."

"Best offer I've had all day."

CHAPTER FIFTY-TWO

LISETTE SEYDOUX FOUND the gate to Villa Ciel open and took it as an invitation to enter.

It was another gorgeous, oppressive August day. She had closed the shop for the hottest part of the afternoon and had decided to stroll to the villa to see how Beau and Nathalie and their friends lived. She had visited the villa twice before, both times for parties thrown by the baroness who owned it, but she had only been a girl at the time, accompanying her parents, and she hadn't been beyond the front gates in years.

As she walked up the hill, she heard voices in the former servants' quarters on the other side of the gardens, and followed them to find Dieter, Cesare, and Grigorii arguing in a circle around a huge, tripod-mounted motion picture camera.

"But that is the effect I am trying to capture!" Dieter said. "It is metaphorical!"

"You cannot shoot into the sun!" Cesare shouted. "The film is too sensitive. It will wash out."

"But I cannot run in other direction," Grigorii said. "I must escape into trees. There is no sea in western Russia!"

"He is running to the *light*," Dieter said to Cesare. "How can you not recognize the symbolism?"

"Excuse me," Lisette said. All three turned toward her reflexively, as if noticing her for the first time.

"Who are you?" Dieter asked.

"Lisette Seydoux. From the village. I'm looking for Monsieur Beau."

"On the terrace." He stabbed a finger at the house and launched back into Cesare. "This is my film, and we will shoot it my way!"

"We will shoot it both ways, and you will see I am right!"

"You would shoot up half our stock just to make a point!"

Lisette left them to their argument and found the path around to the front of the villa. The door was open, allowing the cooling sea breeze to flow through the house. Lisette knocked twice on the jamb, but nobody answered. The sound of clacking typewriter keys echoed down the main staircase. Translucent sheers billowed in the French doors leading to the terrace.

She found Beau on the terrace, at his easel, slashing away with a palette knife nearly dripping with paint, leaving thick gobs on the surface of his canvas. Several feet away, Nathalie sat at a wrought-iron table, holding a glass of wine, one foot on the ground and the other on the seat of the chair next to her. A bottle was on the table, beside a plate of cheese and charcuterie and a small vase of daisies. Nathalie's wide-brimmed woven grass hat flopped across her face, hiding all but her chin and lips as she gazed out over the Mediterranean. She also wore a pair of black high-heeled pumps, and a long string of pearls fell across her belly and hung between her legs. Otherwise, she was naked.

"Oh," Lisette said. Beau and Nathalie both turned to her at the same time.

"Did we order stationery, darling?" Nathalie asked, her voice thick and smoky.

"Be polite," Beau said. "Mademoiselle Seydoux. What a pleasure to see you again."

"I'm sorry to interrupt," Lisette said. "I didn't know you were painting her."

"He isn't painting me, darling," Nathalie said.

"This is a landscape." Beau sounded a little hurt.

"I don't see the point in wearing clothes in this oppressive heat," Nathalie said. "I'm a model and an actress. Everybody here has seen me naked dozens of times. Why be miserable? I wanted a glass of wine, and I decided to keep Beau company while he painted. Please, have a seat. The breeze is delicious in this spot."

Lisette sat hesitantly, and Nathalie walked into the house. She reappeared seconds later with two glasses. She filled one for Lisette, who tried to keep her gaze on Nathalie's eyes as she took the glass.

"Beau?" Nathalie asked.

"Why not?"

She poured Beau a glass and returned to her seat and stared at Lisette over the lip of her wine glass. Lisette sipped uncomfortably.

"I think we've embarrassed her," Nathalie told Beau.

"Speak for yourself," Beau said.

"I'm not embarrassed," Lisette said. "I simply did not expect to find you nude. I was surprised."

"You should try it," she told Lisette. "At least, get out of that black dress. You must be roasting in this heat. Don't be shy. Undergarments are practically formal wear around here."

"So it seems."

"I'm happy you dropped by, Mademoiselle Seydoux," Nathalie said.

"Please. Lisette."

"Lisette, then. Ever since Lady Bish left, I have been lonely for intelligent feminine conversation. Cesare's girlfriend Amelie is sweet, but she is allergic to the inside of a book and hasn't had an original idea since she was whelped. And, anyway, when Cesare isn't arguing with Dieter, she's fucking him, and when he is arguing with Dieter, she's sleeping it off. We don't see each other often, and when we do, all she wants to talk about is Cesare's cock. I grow weary for female companionship."

The surprise of Nathalie's nudity had worn off, and Lisette relaxed. "I would be fascinated to learn what you and I might have in common," she said.

"She thinks I'm a whore," Nathalie said to Beau.

"Are you projecting, darling?" Beau asked without looking away from the canvas.

"Not at all," Lisette said. "You misread my meaning. I am genuinely curious to find out what experiences we share that would promote feminine intimacy. After all, you are Beau's model and lover, and yet he has made overtures toward my presumed honor. You and I are both women and know men are drawn to the same type of women again and again. If he is attracted to you and to me, we must have some qualities in common. As a curious person, I would be fascinated to find out what they are, because as of yet I am entirely uncertain."

425

Nathalie smiled and drained her wine and placed the glass back on the table.

"Fuck all, Beau. This is no fun. I like her."

"Thought you might. Try to bear up," Beau said. He slashed away at the canvas for a few minutes more, ignoring the newly friendly chatter at the table. Nathalie described French-speaking North Africa. Lisette hung on each word as she described the beauty and cruelty of the desert.

Beau allowed himself to drink in the contrast between Nathalie's brown skin and Lisette's Monegasque olive complexion, Nathalie's sable bob and Lisette's flowing auburn locks, Nathalie's sharp corners and Lisette's softer curves, and the stark absurd incongruity of the two of them chatting away, one as naked as the day she was born and the other swaddled in mourning clothes. He yanked the canvas from the easel, substituted a fresh one, and grabbed a stick of charcoal.

"Stay right where you are," he said. "Mademoiselle Seydoux, will you be required at your shop for the next couple of hours?"

"I believe, under the circumstances, you can call me Lisette. It's my shop. I can open or close it as I please. Are you…are you drawing us?"

"I can't resist. You are so amazing together. Please. You said I could paint you."

Lisette turned to Nathalie, "And here I thought he wanted to get me out of my clothes."

"C'est jeunes hommes," Nathalie said.

"Oui," Lisette agreed.

"And it's still early in the month," Nathalie added. "Give him time. But, please, Beau tells me your family owns wineries. That must be the most interesting world—and how wonderful it would be to get all the wine you want for free! Did you grow up on a vineyard?"

"For the first ten years or so, until my father decided to move us to the Paris house. He has directed the wineries from the city ever since. Living in a vineyard is a contrast with the city, indeed. However, I believe the romantic notion of owning a vineyard may not accurately reflect the truth. Yes, we produce the nectar of love. I believe that alone affords our business an aura of eroticism. When you get down to the basics, though, it's just farming."

The afternoon had turned out differently than Lisette had expected. She had planned to tell Beau she wanted to schedule a sitting for a painting, but she had never expected to begin it that afternoon. On the other hand, it was the south of France, and the summers were hot and steamy, and she had adjusted quickly to Nathalie's nudity, so she resigned herself to an afternoon of leisure. The wine helped.

Beau sketched quickly. He told them he had already decided to drop back to his impressionist roots for this painting, modern conventions be damned. He wanted people to look at the two beautiful women in the painting and know beyond a doubt they were women.

Nathalie coached her in posing, telling her to find a comfortable position, because she might be holding it for a while. They laughed and chatted and drank the entire bottle of wine and most of another. Cesare and Dieter and Grigorii strolled through late in the afternoon. They smiled and waved and moved on.

Finally, Beau finished for the day.

"Is it done?" Lisette asked.

"Good lord, no," Beau said. "But I captured everything I needed to. I can add the fine touches later." He took her hand in his and kissed it. "Thank you for posing. You were every bit as lovely as I anticipated."

"Thank you," she said.

Nathalie took her hand and pulled her in for a long embrace. Nathalie was long and lean and lithe, and Lisette felt the angles and blades of her bones through her perfect soft skin. "I am so happy to have a new friend. Won't you join us for dinner?" Nathalie asked. "I think there may be a bottle or two of wine left in Cagne-sur-Mer. We should put them out of their misery."

"I would not wish to impose," Lisette said.

"Dear Lisette, you have posed for the great Beau Shipley," Nathalie said. "You are now part of the *Salle* family."

"Please do," Beau said. "We'd love to have you."

Yes, Lisette thought. *I believe you would.*

———

Keeby found a stopping place in his novel late in the night, long after Beau and Nathalie had returned from their dinner with Lisette Seydoux in the village, and long after Cesare and Amelie had finished fucking for the night, and after the lights were out under Dieter and Grigorii's door.

He padded to the kitchen, poured himself a glass of wine, and walked out onto the terrace to smoke a cigarette in the cool night air. He had no idea what time it was, but most of the lights were out in the village below. A cone of light from the newly risen moon searched across the nearly-still waters of the Mediterranean.

The novel was going badly. He couldn't balance the sense of loss and the tragedy of survival for his lead character, who kept coming off alternately as peevish, spoiled, and naïve. He wasn't particularly worried, as he already had one novel under his belt and had learned through frustrating experience that all first drafts were garbage. *The goal of a first draft isn't to get it right*, he reminded himself. *The goal is to get it done.* There would be plenty of time during editing and rewrites to get it right. Even so, he dreaded the process of typing and retyping the manuscript when the only mystery remaining was whether the damned thing was any good in its final form. Someday, he mused, someone will invent a device allowing a writer to correct a story on the fly. He flicked the cigarette over the stone terrace wall into the Mediterranean below and decided a toy like that would only make writers lazy. Better to just roll up your sleeves and do the work.

He had looked out his window earlier in the afternoon and spied Beau painting Nathalie and a young woman he didn't recognize. *The shopgirl from the village*, he surmised. Nathalie was naked, but the girl remained in her black dress, and Keeby recognized the artistic message Beau was trying to convey. Contrast and conflict drove both painting and writing.

He had gazed at Nathalie for a minute or so, recalling their tryst years earlier, and felt a pang. Lady Bish was painting Paris red with their mutual paramour Monique Rothe, and he was odd man out at Villa Ciel. He recalled the touch of Nathalie's flawless skin, the scent of her hair, and the things she used to whisper in his ear as they made love.

Well, she was with Beau now, and in a few months she'd be with someone else, because that was her nature. He didn't resent Beau or envy him. It was just coincidence and fate in action. His affair with Nathalie had been every bit as accidental as hers had been with Beau. Coincidences happen, and sometimes they were rotten and made you feel empty and fatalistic.

He poured another glass and drank and smoked and listened to the sounds of the night, and he wondered whether his feelings toward Nathalie were influencing his novel. The main character, Rhett, was based on Beau after all. He considered the possibility his resentment toward Nathalie might have caused him to unconsciously emasculate his protagonist as covert revenge against Beau. Maybe he had a difficult time writing Rhett because he *was* jealous of Beau and Nathalie but admitting it would threaten his perception of himself as *so* Parisian and sophisticated.

That was the problem with Paris, at least the part of Paris Keeby populated. Without Bish at his side, Keeby had a lot of time on his hands to think about it. Nothing was permanent. Of all his friends and acquaintances in Paris, he couldn't think of five couples who had been together for decades. Love— the true, lasting, romantic love poets extol, and novels glamorize—seemed nonexistent. Ross Twinings smirked and claimed to love Bish so madly that he'd gleefully share her with any young consort of whom he approved. Amedeo Modigliani and Suguharu Foujita took their spouses to Cagnes-sur-Mer, perhaps to this exact villa, and fell into a fleshy lump together. Nathalie had abandoned him and was now shamelessly fucking his best friend, only doors away from his bedroom. Every moral tenet he was taught as a child was routinely violated and superseded by the damned Parisian insistence on sophistication and *savoir faire*. Nothing blasé or bourgeois was acceptable. The world had stopped in place for four years while the inbred crowned heads of Europe turned the countryside into an abattoir. Now, the war a fading memory, hedonism and celebration consumed Paris with a vengeance. Most poor suckers were just pulled along with the undertow.

"That's good," he whispered to himself. "I should use that."

Somewhere around the side of the house, he heard glass breaking, and a short, sharp cackle, and the silence of the deep night returned. Curious, Keeby crushed his cigarette underneath his heel and walked around to the former servants' quarters. The cottage Dieter had been using as the location for the farmhouse in his film, farthest from the house, was brightly lit inside.

He didn't remember Dieter saying anything about filming that evening, but he recalled Grigorii did steal away in the middle of the night when he abandoned his imaginary farm girl lover, so perhaps they were shooting his preparations to sneak off into the darkness.

Dieter stood behind his camera, cranking at the machine and issuing commands. The room was ablaze with light, and heat and wisps of smoke from the carbon arc lamps rolled from the doorway left open to allow cool air inside. Keeby leaned against the door jamb to watch, and almost dropped his cigarette.

Grigorii and Nathalie were on the bed, naked. Nathalie straddled Grigorii's hips. Every time she lurched forward Keeby could see him deep inside her, thrusting athletically and rhythmically with a member that demonstrated how eminently qualified he was for his profession. Nathalie gasped and moaned and cried in the way Keeby so sorely remembered.

"What the hell!" Keeby shouted.

Dieter immediately stopped cranking. Nathalie rolled off Grigorii and stood next to the bed. Grigorii lay nonchalantly on the bed watching the drama, his improbable phallus still at full mast.

"Keeby!" Nathalie said. "What are you doing here?"

"What are *you* doing here? Does Beau know about this?"

"I can explain," Dieter said.

"It's just acting, and what does it matter whether Beau knows?" Nathalie shouted angrily. "I do what I want to do! You are being provincial about this, and I do not like it!"

"May I explain?" Dieter said.

"What?" Keeby said. "How you're filming Grigorii and Nathalie fucking? I don't recall writing anything that explicit in my novel."

"This isn't for your movie," Dieter said.

"It's not going to be anyone's movie," Keeby shouted, and he pushed the camera and tripod over onto the floor.

"My camera!" Dieter howled, and he dropped to the floor to check it for damage.

"What the hell are you doing?" Nathalie screamed. "You are such a child!"

Grigorii lazily rolled off the bed and casually put on a satin robe. "I agree with her, Keeby."

"Who gives a shit what you think? You're nothing but a man whore. I wish I'd never met you," Keeby told him.

"Your fucking bullshit story ruined my career. I ought to toss you into the Med."

"Just the thing!" Grigorii said, tossing off the robe. "A late-night swim! Who wants to go?"

Keeby grabbed him by the arm and stared into his eyes. "What are you on?"

"What does it matter?" Grigorii said.

"Would you *please* let me explain?" Dieter said, as he righted the camera.

"What?" Keeby said. "What explanation is there?"

"If I didn't do this, there would be no film of your novel!" Dieter said.

Nathalie leaned against the door jamb, still naked, smoking a cigarette. Grigorii walked by her. "Going for swim. Want to come?"

"No," she said.

"Suit yourself." He took the path toward the house.

"What do you mean?" Keeby said.

Dieter inspected his camera as he said, "I could not purchase enough short end film stock to complete the picture. A man at the studio heard I was trying to acquire it. He took me aside. There is a lucrative market for films such as this—" He patted the side of the camera. "He sold me the film stock at less than wholesale. In return I make this movie on the side for him to sell to his rich collectors. He will make far more from them than he would selling the film stock to me at market price."

"And what do Grigorii and Nathalie get out of it?"

"They get to make the other movie as well. Your movie."

"And you're okay with this?" Keeby asked Nathalie.

She took a drag from her cigarette. "It's only fucking," she said.

"What in hell is going on?" Beau said as he came around the corner of the house. "I heard shouting and I ran into Grigorii walking naked toward the beach. Hey, have you guys ever seen his—" He stopped when he saw Keeby in the doorway with Nathalie. Dieter had extinguished the floodlights and was putting away his equipment. Only the glow from the single bedside lamp and the ember from Nathalie's cigarette shown in the night, but it was easy to see she was as naked as Grigorii.

"Throwing a party without me?" he asked.

"Won't even try to explain," Keeby said, and he walked past Beau toward the house. Nathalie took another drag from the cigarette and waited, staring defiantly into Beau's eyes.

"You're on opium," he said.

"Want some?" she asked. "I have a little left."

"I smelled sex on Grigorii as he passed me on the way to the water. I smell it here."

"Probably because I was fucking him," she said coolly, and she took another puff from the Gauloise.

"Yeah. I'm a pretty quick study. I put it all together."

"I can explain," Dieter said. And he did, as Nathalie tossed the cigarette butt out into the garden and pulled a silk kimono around her body. When Dieter was finished, Beau shook his head.

"I paid for the film stock," he said. "You're turning me into a pornographer."

"It was the only way," Dieter repeated. "We never would have been able to purchase enough short ends to complete the picture. We might have shot half, maybe two-thirds. Who knows when we would have been able to film the rest? I'll use maybe two hundred feet on this side project, and the rest of the stock is ours to do with as we please. There's plenty left over to finish filming Keeby's book."

"And Grigorii and Nathalie? How did they get involved?"

"I asked them. Beau, I know this is uncomfortable, but—"

"Oh, fuck, Dieter," Nathalie interrupted. "Come right out with it. Beau, this is not my first time fucking in front of a camera. Same for Grigorii. You fucking puritan American rich boys, you know nothing of survival in this world. I have told you before, and you do not hear it. Sometimes life is all about the least worst choice. You give me a choice between screwing someone I like on camera and screwing some fat, sweaty stranger in an alley? I ask which way to wardrobe. Sometimes it comes down to those two choices, or ones equally onerous. You will never understand."

"Don't I?" Beau said. "Remember how I paid for this trip, Nathalie."

"And even then you let Grigorii do your dirty work for you. I'm taking the empty room tonight."

"Do what you want. I'm returning to Paris tomorrow or the day after."

"You want to stay around long enough to put it to your shopkeeper, don't you?" she asked.

"Right now, romantic entanglements are the farthest thing from my mind."

Dieter hustled between them after securing his film equipment. "I am sorry again, Beau. I do appreciate you coming through with the money for the film. I only wanted to make my own contribution."

"We'll talk later, Dieter," Beau said. "Now's not the time."

"A wise suggestion. I will see you in the morning—oh, wait. It is already morning. We will talk in the afternoon. Good night—er, morning." He hurried up the path to the main house.

"That was a cheap shot," Beau said.

"About the shopgirl?"

"Yes."

"Roll with the punches, Beau." She placed a warm hand on his shoulder as she passed by him to return to the villa house. "For what it's worth, I like her. We knew this was never going to be permanent. We both know our time is coming to an end. It was inevitable."

"It's your nature," he said.

"You may be right. Perhaps a clean break is best, and after tonight we have good reason to end it. But you'd better bed the shopgirl, or I will."

"For Christ's sake, Nathalie. Does everything have to be a competition with you? And, anyway, I saw her first."

"Many international conflicts have been settled on less. Let's go to bed. You have a lot to do tomorrow if you're returning to Paris."

———

Shortly after sunrise, Amelie's screams for help woke everyone in the Villa Ciel. In various stages of dress, the vacationers dashed from their rooms and followed her cries to the veranda, where Amelie stood at the stone wall overlooking the cliff.

"Help! Oh, dear God help him!" she screamed. Keeby arrived first and peered over the wall.

"There's someone in the cove!" he called to Beau and Cesare as they bounded out of the house, followed by Nathalie. Dieter stayed inside the house calling for Grigorii.

Beau stretched over the wall and looked. "He's not moving. Let's get down there."

Keeby, Beau, and Cesare scrambled over the rocky path to the beach, slipping on gravel and stray twigs. Cesare fell once and scraped his leg. As they reached the bottom, Beau said, "Over there!"

They rushed to the side of the prostrate figure in the sand, a naked man with jet black hair, a pencil-thin mustache, and a tight goatee. His sideburns were worn long and trimmed to dart-like points.

"Jesus," Keeby said. "It's Grigorii."

There was no point in trying to revive him. His ashen skin and filmy dilated eyes made it obvious he had been dead for several hours. The skin against the sand had turned purple with pooling blood.

"He was headed to the beach for a swim when I passed him," Beau said. "He invited me to come along."

"He was on something," Keeby said. "I saw it in his eyes."

"Nathalie was using opium last night. He was as well."

Keeby said, "He was high, and he went swimming and became disoriented and drowned. The receding tide left him here on the sand. What a lousy way to go. We need to call the police."

"Someone should stay here with the body," Beau said. "It's common decency."

"I'll stay," Cesare said. "I was a corpsman in the war. Bodies don't bother me. This one is even intact."

———

Beau had expected the discovery of a drowned man on the beach of Cagne-sur-Mer would cause a stir and would have Villa Ciel swarming the gendarmes within an hour.

A single officer arrived two hours after they discovered Grigorii's body. Dieter sat in the living room, half a decanter of brandy in front of him and half in his belly. He stared into space, a continuous dribble of tears staining his cheeks. Nathalie and Amelie sat on either side of him, trying to offer comfort. Amelie's face was tear-streaked as well. Only Nathalie among them appeared to be composed.

The gendarme identified himself as Dorleac and asked to see the body. Beau and Keeby first showed him the view over the terrace wall.

"This is where Amelie—" Beau pointed inside the house. "—first saw the body."

"Was the deceased intoxicated, Monsieur?"

Beau and Keeby looked at each other.

"Yeah," Beau said. "He was intoxicated. We don't know with what. Alcohol. Possibly opium."

"This is a bad combination, Monsieur," Dorleac said.

"Sure was for Grigorii," Keeby said.

"And the man sitting next to the body?" Dorleac asked.

"He's one of the guests here, Cesare. He was inside the house when the body—Grigorii, that is—was first discovered."

"Please accompany me to the beach." As they made their way along the path, Dorleac said, "I should tell you this is a routine occurrence along the Riviera, especially in August. People crowd into the Cote d'Azur from the cities, and they abandon their inhibitions. They drink too much, use drugs when they are not accustomed to them, and think they can challenge *la Mer. La Mer* always wins, my friends. Remember."

They arrived at the beach and made their way to where Cesare sat with Grigorii's body.

"Been dead for several hours, it appears," Dorleac said. "What time did you say he went into the water?"

"I don't know," Beau said. "I didn't check the clock. It was late. Well after three, I'd say."

"And how did you come to encounter the dead man walking toward the beach?"

Keeby broke in. "We were having a party in one of the cottages. Our friend Dieter makes movies and was shooting late last night. When we finished, we decided to let off a little steam. I guess Grigorii let off a little too much."

Beau picked up on Keeby's glossing over of exactly what kind of picture Dieter was shooting. "The noise woke me," Beau said. "I wanted to see what was going on, so I walked around to the cottage. That's when I ran across Grigorii."

"And he was clothed at the time?" Dorleac asked.

"Ah, no," Beau said. "He was already naked."

"I see. All right. I simply need to obtain all the needed information on the deceased. I will send a crew to collect the body, and there will be an autopsy performed later today, perhaps tomorrow, possibly the day after."

"Kind of uncertain, isn't it?" Beau asked.

"It is August in Cagne-sur-Mer," Dorleac said. "I suspect this is not the only drowning we will encounter today. Please accept the condolences of the Cagne-sur-Mer Constabulary on the demise of your friend. I will be in touch shortly with the results of the examination."

———

"Did you say Prince Grigorii Romanov?" Lisette Seydoux asked Henri Carosel.

They sat in Lisette's office at the stationery shop. It was middle afternoon, and she had turned the CLOSED sign out to afford them privacy. Gwynna Tudor stood to the side, as if hovering over Carosel without trying to look like it. Lisette couldn't decipher the emotion on Gwynna's face, but the plump blonde woman never took her eyes off the detective.

Carosel and Tudor had arrived in Nice on the overnight train from Paris, taken an early lunch—which Carosel had left mostly uneaten, complaining of a lack of appetite—and hopped aboard a local bus to Cagne-sur-Mer. Neither had brought baggage, as they did not intend to remain on the Cote d'Azur for more than a night at most. They arrived at Lisette's shop shortly after five o'clock.

Lisette was surprised to the see the detective, especially in the company of the blonde stranger, but also because he seemed to have shrunk in the several days since she had hired him. His face was gray, his eyes sunken. His hair hung limp, and droplets of sweat dotted his upper lip. His eyes were bloodshot, but his voice was strong as he described his investigation.

Carosel drew the candy box Messier had given him from his bag and slid it across Lisette's desk.

"Your stepmother's jewelry. My contact in Paris reported he purchased them from Grigorii Romanov. It fits with the assumptions we made when we spoke in Paris. Romanov lives in the Montparnasse neighborhood, as we suspected, and he would have run in exactly the direction you described to return to his apartment after stripping your father and stepmother of their valuables. As a gigolo, he already had a network of resources to sell valuables, and I was fortunate enough to locate the precise man to whom he sold these. Mademoiselle Tudor here is acquainted with the prince and can identify him. Prince Grigorii informed Mademoiselle Tudor's neighbor, a close friend of the prince, that he could be located as the Villa Ciel in Cagne-sur-Mer. Ironic, is it not, that our quarry should come to you, Mademoiselle Seydoux?"

"More than you know. The watch is still missing."

"Unfortunately, yes. My contact in Paris told me Prince Grigorii Romanov retained the watch."

"So it is still in his possession?" Lisette asked.

"I believe this to be the case, Mademoiselle. We shall visit him at the Villa Ciel and attempt to retrieve the watch. The only remaining decision you will need to make at that point is whether you will take out charges against the prince for the theft."

"Monsieur Carosel, charges will be wholly unnecessary, and in fact impossible. I am afraid I am about to complicate your case. Prince Grigorii Romanov is dead."

"Oh, my God!" Gwynna gasped. "The poor man!"

"This is a surprise," Carosel said, and his chest heaved. He grabbed for his handkerchief and pressed it to his mouth as he coughed until his face turned crimson and his vision blurred. Immediately, Gwynna was at his side, tears flooding her eyes, her hands on his shoulders as they rocked. Finally, the fit rolled to an end. He stole a surreptitious glance at the cloth before closing it in his fist. Still a good day. "I apologize, Mademoiselle. The condition I described to you in Paris…"

"The gas. Yes. It seems worse since we last spoke."

"It is a progressive affliction, I am told, and mine has been progressing for some time. Thank you for your concern. Please, tell me more about Prince Grigorii."

"Yes," Gwynna added, dabbing at her eyes with her own handkerchief. "I am in complete shock. How did he die?"

"He drowned, sometime night before last. They found him yesterday morning on the small cove beach at the base of the cliff below Villa Ciel. I met him briefly when I visited the villa several days ago. His death was a shock."

"Drowned, you say?"

"I have become friendly with a couple staying at the villa. They told me he had been drinking and using opium. The police were planning to perform an autopsy, but I haven't heard any more."

"It is indeed tragic, and perhaps a problem for our case. However, all is not lost. How did the unfortunate prince drown?"

"He went swimming in the Mediterranean and passed out from alcohol and drugs."

"If he went swimming, and if the watch was in his possession here in Cagne-sur-Mer, it is unlikely he took it into the water with him. If he did, it will be among his effects at the constabulary. If not, it should still be in his lodgings at the villa. I saw the constabulary on the way to your shop. With your indulgence, I would like to check with the gendarmes first, to see if the watch is among the prince's effects. Failing that, we shall pay a visit to the Villa Ciel."

CHAPTER FIFTY-THREE

LIKE MANY OF the local police stations along the Riviera, the Cagne-sur-Mer constabulary was a quiet office in an ancient building several streets back from the beaches. Henri Carosel and Gwynna Tudor only had to go through three officers to reach Constable Dorleac, who had conducted the initial investigation into Prince Grigorii's drowning.

"The results of the autopsy arrived only an hour ago," Dorleac told them. "And while I am not typically inclined to share such information publicly, there is nothing in the report suggesting anything other than accidental drowning. The man went swimming when he was intoxicated, and either became disoriented when he was swamped by a wave or simply passed out. It is a tragic case."

"Before he came to Cagne-sur-Mer," Carosel told him, "Prince Grigorii came into possession of a singular watch, manufactured by Bell and Ross, which belongs to my client's father. My client would like to recover the watch to return it to her father, who is incapacitated by an automobile accident and may not survive."

"I regret I cannot be of service," Dorleac said. "The deceased had no jewelry when he was discovered. He had nothing at all, save for the skin in which he was born."

"He was naked, Monsieur?" Carosel asked.

"Apparently, he preferred to bathe at night in the nude. It is not unheard of on the Cote d'Azur."

"In the absence of evidence of foul play, I presume you expect the death to be ruled accidental?" Carosel said.

"That is my expectation, Monsieur. I have been surprised in the past, but only in the rarest of circumstances. This does not appear to be one of them."

"You do not anticipate searching or examining Prince Grigorii's lodgings at the Villa Ciel?"

"I can see no reason to do so. I believe I know your intent, Monsieur, and that is between you and the late prince's estate, to the extent he had one. From what I can gather, he lived hand to mouth as a gigolo in Paris. In any case, the disposition of a watch in the possession of a dead man who has no identifiable survivors is of no interest to the Cagne-sur-Mer Constabulary."

————

Henri Carosel was fatigued after his interview with Dorleac, and asked Gwynna whether she would mind sitting in a café by the sea to enjoy a glass of wine and rest for a bit before making the trek to Villa Ciel. It was late afternoon. The sun angled across the rocky shore. The air was thick with moisture and salt stung Carosel's sinuses. The server delivered their wine and a small basket of bread.

"This is so beautiful," Gwynna said, beaming. "I've never been to the Riviera."

"I have been here—" He counted on his fingers. "—six times, save for our present visit. I have not returned since before the war, and I have never been in Cagne-sur-Mer."

"Where are your parents now?"

"Dead, both of them. Influenza."

"I'm so sorry."

"It was some time ago. I have adjusted."

"My parents used to take me to Cornwall or Sussex for holiday," she said. "But it was different, of course. Not at all like this. I don't recall a warm day before I came to France, not a truly warm one where the sun penetrates your skin and muscles all the way to the bone. A day like this."

"And why did you move from Wales to Paris?" he wheezed.

"You already guessed it when you read me my life story yesterday. I am recently disappointed in love."

"How recently?"

"Not so recently, in fact. The man in question was Parisian. I lost my head and moved to another country for a man who turned out to be nothing but a scoundrel. He lied and cheated and even stole from me. His only grace was he never struck me, but he might as well have, the way he made me feel. Then it was over. But I was in Paris, which beats all hell out of Swansea, by the way, so I decided to make the best out of a horrible situation. Now I'm on the Riviera, drinking wine and soaking up sunshine. Things are looking better."

"And perhaps this is a good time for you to tell me the real reason you accompanied me on this adventure on the Cote d'Azur."

She sipped at her wine and dredged a chunk of bread through olive oil. "I don't believe anyone should die alone," she said.

"Ah," he said. "And here I thought you wanted to spend the rest of your life with me." He chuckled, which triggered a brief coughing spell he stifled with his handkerchief. Still a good day.

"No, but I'm happy to spend the rest of *your* life with you," she said. "I told you I've seen cases like yours before. They all end the same way. Your time is close, Monsieur Carosel. Nobody should face that without someone to hold their hand."

"Are you some sort of angel?" he asked.

"I'm just a girl from Swansea, silly," she said.

"I have never been to Swansea," he said. "Pity."

———

Dieter was still in shock at the Villa Ciel. He sat on the couch hour after hour, staring off into space. The bottle of brandy was long gone, but he still gazed stonily at the walls as if too inebriated to move. Everyone had considered the thing between him and Grigorii to be a fling, the sort of affair that frequently took place between directors and actors. Apparently, Dieter had thought otherwise.

Amelie was finally calm after her early morning shock. Cesare had taken her back to Paris earlier in the day. The glow of the August vacation at the Cote d'Azur had faded to black. Nobody wanted to remain.

447

Keeby sat on the beach, near the spot where they found Prince Grigorii's body, for most of the afternoon. He was twenty-seven years old, and he had seen more death than anyone should be subjected to in an entire lifetime. Bodies blasted to pieces by artillery. Heads drilled through by machine-gun bullets. May Day rioters stiffening along the Champs-Elysees. Boys who died of dysentery in the trenches, lying for days in their own shit in the mud waiting for the overworked graves registration pukes to come along and cart them off. Now, Prince Grigorii.

He had never particularly liked Grigorii. He found the prince self-aggrandizing and pompous and opportunistic and a little conniving. No doubt he overheard a story about some poor fellow trying to escape to Poland and appropriated it as his own. It was like him to steal his own biography. He was extremely envious of other people's adventures.

On the other hand, was Keeby any better? He had taken Grigorii's lie and turned it into a novel. He was in the business of appropriating other people's lives because he hadn't lived much of one himself to draw on. He recalled a teacher in college who told him he should write what he knew. Based on that advice, Keeby could write about war, and drinking, and screwing models and actresses and noblewomen, the sum of his life experience.

To keep from thinking about Grigorii, he had thrown himself into writing. He had started early the previous afternoon, and had continued through the night, stopping only to hit the toilet or briefly nod off as the sun peaked over the horizon. Each time he allowed himself to drift away, even for a few seconds, Grigorii's bloodless face and filmy eyes and salt-matted hair appeared in his dreams, and he would shudder himself awake and force himself back to the typewriter.

He had finally run out of gas around nine in the morning. There were no words left. He had used them all. He stared at the last period he had typed and waited for the next sentence to manifest itself from the ether, and his gears ground away in neutral. He had lost his literary traction. Sleep was still out of the question, so he grabbed a bottle of wine from the cellar, tossed his shoes aside, and made his way along the cliff trail to the beach where Grigorii's body had been discovered, and he sat and watched the waves and drank.

He knew he looked a mess, with his raven hair strewn and windblown, his skin pallid from exhaustion, and the enormous dark circles under his eyes. Even with the breeze blowing in off the Mediterranean, he could smell his odor. His skin was hot and tight, and it itched.

He couldn't erase the memory of threatening to toss the prince into the sea only moments before Grigorii did the job himself. He wasn't even certain why he was so furious when he discovered Dieter filming Grigorii having sex with Nathalie. What he had with Nathalie had ended years earlier. He'd enjoyed his share of entertainments since, and he looked forward to exploring possibilities with Monique Rothe as soon as he returned to Paris. And, of course, there was always Bish. He had no hold on Nathalie, no claim to her. In fact, he hadn't thought of her romantically since about ten minutes after she walked out on him in 1919. After Lady Bish took him under her wing, he almost forgot her until he turned the corner onto Rue Montparnasse and found Nathalie sitting with Beau at the café.

He had been surprised. Shocked, even. He had resigned himself years earlier to never seeing her again. He presumed she had died, or had become a nun, or was in America making movies for Lasky or Edison, or off at Giverny blowing Monet. Wherever she was, she was a pragmatist, so being there benefited her in some way. In any case, it wasn't where Keeby was, and he had grown to prefer that.

Then, without warning, she was back in his life.

Besides shock, he might have experienced any number of emotions when he saw her with Beau. Envy came to mind. Suppressed anger as well. He had not expected sadness. His and Nathalie's past granted him a form of clairvoyance. He saw the future, and Beau did not fare well in it. His friend was destined for heartbreak.

He had debated how to advise Beau about Nathalie a dozen times after seeing them together in the café, but the right words never came—curious for a man who made his living with words. And now, it was too late. After the confrontation at the cottage, Beau and Nathalie had been cool toward one another. Beau would forever be a slave to his Low Country chivalry, but the conversations between them sounded too formal and far too reserved to describe anything other than the end of the affair.

So, Keeby had botched that as well. He recognized the expression on Beau's face all too well, having memorized it in his shaving mirror. It was the same look they had seen in the trenches on men who had survived too many sorties, what the long-moldering Wally Smith had dubbed the *thousand-yard stare*. It was too late to warn him. Now, as Beau did in the Meuse-Argonne, Keeby was obligated to take the shrapnel.

His bottle was empty. Staggering a little in the shifting sand, he pounded the cork into the bottleneck with his palm, walked to the waterline, took a couple of practice swings, and flung the bottle as far as he could out into the surf. It sank for a second or two before bobbing back to the surface. Keeby watched it, making bets whether the undertow would drag it out to sea, or the waves would return it to him in the weirdest game of fetch ever.

The bottle rose and fell with the waves, but it didn't come closer. Slowly, it grew smaller. The current had embraced it, and now it was headed for God knows where. Keeby imagined the glee of some kid finding the bottle washed onto the shore, hoping to find a message inside, and the kid's confusion when he discovered the only thing in the bottle were wine dregs long since turned to must and vinegar.

He leaned his head back against the rock on which he had propped himself, closed his eyes, and listened to the rhythm of the waves lapping on the Riviera shore.

Now there's a story, he thought. *But it's only the prologue.* He allowed his mind to wander in its inebriation. *The kid finds the bottle, but it's empty. Seized by his imagination, he becomes an explorer—*

And the story collapsed in his head. He couldn't go any further. Within seconds, his sodden brain had forgotten the premise.

He needed a nap. He decided to risk intrusive nightmares of Grigorii's dead face and go to his room, fall into his bed, and try to set a new world record for the number of hours asleep.

The bottle had disappeared around a small stony point. He only saw waves now. Rising to his feet, he trudged up the hill to the villa, and the flight of steps to his room. He was ready to drop into bed when he saw his door ajar. He was certain he had closed it when he left.

The door creaked when he swung it open. Beau stood over his typewriter. The manuscript to Keeby's new novel sat on the desk and Beau had it thumbed open about halfway. He looked at Keeby when he heard the door and allowed the pages to fall together again.

"Knock knock," Keeby said.

"I was looking for you. Nathalie is leaving on the night train out of Nice. You might want to say goodbye."

"Why?"

"Because I don't think either of us is ever going to see her again, pal. She's about to do her Houdini act. First, we need to talk. What in hell is this?" He slapped the sheaf of papers on Keeby's desk with the back of his hand.

"You read it?"

"Parts of it."

"You had no right! This is invasion of privacy."

"That's a laugh. You might call your hero Rhett, but that's about all the fiction in it. I told you this story in confidence. You had no right to turn it into melodrama."

"Everything is grist for the mill, Beau," Keeby said. "I've always told you. I always tell *everyone.*"

"My God, Keeb! It's all here! Sophie. Victoria. The suicide. The riot. Father's indictment. Anybody who had anything to do with this story is going to know exactly who they are. Who *I* am! You can't publish this."

Keeby waved at the air. "It's a first draft. I'll disguise it better. I'll… I'll set the story in France and make the soldier French. Damn it, Beau, it's a hell of a story."

"It isn't yours!"

"It's all I have!" Keeby cried back, and the exhaustion overwhelmed him. He sank to his mattress and covered his face with his hands. He sobbed as he spoke through them. "I stare at the paper, and nothing comes, Beau. Nothing. It's a void. You know the old saying? Everyone has a novel in them? Well, it may be true, buddy, but very few people have a *second* novel in them. Looks like I'm not one of them."

Beau poured him a glass of wine from an open bottle on the table and sat in the chair next to the bed. Keeby didn't touch the wine, but he slowly composed himself.

"When a genuine idea finally pops into my head, I realize I read it in a book six months ago," he said. "Armitage Knox said he would help me if I had a good idea for a second novel. Only problem—I didn't have one. I panicked. I haven't done anything, Beau! I mean, I nearly got my guts blown out in the war, and I went to college, and I lived in Paris for a few years. Sounds like a lot, but I try to weave it all together, and it's all shit. I shouldn't be writing novels. Not for another twenty years at least. I need to grow a life first. I need to do something real before I can write fantasy. Knox put me on the spot, and the only story I could dredge up was yours."

Keeby placed the manuscript in Beau's hands. "Here. It's your story. Take it. Stick it in a chest or a drawer somewhere, or toss it in the Med, or use it for fireplace kindling. I don't care anymore. It's all shit, anyway. I don't know enough to write your story or anybody else's. I'm taking the train to Paris in the morning. Cagne-sur-Mer doesn't smell so good anymore. See you back at the ranch."

"What will you do?" Beau asked.

"I have some money saved. Quite a bit, as a matter of fact. I have my syndicate contracts, but I can fulfill those working one day a week. I think I'll take some time to find myself. There are two women in Paris who can help me. One of them might be special, someday. Not yet though. I'm not ready for any sort of commitment. I'll try to arrange some new contracts in the US writing for travel magazines and make my way around the world the slow way, writing as I go. I need to see the world fresh, recovering from tearing itself apart. Or, maybe, I'll do nothing at all for a while. Hey, there's an opening for a gigolo in Paris. Maybe I have a shot. A life of symphonies and ballets and parties and sex with highly experienced women sounds attractive right now."

"First things first," Beau said. "Let's say goodbye to Nathalie."

They found her in the entry hall wearing a lightweight tweed traveling suit. Her luggage was in the doorway.

"You're sure you want to leave?" Beau asked.

"I am," she said.

"We're never going to see you again, are we?"

"One can never tell," she said. "Paris is the greatest small town in the world. Our paths may cross."

She kissed Beau like a lover, and kissed Keeby on both cheeks like a Parisian. If Keeby was disappointed, he didn't show it. Beau watched her walk to the taxi.

"Well," he said when she was out of sight. "I'm sure there's a bottle somewhere around here that's done something unforgivable. Why don't we execute it?"

"None for me," Keeby said. "I need to dry out. I'm going upstairs and sleep until Christmas."

They were interrupted by a knock on the open front door of the villa. They turned to find two people, a man who looked as if he were wearing Dieter's chalky film makeup, and a perky, buxom, blonde woman with a round face and green eyes.

"Please, excuse the intrusion." The man wheezed after walking the hill from the village. "My name is Henri Carosel. This is Gwynna Tudor, my assistant." He handed Beau his business card.

"A private investigator?" Beau asked, after examining it.

"Yes. I am here to have a conversation with Dietrich Heyder regarding the late Prince Grigorii Romanov. Might he be available?"

CHAPTER FIFTY-FOUR

"PRINCE GRIGORII?" Beau asked. "The police already investigated the drowning."

"My interest is in Prince Grigorii," Carosel wheezed. "However, not about drowning. Is Monsieur Heyder here?"

"He is, but I'm not sure he's able to answer questions, especially about Grigorii. They were close, and it was quite a shock."

"Of this I am aware, Monsieur. Mademoiselle Tudor is Monsieur Heyder's neighbor in Paris and was privy to the relationship between him and the prince."

"I thought she was your assistant," Keeby said.

"Only of late. Her status as Monsieur Heyder's neighbor predates her employment by my agency."

"That's convenient," Beau said.

"Not at all, Monsieur. I encountered Mademoiselle Tudor while attempting to interview Prince Grigorii at Monsieur Heyder's flat. She volunteered to accompany me to Cagne-sur-Mer, partly because she could identify the prince and I cannot. Also, she has nursing experience and—as I am certain you have observed—I am not in robust health."

"You do look a little peaked," Keeby said. "Maybe you should sit for a bit. It's a haul here from the village."

"An excellent suggestion," Carosel said. "However, my business is urgent, and there will be time to rest when it is completed. I will ask you again, Messieurs. May I have a word with Dieter Heyder?"

"Why don't you see if he's awake," Beau told Keeby.

A few minutes later, Keeby reappeared at the top of the stairs with Dieter, disheveled and puffy from crying and sleep and dissipation. He had fallen into bed in his clothes, and his linen trousers and cotton shirt were now roadmaps of wrinkles. His blond hair hung in random strings. He and Keeby, who was still drunk, helped one another down the stairs to face Carosel and Tudor.

"What is this?" Dieter asked Carosel drowsily. "Who are you? Gwynna? Why are you here? Has something happened to my fish?"

Carosel again made introductions and handed Dieter one of his business cards. "Your neighbor asked to accompany me to the Cote d'Azur when we met in Paris. Please allow me to express my sincerest condolences on the death of Prince Grigorii. It was tragic. As it happens, it was Prince Grigorii whom I hoped to interview, not you."

"About what?"

"I represent a client whose father barely survived a horrible automobile accident, which also killed his wife, my client's stepmother. In the aftermath of this accident, some valuables belonging to the couple vanished. My client hired me to recover them. I have returned the valuables to my client except for a Bell and Ross watch which belonged to her father. I know this is an unfortunate time to deliver news such as this, and I intend no disrespect to the late prince, but the person from whom I recovered the valuables in Paris

457

informed me he purchased them from Prince Grigorii Romanov."

"Please excuse me," Beau said. "I need to arrange my luggage for the trip back to Paris." He dashed for the stairs, hoping nobody noticed how suddenly pale he was.

"Yes," Dieter said. "I am aware of Grigorii's friends. He frequently sold jewelry and other valuables his clients gave him. I am not surprised to hear this, Herr Carosel. What I am surprised and disheartened to hear is your subliminal suggestion that Grigorii stole these valuables and this watch from the unfortunate couple in the automobile accident. He may have been a gigolo, but he had his principles."

"And if he were highly inebriated, Monsieur? A man in such a condition might respond to impulse, and only discover later what guilt it conveys. I am not suggesting malice. I am suggesting weakness in the moment, human frailty. We are all fallible creatures. We are all subject to temptation. But his motivation or guilt is not the matter here. I have consulted with the local constable investigating his case, who has expressed no interest in it whatsoever. The police in Paris have shown equal indifference. My only concern is in recovering the watch, which rightfully belongs to my client's father. Beyond the fact it is stolen property, it has strong sentimental value, having been a gift for my client's brother, who was killed in the war. My informant—" Carosel stopped to gasp several times, having suddenly run out of wind. "Pardon, Messieurs. I was also a victim in the war. Gas. It affected my lungs. It is difficult for me to speak at length. Please allow me to continue. My informant told me he saw the watch in Prince Grigorii's possession, but at the last moment the prince decided to keep it for himself. So,

Mademoiselle Tudor and I traveled to Cagne-sur-Mer to meet with Prince Grigorii with hopes of recovering the watch. However, meeting with the late prince is no longer possible, so my next option is to ask you, Monsieur Heyder, if you can help us."

Dieter took a deep breath and shook his head. "I regret deeply that I cannot. I am not familiar with the watch. Grigorii was not in the habit of sharing that side of his life with me openly, though it was not a secret between us."

"Would you allow us to inspect his belongings, to see if the watch is among them?"

"I haven't touched his things since he was found. I couldn't bring myself to do so. I will show you where they are. I should caution you, I have no recollection at all of this watch you're describing. If you locate it, though, please return it to your client."

———

In his room, Beau lay on the bed he had recently shared with Nathalie Bel, and he tried to calm the slamming of his racing heart and the roar of panic in his ears.

The black shadow of guilt over his callous thievery welled again. He had allowed himself to crumple it into a wad and stomp it into a distant corner of his mind after Grigorii had delivered the money. He had put the most sordid episode of his life behind him, but now it had returned with a vengeance. Worse, he recognized how closely he had come to being arrested and imprisoned for the theft. Dieter had spoken floridly about Grigorii's principles, but Beau had no doubts at all the prince would have given him up the second Carosel showed at the door, had he not conveniently drowned.

That wasn't the worst. Something Carosel had said stuck in his mind like a burr. His client's stepmother had died in a car crash before being stripped of her jewelry. Lisette wore black because she had buried her stepmother in Monaco days before Beau arrived in Cagne-sur-Mer. She said her father was ill and might not survive, forcing her to take over the family business. It could be a coincidence. *A hundred stepmothers must die in France every day*, he thought.

He liked Lisette. He had only known her for a week or so, but there was a strong attraction he couldn't deny. At dinner the night after she posed with Nathalie, no longer deep in his creative reverie, Beau had allowed himself to devote his attention to what she said and not how she looked. They had talked late into the evening, until the waiters and bartends glanced at their watches impatiently, and the three of them had strolled on the beach at Cagne-sur-Mer, arm in arm in arm, laughing and singing bawdy French songs to drown out the waves. The more he talked with Lisette, the better Beau liked her. He could tell Nathalie was attracted as well, and he was well aware of Nathalie's fluid romantic tastes, but he had no idea how Lisette would take to that sort of notion. Now, with Nathalie little more than a pleasant memory, it was a moot point.

When Nathalie left, she again warned Beau that if he didn't bed Lisette, she would. It wasn't a warning at all, but couched advice. She had seen a glimmer between Beau and Lisette, a spark of something greater than infatuation ready to be fanned into more than an affair. Nathalie, Keeby had told him, was compassionate in her cruelty. She never disappeared from your life without providing an opportunity to fill the void.

Beau recalled the conversation with his father years earlier in Charleston. Gordon Shipley had told him he chose Beau's mother from the circle of available women in Charleston not because of her beauty, but because he found her agreeable. With each passing day, and as their time together grew, Beau had found Lisette intensely agreeable.

He had no idea how something like this would work, living in Paris with Lisette chained to her stationers shop on the Riviera, especially with his new obligation to the import business, an obligation he admitted he had placed on himself. Now it impacted not only on his time for painting but also for any new romantic entanglements.

It was all too confusing. He needed time to sort through all the loose lumber in his head and figure out how he intended to spend the next fifty years or so. Returning to Paris would only befuddle him more. The villa was paid for through the month. With everyone else in Paris, it might afford him the peace and quiet and solitude he needed to steer his life back on track.

And, he noted, he needed to learn more about Lisette and her dead stepmother.

———

"Our search," Carosel announced to Lisette, his voice a barely audible whisper, "was, sadly, not successful."

"Are you all right?" Lisette asked, ignoring the news about the watch. "You don't look well at all."

"I have enjoyed better health," Carosel said. "No matter. I am here to report on your case. I was gratified to recover your stepmother's lost jewels. However, the watch has proven to be a challenge. It does not appear to have been in the possession of Prince Grigorii while he was in Cagne-sur-Mer. A search of his belongings yielded nothing. We can attempt to access and search his apartment in Paris, but failing that, I do not see other options for recovery."

"But Prince Grigorii did have it when he was in Paris," Lisette clarified.

"Most assuredly so. My contact there saw it on his person. It is possible the watch will be in the prince's flat in Montparnasse. Indeed, I have already visited there, but was unable to enter the apartment due to the prince's absence. As he has now died, the landlord may allow me access."

"My father is still in hospital in Paris, but the reports from the doctors suggest he's declining. His injuries have led to infections and other damage. I plan to close the shop and travel to Paris later this week to be with him. I would be so thankful if there is any way to recover the watch. Please do search Grigorii's flat. If you do not find it there, I will resign myself to the fact it is lost. I will be staying at my father's home in Paris." She wrote the address and handed it to him.

Carosel and Gwynna left minutes later.

"I wish to see the water," he whispered, as Gwynna held him steady.

"Then let's see the water," Gwynna said.

He staggered clumsily, as if he expected his legs to collapse at any moment. She supported him, and together, step after laborious step, they arrived at the shore and found a vendor renting chaises and umbrellas. Carosel fumbled in his pocket for the correct change, and the vendor unfolded and placed the chairs and umbrella in a relatively unoccupied portion of the beach.

"I think a glass of wine would be nice," Gwynna said. "How about you?"

"A cold glass of water will suffice for me," he said.

"There's a café. I'll be right back."

As she trudged through the sand and rocks toward the café, he focused on the distance. While the sunlight on the beach was crisp and brilliant and hot, clouds had gathered on a horizon so gray and hazy it was difficult to determine with certainty where the water stopped and the sky began.

Carosel's body had grown impervious to warmth. Even in the heat of the day, lounging in the Mediterranean sun, he was chilled to his marrow, as if all his inner fires had burned to scattered embers. He took a deep breath, and the sudden rush of air into his lungs triggered a spasm of coughing. He grabbed his handkerchief and pressed it to his mouth and waited for the convulsion to stop. He glanced at the handkerchief and moaned.

It was a bad day.

There was blood in the handkerchief. Far too much blood.

He had pressed himself too hard, searching for Lisette Seydoux's family valuables. He had driven himself to the point of exhaustion, buoyed by the newfound confidence that if he faltered Gwynna would be there to pick him up. He crumpled the handkerchief, wiped at his mouth with the wadded cloth, and stuffed it into his pocket as Gwynna returned with their drinks.

"I told the waiter where we were. He said he'd be out in a bit to see if we needed our drinks refreshed," she said chattily as she placed his water on the small tabouret between the chaises. "Wasn't that the politest thing? I believe I could get used to Cagne-sur-Mer."

"I need you to do something," he whispered. She could barely hear him over the lapping of the waves.

"What's that?" she asked.

"Come closer," he said. She leaned in toward him, and she saw the color of his lips, and she checked his nails. She smelled a coppery sourness on his breath, and she knew something catastrophic had taken place inside of him. The nurse in her took over.

"Tell me what you're feeling," she said.

"That is unimportant."

"The hell it is," she argued.

"Please," he said. "Listen to me."

He pressed a key into her palm with a pale, shaky hand.

"This is the key to my office. Do with it as you will."

He gave her a second key. "This is the key to my apartment. This is important."

"Maybe you should rest and tell me later," she said.

"In my apartment, in the back of my closet, is a small file cabinet. My case files are in my office. However, in the course of surveillance, especially the surveillance of people of importance, one occasionally uncovers secrets about *other* people of importance, unrelated to the case. What am I to do with such information? I deal in information after all. The more I know, the more effectively I can do my job."

His chest heaved twice, and he grabbed for his soiled handkerchief, which he held against his mouth. Gwynna saw the blood stains on the cloth and stopped arguing.

"All right," she said. "And the files in your closet?"

"The compilation of my—ah—ancillary investigations. On occasion, having accidentally learned of the indiscreet behaviors of important people, I compiled files on them despite not having been hired to do so. I imagined the files might be useful at some point in the future. A less scrupulous private investigator might have used them to extort money, and I have known some who would. In any case, they are there. Those files contain information which, used illicitly, could complicate the lives of many of Paris' most illustrious citizens."

"Why are you telling me this?"

"I have made a living being a shrewd judge of character. I believe you are a good person, Mademoiselle Tudor. Why else would you accompany a sick man on a futile journey in search of a hopelessly lost watch?"

"You needed assistance."

"And I still need it. I believe I can trust you, even after only the short time we have known one another. Something must be done about those files. I never intended them to do harm, and in the wrong hands they could do nothing else. Burn them. I do not wish my work to reach out from my grave and ruin anyone's life."

"It's already done," she said. "Only, could I read them first? I love a salacious read."

He couldn't help but laugh, which again brought on uncontrollable waves of coughing. He didn't try to hide the crimson on the handkerchief as he drew it away, but he

Richard Helms

folded it to hide the fresh blood and wipe at his lips to remove any flecks.

"You may follow your conscience," Carosel whispered. "I am disappointed my last case ended in failure, but on the whole, I believe I have played the cards I have been dealt well. Please, allow me to thank you for your assistance and your care. I did fear dying alone."

"I know," she said. "Everyone does."

He reclined in the chaise and listened to the sounds of the water and the seabirds and children laughing on the beach, and she sat next to him as the sun dipped and the most brilliant oranges and reds and violets filled the sky and the sailboats on the salt tacked toward shore for the evening, and she held his cooling hand in her own until long after dark.

466

CHAPTER FIFTY-FIVE

THE HOUSE WAS EMPTY, save for Beau. He had told the housekeeper to take the day off. He found an interesting book in the villa library and opened a bottle of the wine Lisette had told him came from one of her father's vineyards. He lounged on the veranda overlooking the Mediterranean, cracked open the book, and endeavored to lose himself in someone else's hell and drink himself into torpor.

He chuckled, recalling Georges Braque's advice that he would eventually embrace the symbiotic relationship between art and intoxication.

"Well, here's to fermentation," he said to the Mediterranean beyond the veranda.

"And the fruits of the vine," someone said behind him. Lisette stood in the French doorway.

"Hello, stranger," he said. "Pull up a chair. I'll get another glass."

He returned moments later with a glass and a plate of sliced cheese left over from dinner the night before. She had pulled one of the other chaises next to his and sat on it waiting for him. She looked different. It took Beau a few seconds to realize it was the first time he had ever seen her in any color other than black. Her blousy trousers and wedged sandals were white, and she wore a scarlet silk blouse, and when the breeze pressed the silk against her skin, he could tell that was about it. The blouse and a knotted silk scarf around her neck set off the lighter red highlights in her rainbow auburn hair.

"Where is everyone?" she asked.

"Returned to Paris." He poured a glass and handed it to her. When he pulled the bottle away, she rested his hand on his to stop him, and she examined the label. She smiled.

"You remembered."

"Saw the bottle in the cellar," he said. "It looked familiar."

"No. You remembered."

"Sure I did. Guilty as charged. I'm happy you came to visit." He returned to his own chaise.

"Why?"

"Do I need a reason? I enjoy being with you. This place is creepy with everyone gone."

"Why did you stay?"

"Had some stuff to sort through." He thumped at his skull with his index finger. "In here."

"Nathalie did not stay to help you sort through your stuff?"

"Staying isn't exactly Nathalie's strong suit. We always knew it was temporary. Time's up. She's in Paris, probably stripping her apartment down to the wallpaper before moving to the Twenty-First Arrondissement."

"There are only twenty."

"Exactly. If we ever see her again, it will be an accident."

"How sad," she said.

"I've had better weeks."

"I am not sad for you. If what you say is true, it is better for you she is gone. The end of an affair is always difficult. But you will someday find a person who will not leave, and you will fall deeply in love, and you will have a happy life. Nathalie has rejected hope for her future. She truly believes nobody will ever love her—truly love her, in the way everyone wants to be loved—so whenever she makes herself vulnerable and allows herself to become involved, she tests the limits. If her lover doesn't reject her, she increases the pressure. She sabotages her own happiness to test the devotion of her lovers, and eventually they will always fail, which gives her permission to move on. She is a lost woman. She is a Flying Dutchman. She yearns for freedom, so she abandons trust. Someone hurt her terribly. Repeatedly. Now the act of love is a transaction for her, the coin of the realm for temporary solace from her loneliness."

"I never thought of it that way."

"You have never been a woman."

"Well," he said. "You're almost right. There's more, though. It isn't all solace. She runs her own table. She told Keeby, and she told me. She's a pragmatist first and foremost. She's a survivor. She told me never to let her know my weakest point, because she'd use it to destroy me. That's when I knew we had no future. You don't threaten someone who fills the empty places in your heart. Yeah. Someone hurt her, and it was wrong in every way I was ever taught. But she's done her share of hurting in return. Maybe it's for the reasons you said. I wouldn't be a bit surprised."

"Beau—"

"In the end, though, you're right. It is sad. Anyone so fucked up is due a little pity. I knew it was coming sometime.

I guess it hurts a little less this way. Like anticipating a shot at the doctor's office. Then, a little stab, and it's over."

"So, if you are over it so easily, why are you still in Villa Ciel and everyone else is back in Paris? Perhaps the stuff you need to sort out in your head is not entirely about your love life?"

"Man, you hit it on the head," he said, and he launched into the conflict he between painting, which he wanted to do, and the import business, which he seemed fated to run instead. He told her the story of his return to Charleston, and she described a similar experience in Paris, and they talked for almost two hours before either knew a minute had passed, and the bottle was empty along with another.

"Oh!" Beau said, his voice sluggish. "I finished the painting."

"Which painting?"

"The one with you and Nathalie. It's inside. Come look while I find another bottle."

She followed him through the French doors, both stepping carefully to maintain balance. Beau had set the canvas on an empty easel inside the parlor to cure.

"It's there," he said. "I'll be right back."

She gazed at the painting. It was so much better than she had expected. The contrast between her widow's-weeds black dress and bare auburn hair, and Nathalie's flawless umber nude body, with its edges and lines and angles, and her face hidden by the floppy hat, in an otherwise tranquil French coastal garden sharing an afternoon tea. It was whimsical and charming and daring at the same time.

"I don't know what to call it," Beau said as he reappeared at the top of the stairs.

"*Afternoon Tea at Cagne-sur-Mer*," she said. "Nothing else is needed."

He set the bottle on the table and stood next to her, looking at the painting. Reflexively, she grabbed him by his shirt, pulled her to him, and kissed him hungrily. Without letting go of his shirt, she pushed him away and stared into his eyes.

"You must continue painting," he said. "I love this *Afternoon Tea at Cagne-sur-Mer.*"

"It's impressionist tripe," he said. "Might have been something when my father was a boy."

"I am not joking, Beau. I see something here. You could make a mark in the art world."

"If I don't starve first. But let's get back to the kissing thing."

"I want you to paint me," she said. "When you said you wanted to, I thought you only wanted to get me out of my clothes and into your bed. I thought you were one of those hundreds of marginally talented children of privilege who flock to Paris every year to buy a place in the art world."

"I am exactly what you just said. Every bit of it."

"But you have more potential than most, and you must not toss it aside. I want you to paint me in this style." She pointed at the canvas. "Then you can go back to Paris and paint all the Cubist and surrealist shit you want. I want something good and beautiful to come out of this terrible summer. I want you to paint me and I will keep the painting to remind me that, even in the worst of times, some beauty can flourish. Please, Beau. The world has been filled with such ugliness for so long. Show me something beautiful."

He wrapped her in his arms, and he pressed his lips against hers. She welcomed him and placed her hand on the back of his head, pulling him into her. He could feel her hot breath and her hands caressing him, and he experienced the most exquisitely conflicting feelings of lust and guilt. He was twenty-seven years old, so there was little doubt which of the emotions would win out in the short run.

He gathered her in his arms.

"Take me to your room," she said.

"The whole house is our room," he told her.

———

She woke later, lying on a bed, underneath an arched window with jalousie shutters thrown open, the pinks and oranges and violets of the sunset reflecting off the stark white walls. She lay on her side, half under and half out of the sheets, her hair tousled and splayed across the pillow.

"Don't move," Beau said.

She opened one eye. He stood a few feet away, naked, sketching on a blank canvas with a stick of charcoal.

"I just want to capture the basics."

"You're painting me like this?"

"The boudoir portrait is a time-honored artistic subject."

"Take your time," she said. "I'll enjoy the view."

"Oh my God!" he said. "I'll put on a robe."

"No need. We've both seen the entire show already."

He smiled and returned to sketching. "Now I really am happy you visited today."

"Makes two of us. But I'm growing hungry. I don't want to rush you—"

"Won't be a rush at all. I'll be finished in just a few minutes. We can go to the village and eat. You never said what brought you to the villa today. Who's running the shop?'"

"Nobody is running it. I've shuttered it. I came to tell you and Nathalie I am leaving for Paris in the morning. I did not know you were alone."

"Why Paris?"

"My father needs my assistance. I mentioned my stepmother died."

"Yes. You didn't say how."

"An automobile accident," she said. "In Paris. It happened in July, on the morning after the final leg of the Tour de France."

The room swayed. For an instant Beau thought he might pass out.

"We never opened the wine," he said. "I could use a glass. You?"

"Please," she said.

He staggered out of the room to the stairs. He had left the robe crumpled on the floor, but there was nobody in the villa to care one way or the other. His head spun. He grabbed the handrail on the stairs to keep from lurching down the steps and breaking his neck. He located the bottle, still on the table next to the curing portrait of Lisette and Nathalie, and he quickly pulled the cork. Their glasses were also on the table, but he didn't dare try to fill them yet. The chances of even a drop making it back up the stairs were not encouraging. He poured half a glass and reluctantly pounded it back.

His worst fears were confirmed. The couple he had robbed after the accident were Lisette's father and stepmother. Apparently, the man—her father—hadn't died after all. Beau wasn't certain why, but that made stealing the watch even more shameful.

"Why can't it ever be easy?" He transferred the glasses and bottle to one hand so he could cling to the stair rail on the way back to the bedroom.

CHAPTER FIFTY-SIX

KEEBY HAD BEEN BACK in Paris for three days. Two of them were spent in bed with Bish and Monique for most of the day and night, with occasional breaks for sustenance to keep the fires of ardor burning.

He stopped first at the apartment at 22 Rue Montparnasse to deposit his bags and typewriter. Before Keeby left Cagne-sur-Mer, Beau had placed the manuscript back in his hands, with an admonition penciled in the margins. If Keeby was going to borrow Beau's life, he needed some rewrites. He trusted his friend to do the right thing, which Keeby interpreted to mean exploiting Beau as little as possible. Before leaving to see what Monique and Bish were up to, Keeby stowed the manuscript in the bottom desk drawer where he relegated all his back-burner projects. It would always be there if he became desperate enough to use it.

Monique answered the door at Bish's *pied-a-terre*.

"You live here now?" he said.

She wrapped her arms around Keeby's neck and her legs around his waist and kissed him deeply. He took the opportunity to carry her inside the door and close it to frustrate the looky-loos.

"Aw, you missed me," he said.

"Of course I did." She crossed directly to the bar to pour two drinks. "Was it terrible? Prince Grigorii?"

"It was bad. Strangely, though, I had seen worse."

"In the war. Of course. You just missed Bish. Out shopping. She'll be back by tea. I spent the night here after I received your telegram, and this is closer to the theater than my apartment, so I decided to stay. She took the news badly. You know she and Grigorii were lovers?"

"I didn't consider how the news would affect her."

"She was heartbroken. She said Grigorii was a sweet and attentive man who never failed to make her come."

"We'll chisel that on his gravestone," Keeby said.

"You know what? He'd like that."

"He'll be a giant among gigolos."

"Are you all right?"

"No," Keeby said. "I haven't been all right for a while. But I'm getting better. The time I spent in Cagne-sur-Mer showed me I've been running full-tilt through a strange pitch-dark house blindfolded. Blunders weren't only predictable, they were inevitable. My first novel failed because I wasn't ready to write it. I shit-canned the second because publishing it would violate the trust of my best friend. I don't believe I'll be writing novels for a while."

"What will you do?"

"It's time to see how the rest of the world is healing. I'm going to travel and write about what I see. It'll be hand-to-mouth, but maybe that won't be so bad either. At least it will be honest and true."

"Strange. I heard another writer use those exact words at Gertrude Stein's salon the other evening. Can't recall his name. Lovely wife, though. Americans."

"Well, whoever he is, I hope he has better luck than mine. Right now, I feel like stuffing the loud end of a shotgun in my mouth."

"We can't have that," she said. "But it does give me ideas. Come upstairs. I'll draw a bath and give you a massage and help you forget Prince Grigorii and Cagne-sur-Mer and writing and everything else. It's August. In Paris, all troubles are required to be postponed until the first of September. As of this moment, Keeby, you are on vacation."

Bish arrived exactly at teatime, as predicted. By then, Monique urgently needed a shower and to wash her hair before dashing to the theater for her evening performance. She rolled off the right side of Bish's bed to pad to the bathroom. Seconds later, Bish lifted the sheets and rolled onto the left side. She lay against Keeby, crossing his chest with her arm, and placed her head on his shoulder. He wrapped his arms around her and pulled her to him and she sobbed. Hot tears fell on his shoulder.

"He was drunk and high on opium. He never even knew he was drowning," Keeby said. "And the very last thing he did was fuck a beautiful woman. All things considered, it's not a terrible way to go."

"I know. We will make love in his memory. It was the thing he did best. And after the performance you and Monique and I will go to a midnight supper, and we will raise a glass to Prince Grigorii, and afterward we will never mention him again. Are we agreed?"

"Sure," Keeby said. "Whatever you say. I'm happy to let someone else drive for a while."

Three days of vacation with Bish and Monique had proven exhausting, and a little chafing. Keeby came up for air on the fourth morning, heavily hung over and sore in places he had forgotten could be sore. The house was empty. Monique and Bish must have risen earlier and gone out for brunch. He checked his watch and whistled. One-fifteen in the afternoon.

"Must have tied one on last night," he said after bathing, as he finished dressing and took the stairs to the small living room.

"I'd say you did," someone said.

Keeby hit the bottom of the stairs and saw the back of a man's head. The man sat in the small loveseat in front of the cold fireplace. He held a glass of red wine.

"Ross? Bish didn't say you were coming."

"No," he said. "I asked her not to. She and Monique have gone out."

"So I gathered. Is this the part of the story where the jealous husband kills the young homewrecker?"

Ross laughed. He stood and turned around. "Hair of the dog, Keeby. You'll need it." He pointed to the bar. Keeby poured a little vodka in a glass and filled the rest with orange juice. He swished the glass to mix it and took a sip.

"Okay," Keeby said. "What's this about?"

"Have you ever wondered how I retained my military commission with an empty sleeve?" Ross asked.

"Figured you were grandfathered in, or it was an honorific, or they simply don't let you anywhere near the shooting anymore. I never gave it much thought. Admiral Nelson only had one arm, right?"

"British military regulations have changed a bit in the last century. You were closer with your last guess. I no longer serve in a combat capacity. You might say my role these days is more, ah, ceremonial."

"Window dressing for King George? A warm body to fill out the entourage in all the royal photographs and speeches?"

"Sometimes. In fact, you are only likely to find me in public at exactly those types of functions. Otherwise, I do not play an openly public role in the military. My commission is more…covert."

"You're a spy," Keeby joked.

"No. I am not, personally, a spy."

"Well, that's a relief—"

"I manage them. You might say I give them assignments and keep an eye on them as they complete them."

Keeby killed the entire drink and crossed to the bar to make another. "Pull the middle one next."

"The empire was caught flat-footed in 1914. We didn't see the war coming. The nature of military intelligence was not something to be proud of after the Boer War ended." He unconsciously touched the empty sleeve of his jacket. "After the Great War, high-ranking officials of the military and the government met and debated and talked and talked and fucking talked some more, but in the end, they came to a unanimous conclusion—Great Britain needs to know everything that happens on the Continent and beyond."

"Spies," Keeby said.

"We don't use that word. I represent a new agency, created only in the last few years, called Secret Intelligence

Service. It is presently under the direction of Sir Mansfield George Smith-Cummings."

"A lot of name to carry around."

"Nothing compared to the weight of his mission, I'd imagine. I do not envy him."

"What does this have to do with me?" Keeby asked.

"Bish called the other evening. You were asleep. She told me about your crisis of confidence and your belief that you need to —how did she put it? —*grow a life* before you have the breadth of experience necessary to write convincingly about the human condition."

"My version was more profane, but yeah. She reported it accurately."

"You plan to travel and write for American periodicals about the places and people you see on your journey." He said it as a statement.

"You and Bish had quite a conversation," Keeby said.

"I like you, Keeby," Ross said. "Yes, I know. You're putting it to my wife. It is remarkable the privilege a spouse will relinquish to keep a marriage going for a quarter century. One little unconventional compromise. We both know it looks strange to those on the outside, but it works for us. Bish and I discovered decades ago that we function much better as a couple when we seldom see one another. The time we are together is always filled with passion. I manage to return to my professional life before either of us can feel any discontent whatsoever, and in that respect, we have the happiest of marriages. If it means I share my wife's body with men I personally endorse, I am comfortable, as the privilege extends to both of us. Bish tends to take advantage of our arrangement more than I. More leisure time I'd imagine, but I have my own friends as well. A uniform and a few medals still open boudoir doors. She takes on projects, good-looking young men in whom she sees potential. You've lasted longer than any of them. I suppose I should be jealous, but Bish and I both know one another well enough. I have no fear of being supplanted in her affections."

"You're fine with her having boyfriends, because you've discovered a different kind of fidelity," Keeby said.

"Precisely put! I do enjoy your economy of language. I read your book, you know. I liked it. Can't imagine why it failed."

"Makes two of us."

"Let me put this straight. You want to travel and write. I believe the Foreign Office can help you."

"I think I know what you're suggesting," Keeby said. "I travel around the Continent on your nickel."

"Nickel?"

"Shilling."

"Ah! I see. Yes. With you so far."

"Every once in a while, I may find myself, entirely by chance, in the vicinity of people or an event you want to know more about."

"I see you are already two steps ahead of me."

"In the course of recording my travels, I might include information you would find interesting."

"Capital! Bish always said you were a sharp lad."

"I suppose meeting Bish wasn't entirely an accident, either."

"It wasn't an accident at all, Keeby. There are no accidents in my line of work. Only happy and sad coincidences. Bish keeps an eye out for promising young people in whom I might be interested. She has no official role with the SIS, but she has directed more than one operative our way."

"Let's cut to the chase. I travel around Europe, collecting random stories, and occasionally I will randomly choose to write about something of interest for you. In return, the Foreign Office would surreptitiously underwrite my private travels."

"That would be one benefit."

Keeby considered it, as he sipped his second drink. "There are specific markets I'd like to sell stories to in both Britain and the States. Anything you can do about that?"

"Not all at once, of course. Too suspicious. Over time, as your work becomes better established, you should find enthusiastic access to the better-paying presses in both countries. I believe we can assure you will be a regular contributor to the *National Geographic Magazine*, for instance. Gradually, over the course of two or three years, I would say you can expect to become quite the noted travel writer, with a commensurate income beyond your sponsorship by the SIS. The more dramatic your stories, the better. The salacious stories you can sell to the pulp magazines. We'll assist with that as well."

"Don't think I'm not appreciative. But, all the time, I'd be spying for the British government?"

"Not *all* the time. As a Canadian American, you have suitable cover. You are only tangentially a British subject. Eighty percent of your work would be legitimate writing to fulfill your syndication requirements. The other twenty percent would be gathering information regarding specific individuals and organizations in which the British government is interested. Your press credentials should assist you in gaining access to specific individuals for interviews, or to cover events."

"What sorts of events?"

"Oh, rallies, mass assemblies, riots, the occasional insurrection. Revolutions if they happen. Civil wars. All terribly fascinating stuff. In the wake of the war, Europe is walking on eggshells. The treaties signed in Versailles are far from cast in concrete. Economic problems across Europe threaten security. If people become hungry enough, bad things happen."

"Russia?"

"We believe they are a threat, yes. In fact, we would be exceptionally pleased should your travels at some point lead to Moscow. While he was a raving Bolshie, the information we received from the American Jack Reed proved extremely useful. Pity he died. We have some agents in place living in various Russian cities—"

"Wait. Agents in place?"

"People we have sent to Russia to live. They assimilate into the Russian culture, mostly in relatively insignificant positions, and they send information back."

"People like Karl Frankl?"

Ross smiled. "Gad, you are a sharp lad. I do admire your mind."

"I'm also good at asking the next question. I always wondered how Karl Frankl knew about my writing. According to Nathalie Bel, he was a rich discontent who ran a solitary Bolshevik cell-of-one out of a tawdry apartment in the Montparnasse. I didn't see him as a regular reader of the *Times of Montreal.* Now I know. He was working for you. Your

SIS targeted me. Establishing Karl as a Bolshevik revolutionary in Paris was the perfect cover for placing him in Moscow. He arrived with a portfolio of revolutionary broadsheets as his calling card, and I wrote half of them. He claims credit for the entire thing and is accepted as a true poet of the revolution."

"What do you care? You were paid generously for your contribution. As long as the check clears, right?"

"The money came from you, of course."

"You are welcome."

"And Nathalie? The ultimate pragmatist?"

"Pragmatists make the best operatives," Ross said. "They do what has to be done and they don't cry a lot about it afterward."

"It was all theater," Keeby said. "Karl and Nathalie were both playing roles. Following Karl opened the door to Nathalie. When Nathalie finished softening me up, she exited and handed me over to Bish. I was the only performer in the play without a script."

"It wasn't entirely unpleasant, was it?" Ross asked.

"Nathalie fucked me as part of her *job?*"

"Well, and because she truly enjoys it. She's another of Bish's finds. Bish reads a lot of Freud, you know. Everyone does these days. All the rage. She said Nathalie is what the psychoanalysts call polymorphous perverse. Big words for *anyone in any bed.* Highly damaged. Horrible childhood. Stuff you really don't want to know. Her analyst says she has made remarkable progress. She is now merely promiscuously neurotic and mostly absent a conscience. One might blame her childhood, but I also hear these things can pass from parent to child genetically. Shame we have no idea who her parents were."

"Nathalie was with Beau Shipley. Are you recruiting him as well?"

"Why? Do you think we should?"

"His family owns a shipping business, and they're getting into aviation. I'd think he'd be a prize."

"But he has no ties to Buckingham, does he? At least half of you is a British subject. I do agree about the advantage of cultivating a relationship with him. We were hoping you might be our conduit. After all, the two of you are very close."

"How many moves ahead are you playing?"

"Depends on the day."

"Did you kill my novel?" Keeby asked.

"No. In fact, we were disappointed it wasn't more popular. People of some renown also make great operatives. Nobody suspects them. Bish tells me you don't feel competent to write a novel right now, because you need to grow a life—I do love the term, by the way. So? Grow it on our shilling. Go where you want, mostly, and write what you want, mostly. In a few years, make another stab at a novel when you are more worldly and sophisticated. In the meantime, any stories you sell—and we will see to it you *do* sell them—are pure profit, because you didn't pay a penny to write them."

"I'm not keen on Russia," Keeby said. "It's cold and the food is shit."

"We have people in Russia already. Before I say more, I should caution you. Everything I've told you to this point is, as should be patently obvious, secret. Should you divulge

485

what I've told you, it would inconvenience me greatly, and would get Karl Frankl killed, but that would be the end of it. They know we keep an eye on them. We know they keep an eye on us. It's all terribly cordial and courteous until the moment you're caught with your hand in the cookie jar. Nathalie is too valuable an asset to lose, but we'd have to give her another new identity. She would not be compromised as much as I would."

"I see."

"Oh, and I would kill you, of course. Unpleasantly." Ross kept his expression entirely flat as he said it.

"Perhaps you should have mentioned that before you put the noose around my neck."

"I have been accused of the error before. I should work on it. If you are looking for other incentives, you would continue to fuck my wife for as long as it pleases her. It could be a while. She apparently likes you quite a lot."

"What about Monique? Is she in on the game?"

"No. She is—what is the term? —window dressing. And Bish likes her. No reason why you couldn't continue your liaisons with either of them."

"Going to be difficult if I'm thousands of miles away, wandering the countryside."

"Sounds to me like you are already nine-tenths of the way to a decision," Ross said. "What I am about to tell you will result in your painful death should you divulge it to anyone. There is a disturbing trend across Europe. The Bolsheviks are troubling, yes, but it appears for now that inefficiencies in their bureaucratic system will allow some years, perhaps a decade, before they constitute a significant threat to the region."

"I came to the same conclusion three years ago."

"Yes. Nathalie told us."

"Three years ago? And you're only approaching me now? You people are patient."

"We plant seeds. Lots of seeds. Only some of them germinate. When you told Bish you were abandoning novel writing and planned to travel the Continent, I knew one of our little seeds had sprouted. If your novel had been a success, we would have made our move earlier."

"Okay, let's say I'm in. What do you want me to write?"

"At the moment, we have several pressing areas of concern. We have never experienced a war as widespread and catastrophic as the one we recently completed. The reverberations are still rippling through every world government. Some are handling it more effectively than others. At the present, we are concerned about Germany."

"Germany? I seem to recall pummeling them a few years back."

"And the treaties signed at Versailles punished them severely. The economy in Germany is in poor shape as it recovers from the war. Hungry people are dangerous. There is a sharp increase in right wing ultranationalism among some of the younger students. We have been observing the activities of several organizations, but the one which worries us most is *Nationalsozialistische Deutsche Arbeiterpartei.*"

"I don't speak German."

"We'll teach you. It translates, roughly, to National Socialist German Workers' Party."

"Like France's SFIO?"

"Don't let the word *socialist* fool you. Any resemblance between their beliefs and those of our friends in St.

487

Petersburg or here in the SFIO are purely coincidental. The two camps detest each other. I suppose part of travel writing might include some notion of the local politics and what people think about them. If possible, we would very much like a personal interview with one of their leaders."

Ross opened a briefcase next to him on the loveseat and took out a picture.

"We are particularly interested in this man. He gave a speech in Munich a few months back. Here's the transcript."

Keeby read over the typewritten English document.

"I see what you mean. This boy really hates Communists," Keeby said.

"He isn't fond of Jews either. Or anyone who isn't white and European. His intent is clear. If people who believe as he does come to power in Germany, the Foreign Office believes the country could become the right-wing authoritarian equivalent of Bolshevik Russia. Two sides of the same coin. All the misery of both."

"What's this guy's name?" Keeby said, flipping the picture over. "Jesus. The damn name is a foot long and only has three vowels."

"It's Schicklgruber," Ross said. "He's changed it. Calls himself Hitler now. Adolph Hitler."

"You want me to do a sit-down with this fellow and interview him?"

"When you get to Berlin. Take your time. Work your way there, so it looks as if you didn't make the trip specifically to interview him. Ingratiate yourself to him in the process. Our psychoanalytic experts suggest he likes to be fawned over. He's a glutton for attention. He thinks better of people who compliment him and agree with what he says. At some point, we may need someone to facilitate an invitation. In any case, your access to him gives us an ear inside the castle, if you will."

"The fly on the wall," Keeby said.

"An appropriate analogy."

"As long as I don't get swatted." Keeby raised the glass, but thought better of it, and placed it back on the table. "I don't want the booze to make my decision for me. I'm in. It seems the arrangement you describe serves a multitude of purposes."

"Plans work best when everyone stands to gain," Ross said.

"Sure," Keeby said. "I'm going to hold your feet to the fire on the *National Geographic,* though."

CHAPTER FIFTY-SEVEN

DIETER OPENED THE DOOR to Grigorii's apartment with the key the prince had given him before they departed for Cagne-sur-Mer. Gwynna Tudor followed him inside.

"I never spent the night here," Dieter said. "I only visited once or twice before we left for the Cote d'Azur. I am not familiar with where he kept his valuables."

"I will be respectful," she said. "But if the watch is here, I must locate it."

"May I ask why you are pursuing this?" he asked. "You are not a detective. You are a nurse. Your client might as well hire a plumber to paint a house. I am terribly sorry to hear Carosel died. I had nothing against the man. But once he died, it seems to me the case was over."

"For the most part, you are correct. I have collected the bill due from our client for the items already recovered. Once we locate the watch and return it to the client, I shall liquidate Henri's business and destroy his records as he requested. Then, and only then, the case will be over."

She checked the obvious places first—the bedside table, the dresser, under the bed, the bathroom closet. She came across expensive gold cufflinks and shirt buttons and a few rings, one of which sported a handsome diamond. There were two or three watches, but none by Bell and Ross.

"*Mein Gott!*" Dieter exclaimed. Gwynna rushed into the living room, where he stared at a picture on the wall.

"What did you find?" she asked.

"This sketch. It is a Monet original."

"Huh. So it is. I don't suppose there's a safe behind it."

"Do you hear me? A Monet original. Can you imagine what it might bring at auction?"

"He must have kept it as insurance against hard times."

"You can get something like this for fucking?"

"You would know better than I. He never got that far with me. You want it?" she asked.

"What do you mean?"

"Grigorii is dead. All his closest relations went up against a wall in St. Petersburg years ago. You were closer to him at the time he died than anyone else. Nobody's coming for his belongings, except perhaps the landlord once the rent is overdue. If you want the drawing, take the drawing. Take it all, if you want. All I care about is the watch."

Dieter sunk onto the sofa. "I never thought of it that way. He truly had nobody, did he?"

"He had half the dowagers in Paris, from what I hear, but I don't think he had many friends like you. Take the drawing. I'll never tell. Who's going to ask?"

She searched the apartment for another half hour before giving up. She had checked every drawer, cabinet, and even in the tank of the water closet. She looked underneath every table, chair, and chaise, and behind every picture on every wall in every room of the apartment. She had even tapped at the floorboards with a fireplace poker, hoping to find a loose board and a cache of goodies underneath. She found nothing. Reluctantly, she and Dieter locked the door behind them an hour after arriving and walked away. Dieter had wrapped the little Monet in a bath towel and placed it in a burlap grocery sack to carry home.

"Who can say?" Gwynna said. "Maybe he had second thoughts after deciding to keep the watch, and he sold it to another buyer. It isn't inside his apartment. I'm no expert, but I can't imagine any other places we could have looked."

"I feel guilty taking this," Dieter said.

"You'll get over it when you see how it looks on your apartment wall. He didn't tell you who gave it to him?"

"I didn't even know he owned it. I would suspect it came from the baroness. She was especially generous, according to Grigorii."

"I'm sure he would want you to have it. Or we can always give it back to the baroness if you want."

"I am certain she has forgotten it," he said. "Better it stays with me."

———

Lisette had left for Paris the day before. Beau finished packing, except for his traveling clothes. He'd spend one more night at Villa Ciel and take the train back to Paris and the stark reality that faced him. He would meet Lisette at her parents' home the next evening. Keeby had talked about his girlfriend Monique in Paris. Her play was still running. They planned to see it and take in a late dinner.

Until he left for the train station the next day, he was on his own. He relaxed on a chaise on the veranda, sipped at a glass of wine, and stared vacantly at the Mediterranean while he allowed his mind to wander aimlessly.

He was dozing in the afternoon heat when the villa telephone jangled. He considered letting it ring on, but with everything that had happened in the last month, it might be something important. He pulled himself from the chaise and found the telephone inside the French doors.

"This is Alphonse Rimbaud. Can you hear me?"

"I can hear you fine," Beau said. "How's the weather in Paris?"

"Raining. Stay at the coast."

"Too late. Coming home tomorrow."

"Well, perhaps tomorrow will be sunny."

"Do you have news for me, Alphonse?"

"I have news indeed," Rimbaud said. "Our first ship landed at Marseille. The tobacco consignments have all been delivered as scheduled, and I am pleased to report you were correct. I was able to line up enough buyers in Marseilles. We sold our entire cargo of rum at wholesale the instant it offloaded. When all is said and done, this shipment provided a healthy profit, and I am depositing the money into our French banks so I can reinstate your allowance immediately."

"Good news indeed," Beau said.

"Your father said so as well. He has authorized me to release the other two ships from their Charleston moorings as soon as we can assemble crews. They will steam directly to Havana and from there to Kingston before setting course for Marseilles. We have approximately seventy-five percent capacity on scheduled cargo for the return trips and will have the ships full by the time they dock in Marseilles. All in all, your first venture as an importer is a rousing success. Your father sends his congratulations."

"He got his wish," Beau said wistfully. "I wound up in the family business after all."

"I have discussed this with your father. He believes if he concentrates his shipping activities to the Caribbean and Europe only and promises never to import alcohol to the United States again, they may expedite his trial. The concessions may reduce any penalties. He would have to import tobacco products to Charleston as cargo with independent carriers, and he'd still have to agree to have his cargo landing in Charleston searched thoroughly for a while, but that will be necessary for him to meet the demand for cigars there. On the other hand, he will not be out of business. And neither will you. In fact, he anticipates an exciting expansion. Your father has asked if you would accept the title of Vice President of European Operations."

"He doesn't want me to come home?"

"He believes you are more valuable in Paris. I agree with him. Of course, I will carry the lion's share of the burden to make our new French markets successful. While you were blessed with a remarkable amount of beginner's luck, there is still a great deal for you to learn about this business. I will show you what you will need to know as we grow. Within a year or so, you will be able to take it over yourself."

"A year or so," Beau said. "What the hell? I'm only twenty-seven."

"You'll be a millionaire by thirty, at the rate you're going."

"Sure," Beau said. "I suppose that would be a consolation. I'll be back in Paris tomorrow afternoon, but I plan to take a day or two to rest and prepare for what's coming. I should see you in a few days. Carry on. You're doing great. I won't forget it."

―――――

"That's terrific news," Keeby said the next afternoon when Beau told him about the ships. They sat in the living room at 22 Rue Montparnasse. Beau had opened a bottle of Lisette's family vintage, and they talked about how horribly their planned exotic vacation had gone.

"You know the detective who came looking for Grigorii?" Beau said sometime during their second glass.

"Of course. I was drunk, but I remember him."

"He died."

"I didn't like his color. He looked like someone about to kick the bucket."

"The British girl accompanying him visited me at Villa Ciel the next day, before she returned to Paris. He had some sort of fit and died on the beach at Cagne-sur-Mer."

"There is the essence of irony somewhere in there, but I'm too tired to figure it out," Keeby said. "No word from Nathalie?"

"I think neither of us will hear from her anytime soon. Do you recall the girl from the stationer shop in Cagne-sur-Mer?"

"The one you painted with Nathalie? I watched from my window. She's cute."

"Her name's Lisette. She might be the one."

Keeby freshened Beau's glass and his own. "Throttle back a little, buddy. You've known her, what? Two weeks?"

"I barely know her at all. We're going to see your girlfriend's play tonight. Our first official date."

"But you've slept together."

"It's obvious?"

"Yeah. It's obvious. What the hell? It's Paris. They've been putting the cart before the horse around here since the Renaissance. Good luck, Beau. I mean it. And don't be so sure Nathalie is out of your life entirely. She has a funny habit of popping up from time to time."

"Never is too soon. Once burned."

"I'm leaving as well," Keeby said.

"Where are you going?"

"Don't know yet. I'll hop a train and get off when it stops and walk around and talk to people and write about it, and I'll hop back on the train. When I get to where the trains don't run, I'll find a donkey cart. I'm going to become an itinerant writer. I'll keep my room here, since I'll base out of Paris, but we'll go months without seeing each other."

"Is there a downside to this?" Beau asked.

"Fuck off, Johnny Reb. You'll miss the hell out of me."

"I will. When do you leave?"

"Soon. Tomorrow. The day after. Don't worry about the rent. It will be paid in advance."

"I'll be in Paris for another couple of years, breaking in my new title," Beau said. "Sooner or later, I'll need to find some place more permanent. You may discover a new roommate when you return."

"Make it someone cute and curvy," Keeby said. "This Lisette. Why do you think she might be the one?"

496

"Something my father said a few years back. She's agreeable."

"Let out some slack, brother. You're about to heel over into the drink."

Beau laughed. "I know. It sounds boring as hell. It isn't. She's been in bed with men before. It shows. She knows what goes where and how. In that way, she's like any of a dozen other women I've known. I look forward to our conversations, though. She's witty and educated and fun. When I touch her hand, I feel electricity."

"Wool crinolines. They'll get you every time."

"I have as much fun with her outside the bedroom as I do in it. An interesting sensation. I'll never know whether it's real if I don't try," Beau said.

"No, my friend. You won't. Seems to be a lot of that sentiment around here lately. You're ditching painting?"

"Not a chance. With my windfall, I'll continue to sponsor The Salle, and I'll be an active part of it. I'm lucky to have Alphonse Rimbaud to do the heavy lifting. I need to learn every aspect of the business, though, and I might even have to do a run or two on the ships, so there won't be as much opportunity for painting. I'll make time, though."

Keeby lofted his glass. "If it's important, you will always find the time."

"Hear hear," Beau said, and they both drank.

CHAPTER FIFTY-EIGHT

THE PLAY WAS MARVELOUS, Monique was alternately hilarious and tragic, dinner at Le Comptoir de la Gastronomie was delicious, and the evening was balmy and clear-skied. It was time for Beau to take Lisette home. Since they were already on the Boulevard Montmartre and it was a short walk, they strolled and took in the sights of Paris after midnight, until Lisette took his hand and said, "This is my home."

They had stopped in front of an ostentatious Haussmann style building, three stories high and thirty yards wide. The front façade was stone, interrupted by ornate concrete cornices and window jambs and wrought-iron faux balconies in the windows and along the terraces. A heavy oak double front door stood at the top of stone steps, and it opened with massive bronze knobs. Lisette unlocked the door and opened it for Beau. He had expected to step into a marble-tiled entry foyer. Instead, he found himself in a terrazzo courtyard lined with beautiful flower gardens, and an imposing stone fountain in the center. Three wrought-iron benches had been placed around the fountain to facilitate conversation. The living quarters of the house wrapped around the courtyard, affording every room a view of the fountain.

"As *pieds-a-terre* go, it's not bad," Beau said. "Your father has an apartment here?"

"My father has everything here. This is our family house. My grandfather purchased it fifty years ago. My father and stepmother had their suite there—" She pointed to a third-story corner. "My suite is on the diagonal corner." She pointed to a second-floor window.

"Suites."

"Yes."

"Not bedrooms."

"No. We all had our own bedroom, a sitting room, a dressing room, and a bath."

"It's important for families to remain close," he said.

"You're a little overwhelmed."

"Are you kidding? We live on plantations in South Carolina, remember? Why, we could plop this entire house in the middle of our smaller ballroom and still have room to encamp a Confederate brigade."

"Maybe you can understand why I fled to Cagne-sur-Mer. I love my father, and my stepmother was wonderful to me—she's the only real mother I've ever known. I should have been happy here. It is every little girl's dream to live as a princess in a castle, is it not? I've never been comfortable here, though. I can spend a few nights, but after a week or so I start to look in the newspaper for train schedules and loiter in travel agencies perusing brochures about places far away."

"A mink-lined mousetrap," Beau said.

"It is as you said. Our lives were not our own, from the moment we were born."

"We tried to break away."

"We believed it, didn't we? I wanted something to call my own. I didn't have much money that wasn't controlled by my father, but it was enough to buy the shop."

"That's an achievement."

"It's a failure, Beau. I haven't made a profit in a single month since I opened it. I prop it up with the monthly money that appears magically in my accounts whether I wish it to or not. I'm play-acting in Cagne-sur-Mer. I pretend to be a self-reliant businesswoman, but I'm still living off Daddy's allowance."

Beau gathered Lisette in his arms and held her close, and he pressed his lips against hers. She responded unhesitatingly, losing herself in his arms.

"You take my breath away," she gasped as they paused.

"We've been living parallel lives," Beau said. "Our paths never should have converged. I am about to say something you will find entirely senseless and befuddling, but it means something profound. Lisette Seydoux, I find you a most agreeable woman."

She kissed him again, and said, "That may be the sweetest thing anyone has ever said to me. And my inescapable wealth does not frighten you away?"

"According to my Paris business manager, I should be able to buy this house and the one next door in three or four years, before I'm even thirty. I am afraid, my darling, we are forced to embrace the sad and incontestable fact that we are doomed to obscene wealth."

"Merde," she said. "What rotten luck. And, despite your detestable riches, I must confess I find you a most agreeable man. Shall I show you the house?"

"Let's start there," he said, pointing toward the second-floor corner suite.

"Oh, I do hope you like stuffed animals," she said.

———

Beau and Lisette separated the next morning with a promise to meet for dinner. He hustled across the Seine to Montparnasse and his apartment. The morning was already oppressively hot and humid. The sky was puff-bombed by thick ropy clouds and portended afternoon thunderstorms. Beau made a quick list of chores to which he had to attend, and the algebraic equations ran through his brain as he tried to figure out if he could complete them all before the heavens opened in late afternoon. It gave him a headache.

If he had harbored any doubt before he left Cagne-sur-Mer, it had disappeared overnight. She had held his hand throughout the play, and he hadn't minded a bit, even when his fingers went numb. Their conversation at dinner had come spontaneously and without artifice, and they had made each other laugh again and again. As they strolled toward her enormous—even by Paris standards—house, her arm felt right in his. Later, in bed, after they had exhausted their carnal desires, they lay awake in each other's arms and recited their individual biographies, frequently interrupting one another to note how coincidentally similar their experiences had been.

He wanted to be with her. He was elated each time he spied her, and his heart fell each time they parted. Even as he hiked across the Seine, only minutes after closing her door behind him, he wanted to turn and run all the way back to her and suggest they waste the entire day finding new ways to make each other giggle and scream, and then talk until the sun rose again.

If he had any doubts before, there were none now. Lisette Seydoux was the one.

Beau frowned as he resisted the inevitable next thought. He might only find happiness with her by living a lie. As he had stripped the jewelry from Madame Seydoux's cooling body, he had cursed himself. The moral center of his brain not already poisoned by alcohol had tried to warn him he would regret this act for the rest of his life. Fate, circumstance, and the interconnectedness of all things had manifested a special circle of hell just for him.

In time, had he never met Lisette, he would have glossed over his shame about the theft. The gloss would become a shell and then a spore, and finally would ossify over entirely, the gleaming red-hot shame trapped inside like a geode. With the passage of months and years, he would relegate it to the darkest part of the mind where we stow our minor crimes and misdemeanors, far from our consciousness, so they won't keep us awake at night. In decades, he might even have forgotten it entirely.

If he gave in to Lisette's undeniable gravitational pull, he would wake every morning to her lovely face, and never forget an instant of his shameful act, and his self-loathing would remain an oozing gaping wound that would torment him for as long as they might be together. This would be his penance for the privilege of living with someone for whom he was plainly intended.

They would live someone else's lives, never have to worry when the bills came due, raise beautiful children, and pass the soft velvet jaws of the family bear trap to a new generation. With each passing year, the obligation to serve the interests of their family wealth would grow, until it would swallow all their time, leaving nothing for art and music and beauty and reveling in their love for one another.

That was the price. Nothing of great value came without one. They would live the lives they never wanted, but they would live them together. They would carve out a hollow in the stultifying obligations fate had handed to them and it would become their secret sanctuary where they could be Beau and Lisette, together again alone in the Villa Ciel at Cagne-sur-Mer, wrapped around each other waiting for their hearts to synchronize, and marveling each time it happened. For a while, only an hour or two each day, they'd always have their covert retreat to remind themselves they were still good people, and they hadn't abandoned all of their ideals and dreams on the altar of duty.

Or, perhaps, there was another way. Lisette's father was in decline. The ravages of the automobile crash on his body were too severe for the doctors to repair. Each time they resolved one crisis, another would arise. It seemed inevitable he would die, more likely sooner than later. Perhaps, after a suitable time to settle her family affairs, Lisette could break the generational shackles that bound her to the stone and wood castle in Paris. She had told him about their vineyards in the south and their lovely villas, far from the bustle of Paris city life. The telephone and the telegraph had liberated people of business from urban confines. There was no reason Lisette and Beau couldn't manage their individual fiefdoms electronically from a veranda overlooking the verdant vineyards of southern France. If telephones and telegrams didn't work, couriers were cheap.

It was a fantasy, and he never imagined otherwise. Fantasies could be nice, though. There were a thousand lives he and Lisette could live together. All but one required them to bring an end to family concerns that had endured for generations, an act almost as egregious in some circles as not carrying on the family name.

Beau was so lost in his reverie that he was surprised when he found himself in the lobby of 22 Rue Montparnasse. He trudged the four flights of stairs and unlocked the door to their lodgings.

Keeby's desk was cleared, save for the tattered and ink-stained blotter. Beau checked his roommate's bedroom. The bed was meticulously made. The closet stood open and empty. The empty dresser drawers hung half-open to air out.

Keeby had taken off on his romantic world journey without saying goodbye.

Beau looked back on the time they had spent in their top floor bower and how little of it had been spent together. They might have both encamped on the same night once or twice a week. Otherwise, they had frequently passed the night with lovers across the city. He'd been alone in the apartment more often than not in the last three years. Even so, knowing Keeby wouldn't trot through the door at any given moment made the silence more intense. Beau could almost feel it pressing in on him.

A note was pinned to Keeby's pillow. On the outside, he had penned *Rhett*.

"Fucking writers," Beau whispered as he unfolded the envelope. Inside, the message was brief. Keeby had typed it on his machine before stowing it for travel.

REMEMBER: CUTE AND CURVY.
KEEP YOUR HEAD DOWN, SARGE.
SHRAPNEL CAN RICOCHET
ANYWHERE.
LEFT SIDE OF DESK. BOTTOM
DRAWER.
KEEP YOURSELF WARM THIS
WINTER.

KEEB

Beau opened the lower left drawer of Keeby's desk. Lying on the bottom was the manuscript to *Faded Oleander*, the pastiche Keeby had written about Beau's trials in Charleston. Across the nearly blank title page, he had scrawled, *Some things aren't grist for the mill. K.*

"Maybe yes, maybe no," Beau said. He dropped the manuscript back into the drawer, closed it, and took to his bed for a long, well-earned nap.

CHAPTER FIFTY-NINE

LISETTE'S FATHER DIED alone in the middle of the night on the first Tuesday in September. Beau was in bed with Lisette at her Paris mansion when the telephone rang. She had visited him the previous morning, and at the time his condition seemed no better or worse than it had for several weeks. *The type of injuries he had are unpredictable*, the doctors had cautioned her. *Sometimes something vital breaks without warning and too rapidly to be corrected.*

Something vital had broken in her father. He had died in seconds. He had been sleeping, and never knew death had arrived for him.

Beau could hear the other side of the conversation on the telephone. He placed a hand on Lisette's hip to let her know he was there. She told the hospital she would be by in the morning to arrange to transfer the body to Monaco, and she cradled the telephone. He thought she might be distraught, and he prepared to comfort her, even as his mind couldn't erase the memory of her father's ashen face, his chest crushed by the steering wheel of his overturned car, as Beau slipped the Bell and Ross watch off his wrist. He shoved the awful memory as deeply into the back of his mind as he could and focused his attention on Lisette.

Remarkably, she was composed. She rose, pulled a lace robe around her, and sat in the chair next to the bed.

"I have decisions to make," she said. "I dreaded this moment. As long as my father lived, I could lie to myself that he would recover, and I would buy more time to be the person I want to be. I liked my little fucking failure of a stationer shop. I liked the person I was in Cagne-sur-Mer. I am the only Seydoux left. Now I am my family, and by extension I am now my family business. Everything changes on a single telephone call."

"What can I do?" he asked.

"Take notes. Whether you have recognized it or not, we are in the same boat."

———

A week after the funeral in Monaco, which Beau reluctantly attended as Lisette's escort, he was summoned to Alphonse Rimbaud's office.

"Good news on good news, Monsieur Vice President!"

"I haven't accepted the title yet," Beau said.

"Perhaps we can remedy that. The second two ships have arrived in Marseilles, offloaded their cargo, loaded their return shipments, and are now steaming for Havana. I have settled the accounts for our first three European Operations deliveries and the fees for the return cargo, and I have made all the necessary corporate and personal bank deposits. You might like to see your current statement."

He slid a small leather-bound book across the desk to Beau. When he read the numbers inside, Beau raised an eyebrow.

"This is a great deal of money."

"This may be a good time to review the standard provisions of the contract you would sign with your father should you accept the vice president position." He extracted a thin sheaf of papers from his desk drawer and handed them to Beau. "I would draw your attention to the section regarding compensation. By accepting the Vice President of European Operations position, you would immediately acquire one third share ownership in the Shipley Company. As an owner, you are personally entitled to shares of the profits of each voyage. It's a shipping tradition I imagine goes all the way back to the Phoenicians. In lieu of a salary, you receive these profit shares. We have enjoyed three highly successful round trips so far. This is your share of the profits from those voyages."

"Holy cow," Beau said. "This is for only the last month?"

"Correct."

"This mousetrap has some pretty thick mink."

"I do not recognize the metaphor, but its meaning is easily interpreted. Yes. Your father anticipated accepting this position would have some significant negative impact on your plans and may force you to abandon your professional artistic pursuits. He says you will remember how he knows what a sacrifice that will be for you."

"Yes. I do."

"And, in recognition of your sacrifice, he wants to make your landing a soft one."

"By lining the eyrie with well-worn cash."

"If it is any consolation, his own nest is heavily padded as well. Which brings us to the second piece of happy news! I have saved the best for last."

"I'm getting polio?"

"I am delighted you can retain your sense of humor. No, this is exciting. I received the cable only this morning. Your father's trial has ended."

Beau sat upright. "What?"

"The recent modifications in our shipping schedules and removing our ships from United States ports convinced the government he did not intend to continue his smuggling activities in the country. He may continue to import cigars to the United States using independent carriers, with the provisions we anticipated. A government customs agent has been assigned to inspect every crate Shipley imports as it is removed from the carrier. It is a minor inconvenience. In return, your father pled guilty, and was issued the maximum monetary penalty."

"How much?"

"A thousand dollars. He could have been imprisoned for six months, but his sentence was reduced to time served— only a few days, since he had been out on bail while he awaited trial."

Beau collapsed back into his seat.

"I...I don't understand."

"What is it you don't understand?" Rimbaud asked.

"A thousand dollars? Only six months? That was the worst he ever faced?"

"As it turns out, the penalties outlined in federal law for violation of the Volstead Act are surprisingly lenient. It's almost as if even the lawmakers don't take it seriously. In any case, the answer to your question is yes."

"And all I faced if I returned to Charleston after his arrest was *suspicion* of involvement?"

"Correct again."

"Suspicion of involvement in a crime that would only cost me a thousand dollars and maybe a few days of jail time?"

"Well, there would be a permanent criminal record involved."

"You manipulated me. Both Father and you. I didn't face any real risk at all. I didn't have to stay in Paris. You don't understand. You have no idea what I did."

"What? What is it?" Rimbaud asked.

Beau dashed to the window, raised the blinds, threw open the sash, and leaned out to gasp fresh air. He needed time to think. When he finally pulled his head back inside, Rimbaud stared at him with a look of mixed fear and worry.

"Our ships in Marseille," he said.

"Yes?"

"They offloaded cigars and processed tobacco and rum, right?"

"That is correct. Is something wrong?"

"And that's *all* they offloaded."

"What do you mean?"

"Don't jerk me off, Alphonse. Your answer to my next question may well determine whether you work for this company an hour from now. Is there anything I've said you don't understand?"

"No, Monsieur Beau. I heard you clearly."

"What else was offloaded from those boats? Besides tobacco and rum? After everything else my father has experienced, is he still smuggling?"

"There may have been two or three hundred kilos of Jamaican cannabis, but it is not illegal in France, so it is not technically smuggling."

"If it isn't technically smuggling, what exactly is it, technically?"

"The market in France for cannabis is complex. Most of the product comes from places like Afghanistan and India and is strictly controlled by cartels. Those cartels do not approve of interlopers, but there is a thriving underground economy in the product. They purchase their supplies from only three sources, and we are selling to one of them."

"And if those cartels discovered we were moving in on their territory?"

"They would not be amused. If their irritation grew large enough, they might push back. But our imports constitute much less than one percent of the product being imported into the country for the independent contractors, and we are several levels of distribution away from the cartels. I believe we are adequately insulated from reprisals."

"How much of the deposit in my account came from smuggling?"

"Perhaps ten percent."

"I see. Thank you for being honest. All right. I can live without that ten percent. Wire my father. Tell him I'll accept the vice president position on one condition. The smuggling stops. He didn't want me to be part of that business? He gets his wish. As of today, if he wants me on board, the Shipleys only engage in legitimate import. We'll stick with the legal products that have been our bread and butter for decades. If he argues, tell him the increased tobacco and rum market in France will more than cover the loss. If he argues more, tell him to stick his vice presidency up his ass, because my demand is not negotiable."

"Would you be too terribly incensed if I were to moderate your language?" Rimbaud said.

"Put it any way he'll hear it."

"There is one other matter to discuss. Now that his legal entanglements have been disposed, your father wishes to move ahead with his long-held plans to enter the aviation field."

"Not letting any grass grow under his feet."

"He wants you to spearhead the aviation operations in western Europe."

"And the noose tightens."

"There is an airplane manufacturer near Paris named Bleriot. They are developing a multi-passenger aircraft capable of long-distance flights. Your father would like to explore establishing a daily commercial route between Paris and London using Bleriot's aircraft."

"He isn't asking much."

"I expect the reward will be worth the effort."

"One more condition, then. I want you as Chief Operating Officer."

"Beg pardon?"

"I need someone to handle the day-to-day shipping operations, and to extend our market here in France. I need someone who knows which palms to grease and where the bodies are buried. You know who to talk to and how to do it. You could have lied to me about the hop, but you told the truth. I can trust you. Your experience trumps my family ties. I'll make the big decisions. You get dirty with them."

"I'm honored," Rimbaud said.

"Wait until you see your new salary."

"I believe if he could see you today, your father would be proud of you."

"Shame it doesn't run both ways. Send him my terms. If he agrees, we'll talk about what happens next."

CHAPTER SIXTY

REALITY HIT LISETTE that evening. She and Beau had spent a quiet night at home after dinner. The world had been spinning at triple speed since the night a telephone call informed her of her father's death. It was the first chance they had found to explore what would happen next in their lives.

Beau wanted to talk about the decision he had made and the ultimatum he had delivered to his father. He was frustrated and disappointed at the way he had been led to believe Gordon Shipley faced years of prison and financial ruin.

Lisette had been quiet at dinner. Beau could tell something was on her mind. Several times, she acted as if she wanted to start a conversation but thought better of it. As soon as they arrived at Lisette's suite in her family home and sat on the sofa, tears welled in her eyes and she burst into sobs, crushing her face into Beau's lapel. He held her closely, waiting.

"I...I don't know why I did that," she said. "I walked into this room, my childhood room, and suddenly I was overwhelmed. Since my father died, I have been numb. I lay awake at night worrying whether I should be more devastated. I have waited for grief to come, and now it has arrived."

The tears welled again, and he rocked her as she didn't speak for a while. "Is it the house?" he said as she slowly recovered. "We could go to my apartment. Keeby has left. There are no memories there to trouble you."

"I detest this house," she said. "I intend to sell it."

"Where would you live?"

"On one of the vineyards. We have telephones now. I don't need to be in Paris to manage the winery operations. Paris was my father's fascination. He loved the bright lights and the rushing around. I love it as well, in small doses. My heart is in the vineyards, though. I will move from one to another across the year. One for every season. What do you think?"

"You've been reading my mind. Is this what you wanted to discuss at dinner?"

"At dinner I was about to burst into tears. I wanted to talk, but I knew if I said even a word, I'd flood the tablecloth. I barely made it home. I miss my father and stepmother. I miss the life I had in Cagne-sur-Mer. I hate this house. My entire life has been turned inside out in only a month or two. And then there's you. What in hell am I going to do with you, Beau?"

"I'll give you fifty years to figure it out. Deal with the other stuff first. This must be the day for big decisions. I tentatively accepted my father's offer today. If he agrees to my conditions, I'll be the Vice President of European Operations sometime next week."

"Destiny will not be denied," she said. "Neither stationer shop nor artist's studio can withstand the onslaught of fate. What were your conditions?"

He told her. When he said he had demanded that The Shipley Company get out of the smuggling business, she threw her arms around his neck and kissed him deeply.

"You make me so happy," she said. "The romance in being the lover of an American gangster wears out quickly."

"Turns out I'd have been a pretty minor gangster. The penalties for smuggling booze into the States amount to a slap on the wrist and a warning not to get caught again. I was worried about nothing."

"Yet, had you returned to America when your father was arrested, we never would have met."

"You know, my agent's office here in Paris has a telephone."

"What are you saying?"

"What I told him. Until I know every nut and bolt in my family business, I'll make the big decisions, and he'll handle the details. I don't have to live in Paris, at least not all the time. I could run the business from almost anywhere. Why, even a vineyard in the south of France."

"I see," she said. "Do you own a vineyard as well?"

"In a year or so, I'll buy yours."

"Oh, s'il vous plait monsieur, ne me menecez pas de bonheur."

"Wait. Wait. I think I caught that. *Do not threaten me with happiness?*"

"I have not considered selling my family vineyards. But should some shipping tycoon appear with an obscene offer, preferably involving obscene behavior, I might be tempted. I shall not sell you one vineyard, however. My favorite."

"Which one?" he asked.

"The smallest one. In Arcachon, on the Atlantic coast. Only a hundred acres or so, but the villa is stone with heavy oak beams and massive fireplaces in every room, and it sits high on a hill overlooking the vineyards and the ocean in the distance. We grow Bordeaux—both red and white—and Médoc. Behind the fields is a grove of olive trees, and we press our own oil at the end of the season. Arcachon has the best oysters in the world. Sometimes, you can find the entire world in a plate of oysters, some bread and butter, and a lovely glass of wine grown yards from your table."

"Followed by a fine cigar. You make it sound enticing. I'd like to see it."

"We can go next week if you wish. As the new owner, I am obligated to inspect the property in any case, though, I cannot imagine it would take more than a day. The rest of the week would be ours."

"I have no plans for next week."

She kissed him.

"Make some," she said.

———

Beau called a meeting at The Salle to discuss the changes he saw on the horizon. Everyone arrived early except Dieter. When he hadn't shown by ten minutes after the appointed time, Beau launched into an explanation of his new role with The Shipley Company.

As he was about to announce his new position, the door banged open, and Dieter lurched into the studio. He grabbed at one of the barres left over from the old dance studio to keep from losing his balance. His hair was askew, and his eyes were red and rimmed with dark bags. His approach was announced by a wave of alcohol odor that preceded him. When he spoke, his speech was thick and slurred.

"Sorry I am late, my comrades," he said, a little too precisely and a little too loud. "Oh, my apologies. I should not use that term. We are already a collective. We do not wish to alarm the authorities!" He collapsed in giggles against the wall.

"I do not believe he is handling Grigorii's death well," Cesare told Beau.

"No shit. Help me pour him in a chair."

Together, Cesare and Beau deposited Dieter in a battered loveseat used by some of the models, because he would have fallen out of any of the other chairs.

"Maybe you should have stayed home," Beau said.

"Been there all week. Can't take it anymore. Needed some air."

"Some water and a little soap as well wouldn't have hurt," Beau said. "You aren't going to throw up or anything, are you?"

"Haven't eaten since…" He counted on his fingers. "…Tuesday. Nothing to throw up."

"All right," Beau said. "When we're done here, I'll take you out to eat. If you don't eat, and keep drinking like you are, you're going to die."

"And my genius will never be recognized!" Dieter lamented.

"Well, you won't care because you'll be dead. We're going to prevent that."

"You're a good man, Beau."

"Sure I am. I'm a regular Saint Francis. Relax here and try to follow the conversation. If you pass out, I'll fill you in later."

Beau finished outlining the changes for the other Salle artists. Most of them were so far in the background, the artists themselves would never know a change had been made. He assured them the new arrangements meant the Salle would continue to operate, but Beau would not be around as often. He had planned to announce that day-to-day decisions going forward would be made by Dieter, but when he glanced over, the German snored quietly in the loveseat, and thought better of it. They could always make the announcement later when Dieter was in shape to say something about it and to inspire greater confidence.

Beau concluded the meeting, and the artists wandered off to various places for lunch leaving Beau alone with Dieter and Cesare.

"You want me to stay?" Cesare asked.

"No," Beau said. "I can handle him."

He sat next to Dieter and shook him. Dieter snorted and jerked awake.

"Direkthilfe?" he demanded.

"In English, pal," Beau said. "I was too busy dodging German bullets to learn their language."

"Beau." He looked around. "The Salle. I remember now. The meeting. Am I early?"

"It's over. You slept through it. Don't worry. Nothing huge. I'll tell you all about it at lunch. You need food."

"I am a little hungry."

"You haven't eaten since Tuesday."

"Is that a fact?"

"It's what you told me."

"And what is today?" Dieter asked.

"Eating day." Beau helped Dieter to his feet. When he did, the German's cuffs receded, and Beau saw the gold Bell and Ross watch on Dieter's right wrist. He held Dieter's arm and pulled back the sleeve.

"What is this?" Beau said. "This is the watch. The one the detective in Cagne-sur-Mer was looking for. You knew we were looking for it!"

"It is not," Dieter said, trying to stand right and look indignant. "You are mistaken."

"I'm not. Look. Here. The corner is abraded, as if it rubbed against a concrete sidewalk, which is exactly how this happened."

"You cannot know that," Dieter said.

"The watch doesn't belong to you."

"It was Grigorii's. I was all he had. There is nobody else. He gave it to me."

"It wasn't his to give. This watch is stolen, Dieter. That's why the detective was looking for it."

"I cannot believe you. I do not believe Grigorii would steal."

"He didn't. *I* stole it."

"It does not belong to you either, then."

"It belongs to the person I stole it from, and I'm going to give it back."

"You will have to take it from me."

"Look at yourself. You think I can't?"

"I would remind you we are friends."

"Friendship will make it easier to reconcile later if I have to rough you up." He grabbed for the watch band. Dieter jerked his arm away.

"Please," Dieter said. "I beg you, Beau. I know what Grigorii was, and I know what a comical pair we made, and I knew from the start he would desert me the second a more profitable opportunity presented itself. I know all these things. But I also know I have been terribly lonely since moving to Paris. Grigorii took loneliness away. The greatest joy I have known since leaving Berlin was the time we spent in Cagne-sur-Mer, filming and simply being together. Now my film will never be completed. Grigorii died in disgrace and his story will be forgotten."

"It wasn't his story," Beau said.

"What?" Dieter asked.

"The book. Keeby's book. It wasn't Grigorii's story. It was a lie he told. He was in Nice when the Bolsheviks took over Russia. The only flight he took was hopping the first-class rail car to Paris with a wagonload of luggage and a title."

Dieter stared at Beau, bug-eyed. "Do...you...think I do not know this?" he asked. "Does it matter at all? Do you believe for an instant any of us in this goddamned city is who we say we are, Herr Shipping Magnate? We are all living a lie. I lied to you on the night we met, and I have lied to you every moment since. I told you I was a clerk in Berlin during the war. It was a lie. At the Meuse-Argonne, I was behind the trenches, along the howitzer line. From three kilometers away, we rained fire on you. We cheered every time the huge gun spat and recoiled. I got hard in my pants. I loved it."

"Why lie?"

"We lost." He shrugged. "There is no great honor in getting a hard-on while fighting a losing cause. I lived in a city filled with people I had only recently tried to murder. Would you boast of such a thing, Beau?"

"No. I suppose I wouldn't."

"But you admit to being a thief. I suppose now we know where your moral boundaries lie."

"Give me the watch," Beau said. "I'm not a thief. I made a horrible mistake, and I'm trying to make it right."

Tears welled in Dieter's eyes again. "It's all I have left of him, Beau," he whined. "Can you not leave me one memento of our short time together?"

"No. It wasn't his and it isn't yours. Hand it over. This is a new shirt. I don't want to get it bloody."

"You wouldn't dare."

"The watch belongs to the woman I love. It was her father's. He died after I took it off his wrist. Tell me again I wouldn't dare."

Dieter sunk to the couch under the onslaught of Beau's arguments. He raised his hands instinctively to protect himself. Beau unfastened the watch band and removed it from Dieter's wrist.

"That wasn't so bad, was it?" Beau asked as he pocketed the watch.

"I will never forgive you."

"I'll survive."

"Of course, you understand our partnership is at an end."

"I'll survive that as well."

"According to our agreements, I demand you buy out my share."

Beau chuckled. "I'll have the check to you tomorrow, you sanctimonious lying little prick. If you hadn't demanded, I'd have bought you out anyway. I lost a good buddy at the Meuse-Argonne. If you'd told me you were a gunner there from the beginning, it wouldn't have been a problem. Battlefield honor and all that bullshit. Awkward, maybe, but not a problem. Lying about it is a problem. Clear out your workstation. Come by tomorrow and I'll pay you for your share."

He turned to leave. As he approached the door, Dieter let loose one last volley, screaming at Beau's retreating back. "You smug rich boy piece of shit. You don't have the soul of an artist! You are a dilletante! A dabbler! You are a Johnny-come-lately! Go paint your stupid fucking landscapes and your naked models and your whore of a girlfriend. You can line your walls with your unsold canvases! Your art career will be a footnote on a footnote! Do you hear me? You will never know the suffering of a true artist. You have never suffered a moment in your life. You have always had a lifeline. I detest you! I have always detested you! Go! Walk away, you coward! You make me sick!"

Dieter was still screaming when Beau hit the street and turned toward the river.

"Tell me something I don't already know," Beau said.

CHAPTER SIXTY-ONE

ALICE TOKLAS ANSWERED the door at 27 Rue de Fleurus when Beau knocked.

"Hello, Alice. Is she available?"

She led him back to her salon, where Gertrude Stein lounged imperiously, reading a book and sipping a cup of tea.

"Young artist Shipley," she said. "So nice to see you again. How did the showing go at The Salle?"

"Funny thing. You might have mentioned something about the Tour de France when I told you about it."

"It amused me not to. And what favor can I bestow on you today?"

"None at all. I've come to thank you."

"You're welcome, for whatever it is I did."

"When we first spoke, you asked whether the import business was still on the table."

"I recall."

"It was never off the table. A...a series of reversals and other circumstances have required me to give up my aspirations to be a professional artist and rejoin the family business."

"Am I to be thanked for this?"

"Not at all. I apologize for suggesting it. No. I want to thank you for something else you said in our conversation. You asked whether I was a craftsman or an artist."

"And you declared yourself to be an artist."

"I did."

"And not a craftsman."

"No."

"Nor a shipping magnate?"

"Not at the time. I'm thankful you left the option open. I might be an artist. You encouraged me. You'll never know how I appreciate it."

"And I don't believe you know how happy I am to hear you have returned to your family business."

Beau sat back, surprised. "I don't understand."

"Walk with me," she said. He followed her as she strolled through the rooms of her salon, pointing out various artists hanging on the walls.

"What does it mean to be an artist, Beau?" she asked.

"It's about expression. It's about adding a little beauty to an ugly world. It's about challenging people's strongest beliefs. It's about trying to make sense in a violent, uncaring world. It's a way of preserving a moment in time people can see hundreds of years later and know how we lived."

"And you can only do these things if you are doing nothing else?"

"I suppose you can find time to do anything if it means enough to you."

"Even if you are running a shipping business?"

"I'm already trying to find a way."

"Keep looking," she said. "You have missed the point entirely. Don't let life make you angry or inadequate. You aren't alone. I am keenly worried about the postwar generation. Having seen death and destruction on a scale unimagined in human history, you return to a society that, largely, watched the conflict from a distance and has no idea what it was like. Returning soldiers like you are as strange to them as if they had jumped out of some Edgar Rice Burroughs novel about Barsoom. The soldiers themselves, however, are damaged far beyond any known tolerance. You—all of you—are so lost. Having mortality rubbed in your faces and not stick has left you with a sense of invulnerability. You flaunt every rule, break every commandment, violate every moral. You are hedonistic and uncontrolled. You drink yourself into stupors and smoke opium until you can't remember your own name. You sleep with anyone who even hints at receptivity. You are licentious and reckless and animalistic. You are on a nonstop party. Many of you will not survive. I am happy you are returning to your family business. It will provide you with grounding that may allow you to escape the waste and carnage I believe will claim many of the young artists I meet today in Paris."

"You have so little faith in us?"

"I have little faith in the world. The war was a horrible thing, and it caused horrible suffering. Your entire generation is marked. You might be lucky. You may escape. Keep painting. You have talent. I never thought you were likely to challenge Picasso or Modigliani or Braque. On the other hand, you would not wish to spend five minutes inside any of their tortured heads. There is a price for genius. Fortunately, you are no genius. On the other hand, when you came begging for help two months ago, I feared you had fallen victim to the insane competition between artists in this city. I am gratified to discover you were only struggling against your inevitable destiny."

"You knew I'd go back to the business?"

"I knew it when we first met. Remember, I listed it among your options," she said.

"Yet you encouraged me."

"Did I? I humiliated you, if you will recall. When you came for help in July, I turned you away. I purchased your three paintings not because they were worthy of money, but because Braque suggested I do so, and I was courting him for another matter at the time. I could have warned you your show was doomed to failure because of the Tour de France, but what fun would that have been? At what point in all the time we have known one another, as short as that has been, have I been in any way encouraging?"

"Perhaps I wanted to see it."

"I am not responsible for your perceptions. If you are grateful for the attention I have bestowed on you, you are welcome. Now, we have settled it. You will become a shipping tycoon and you will paint when the passion strikes, all that is necessary to be an artist. Forget fame. Forget hanging in the Louvre. Piss on posterity. The greatest art comes not from working at it twenty-four hours a day, year after year, but in the momentary inspiration that transports you to a place where there is nothing but you, the brush, and the canvas. The art is in losing yourself, not in whatever you slap on the cloth. You've made your first steps. Art will always be with you now, any time you need to tell the rest of the world to fuck off for a while."

Beau left Gertrude Stein's salon even more confused than when he had arrived.

The watch weighed half a ton in his pocket and reminded him of one last great decision he had to make.

He had already decided. He couldn't live a lie with Lisette. If she was the one, and Beau believed with all his heart she was, despite the short time they had been together, it was no use trying to keep anything secret from her. Giving her the watch was one thing. But he'd have to explain how he came across it, and he'd have to explain how Prince Grigorii obtained it.

He could toss the watch in the river, watch it disappear into the muck, walk away, and never talk about it again. Lisette already believed the watch was lost. She had already grieved for it.

But then he'd be back to lying.

September in Paris was beautiful. The air was crisp. The leaves had burned in the sun to a rainbow of yellows and reds and purples and oranges.

He stopped at a bench across from the Notre Dame cathedral and allowed the afternoon sun to bathe his face, and he thought for what seemed like hours.

He had to give her the watch. There was no other choice. He had to tell her the truth. He had no choice in that either. He knew she would be hurt and angry. There was no escaping the betrayal she would feel. He would prostrate himself before her and beg for her forgiveness. Tears would flow like floodwater. None of that mattered. The only thing he knew was he would not begin their life together on a lie, even if that meant destroying the fragile love they had grown together.

Casual strollers passed, unaware of his internal torture, as he envisioned two futures. In one of them, with an enraged and vindictive Lisette no longer part of his life, he browsed Paris society parties, hobnobbed with theater and film stars and athletes and politicians, and garnered respect wherever he went because of his wealth, but was utterly empty and bored inside the entire time. He saw years of drinking and empty sex and dissipation and ennui so intense death would become a welcome alternative. He could easily imagine a life so devoid of emotion and commitment, but he couldn't imagine any way he might continue to paint in such a life.

In the other vision, he awoke beside Lisette in their enormous bed in their medieval villa bedroom in Arcachon, with a huge window overlooking acres of winding grapevines, and the green Atlantic in the distance. They made love casually to start the day, bathed and dressed and breakfasted on croissants and Normandy butter and sweet French fruit preserves. Beau spent an hour or so on the telephone with Alphonse Rimbaud, making the big decisions, and Lisette did the same for an hour with her vineyards, and the rest of the day was theirs. They'd walk on the beach and tour the fields and he would paint, and she would read and at the end of the day they would open a bottle of their own wine and enjoy a delicious dinner and spend the evening on the veranda watching the sun set over the ocean and believe beyond any doubt they were the most fortunate of people living the best possible life.

Beau stood and walked. He knew he had no control over which of the futures he envisioned might come true. It was entirely out of his hands. No matter. He was not only willing to roll the dice; he was committed.

At last, there was no time left. He stood outside her house off the Boulevard Montmartre. He checked his pocket one more time, hoping the watch had fallen through an unrepaired hole and dropped into the streets. No such luck.

The universe was not going to let him off the hook.

Not this time.

Two futures. One or the other. In a few minutes, he'd know how the rest of his life would play out.

He walked up the steps and rang the doorbell.

CHAPTER SIXTY-TWO

2024
New York City

THE AUCTIONEER WORE a perfectly tailored summer wool suit and white cotton gloves, even though he hardly ever handled the artworks as they were presented. That was left to the union techs. He was a fastidious man, though, and he believed wearing the white gloves gave him an air of sophistication and erudition. Not everybody could get away with wearing white gloves in this day and age. He thought he pulled it off handsomely.

"Our next item, ladies and gentlemen," he said into the microphone as the techs placed a simply framed canvas on a glossy brass easel on the raised stage, "is an entertaining bit of artistic mystery, a detective story in process, if you will. This is lot number FB1074, a painting entitled *'Grief'* by an artist named B. Shipley."

He waited for the murmuring to settle in the crowd. "As you can see, this painting is in the late Impressionist style, and is a moving portrait, depicting a woman dressed in black, grasping at the wrought iron fence of a cemetery as she stretches one thin hand through the iron for a lost loved one.

We have almost complete provenance on this lot number. It appears first in the listings of the late Gertrude Stein, who purchased it from the artist in 1920, and was included in the extensive collection of artworks in her possession when she passed away in 1946.

"Very little is known about the artist, however. Some research has been made into the matter, and an artist named Shipley appears in a few obscure references to Paris during the 1920s, but there are no definitive sources that categorically identify him—or her, as the case may be. Many records, as you may be aware, were destroyed during the Nazi occupation. We simply don't know.

"One reference describes an artists' workshop in the Marais that operated between the years 1921 and 1924. No particularly notable painters or sculptors are associated with the workshop, but this isn't uncommon. Paris a century ago was flooded with would-be artists, writers, poets, and filmmakers. Many passed through the decade and created hardly a ripple in the ocean of the art world.

"It is possible our B. Shipley was one of those young expatriates whom Gertrude Stein included in her now-famous 'lost generation'. We are all familiar with the greatest names of the era—Hemingway, Fitzgerald, Dos Passos, Picasso, and the like. Their lives in Paris in the 1920s are the stuff of legend. Let us journey back in our imaginations to evenings along the Saint-Germain des Prés on the Rive Gauche. A crowded sidewalk café at Les Deux Magots. Women dressed in their finest gowns and yards of pearls. Men in evening wear and white ties, ordering drinks and smoking as if there were no tomorrow. In the distance, a band plays jazz. A heady

Charleston contest breaks out. It is Paris and the war is a distant memory, and people are celebrating life again.

"Perhaps our friend, B. Shipley, whomever he or she was, was in the middle of it, laughing uproariously, quaffing champagne like soda, and knowing beyond a shadow of a doubt there was no better or more perfect place or time in history.

"But, as I said, we don't know. This is an opportunity, ladies and gentlemen, to purchase a true artistic mystery. See in your mind's eye the conversations you can have with friends, imagining who the real B. Shipley might have been. Perhaps you can buy a deerstalker hat and become an art detective yourself. Or, if nothing else, you have a striking and emotional work of art to enjoy for years to come.

"So, Lot Number FB 1074, *"Grief"*, by B. Shipley, is offered for auction today. We will open bidding at five hundred dollars. Who will make the opening bid? Ah, I see you in the corner. I have five hundred dollars. Will anyone bid five-twenty-five? Anyone at all?"

———

Arcachon, France
This morning...

A Bell executive helicopter swept over the vineyards and hovered above the helipad installed behind the bottling facility, which also housed the winery offices. As the blades spun down, two men and a woman emerged from the plush leather-upholstered cabin. The woman was obviously in charge, as the two men fell into step just slightly behind and to each side of her. One of the men carried a briefcase chained to his wrist. The other kept both hands free, as his eyes swept the perimeter, never resting on a single spot.

They were greeted by a man in a meticulously tailored suit. He wore round wire-rimmed glasses above a silver mustache. His head was shaven to the scalp and gleamed in the coastal sunlight. He shouted over the whine of the jet helicopter engine.

"Madame Clement, please allow me to welcome you to Chateau Arcachon. I am Miles Allegretti, the executor of Monsieur Proulx's estate. I am also an attorney and the current vice president of Chateau Arcachon. For all intents and purposes, I am in charge. Will you accompany me to the conference room?"

Inside the bottling facility, he directed them to a room that looked more like a first-class airport lounge than a conference room.

"Please make yourself comfortable," Allegretti said. "As you might imagine, Monsieur Proulx did not believe in rigid structure and sitting around tables and the like. Would anyone like a glass of wine?"

Madame Clement took a glass. The two men remained standing and declined to drink. Allegretti had expected no less. He produced a bottle of Chateau Arcachon's Medoc, from one of their best vintage years. After pouring, he sat across from Madame Clement.

"As you are aware, Monsieur Proulx died without issue," he said. The subtext was unnecessary. Caleb Proulx's status as a proud openly gay man had been well-documented for decades. He had never married, and to the best of anyone's knowledge had never even slept with a woman. The potential for heirs at the time of his death was unlikely. "Chateau Arcachon has been a family-held winery for eight generations. However, there is no family left. As their representative, it is my final duty to ensure their legacy is maintained by new owners of the highest possible standards. I am gratified you have arrived today. I should tell you, among the various suitors for the vineyards, I was most enthused by your proposal. I take it we are in agreement?"

Madame Clement made a quick hand gesture, and the man with the briefcase removed the chain and unlocked it, placing it open on the coffee table in front of Allegretti. After taking several minutes to read over the papers inside, Allegretti signed the documents, and then stowed the pen.

"I wish you the greatest success," he said. He stood and bowed. Madame Clement shook his hand. She and the two men boarded the helicopter, which immediately accelerated the engines and lifted off the helipad seconds later.

It was done.

Allegretti folded his copies of the sales agreements, and retreated to the main house, where Caleb Proulx had kept his personal office. The main house sat a few hundred yards from a cliff that overlooked the Atlantic Ocean. It was a classic French cottage, built of stone and fumed oak beams and lead casement windows and a tile roof. The bowed window in the office looked out over the ocean, and the mist-shrouded Île aux Oiseaux in the distance. The walls were oak wainscoting below plaster and lath. The plaster ceiling was supported by beams hewn when Louis XVI was still a boy. The house itself had stood largely unchanged since the middle of the nineteenth century.

Allegretti filed the papers, poured a glass of wine, and settled into the sofa that lined one wall. He had spent almost forty years in the service of Caleb Proulx, and he had to admit they had never been boring.

And now they were over. For the first time since before the French Revolution, Chateau Arcachon had passed from family control. It was just another corporate entity now, a cog in the vast economic machinery of profit and loss. Chateau Arcachon had become a commodity.

He would miss the office, with its magnificent view and its oddball collections of family memorabilia, the model ships and airplanes, a long-stopped gold Bell and Ross watch that rested permanently under a glass dome on a small walnut pedestal, and especially the strange painting that hung behind the desk. It depicted two women, one nude and one clothed in black, chatting at a table overlooking the blue waters of the Mediterranean. The naked woman's face was mostly hidden by a huge round sunhat. Despite the contrast, they both looked perfectly natural and relaxed. A brass plate screwed into the frame identified the painting as *Afternoon Tea at Cagne-sur-Mer*.

It was a curious decoration for an office, but it had hung in place ever since Allegretti could remember, almost forty years, and as far as Allegretti knew it had hung there for decades before. According to Caleb, his mother had insisted on it, as had his grandmother, and Proulx was too focused on his hedonistic life to bother with changes to an office he visited perhaps twice a year in one of his several wineries.

No matter. It had been sold along with the rest of the estate. It was someone else's painting now, as were the framed canvases that lined the hallways and decorated the walls of the study and the bedrooms and even the kitchen. Most of them were originals. Many of them, Allegretti knew, had been painted by the same artist.

He sipped his wine and gazed out the bowed window, as clouds pulled together over the ocean, and he sipped from the wine. He wondered what the new owners would do with the private family plot that stood sentry over the ocean near the edge of the cliff. It was enclosed in a wrought iron fence, and was becoming crowded with the addition of Caleb Proulx, who had been laid next to his mother Nathalie and his father Charles. On the other side was his uncle Alphonse, who hadn't survived infancy. Several feet away lay a marker over an empty grave, commemorating Caleb Proulx's namesake, his grandfather's closest lifelong friend, a writer of some renown whose airplane disappeared over the Black Sea during the Second World War. Nobody had ever explained what he was doing there.

Nearer the cliff stood two other gravestones, so close they nearly touched. Caleb's grandparents, who owned and ran the winery for many years. On certain days, the sun setting over the western Atlantic beamed between the two stones and shot laser-like through the casement windows of the office to bathe the Bell and Ross watch in a heavenly light, almost as if they had been designed to do so.

It was a curious thing, and probably nothing more than a great coincidence.

On the other hand, Allegretti mused, sometimes wonderful miracles can be reflected in a single moment of serendipity.